NOW AND ALWAYS

LEE DAWNA

LeeDawna Books

This is a work of fiction. Names, characters, places, and incidents either are the product of the author's imagination or are used fictitiously. Any resemblance to actual persons, living or dead, events, or locales is entirely coincidental.

Copyright © 2021 Lee Dawna

All rights reserved. No part of this book may be reproduced or used in any manner without written permission of the copyright owner except for the use of quotations in a book review.

First edition

Cover design by Premade Ebook Cover Shop
www.premadeebookcovershop.com

ISBN 978-1-949192-04-9 (paperback)
ISBN 978-1-949192-03-2 (ebook)
ISBN 978-1-949192-05-6 (audio)

Published by LeeDawna Books www.leedawnabooks.com
leedawnabooks@suddenlink.net

~

This book is dedicated to my fans. You amaze me every day, and without you, my heart wouldn't be whole.

~

$$\sim 1 \sim$$

I'm photogenic. Or so say the stack of surveillance photos in my hand. They were undoubtedly taken by some creepy dude holed up in a rusty sedan, his telescopic lens clicking away trying to catch me in the *act*. But just like the jerk who followed me around in Europe, the cheater-catching private eye providing these headshots is going to be disappointed. My days of being dumb enough to bury my sorrows in a woman are long gone.

To this buffoon's credit, while he wasted time snapping photos of my lone face peering out of my third-floor bedroom window, he made the building I'm living in look a lot nicer than it actually is. The whole three-floor structure is dusty and dated, with doors falling off hinges and carpets stained any place they aren't torn. But from these photographs, you'd never know the ruin surrounding me.

Working out of an office on the first floor of the same building compounds my dismal living situation. Knowing who's behind these impressive photographs is equally repulsive. I wish I could divorce her. But my overpaid lawyer says I'm not getting out of this marriage without opening my wallet, so we're staying hitched. Whether Cassie likes it or not.

"Shred these for me." I hand the flattering mail to the clerk and walk out of the cramped post office. I didn't notice anyone tailing me earlier and I don't see anyone now, but I'm new in this quaint city, so unless the voyeur is openly pointing a camera at me, I'm not going to spot them. And that's what Cassie wants—for me to live with powerless awareness that I'm being watched.

I'm not moving again, though. Huntington, with its colonial architecture and small-town feel despite being a bustling metropolis, beats the heck out of being exiled in Europe. A man can only endure cookies masquerading as biscuits for so long. Three days ago, my first meal back in the States was a big fat plate of buttermilk biscuits doused in sausage gravy, with a side oath to never drink tea again.

Hopping into my Land Rover, I shoot Cassie a text. **Congratulations. You found me. But I've avoided giving you a single cent for over seven years. I'm not going to cave now. Especially over more stupid photos.**

What are you talking about? Her words ping my screen. **What photos?**

Playing stupid doesn't mean you are, I type back. **Stop trying to harass me. And leave my family alone while you're at it.**

You leave them alone, Avery. And sign the divorce papers while you're at it!

If she wants me to sign a single piece of paper related to our marriage, she knows my terms. And since she'll never agree to them, she can go to her grave still being my wife. **Just go away, Cassie. Never hearing from you again is too soon.**

~

I'm well aware that Dad's dabbling in Huntington hasn't led to anything more than a lone secretary set up in a single office, and that he only gave me the East Coast operation of Kingwood Properties to get rid of me again. But just like the Kingwood family built their fortune in commercial real estate along the West coast, I'll prove I can build mine here. Plus, Dad and I get along about as well as Cassie and I do, so moving across the country is the only option that lets me be *home* without actually being home.

It isn't fair that my brother gets to actually stay home in California, but Curtis has always been Dad's clone, so Curtis is the one inheriting the keys to the kingdom while I'm shuffled off to every dark corner they think my name can be buried in. Too bad for them I figured out the game. I intend to capitalize on my time in Huntington. The properties Dad and his perfect son don't want will be added to *my* company's holdings. Once A.K. Investments rivals Kingwood Properties, they'll see I know the business of buying, renting and selling better than Curtis, and certainly better than my self-righteous sister's podgy husband. The only thing Byron knows how to do is suck up to Dad, and that's why he's such a good match for Lila.

The first order of business in Huntington is attending a charity event at one of the properties Dad *did* manage to acquire during his brief interest in this side of the continent. The flat-roofed banquet hall adjoins a golf course, butting up to the overgrown fifth hole. Driving around the tan-sided venue, I park in the back, in front of a row of ground-level windows. From what I recall of my one and only tour of the place two days ago, these three-foot-tall panes lining the wall provide light to a hallway that slopes down to the basement.

Behind me, draped over my backseat, is a notched-lapel single-breasted suit. After three sleepless nights I considered not attending tonight's Veterans' Banquet, but it's a toss-up as to what will make the vein in Dad's neck bulge more, and I'm banking on my presence here doing greater damage than skipping.

In case he's the one bankrolling Cassie's voyeurism, Dad can also choke on how I'm getting ready to strip down to my birthday suit in a public place. I throw open my door and step out onto the scorching pavement, dropping my drawers. If they're watching, Cassie can eat her heart out over what she can't have, and Dad can stay jealous of the surfer's body he's always complaining I spend too much time on. Which is a joke, because I spend zero minutes on my physique. He'd know that if he actually cared to ever talk to me. But conversation with me doesn't interest him. All he's ever done is declare me to be a long line of grief and screw-ups. So now he has something new to add to his list. Public indecency isn't the most moronic thing I've ever done, though. Marrying Cassie without a prenup takes that title.

Snatching my baggy shorts and t-shirt from the pavement, I toss them into the Rover and look around. The golf course is rundown, the dozens of cars around me appear empty, and I doubt anyone passing through the hallway would bother glancing out to the parking lot. But the longer I stand here naked, the dumber I feel. The Kingwoods may be the reason my life is a cesspool of oozing agony but I don't need to confirm their every judgment.

Covering my dangling jewels, I lean toward the backseat. Movement draws my eyes to the right. There's a shadow silhouetted in one of the building's windows. I face the glass and drop my hands. Judgement or not, no one is going to intimidate me.

~2~

Growing up in a family like mine means wearing suits more often than not, but being worse than a black sheep means not being forced to attend events. At twenty-nine and not really part of my family anyway, I need to start forcing myself to go out. I've got to build a social network to convert to business leads. Tonight's charity banquet isn't ideal for that because it's for the actual people in need, not the stuffy elite. But I can barely tolerate being around the *upper* class, so as far as I'm concerned, tonight is utopian. I'm just not sure I got the time right.

The insomnia started right after my very short marriage imploded. I was a naïve twenty-one then. Now, my weeks all run together, and when the battery on my phone dies, I lose all hope of even knowing what decade I'm in. I'd put myself out of this misery if the witch I'm hitched to wouldn't get all my money after I died.

Sun blazing its last rays of day, I stare at the low bank of windows while yanking on my suit pants, imagining Cassie burning through my bank account before my body is even cold. I drag the crisp white button-up over my bronze arms, slowly sliding the buttons into place. Turning from the shadowed glass, I shrug into the suit jacket and smooth my hair in the side mirror. I didn't bring a tie. I hate them so I only own one, and I was wearing it my first day in town, when I met with Joan, the tight-laced lady who runs the nonprofit hosting tonight's event. While she explained her organization's work in helping veterans return to civilian life, I sat in front of her with gravy splotched on my shirt like a toddler. After she left, Gladys, the brave lone secretary keeping my family's affairs organized, informed me Joan has connections with deeper pockets than my own. Her point was to advise me of the need to make better impressions. I glance at the windows of the building. If that shadow is Joan's, I hope my show impressed her.

Rounding the banquet hall, I regret letting my temper get the best of me; I should have changed *inside* the blacked-out Rover. I reach for the handle of the exterior door and my gut somersaults, Joan is already on her way into the foyer to meet me. I guess this confirms she *was* the shadow.

I step into the tiled foyer and take the hand she's extending, a brief firm shake, and then palms at my sides. No need to acknowledge me stripping for her. "Good to see you again. How are tonight's final preparations coming along?"

Her head tilts. "They're fine, but I didn't expect to see you. Is everything okay? We're still permitted to use the building, I hope?"

"Of course…" I stumble over my tongue as my eyes catch a glimpse of the all-smiles woman strolling toward us. I avert my gaze. The curve of her swaying hips draws me back in, and now that she's standing next to Joan, I can't help but *know* her skin smells as delectable as she looks. A flash of me digging my fingers into her shoulder-length honey hair and kissing every bit of that red lipstick off her hits my frontal cortex. I clear my throat, pinning my hands together. I've sworn off women. I've even sworn off alcohol to make sure I rid myself of all female mistakes. I'd rather stay celibate than get mixed up with another Cassie. "Joan, you mentioned always needing help, so I'm at your service. And don't let the suit fool you, I'm not above emptying the trash."

Sweat builds under my collar as the unidentified drink of dead and bitter dreams on Joan's left provides the answer. "We never turn away volunteers. Especially tall, dark, and stallion ones."

I force my eyes off her lips again, staring directly at Joan. I'm not here to flirt. No matter how much the luscious woman strokes my ego. Joan saves me from having to launch a response, her narrow blue eyes twinkling. "Mr. Kingwood, allow me to introduce you to the person solely responsible for making tonight's event happen. She isn't tall, dark, or a stallion, but she's equally impressive. This young lady is *the* Miss Sheila Beller."

"Beller?" Moisture breaks out across my entire body. "Of the John Beller family?"

"Guilty." Sheila laughs, the sound tickling over my ears like a soft summer rain. "But I don't want to know what you've heard about my family, particularly my brother, unless you're willing to give me the chance to dispute it over dinner. Say, next Thursday at six?"

The primary order Dad gave me was to make the acquaintance of John Beller. But billionaire or not, the one thing I'm *not* doing is following Daddy's orders. Every member of the Beller family gets my cold shoulder. Even the beautiful ones. I only wish I kept up with society columns. I could have used a heads-up before running into Sheila's sleek legs. From the tip of her pointy-toed shoes to the crown of her honey-hued head, she's a work of art. And her amber eyes openly admire me, digging in like their purpose is to read my soul.

"No need for dinner. As far as I'm concerned, your family's reputation is none of my business." I level my eyes on Joan again, waiting. Despite the fact that Kingwood Properties chose Huntington solely because it sits halfway between the Potomac River where the Beller estate is located and the secluded inland property where John Beller built his home, I will *not* engage Sheila.

~

Of course Joan partnered Sheila and me together. It's what Sheila wanted, and like all wealthy people, she gets what she wants. "Need anything else, Miss Beller? I just put two cushioned chairs at the table in the foyer."

"I can see that." She hands me half the stack of programs in her arms, pivoting away from me to walk back out the clear glass doors and into the foyer where we've been setting up the hostess table. She stacks her programs on her side of the table and I follow suit on mine. "You're in luck, Mr. Kingwood. I assume the standoffish attitude you have with me is because my brother's reputation precedes him. The infamous man himself will be in attendance tonight, so you'll have a chance to quell your nerves. And my pushy mother is in the kitchen at this very moment, no doubt telling the chef how to do his job." Her hand rests on my forearm. "Don't worry, my sister-in-law will also be here. She makes up for the shortcomings of the rest of us. The icing on our otherwise bitter cake."

I remove her hand. "I've always liked icing better than cake."

"Most men do." She isn't fazed by my rejection. "Be warned, my brother does *not* take kindly to anyone touching his breadbox. Try even the tiniest lick of her sweet icing and he'll have your head."

Her attention turns to straightening the table and I feel a tug in the pit of my stomach. It's better when her eyes, and all her attention, are on me. "No licking icing or touching breadboxes. Sounds easy."

"Say *all* the boys before their heads are chopped off." she chides, glancing at her watch. "The guests of honor should be arriving soon and I'm not talking about my family, so let's check in with Joan one last time."

"After you." I wave her on ahead of me and follow her enticing vanilla scent. A few steps in and it's clear that walking behind her is a mistake. The woman's curves have curves. And my eyes want to glue themselves to every move they make.

Forcing my feet forward, I fall in beside her. "You set this whole thing up? The food? Presentations?"

"The finest of food. Cutting-edge presentations on new medical procedures for anything from PTSD to prosthetics and for veterans' issues like reintegration and job training. Employers, as well as those looking for willing participants for medical trials, will be on hand for guests to mingle with after the meal."

"Impressive."

She keeps a steady pace toward the dining room, pointing to the hall where informational displays are set up. "Questionnaires are available so the veterans can let Joan know what they most need help with in their daily life, and what they would like to see at this exquisite expo next year. Assuming they want it at all. Which I'm betting they will." She slides her hand onto the crook of my elbow as we enter the dining room. "Oh, and I also found this banquet hall all by my little self. I guess a beautiful socialite *can* have brains after all."

Those eyes of hers *are* reading my soul. "You think very highly of yourself, Sheila Beller."

"Don't you?"

I let her touch remain; her fingers feel good brushing against my bicep. "Myself? Sure. You? We'll see."

She lets go. "Don't take too long *seeing*. I bore easily."

I move close enough that our arms touch as we walk. "I've been around plenty of socialites and plenty of women. I know what keeps you interested."

"We'll see." She walks ahead of me. "And I won't take my time figuring it out."

$$\sim 3 \sim$$

I've lost every drop of Sheila's attention. I haven't interacted with her since Joan sent me to check on the freshly arrived valets. When I came back, Sheila was busy inspecting the venue as a whole. I maneuvered to watch her as she *suggested* different configurations for every vendor display, and I became so engrossed watching her orchestrate the show, I forgot to even try to avoid her. She didn't notice. Veterans started arriving before she glanced my way again.

I fix my eyes on the clipboard in my hand. She's right beside me, the two of us standing behind the hostess table with the glittery point of her stiletto drawing my attention every time the light dances off it. Then I find my eyes winding their way over her ankles and up her calves. "One last family to check in. Next, we start dinner service?"

"You're a good guesser, Mr. Kingwood." She openly admires my hand as I tap the clipboard with my pen. "I don't see a ring, but maybe you have a girlfriend you invited to join you for dinner?"

"You don't have to fish, *Miss Beller.*" Her formality stinks of home. Where games are played and witches rule. "You can simply *ask* if I have a girlfriend. And if you're going to insist on speaking to me, you can also call me Avery."

"Avery, you may call me Sheila." She grins. "You may also tell me if you have a girlfriend."

We're close enough I can almost taste her, and the desire to do just that is burning a hole through me. I lean in to her ear, breath fanning over the soft hairs of her creamy neck, so near to what my mouth wants. "I don't have a girlfriend. That's why I'm so thoroughly enjoying spending an evening working next to you."

A little flirting won't hurt. It might even ease the searing lust. "Joan chose her hostess well. The veterans are receiving a special treat being greeted by your smiling face, not to mention the white dress you're wearing is exquisite." I pull back and admire the legs I've been trying not to memorize. "And those lip-matching red shoes…what appropriate thing can a man say when this is his view?"

"I'm glad you approve." She turns to the opening door and nudges me. "Speaking of treats. Here's my brother and his sweet Mary."

"You always refer to her as his possession?"

I follow her gaze and freeze. She's talking, but the sound is dull. All my being focuses on the vision in front of me. John Beller is imposing, and his famously gorgeous wife doesn't disappoint, but it's the bundle in her arms that takes my senses. Sheila places a hand on my arm. "Brace yourself. We're bound to be nauseated by this utterly ridiculous duo before the night is over."

"Very funny." John's hand rests possessively on his wife's shoulder. "Say breadbox one time tonight and I'm going to embarrass you in front of all these people."

"Too late." She giggles, winking at me. "They refer to each other as possessions and the longer they're together, the worse they get. If you have a weak stomach, run away."

"They have a baby."

The words fall out of my mouth. I've lost all control of my brain. But Sheila's in command of hers. "This *very* clever man is Avery Kingwood." She pats my back. "Good call on staring at the baby. My brother's bite *is* as bad as his bark. Breathe, though. He really is only a man, no matter what the legends say."

"Still not funny," Mary scolds, passing the baby to Sheila before turning espresso eyes on me. "Kingwood? We sold furniture to a Kingwood a few years ago."

"My father." I extend my hand first to John, then decide not to attempt to shake hers. "I'm Avery. The youngest of two sons, and we also have an older sister." My babbling brain hasn't recovered. "It's nice to meet you both. Dad speaks highly of you."

John studies me. "He was having some health problems when I spoke to him last. How's he doing now?"

"Better. He plans to retire soon and spend his time yachting Mom around the world." Dad's *health* problem is me. "The furniture he purchased was meant to be used in one of our commercial spaces, but Mom took one look and had it shipped home for her personal use."

Mary's face tilts to John's. "She has good taste. My husband is the finest carpenter in the world."

"Thank you, sweetheart." His lips brush hers.

"Get a room." Sheila stuffs the baby into his arms. "And take Mikey into the kitchen to rescue the chef from Mom."

Mary presses a kiss into her husband's cheek for effect and nuzzles her baby before smiling at me. "If you get a chance, join us for dinner. We'd love to hear more about your parents."

I return her smile, eyes narrowing toward her husband, who may have just growled at me. "I'd be delighted to have dinner with you, if your sister allows me a chance to sit down."

Sheila shoos them away. "If you three don't stop adoring each other there isn't going to be a dinner. The chef is liable to walk out any minute."

I wait until they're safely inside the venue and I'm alone with her. "How old is their baby?"

"Johnathan Michael Beller is five months old. His mother is spoken for. In case my brother growling at you didn't tip you off."

"So I didn't imagine that? He actually *growled?*"

"Consider it his first warning." She waves me away as she did them. "Go. You're free to have dinner with them. If John's growl increases in decibel, hide behind Mom."

~4~

Dinner with the Beller family is akin to spaghetti night in a bingo hall. That's what Mom would say anyway. As if any of us have ever been to a bingo hall. And I'd bet half a million that she's never had a plate of spaghetti in her life. Still, sitting with this family who's exactly like mine on paper yet completely opposite in demeanor, all I can do is think of Mom. If she were here, she'd be fanning her face and commenting on the lack of canapes.

On second thought, she wouldn't be here at all. Her charity involvement consists of raising money from deep-pocketed people, not sitting among the people she's giving charity to. She'd have a coronary if the two dozen people who have interrupted our dinner tonight came anywhere near her table. But as these men and women trickle by, thanking the Bellers, *this* family doesn't turn them away. There isn't a whiff of disdain. Instead, the Bellers quickly filled the three open seats at our table with veterans who have no family here. The only vacancy left is beside me, and it's reserved for Sheila. But her presence only exists in the words of those gathered around me.

I seek her out when I can, my eyes drifting to where she's busy making rounds. From what I've seen, she's spoken to every single person in attendance. When she's not talking, she's ensuring all the moving pieces of the night are well oiled, fussing over the tiniest of details. I can't help but think of Mom again. Only, Mom's details are all self-focused. Sheila's too perfectly put together to be anything except the same. Though tonight, somehow, she's managing to focus on others.

When her nephew begins to fuss, she finally graces our table. "Is Auntie Sheila's favorite boy upset?"

"He's hungry." Mary denies Sheila's outstretched arms. "John and I will take him out to the truck."

Sheila sighs. "They do make pumps. Mom and I are offended you won't use one so we can feed him."

"Too bad." John flicks her nose, standing with his wife. "He needs this bonding time with us."

They skitter away and I fight the dull throb that never leaves my heart. The weight of loss is always there, ready to pull me under, to smother what little resolve I have left. If my child had lived, I would have been a dad like John.

To stop my internal descent, I focus on Sheila, pulling out the empty seat beside me. "I guess modern dads like to be a part of the feedings."

Her eyes roll and she ignores my offer, remaining on her feet. "They like to have Mikey grip onto his dad's finger while he's eating so he'll grow up *knowing* both his parents are *always* with him. It's all to cover up the fact that they never leave each other's sight."

Katherine Beller shrugs, her puff of white hair hinting at her age. "At least they give marriage a good name."

Sheila pans the room; dinner service is winding down and the last presenter is being announced. "All they're doing is giving Mikey a reason to grow up wondering why his parents aren't fighting and living in separate rooms like the rest of his friends' parents. The poor kid is in for a life of helicopter parenting that's going to send him straight to therapy."

"Sheila." Katherine's tone scolds. Sheila shrugs, winks at the guests and slips away, those infuriating stilettos drawing my attention to her legs again. I swivel away, focusing on the doctor getting ready to explain sound therapy as a treatment for PTSD. A topic much more important than the shape of Sheila's legs.

~

The toothy doctor with the comb-over runs through his slides. I tune out, palms sweaty against my suit pants. Even when I loved Cassie, I wasn't codependent with her the way John and Mary are. I never wanted Cassie to so much as stub her toe, but it wasn't like I was going to hover over her to make sure she didn't. We both needed time alone.

Away from each other. Like normal people. So why I'm sitting here broiling with the desire to endlessly be near Sheila and her perfectly groomed body is lost on me. And embarrassing considering her mom is sitting five feet away.

I'd excuse myself but everyone else has already left the table. I don't want to be rude and leave Katherine alone. It doesn't appear John is going to bother to bring his little family back, so here I sit, stuck, while the veterans filter out to the many different post-dinner activities—and with images of Sheila's legs walking through my mind.

I tug at my sweat-soaked collar and glance at Katherine. I might as well make small talk. "Why do you refer to Mary as John's breadbox?"

"Me?" She huffs. "Sheila is the only one who does."

I raise a brow. "With the deepest of affection?"

A slow smile creeps over her lips. "Sheila started calling Mary that years ago. John thinks it's even *less* funny now than he did then."

"So Sheila's motivated by annoyance levels?" That explains some things.

Katherine sighs. "Sheila's motivated to amuse herself. The annoyance of others is only a bonus. And you won't have to spend much time around her to figure that out for yourself. She'll find your buttons, and she'll push them."

Spending time around Sheila is the last thing I need to do. The lust from barely being near her tonight is stifling, any more of her and I'm liable to forget women are spawns of Satan. "Thanks for the warning. I'll keep my buttons well hidden."

Katherine stands, laughter flittering across her features. "You might try, but what Sheila wants to know, she finds out. You're only move is to not give her a reason to *want* to know you, Mr. Kingwood." She rests a hand on my shoulder. "Excuse an old woman for abandoning you. I need to check on the kitchen one last time and track down that grandson of mine before it gets too late."

"If you find him let me know, I'd like to say goodbye to his father."

She gives my shoulder a soft pat before moving out of the room and down the hall toward the kitchen. I wait until she's gone before scanning the room for Sheila. Wherever the vixen is, I need to steer clear of her and her shoes. My family has gone to great lengths to ensure my wife stays hidden. If Sheila's a secret-digging gossip, I can't let her push any more of my buttons than she already has.

~5~

My bride and I were carted off to distant shores directly after our elopement, and I was banished from ever stepping foot within the United States eight months later. Not legally, but the threats were clear. First, the marriage was my family's dirty little secret. Now, it's the potential divorce.

My absence provided the Kingwoods an opportunity for less gossip to circulate about me, but they took it a step further, essentially erasing me from their lives. I've often wondered what people connected to them were told about the wayward son. As for the friends I used to have, all they know is the night I met Cassie, I vanished. Wrapped up in a storybook love. When it turned out to all be a lie, they weren't there. Not that I tried to call any of them. I was too distraught; in agony over having the promise of fatherhood ripped away from me and drowning in the guilt of having willingly conceived a child only to have Cassie abort the little girl without giving me a voice in the fate of the life we'd created. I'll never suffer enough in this lifetime for believing Cassie when she said she wanted a baby. For excitedly going along with her desire to get pregnant right away. I was a twenty-one-year-old fool. Since then, I've only endured the weight of my mistakes by remaining resolved to not care about anything—or anyone—ever again.

Instead of bailing on the banquet cleanup just to avoid Sheila Beller, I make myself useful. Boxing up the last of the centerpieces, I nestle the delicate arrangements inside the cardboard cocoons they were delivered in and place them on a dolly. Circumventing the yellow-walled hallway where Sheila is helping Joan sort questionnaires, I duck out a back door and loop around the building to where a floral van is waiting. I load the boxes into the back of the van and consider using the door on my left to

14

re-enter the building. But then I'd have to pass by Sheila, and the seductive woman beats a four-alarm fire through my center. Even in the days of finding myself slung over a barstool I never got this worked up over a woman. I rub my tired eyes. "It must be the jet lag."

"You just got off a jet?" The timbre of her voice washes over me, heels clicking on the pavement behind me. "I didn't expect you to stay for cleanup, let alone the tail end of it."

"I can say the same about you." I keep my eyes to myself, nodding to the boxes of flower vases in the back of the van. "I heard you made arrangements for these to be delivered to the veterans' hospital tomorrow?"

"For patients who don't get visitors." She steps closer. "You did a fine job of packing them. I've never seen anyone take so long, though. You must have been *very* careful."

"The least I can do is make sure they reach their destination looking just as beautiful as they did gracing the tables this evening."

"So, you approve of my dress *and* my choice of centerpieces?"

Her eyes gleam. I can't help but stare into them. Then I move downward, settling my gaze on her lips. I clench my hand to keep it from reaching for her. "If my approval is what you were after, you earned it. For more than your dress and centerpieces."

"Not bad for my first day." She grins. "The night *was* a smashing success. But I can't take all the credit. It was Joan's brainchild, all I did was bring it to life."

I close the van doors, choosing to grab them instead of her beautiful face. "You executed remarkably. And meeting your family was a pleasant surprise."

She leans on the doors. "Really? Pleasant wasn't the initial feeling you gave off."

I look out over the rolling greens of the golf course. "Meeting any member of your family at this old banquet hall took me by surprise."

"Not to worry." She pushes off the van and stands next to me, admiring the view that's not really that great. "They like you. Except for wondering why a grown man would strip in public. My brother was particularly bothered by the news, but I assured him there were no complaints from those of us who watched. My favorite part was when your perfectly sculpted backside bent over to pick up the shorts you kicked off." She faces me. "My least favorite was when you covered your beautiful torso. How does one get so…tan?"

Mortification rips through me. The *Bellers* are who Gladys was referring to when she warned about who Joan was in cahoots with. Just my luck it was one of them I stripped for. "Who else was invited to your peep show? Did you and your friends make popcorn?"

Sheila's eyes twinkle. "I'm not great at sharing. I'm afraid I reserved a seat for only myself."

That's a relief. I only made a fool of myself in front of one person. One beautifully crafted art piece of a woman. "Before you get too carried away enjoying my mistake, I only made it because I wasn't sure I was going to be free in time to make the banquet, let alone be here early enough to help with the finishing touches." I glare at her for effect. "Next time, I'll be more careful about what windows I park in front of. Especially if I know *you're* lurking inside."

She folds her hands innocently in front of her. "Don't be careful on my account. I'm not complaining."

"No, you're just telling your brother I'm a stripper." I run a hand down my face. "That must be why he was short with me when I tried to say goodbye to him."

"*That* was because you talked to his breadbox too much. No matter how hard it is to divert your eyes from Mary's gorgeousness, you have to learn to keep your attention elsewhere."

"It wasn't *Mrs.* Beller who had my attention tonight." My heart pounds, propelled by the delicate shadow the moon casts on her creamy skin. "My eyes were otherwise engaged."

Her head tilts, trickling hair over the curve of her shoulder. "Does that mean you'll allow me to be your tour guide tomorrow? I'll show you around town. And if you're well-behaved, I'll treat you to lunch at my favorite spot."

"I appreciate the offer, but I'm in town to work. You asked earlier if I had a girlfriend and I don't, nor am I looking for one. Or for anything even remotely close to a date."

Her smile flashes. "The best things in life find us when we're not looking for them. And you have to eat. So meet me by the fountain in Miller

Park tomorrow at noon. I'll give you a quick tour and a late lunch, then you can get right back to work, still being just as single as you are now."

My mouth opens, but she's already strolling away in all her glory. Before disappearing around the corner she glances over her shoulder to see if I'm watching. I am. And I'm thinking a tour of Huntington can't hurt.

~6~

Last night was the same as usual. Toss, turn, pace and repeat. Each time I passed the window I thought about Cassie's hired stalker, how I can't ditch her efforts to plague me unless I cut ties with my family altogether. A solution with as many upsides as downs.

The morning light never brings any fresh perspectives, especially after the pre-dawn scoldings Dad insists are company briefings. I walk down the dingy hallway to bathe in a chipped sink, the air is as stale as ever. If business proves to be good in Huntington, both for the Kingwoods and A.K. Investments, getting an apartment will be necessary. Right now, there's no point signing a lease if I'll only have to pay to get out of it later. There's also no point in pretending I don't want to see Sheila again. I tried beating the desire out of my skull earlier, but all that encounter with the wall gave me was a headache.

Wielding the only control I have over my yearning, I'm purposefully fifteen minutes late to meet Sheila. The very fact that the woman texted me at a number I didn't give her is proof her mom wasn't lying about Sheila finding out what she wants to know. All the more reason for me to turn and run. She's the type of mistake I can't afford to make. With any luck, she'll put an end to my angst herself by already being gone.

Wandering down Miller Park's main cobblestone path, I keep my pace slow, taking in the mix of miniature roses dotting the landscape. The smell of the orange and yellow blooms reminds me of home. Mom had dozens of pink rose bushes planted on our estate. When I was little, I'd jab my tiny fingers full of holes trying to pick one for her. Later, I stole more than a few of those prized blooms for Cassie.

"Avery!" Sheila's voice cuts through my memories. I shield my face from the sun with my hand. There's an oval fountain rising out of the center of the park. On its left, where the path winds around the soothing fountain of water and shoots off in six directions, stands the exquisite being from last night.

I take my time reaching her, reminding myself with every step that looks are only skin deep. "Hey."

"Hey yourself." She slides her sunglasses up, perching them atop her head. "Glad you could make it."

"You didn't give me a choice." I motion for her to spin. "That's a beautiful skirt."

She actually obliges me, twirling a step closer. "It's a skort. I'm fashionably bringing them back."

"I have no idea what a skort is, but I like it."

"Thanks. But since I only have you for a little while and you're already late, we can't stand here admiring my outfit." She links her arm through mine. "Come. I have a surprise."

"I don't like surprises."

"Too bad."

On the opposite side of the fountain, she waves toward the tandem bike propped against the stone. "Ta-da! We're going for a ride!"

"On that?" I laugh. "You're serious?"

"I am." She plucks a helmet from the handlebars. "This is a fast way to tour the town. We'll cover a lot of ground before you run back to the real world of all work and no play."

"Keep surprising me and I'll be running back sooner than you think."

I plop the second helmet on my head and snap it under my chin. "Do you want me in the back or front?"

"You'll have a better view from the back." She reminds me I was glued to her backside last night. A reminder I don't need.

"Fine by me." I straddle the back seat, steadying the bike for her. "Let's see how this skirt-skort thing of yours peddles."

She sits on the seat, spinning her legs forward the way I imagine any woman wearing a skirt would. I don't see how that blocks anyone's view of her sweet spot from the front, but that's not my problem. I didn't wear a miniskirt to ride a bike. I raise the kickstand. "Ready?"

She grips her set of handlebars, feet on the pedals. "Ready."

I push off. The bike tilts. Our bodies go with it, Sheila sliding off her seat and dangling sideways. An angle that explains what a skort is. *I might be willing to put all my goods on display, but she has sense enough not to.*

I bring the bike down gently so she can untangle without getting hurt. "What are you doing, Sheila Beller?"

She giggles. "I have no idea. I thought you would warn me before we moved."

"I said *ready.*"

"Yes, but you didn't say *here we go!*"

I set the bike upright and she slides back onto her seat. "How do we do this? Do we count while we pedal? Or sing or something to keep in sync?"

"You got me on this contraption and you've never ridden tandem before?"

She shrugs. "I've always wanted to. Today seemed like the day to try it. And I was kind of hoping you'd done this before?"

"No," I snap. "And I've never wanted to."

"Well, if you're *that* miserable about it, we'll scrap the bike." She plants her toes on the ground. "I just thought it would be a fun way to break the ice. Nothing serious, just a silly bike ride."

Therein lies my problem. At all costs, I need to *want* to avoid breaking the ice with her. "You dragged me out here. We're doing this. So pick up your feet, we'll push off on the count of three."

She groans. "Try to curb your enthusiasm. It's nearly unbearable."

"Like you said, it's just a silly bike ride. Nothing serious." I push off. "Three!"

~7~

I'm not sure I've ever smiled so much and I'm certain I've never laughed this hard. Being an absolute failure at tandem bike riding, plowing through shrubs and toppling over benches, has turned Sheila and me into hyenas. Our chuckling apologies reach the occasional innocent bystander caught in the middle of our inability to steer in the same direction. But the best part of today is Sheila's unlaced disposition. No matter what obstacle jumps out at us, or how inept we prove to be at driving this hunk of metal, she never complains. She only laughs, declaring us pros if we manage to remain incident-free for a whopping two minutes.

It's appealing to be with someone so jovial. Someone so tenacious. She didn't even flinch when our last crash resulted in a nasty scrape along the bottom of her knee. I didn't get a leg under us in time to keep her from toppling off the seat, so instead I went down with her, softening her fall. Lying there underneath her, the cobblestone cool on my back, I waited for tears or for her to blame me. Instead, she took my breath away with one flash of her smile.

Reluctantly, I climbed back on the bike, wishing we were still lying on the ground, my arms around her. "How's your knee feel?"

"It's fine." She doesn't so much as glance at the skinned bit of flesh. "How about you? Can you take a fall or are you hurt?"

"I can take anything you're giving out." My fingers move forward, brushing against her back. She glances over her shoulder. If I don't fill my mouth with something else, I'm going to fill it with her. "Where are you taking me for lunch?"

She faces forward. "We're almost there."

"It looks to me like we're almost back to the fountain."

"See?" She steers us into the interior of the park. "One bike ride with me as your amazing tour guide and you already know your way around."

"I'm not sure you get to take credit for being a tour guide, you didn't tell me anything about the town today."

When we reach the fountain, I put my feet down, steadying us so she can get off without falling this time. She slides from the seat, unclips her helmet and shakes out her silky quaff. "I made you laugh, that's much more important than the history of this stuffy old place."

I put down the kickstand and tug off my helmet. Maybe it's her bright eyes or the locks of honey falling over the soft curve of her shoulder, but I'm persuaded to speak the truth to her. "I've laughed more today than I've laughed in a very long time."

She smiles. "Well then, now I'm going to feed you more than you've eaten in a very long time."

She wheels the bike in the direction of the rental kiosk at the edge of the park. I take a breath and close my eyes for a beat. I can't do this. I can't be here feeling the type of way that will make me blow up what's left of my paltry life.

Catching up to her, I take control of the bike so my hands have something to do other than caress her. "I'm going to pass on lunch. You've wasted enough of my time today, I've got to get back to work."

She takes the handlebars back. "You're free to leave, but I doubt you will."

"Why's that?"

Her feet stop, eyes locking onto mine. "Because if you do, you'll be missing the best food you've ever had. And I'm not only saying that because *any* food you eat in my company is sure to taste significantly better."

"You're full of yourself, you know that?"

"For good reason." She gives me control of the bike and links her arm through mine. "I'm so delightful even the sun shines brighter when I stand in it. Ask around town, the people will tell you. That, and other accolades just as fanciful."

She gets no argument from me about how great she is, and I'm sure everyone in this quaint city feels the same, but I don't need to feed her ego. I need to remember Cassie. The reason I can't have the sunny Sheila Beller.

I return the bike to the kiosk, her touch on my arm draining my will to bail on lunch. *Just one meal.* My fingers find their way overtop hers. "The deathtrap is back in its place, now where's lunch?"

"Right over here." She steps out of the park and we cross the road, heading straight for a food truck.

"You can't promise me the best lunch of my life then feed me a street hotdog. Especially after making me ride that stupid bike."

"What I'm doing, Mr. Kingwood, is being the best tour guide *ever* by feeding you exactly as I promised." She releases my arm and joins the other patrons waiting in line, amber eyes igniting. "This is no hotdog stand, it's a taco truck. And before you say a word, I have to insist you try them. Erase everything you thought you knew about tacos because my friend Alberto is going to blow your mind."

I look over the menu, her essence so near it's hard to read the words. "Order one of everything," she whispers. "If you don't, we'll only have to stand in line again because trust me, you're going to want more."

"That good, huh?" I'm torn between kissing her and ordering. "I don't know if I can trust your opinion since you thought riding that bike was a good idea. I'm only ordering three." There will definitely be no kissing. Of any sort. With anyone. "Chipotle short rib. Cajun chicken. Blackened fish."

"Your mistake." She shrugs. "But all good choices. I see you like it hot, same as me."

My eyes slide from the sign to her legs. "The hotter, the better."

Her lips turn up. "I couldn't agree more."

$$\sim 8 \sim$$

Dousing my fire with a bottle of ice-cold water, I stand aside as Sheila chats with the cooks while we wait for our food. She laughs and smiles so freely it *has* to be an act, the way Cassie was an act. A mirage. The woman I loved melting away each day until seven short months after we said *I do*, there was nothing left of her.

"Is this the first time you've eaten from a street vendor?" Sheila breaks into my rumination, motioning for me to follow her.

I trudge along beside her. "Unfortunately not."

We sit at the only open table on this stretch of sidewalk and I pull out my tacos, splashing the already spicy fare with hot sauce. "I take it you eat here a lot since the owner is your friend?"

"Jealous?"

"Not even a little." I stuff the unusually large Cajun creation into my mouth. She takes an equally unattractive bite, and I imagine the taco goodness sliding all over her tongue. It leaves me wondering what other tasks that very proud tongue of hers can perform. A question I'll chalk up to lack of sleep because a woman stuffing dripping, oozing food into her face shouldn't be this sexy.

Swallowing hard, I force my half-chewed food down with a gulp of water. "Instead of letting you waste my time today, I should have been working. Or sleeping."

She steals my hot sauce and dabs it on her own food. "You're a grown man. I'm not *making* you do anything, you're here of your own accord."

Since she's right, I wolf down my tacos and go back for three more, stuffing them in my face to keep from talking. She watches with amusement as I lick the remnants from my fingers. "What? Haven't ever seen a grown man clean his hands before?"

"Not one who looks so good doing it." She leans forward. "Don't get too clean. You haven't had dessert yet."

My pulse quickens. I want *her* as my post-lunch treat. "I'm stuffed." I rub my protruding stomach. "You were right about these being the best tacos *ever*."

"You haven't seen anything yet." She stands with a wink. "Wait until you try Alberto's calorie-laced dessert."

I force myself to stand, disappointment flooding my chest. "I really can't eat another bite."

"Don't worry," she motions for me to sit back down. "I'm only getting one. It's too decadent not to share."

Putting my mouth anywhere near hers is a plan I can get behind. I shouldn't, but it's really hard not to desire her. A herculean struggle now that she's standing in front of me with chocolaty goodness dripping down her arm. "Is that a *cookie* taco shell?"

"Made to order." She slides the tantalizing treat under my nose, one hand still behind her back. "It's a 'choose your own topping' situation. I made ours a chocolate sundae with fresh strawberry salsa. Still too full to eat?"

I slide over and tap the bench next to me. "I've got plenty of room."

She ignores my invitation and sits across from me again. "I have one more surprise for you."

I stretch out my legs, nestling her knees between mine. "I don't like surprises. I thought we covered this already."

"You'll like this one." She produces what she's been holding behind her back. The thing I didn't care to ask about because I'm too busy trying to convince myself I'm not *this* attracted to her. "We can't call this meal complete unless we finish it with churros."

~

We devour the creamy crunchy dessert taco and sit grinning at each other in a stupefied sugar rush. All that's left is a paper cone of confection, and I know where I'd like to share the churros with her. "Want to take a walk in the park while we finish these?" I have to go that way anyway, it's where the Rover is parked.

"As much as we've eaten today, we'd better." She ignores my outstretched hand and stands of her own accord, strolling across the street, her flesh so near and yet so far from touching mine. "I forbid myself to come down here more than three times a week. If I came every day the way I'd like to, I'd eat Alberto out of business. Not to mention eat myself out of my entire wardrobe."

I step over the curb and onto the cobblestone path. "Unfortunately, I work near here. I guess that means a new wardrobe is in my future."

Her eyes glide to my torso. "You can afford to overeat a little. You don't have an ounce of fat anywhere on you."

"Oh, that's right." I smirk. "You're Peeping Tom."

She shrugs. "It can only be considered peeping if you were hiding, which you weren't. I merely looked at what you openly showed. And it was a *very* nice showing."

She faces me, holding up a churro. My hand moves of its own volition, fingers on a path all their own as they caress the length of her arm, from the curve of her shoulder down to her wrist. I lift her perfumed flesh to my mouth, tongue gliding over skin laced with dribbles of chocolate. Her breath catches. My teeth scrape against her, a pain worse than lust burning through me. I drop her arm. "I've got to go. Thanks for showing me around."

Her lips twist into a smile. "My pleasure."

"Miss Beller." I run my betraying hand through my hair, stepping away from her. "I didn't want to let any of Alberto's delicious work go to waste. And I also never want to ride a tandem bike again."

She rubs the churro on her succulent wrist. "You had a blast with me today, admit it."

I need to admit quite a few things, but enjoying her company isn't one of them. Neither is knowing I'll never get the taste of her out of my mouth. I cross my arms, resisting the urge to lick her now-sugared wrist. "I don't know what kind of *boys* you're used to, but I'm a man. Men don't tandem bike ride or waste their entire day playing in the park."

"Right." She stuffs the churro back into the paper cone. "I dare you, *man*, to meet me tomorrow."

I force my eyes to roll. "Why? So we can spend the day knitting?"

Her eyes narrow. "I'll text you an address. Meet me there at ten in the morning, and don't be late."

"Text me." I walk away. "If I don't have any better offers, I'll think about meeting up with you."

~9~

The obsession I'm developing for Sheila is maddening. I can't stop thinking about the taste of her chocolate-covered wrist. Her smile. The way her hair catches the light when she moves and how the sound of her laugh makes me forget about all the chaos in my life. When she's near, I forget who I am. I simply become a man who's willing to do anything to see her smile. But in the dark of night and the glow of dawn, I *know* what I am. A man without a home. Without a family. A man tied to a wife he desperately hates. I'm not capable of having a relationship with anyone, especially someone as remarkable as Sheila.

When I'm not stressing over my ill-fated attraction to Sheila, I'm fretting over Cassie's recent behavior. In the past, there have been times when she's amped up her harassment, being more vocal and even transparent in how often she has me followed; antics I've learned to live with because they equate to nothing and I refuse to be bullied by her. But there was a time when my mom wouldn't be caught dead taking pictures with Cassie, so the text I just received with a picture of the two of them sitting side by side is alarming. Something is changing between them. **Ticktock, husband. Sign the divorce papers or I start telling Mommy our secrets.**

Cassie's too smart to break the terms of our separation agreement. A document I wouldn't have signed if I'd been smart enough to see how she would use it against me. Before the ink was even dry, she was in my family's ear, telling them lies. And they've always believed the worst of me so they ate up her every word. No hesitation, just full-on belief that I'm capable of being the monster Cassie painted me to be.

At some point over the last seven years I could have told them the truth, fought the lies and saved myself from some small portion of their ridiculing judgment. But why do that when they can't be bothered to give me the benefit of a single doubt? Ever. **You're the one who lobbied for the gag, so go ahead, Cassie, break it. I live for the day my hands are no longer tied by you, or to you.**

We both agreed to the terms and I'm keeping my end, but I can't stop your parents from announcing our marriage. Call me. Please.

Even in this new reality of posing for pictures, my parents will never publicly acknowledge the daughter-in-law they never approved of to begin with. The only reason we're married is because I was dumb enough to elope. All too eager to marry Cassie, then seven months later all too eager to get away from her. A lesson I need to keep in mind when dealing with Sheila. She may seem like a gem now, but there's no way that silver spoon princess isn't running a scam on me. The very fact that I'm even sitting at my laptop looking up the address she texted this morning is proof of Sheila's witchery. The address leads to a racetrack for high-performance cars. The temptress is going to take me someplace fun, act like she's into having fun, then nail me in my coffin when I dare spend too much time having fun.

Closing the laptop, I head to the bathroom for my daily sink bath. When I renovate this place, I'm installing a shower. I'm going to install showers in *all* my commercial properties. As a separated man I can attest to the fact that sleeping in an uncomfortable chair in your office is better by far than spending a night anywhere near your wife. And the lifestyle might be demoralizing to anyone getting ready for a date, but I'm not dating. I'm simply meeting Sheila out of courtesy. After all, she is a Beller. Getting in her good graces will be good for business.

~

Despite the fact that I spent my life savings filling up the Rover's gas tank yesterday, it's empty. Dry. I had to use my insurance's roadside assistance perk to have gas delivered to me and by the time the freckle-encrusted woman showed up, a mock on her lips as I attempted to explain that I do know to put fuel in the vehicle, I was already twenty minutes late to meet Sheila. I shot her a brief text to let her know I'd be there in half an hour, and her tart response was that I should invest in a decent watch.

I hand the now empty gas can back to the waiting freckles and drop into a plank, watching the undercarriage for signs of a leak. "I didn't see anything on the pavement earlier and everything is clear now, so are you getting a lot of calls from people like me?" I lift back to my full height. "People whose gas has been siphoned?"

She looks me over. "A lot of new vehicles are siphon-proof, but I've heard thieves know how to get around that."

Cassie's face flashes in front of me. "When someone wants what you have, they always find a way to take it."

"Or you might just need to pay more attention to the fuel gauge." The woman laughs, climbing back into her pickup.

I jump in the Rover. I don't have time to deal with people who won't bother to listen to the words coming out of my mouth. By the time I get to the racetrack, I'll be an hour late. I don't know what time slot Sheila booked for us, but she didn't tell me not to come, so I'm hoping there will still be a car available for the evasive maneuvering course touted on the website. As for the honey-eyed goddess being mad that I'm late, it isn't my fault, so she'll just have to get over it.

When I lived with Cassie, she used to play pranks. Move my stuff around, pretend I'd done it myself. Little things, like my razor or a book I was reading. I'd find them in bizarre places and she'd swear she never touched them. I believed her. For months. Then, when I was convinced I was losing my mind, she laughed. Hysterical, tear-jerking laughter right in my face. My gas being siphoned feels like one of her tricks. Then there's the container of paperclips I found sitting on the windowsill behind my desk yesterday. I usually keep the magnetic holder in a desk drawer and just assumed I absentmindedly set them down, but now I'm not so sure. I need to check the locks on all the rickety exit doors, inventory the building to see if anything else is out of place, and find out if my wife has been out of California lately.

~10~

Whipping into the sparsely occupied lot of the high-performance racetrack, I park in the first non-handicap space by the door and take in the massive concrete structure. It's flanked by razor-wire topped ten-foot solid fencing that juts off the main building, blocking the view and enclosing the lesser buildings so the arched doorway of the concrete giant is the only way in. Compared to other speedways I've been to, this place is impressively underwhelming. There wasn't a lot of information on the website outside of this being a training facility, but the place looks barren. There's not even signage.

A lanky young man in gray coveralls taps on my window while staring at his shuffling feet. This better not be Cassie's photographer come to confess he stole my gas. I'm irritated enough I might strangle him.

I roll down the window. "Yeah?"

"Mr. Kingwood?" His ball cap is pulled down over his eyes. All I can see is shaggy blonde hair jutting out. "Are you Avery Kingwood?"

"In the flesh. And you are?"

"Earl." His head bobs. "I'm Miss Beller's mechanic."

"Mechanic?"

"She told me to wait for you and bring you on in when you got here." He wipes oily hands on his pants. "Follow me. She's already been waiting long enough."

A humorless laugh escapes my lips. "Funny how women expect us to wait for them but can't give us the same leniency."

The racetrack's arched doorway is no less massive when standing underneath it than it appears from the distance. Mine and Earl's footsteps echo across the empty space of the towering room. "Where are we going?"

"Miss Beller is waiting." Earl's pace quickens, leading us through a set of double doors and into the bowels of the building.

His insistence on rushing pricks a nerve. "Miss Beller may be rich *and* female, which she thinks entitles her to have her way, but we can slow down. Waiting a couple more minutes won't kill her."

"It might kill you, though." His chuckle vibrates against the bare walls, legs pulling back to strides half as long. "We don't get many visitors, this not being an open track and all." His head dips toward the end of the hall. "When Miss Beller is here…" His throat bobs. "I'm her mechanic."

"So you said."

Just speaking her name makes him as nervous as a lamb on slaughter day. "What exactly do you *mechanic* for her?"

A whistle slices through the air, cutting off our conversation. His pace picks up again and before I know it, we're ducking out a door, landing ourselves in a pit area. Directly ahead, three polished Chevrolet SS stock cars lie in wait. Leaning against the only hot red one in the bunch is the dame herself, adoring the three men surrounding her Scarlett O'Hara style.

Piling on the agitation, Sheila doesn't acknowledge me. Neither do the men around her. Two of them are clad in the same overalls as Earl and the other is in jeans and a plain button-up shirt. I step into their midst. "I'm here. Now tell me why. Unless you're too busy telling jokes."

Sheila's hips push off the car, fingers sliding over the wrist of the jean-clad man, checking his watch. "Avery Kingwood, everyone. Late. And he hasn't even blown out his hair or painted his nails."

Their laughter heaps coals on my building ire. "I didn't want to interrupt the *moment* you and your friends were having."

She slides her hips back on the car, smiling at the faces of each of the men around me. "I don't need *his* company. Would any of you be interested in taking Mr. Kingwood's place?"

All of them eagerly agree. I glare at them, especially nervous Earl, then turn the glare on her. "I'm here, so no one needs to take my place. Just tell me what we're doing."

"This right here." Earl taps the hood of the blue metallic car next to hers. "She's gassed up and ready to go. Have you ever driven before?"

I cross my arms. "Not one of these. But I'm sure I can figure it out."

Sheila walks past me, back toward the door I just came out of. "If you've never driven a car like this on a track like this, you'll have to take a class before you get behind the wheel. Do try to be quick about it. You're already holding everyone up."

"Keep giving me attitude and I won't let you ride shotgun." Her men laugh. I scowl at them. "She went through the trouble of setting this up, the least I can do is offer to let her ride with me."

"Mr. Kingwood." She looks back at me. "Suit up, take your class, and maybe if you're a good little boy, I'll let you ride *my* shotgun."

~

According to her suitors, Sheila owns this track. Literally and figuratively. Even the professional NASCAR drivers who train here on occasion don't have a good record of beating her. But I'm not them. I'm not going to go easy on her because of misguided loyalty to a billionaire. No matter how good she looks in her blue jumpsuit with white and red racing stripes running up the sides.

I admire the curve-hugging outfit. "Now I see why so many people let you win. But you do understand there's no crying in racing, right?"

She looks around, sliding fingers over the hood of her car. "Who's going to make me cry? Surely you don't think *you're* man enough for the job."

"This may be my first time racing, but I'm no stranger to speed." I strap on my helmet, already donning the same boring overalls everyone else around here is wearing. "I'm man enough to live without ever seeing your body so tightly hugged again, so don't get mad when I don't back off and *prove* your pretty little face only owns this track on paper."

She smiles. "If I weren't as nice as I am, I would make you put your money where your mouth is. But I much prefer the satisfaction of making your pretty little face grovel." She tugs on her custom swirled helmet. "I hope you're not averse to humiliation, Mr. Kingwood. If you are, give your keys to a man who can handle it."

$$\sim 11 \sim$$

Sliding through my Chevrolet's window, I buckle in and rev my idling engine. We maneuver into position and I watch the signal, unblinking. As soon as the light turns, I'm getting the jump on Sheila.

"Earl!" I scream into the headset when the green flag lights. Sheila's ahead of me, nothing but a blur of taillights. "You're supposed to be *my* eye in the sky. How about some warning next time?"

"Copy." His voice crackles through the mic. "You might want to hit the gas now."

"I'm trying!" I chase after her, shifting through gears and still losing ground. "Don't worry, Earl, your boss is going to lose."

The sound of the other men laughing behind him as he directs my path only makes me push harder. Not being experienced, I shouldn't go this fast and he keeps telling me I'm not going to catch Sheila, but I can't slow down. The speed is intoxicating. The glimpses of her as she whirls around the track, outmaneuvering me at every turn, thrills. I'm electrified.

"Come in on your next pass," Earl orders. "You need new tires."

"Copy." I ride the rush into pit lane, chomping at the bit to chase her again. She whips in behind me. I throw off the restraint and push out the window, running to her car in an excited frenzy. She tugs off her helmet and slides out her window. I trap her against the hot metal of the door, peeling off my own helmet and diving toward her mouth.

Her head turns. "I don't kiss men I'm not in a relationship with. Back away."

My palms shake, adrenaline coursing through me full throttle. I unclasp the top of her car and step back three paces, blowing out a steady breath to quell the euphoric beat of my heart. "I didn't want to kiss you anyway."

She pushes off the car. "Your hovering lips made that very clear."

"I didn't say I *wouldn't* have, I said I didn't *want* to." I shrug. "Kissing you in the heat of the moment after a thrilling race wouldn't mean anything anyway. At least, not to me."

"You think it would mean something to me though?"

"You're a female." I wish the earth would open up and swallow me whole. "You would have thought it meant we were together, which you're not. So thank you for stopping me from doing something I would regret."

She removes the distance between us, staring directly into my eyes. "I've raced tons of men. Not one of them has ever tried to kiss me. So tell your lame excuse to someone who might actually believe you don't want to kiss me as much as I want to kiss you."

"If you want to kiss me, you shouldn't have stopped me."

"I'm not your girlfriend." She studies the cracks in my exterior, the ones I don't want anyone to see. "It appears I'll never be. Both from your own professions and from my increasingly unfavorable opinion of a man who changes his mood from one second to the next." She walks away. "See yourself out, Mr. Kingwood."

I follow her inside the building, where she shimmies out of her racing suit. Underneath she has on black leggings and a pink t-shirt. "Nice." I whistle, ignoring the fact that she just politely kicked me out. "But I liked the suit a whole lot, too." Her eyes roll. I chuckle, hoping to de-pile the mess I've made. "What? Can't a man compliment a woman these days?"

"You've been trying to pick a fight with me all day and now you want to talk about my clothing? Again?"

"I can't help that you have good taste." I also can't help looking at her perfectly formed legs. "You had a custom suit made so it would fit all your curves. And women do that because they want men to notice. I'm letting you know I've *noticed*."

"I have custom suits because I race a lot." She hands the one she just vacated to Earl, whose beady eyes are glaring at me. "I also have them because I want them. And if I desire the notice of a man, I'm sure I'll be more creative."

"Like forcing him to ride a bike with you?"

I've heard of toxic masculinity but never thought it was a real thing until right now. I'm taking my frustrations out on Sheila, insulting her, making her uncomfortable to a point that brings bile to my throat. She has nothing to do with the chaos in my life. I have to stop treating her like she does. "Sheila, I'm sorry. My mouth works without my consent sometimes. Can we have a do-over?"

Her answer comes in the form of storming a path through the building, her trajectory leading me straight to the exit. I don't blame her. But even *if* she's not like Cassie, I still can't give in to our attraction. Cassie and I may be irrevocably separated, but dating someone will only give her fodder to use against me. One slip and my lawyer says it's possible a judge would believe her when she says I cheated in the first months of our marriage. Not because it's true or because she has proof, simply because she's a woman.

All Cassie had to do to get the Kingwoods to dance like marionettes was drop a little water from her lashes. There's no reason to believe a judge won't react the same way. So whatever carnal urges Sheila summons, I have to tamp them down. And manage to do so without tying a noose around my neck. I might not be able to bed a Beller, but I can do business with them. Preferably the one I'm barely managing to keep pace with. "To be as good of a driver as you are, you must *really* like racing."

"And you must be a genius." She stops at the main doors I entered through.

I stand beside her, ignoring the exit. "What draws you to racing?"

My palms itch as I wait for her response. She takes a few beats, studying me, and answering only because she has manners. "It's freeing. On the track, nothing matters. Only the speed. And it doesn't make a difference if I'm racing or driving alone. Some days I just need to feel the rush. So I go out alone and push as fast as I can until whatever bad is in my world doesn't seem so terrible anymore."

"The bright-eyed Sheila Beller has bad in her world?" Besides me?

"Everyone does." She sighs. "Don't start being judgmental on top of everything else."

"I'm not." I hold my hands up in truce. "I'm sorry about earlier. I was caught up in the moment and you've clearly been flirting with me like crazy, so I figured a kiss would be okay. It wasn't, and it's pretty awesome that you don't kiss randomly." Bafflingly cute, actually. "I assume that means you have values and morals and probably wouldn't have sex before monogamy either?"

"Try no sex before marriage." Her arms cross. "And I certainly couldn't care less how you feel about my morals so spare me your opinion on the matter."

I have many opinions. Like, why didn't I think of that? "I haven't meant to offend you. I was only picking on you today to see what you were all about."

"And now you've seen." She nods to the door. "You're free to leave, and with my full assurance that you'll never again be subjected to my flirtation."

I'm unable to have a clear thought around her, let alone string proper words together. "If I'm going to spend my time with someone, I want them to be at the very least capable of a real conversation." I motion to her. "I now know you're capable. So, will you talk to me for a while if I promise to stop being obnoxious?"

Her eyes narrow. "We talked yesterday. So why show up with an attitude today? I have my own money. Yours is of no consequence to me, if that's what you think I'm after."

"I—"

"I'm not finished." She unfolds her arms. "All I wanted from you today was a chance to get to know you better. No strings. No fingers in your wallet. Just two people seeing if they have anything in common."

My lip ticks up. "Since the moment we met, you've made it clear you want more than that."

"Why is not okay for a woman to flirt with a man she thinks is attractive? If you saw me and thought I was pretty, you would have flirted. But somehow, switching it up means I'm throwing myself at you? I'm not. I get sick even thinking about dating, so maybe I'm just great at flirting because it hides the fact that I struggle to get close to anyone. And *maybe* I'm happy in spite of it. Instead of being drab and sucking the fun out of life by picking fights over *every* little thing the way *you* do!"

It isn't my fault I suck. It's Cassie's. Dad's. Mom's. My brother's and sister's. And standing in front of Sheila right now, I hate them for turning me into this. I fixate on the color of her irises. "My intent wasn't to rain on your parade. How about we start this day over? Do it your way. Be friends and see if we have anything other than dating woes in common?"

"You just want to get back inside a race car."

I grin. "I wouldn't mind it. But it's your call, we'll do whatever you want. Except tandem bike riding or knitting."

"Giving exclusions by definition means you're not willing to do *whatever* I want."

I extend my hand. "All good friendships have compromises. From me, you get no more teasing or half-baked kiss attempts. From you, I get a bike-and-yarn-free zone."

~12~

I've never been given the benefit of the doubt from anyone or had them extend graciousness the way Sheila just did. I'm not a fool. She didn't give in to me and let me stay at the track out of the kindness of her heart. She ignored my handshake and let me back behind the wheel of her race car so she could humiliate me all over again. Toying with me. Letting me get close enough to think I had a chance of passing her before she vanished like the magical unicorn she is. But what she didn't do was tell me to take a hike.

I dump a handful of hot sauce packets onto our sidewalk table near Alberto's taco truck. "I didn't know racing was so tiring. I'm worn out."

"And starving." She eyes the food. "Thanks for buying."

"It's the least I could do." I step over the bench and my long legs move to find her, our knees finally touching. "You've been nothing but gracious to me."

"That's me." She picks up a pineapple fried rice taco. "Gracious everywhere but on the track."

"You're ruthless on the track." Still high from the thrill, I'm barely managing not to throw myself at her again. "It's your world out there."

"I warned you not to come into my jungle unless you knew how to play."

I lean toward her. "Just you wait. One of these days, I'm going to plow through your jungle and make it *my* world."

Her teeth sink into her lip. "The first day I *saw* you, I had a feeling you might be the one to do just that."

Electricity runs down my throat. From how this day started, I wasn't sure it was possible to even be her friend. It sounds like this exciting woman *has* forgiven me. And then some. A smile splits my face. "I concede. You own the track." My knee rubs hers, all the things I'd like to do with her front and center in my pulse. "Literally. And figuratively."

She snags a packet of hot sauce. "It's a test track. I lease it out to pro teams and run some driving experiences for the general public, something like what you did today minus having me there."

"Then you're ripping off the general public." I tuck my leg against the side of hers. "I doubt it's even remotely the same without you."

She shrugs. "My relationship with the track is special. I don't want to dilute it. Drive the track with just anyone…"

My breath hitches as she devours her taco, sauce dripping over her fingers. "I'll count myself very lucky then." I hand her a napkin, wishing it were my mouth. "What's so special to you about the track?"

"I used to go there with my dad. It was our sanctuary." She cleans her hands while I stuff a taco into my watering mouth. "The year after he passed away, the place went up for sale so I bought it as a way to honor his memory. It was going downhill and I didn't want to see it close, but in truth, I'm only the owner in terms of footing the bill. The men you met today run things. They know what they're doing and they indulge me when I want to drive, but I don't actually *do* anything there."

"You clearly know what to do, though. I'm guessing you're as quick-witted in business as you are in life, so why aren't you running the show?"

Her eyes go distant. "I don't want to. I enjoy having an outlet when I need it, but running a racetrack isn't my passion."

"What is?"

Wheels turn as if she's considering the meaning of life itself. In this moment, I can relate. She has me questioning everything. "Is Sheila Beller too rich to consider working?"

Her eyes fall over the remaining abundance of food. "I went to school for interior design but haven't tried to make that pan out as a career. Instead, I've invested in lucrative businesses so I have money coming in. Passive income." Her eyes lift. "My dad taught us to make the money we live on so that our net worth remains even, ensuring our family's financial security for generations to come."

"Smart man." I approve of the tactic. "Too many trust fund babies squander what they have, not understanding that if they spend it, it's actually gone."

"Well, I definitely make my own contributions to the family accounts, but at twenty-eight, being a silent partner who sits back and collects checks gets boring." Sadness flashes in her amber pools. "That's why I connected with Joan and some other small nonprofits. I didn't want the same old organizations that are so big their overhead kills the difference they're actually making. For me, it's about doing something important with my life. Not just sticking my name out there to bring in money, but having that money get to the people who need it. I'd rather anonymously foot the bill for clean water systems than give money to an organization that's going to take half of it to pay for their headquarters."

Another tactic I approve of. "No wonder I never see you plastered in the tabloids."

"Ditto." She softens. "What about you? How much do you actually work since you spent the majority of the last two days playing with me?"

I'm in the same situation as her. My family has a lot of money and intends to keep it. These days that means they intend to keep it as theirs and cut me out altogether. Outside of my trust fund, which I've already collected and used most of to buy properties for A. K. Investments, I'm not liable to see a penny of any other *family* money, no matter how hard I work for Kingwood Properties.

I rest my elbows on the table. "I pretty much work around the clock. Both for my family's company and my own. So I figure I've earned a couple days off to play with you." She smiles and I return the sentiment. "I invest in real estate. Commercial ventures, mainly, buying to refurbish and sell with the occasional rental thrown in. That's why I'm here." To prove I'm as deserving as my brother. "My family has dabbled on the East Coast, but the main operation is out west. I came to see firsthand what the market is like and if it's possible to grow financially on this side of the country."

"So, you don't plan to stay? You're just scoping out the place?"

"I'm in no hurry to leave." Especially now that I've met her. "So far, business is good. I've found a few potential projects and I'm converting one of the buildings we've been leasing into my own office space. All we've had here is a single secretary stuffed into an office, but the building lease came up, so I found another property for the leasing firm and moved in with the secretary so we could start making a real presence here."

Her tongue clicks. "Moving in with your secretary. How cliché."

"Socialite with taco sauce dribbling down her chin." I reach over and wipe it off. "How endearing."

42

~13~

I'm only twenty-nine, but sitting here with Sheila, I feel aged beyond the innocence of what this time in her life is. She's just beginning to figure out what she wants, and I've lived long enough to know dreams rarely come true. I'd give anything to stretch out today. Stay in this moment with her. But sitting on the street at the same table where we ate yesterday, I'm acutely aware of each passerby. Especially with our knees entwined this way. I don't need a reporter to spot us and splash this *endearment* across their front page.

Hands on my side of the table and spreading my legs so I'm not touching hers anymore, I wash down my last bite of taco. "I don't need anyone suspecting an affair with my married secretary, so don't go spreading rumors around."

She grins. "I'll see if I can keep a lid on your immorality. No promises."

"Then I'll have to dig up some dirt on you to ensure my safety." I feed her a piece of chicken that fell out of her taco, my hands seeming to work on instinct. Another Kodak moment. "But I bet there isn't any, is there?"

"Dig as deep as you want." She slides the food remnants away. "While you're digging, maybe you can find a building for Mary and John? She has a boutique, but they want to relocate into something larger where she can sell clothes on one side and he can sell furniture on the other. And yes, it *all* has to be in *one* building where they can see each other *constantly* or they'll die."

It's cute the way she hates their intimacy. "I saw how close they were the other night."

"You have no idea." She groans. "Being around them either makes you long to be married or petrified to even utter the word."

43

"Which is it for you?"

She shrugs. "I'm nearly thirty and I want kids, so I'm ready to get married. I'm afraid that if I wait much longer, the pregnancy will either be hard, or I won't be able to get pregnant at all."

Her words stack stones around my heart and cover them in cement. She hasn't been flirting with me for the sake of flirting or because she likes me. She's daddy hunting. But I already let Cassie play that card and she ripped out my soul with it. "You're still young, Sheila. And plenty of women are older than you when they have kids."

She focuses on the space above my shoulder, a whole lifetime away as her cinnamon lips begin to move. "When I held Mikey for the first time, something opened inside me. Every day since, I've heard my biological clock ticking. Loudly. Unbearable some days." She meets my stare. "Then I think about how weird John and Mary are, and the marriage part of the ache quiets down."

"Marriage is overrated." I gather up our trash and attempt to silence the ache in my own heart with a trip to the dessert line. She comes with me. I put an extra step of distance between us. I'm sure I tick off boxes for her, but I'm not knocking her up. I won't ever conceive a child again. Plus, I'm already married, so there's that little snag in her plan. "Speaking of weird, I got a strange invitation this morning for an afternoon tea. Do men in this area go to tea parties?"

"It isn't really a tea." She grins. "And I made sure an invitation was issued to you because men attend to sit around pretending to talk business while they gape at all the beautiful women dolled up to make *sure* they're the ones being talked about. Which is exactly why you'll have to make arrangements to discuss business with my brother some other time. He wouldn't be caught dead there, and certainly would never allow his wife to be on the visual buffet."

"But he's okay with his sister being on the menu?"

"Not in the least." She waves to Alberto as his head pops out to survey the waiting customers. "But we've established I like to flirt, and the dear old lady who hosts the shindig would have a heart attack if at least one Beller didn't show up. Plus, my mom loves to go."

"Seriously?"

"Uh-huh." She faces me. "You see, while the men are gaping at the young women, the older women are gaping at the young men."

"Which is why you had me invited? To give them more eye candy?"

"Don't worry." She winks. "Mom isn't crude and she fusses at the other women when they are. So you won't be *too* objectified. Verbally, at least. And," she leans into me, her hands pressed against my chest as her lips find my ear, "there's bound to be someone leaving miffed after Mom publicly embarrasses them. It's the highlight of the evening."

Summoning all my will, I remove her hands and step away. I have to keep space between us. "This is what you and your mom do? Go to parties and embarrass people?"

"I don't need a party to embarrass someone. Remember this morning's run on the racetrack?" She ducks out of line. "It's getting late, I have to go."

"We haven't had dessert yet."

"No time for it today." She waves. "I'll see you at the tea."

I should order dessert, walk in the park alone and reminisce about the time I got to lick chocolate from her vanilla-scented wrist. I should heed the sorrow I've worn like a second skin since the day I found out Cassie aborted our child. I should keep myself from ever being hurt again by staying as far away from Sheila Beller as possible. But the farther she moves away from me, the less I feel able to breathe.

Catching up with her, I press against her shoulder, filling my lungs with air as fresh as a spring day. "Would you be interested in looking at my office next week? I was going to hire a designer anyway, so if you're up for the job, it's yours. There's a lot of work to be done. The building is only three stories but basically needs to be gutted."

"Hmm…" She taps her chin. "My first real job. And working for you? The moody broody man who's just blowing through town."

"A simple yes or no will do."

She opens her car door. "Show up to the tea looking impressively dashing, and we'll discuss the terms of the job."

"There's a reason I'm broody."

"Do tell."

"All you need to know is that you're *not* breaking me." I curse my gaze for following her legs as they slide into the driver's seat. "I'm not dating. And you're *not* tempting me."

"Is that what I'm not doing?" She grins. The blind couldn't miss my obvious scouring of her body. "I'll see you at the tea, Mr. Kingwood. And do try to be on time. I hate when my friends are late."

I watch her drive away and then turn the corner, no longer in the mood for dessert. The Rover is parked in the alley since she beat me here and took the last space on the street. I make the last turn and see a leather jacket-clad man standing beside my hood. He reaches over and tucks an envelope under the driver's side windshield wiper. "Hey!" I put my feet into gear; this has to be Cassie's hired lens.

His faded brown leather puffs as he runs the opposite direction, nearly losing his ballcap as he jumps into a waiting sedan. The tan car darts away and skids onto a side street. I catch enough of the license plate to memorize a few digits, and run back to the Rover to jot them down.

Sliding the thick envelope from behind the wiper, I rip open the top, already knowing what's inside. Divorce papers. Each of Cassie's offers is more lucrative for her than the last. I shove the fire fodder back inside the envelope and tug out the glossy paper behind it. I'm used to seeing myself, but I'm not alone in this picture. I'm with Sheila, my mouth on her wrist. I steady myself on the hood, the assorted tacos I just ate wanting to make a reappearance. I hope beyond all hope that Cassie doesn't know who Sheila is. Or that if she does, she's smart enough to keep away from Sheila.

My phone beeps. It's another picture of Sheila. This one from just minutes ago, the two of us standing outside her Corvette. **Who's your new friend? She looks fun. I should meet her.**

~14~

Since leaving Cassie, I've remained alone. Lonely. In the short amount of time I've known Sheila, I've started to feel alive again. Let dreams of her resuscitate parts of me I thought were dead. And now Cassie, after already taking away my family and my child, is ripping away the one single happiness I've had in all these years.

Twelve moons have graced the sky since I saw Sheila last. As much as I want to look into her beautiful face, text her, call her and stay up all night talking, I've cut myself off from her. I didn't even answer when she called to thank me for the box of chili spiced chocolates I delivered to her via courier. I've listened to her voicemail, though. Filling my hours with work, and with scribbling her name over my notebook while her message plays in the background.

I tell myself that avoiding her is for the best. All she wants is a baby daddy anyway and that can't be me. But as the days blur together, I still scroll her name alongside mine, and look up specialty confectioner's shops so I can send her petit fours modeled after cars and tiny taco shaped caramels. I have a box of each sitting on my desk, right next to the gold inlayed teacup set that Glady's bought and wrapped for the tea party hostess. Mrs. Smithers' party is today and though I've sworn off tea, I'm willing to drink a jug of it just to be near Sheila again. If I'm lucky, I'll convince her to come back to my office afterward, and give her these treats in person.

Eager to make a better impression than I have so far, I went to Mary's boutique earlier this week and bought a new suit for the party. John helped with the tie selection and the shoes, and I left the store feeling closer to Sheila. If she'd been there, we could have made fun of her brother's relationship together. John and Mary are two separate entities standing in front of you, but they walk and talk as one. I kept wanting to snap my fingers in their faces, but the co-dependency is equal. More importantly, they're happy.

Today, I get to be happy. Attending this afternoon's tea *requires* me to be near Sheila. If Cassie has a spy inside the party and they photograph me standing next to Sheila, so be it. A lot of people will be standing next to each other. The only thing I have to do is control my tongue. I'd rather rip it out than insult Sheila again, and under no circumstances can I lick anything off her delectable body.

Not even Dad's pre-dawn scolding soured my mood. The conversation started badly and ended worse, but all he managed to do was keep me from being the first person to arrive at Mrs. Smithers'. Now that I'm here and have spotted Sheila's Corvette, there's warmth radiating from a place that feels a lot like my heart.

Stepping out of the Rover, I hand my key to the valet and point at Sheila's souped-up machine. "Park me as close to that jewel as you're able to get."

Mrs. Smithers' massive garden rivals the best of what I saw in Europe. Paths jut off in every direction, winding through spectacles of shrubs and flowers. I trek through the crowds gathered around trees where stone benches offer seating to a select few. I pass laughing groups, hear their whispers and feel their stares, but there's only one face I care to see and one woman whose words I want to hear.

I head for the sprawling patio where the bulk of the party is amassed. Two water features bubble over rocks and spread their refreshing liquid into a brook that cuts through the middle of the landscape. To my right is the bar, on the left a trio of musicians wafting mood-setting music over an unappreciative crowd. Ahead of me, silhouetted against the green backdrop is what I came for. Sheila's pale-blue dress is belted around her waist and flows all the way down to her silver shoes. When she moves, the faintest glimpse of knee slides through the slit. I calm my breath and force my feet to not run to her.

"Is that for me?" She gestures to the white shoebox wrapped in pink ribbon cradled in my hands. "Oh, Mr. Kingwood! You shouldn't have!"

"If you don't mind, I'd like you to stop teasing me and introduce me to our hostess so I can get rid of this thing." I motion to the eyes plastered on us. "I wasn't aware the custom here is to not bring the hostess a gift. But after walking through this gawk fest, I won't make that mistake again."

"You poor dear." She straightens my collar and fusses with my tie. "The beautiful box isn't what's making you a spectacle. This is." She pats my cheek. "Because our custom *is* to bring the hostess a gift. So all of these women, and I dare say some of the men, are wishing they were *hosting* you right now."

"I guess that means you'll have to save me from them." I hold out my elbow for her to latch onto. Safe. Innocent. "Since I don't know anyone else here, may I stick close to you today?"

She steps back, eyeing me head to toe. "I touted you very highly to Mrs. Smithers, and you've made me out to be a speaker of truth. The suit is nice. I like the way it hugs your curves."

"Are we going to do this all day?"

"What else are friends for?" She takes my elbow, her touch setting my flesh aflame. "I'll do what I can to rescue you from the worst of the group. Just give me a nod to back off if I keep you from any vultures you'd like to be in company with."

"The only company I'm interested in keeping is yours."

We stroll across the patio and I can't stop my eyes from glancing to her legs as they slide out from under the slit that stops just two inches above her knees. Meaty, curvy, feminine, soft legs. "You're in another breathtaking dress." I tug at my collar. "Later, I'll have you spin so I can see it from all angles."

"If only *I* garnered the praise you heap upon my clothing." She sighs. "Brace yourself, this blue-haired woman coming our way is Mrs. Smithers."

The woman is on us before I can tell Sheila her clothes only get my praise because her body is in them. "Miss Beller!" Mrs. Smithers waves a handkerchief in the air as if we can miss her flowered dress and wide yellow hat. It's just as well she's interrupting us, I don't need to pay Sheila more compliments. Her ego is strong and I'm married. Horribly, horribly married.

"Miss Beller!" Mrs. Smithers is half out of breath. "Is this the young man you spoke of?"

"It is." Sheila releases my arm and angles to see both of us. "This divinely handsome man is Mr. Avery Kingwood. Mr. Kingwood, meet your gracious host. When it comes to afternoon tea, Mrs. Smithers is the best in the business."

The old woman laughs, pretending not to take Sheila seriously but puffing up with pride nonetheless. I extend my hand. "It's nice to finally meet you, Mrs. Smithers. I've been looking forward to being here today. Thank you for the invitation."

"Of course!" She beams, blushing when I bring her fingers to my lips, a trick I learned from watching John kiss Mary's hand a thousand times in the hour I spent with them. "It's the event of the year. Practically, anyway! Everyone always has such a good time, and heavens yes! I would never think to not invite you, Mr. Kingwood. As soon as Miss Beller told me a member of your family was in town, I knew immediately I had to get an invitation out to you. And quickly! The others were sent out some time ago, but I knew that even a last-minute invitation must go out to you because you would *surely* want to be here among the rest of us." She waves her hands wide. "Everyone who's anyone comes to my tea party."

"You do have quite the gathering." I note the crowd again.

"I certainly do." Her nose flares. "If they aren't here, they're not worth knowing." Sheila clears her throat. The old woman flinches. "Well, except for those of us who simply can't make it to such frivolous things. There are many much too busy with important business, like the rest of the Beller family. If you haven't had the privilege of meeting Miss Beller's brother and his pretty wife, you simply *must* beg her for the introduction." She tilts her head and smiles at Sheila. "They're wonderful people. The best you'll ever meet! Just like Miss Beller and her mother, who is an old friend of mine. The very dearest of friends."

"You're too kind." Sheila's lashes bat. "My mother thinks very highly of you too, and I'll be sure to tell my brother and his wife you said hello. But right now there is something of great importance to discuss."

"My goodness!" Mrs. Smithers' hand clutches her throat. "What is it?"

Sheila grins. "Mr. Kingwood has a gift for you. Everyone is dying to know what *such a man* gifts his hostess."

With as straight a face as possible, I pompously present the box. The old lady smiles broadly, glancing around to be sure everyone is paying attention. "Oh, *my* dear Mr. Kingwood. This is for me?"

"It is."

"Thank you." She proudly lifts it from my outstretched palm. "The box alone is exquisite. You have wonderful taste."

"See?" Sheila winks. "All you have to do is look handsome and give us pretty boxes."

"To be sure!" Mrs. Smithers nods. "But we know a man such as yourself would never give an empty box. Surely not!"

"No, ma'am." I have an urge to hold Sheila's hand. "Not even to Miss Beller, who deserves a whole wagon full of empty boxes."

"Make it a car full and I accept." Sheila places her palm on my arm and leans in. "As long as one of those boxes contains a diamond."

~15~

I want to kiss Sheila. Full and hard, right on those brazen lips of hers. It feels good to be close to her again. Even better when we're touching. If my parents see a picture, I'll say it's business. They may even applaud a Kingwood managing to get a Beller on their arm. They'll wish it was my brother's arm, but they'll also tell Cassie to calm down if she pretends to be upset. So for today, this one moment of my life, I get to have something just for myself. If Mrs. Smithers will quit droning on about the Bellers and how no better girl has ever lived than *our* Miss Beller.

I slide Sheila's hand back onto the crook of my arm. "It's a good thing Miss Beller is one of a kind. The world couldn't handle two of her."

"To be sure!" Mrs. Smithers wags a finger. "Her sister-in-law may have beauty and sweetness, but she doesn't come from the same fine stock. No indeed! There can be no mistake that this one here is the *real* heir of the Beller name."

"Careful," Sheila warns. "Your words are dangerously close to insulting Mary. She's fully a Beller, an heir just as I am."

"Of course!" Mrs. Smithers swallows hard. "I didn't mean to say anything else. Everyone knows she is a Beller through and through. And I, more than anyone, think the world of her."

"Which is why I know you'll choose your words more carefully in the future." Sheila places a hand on the woman's shoulder. "Go sit with your friends and open your gift, everyone's eager to see what it is. I'm going to take Mr. Kingwood around the garden and introduce him to your other guests. You can thank him later for whatever charming gift he brought you."

Mrs. Smithers scurries off, the brim of her yellow hat bouncing as she hurries to follow Sheila's instruction. I turn us onto the first offshoot in the garden I see. "That was brutal."

"Our hostess is quite a character."

"She certainly brought out a character in you." I walk slowly, in no hurry to get to a populated area. "It's cool that you take up for your family so fiercely, but she wasn't insulting Mary. She was simply making the distinction between someone born a Beller and someone marrying into the name."

"A distinction that doesn't exist." She pulls me toward a smaller path barely large enough to fit us side by side, circling around a bed of roses and away from the amassing crowd. "Mary is a Beller. Period."

Cassie says the same of herself, that marrying in is the same as being born a Kingwood. It isn't. If I divorce her, she isn't keeping my last name either. "I don't agree with you, but Mary is your family and everyone is on good terms, so you should be looking out for one other."

"Even if we aren't on good terms, we take up for each other. The only people allowed to bust our chops are other Bellers." Our path widens, intersecting three others where a crowd is gathered. "Before you dive into meeting your adoring fans, would you like the skinny on who's single, taken, or willing to sleep around whether they're taken or not?"

What I'd like is to consider this a date and not speak to anyone other than her. "I imagine I'll be able to figure out the consorting on my own."

"Most of it you can, if you're paying attention." Her nose scrunches. "Which I am. But some of it you still need to put your ear to the ground to be aware of."

"That bad?"

She deliberately notices a couple cuddling together in the hedgerow. "Mom and I would rather not know any of the gossip, but it's important to be able to protect ourselves from being too close with the wrong people while still trying to help some of them, if possible." She gently tilts her head to where the couple have disappeared. "Case in point. A lot of the young women are encouraged to behave outrageously in order to land a wealthy man. As if that's what they should aspire to despite the fact that you don't have to look far to see the damage *that* ideology does to everyone involved."

"So you're here to be the voice of reason?" Where was she when I needed reason not to tie myself to Cassie?

She grins. "It's the neighborly thing to do. Plus, I need to see these men in action. I know I'm not the belle of the ball, so I watch to see if while they're flirting with me, their eyes are looking past me to those whose skirts are shorter and bodies fuller. Or to the ones who are *known* for their promiscuity. Speaking of which, would you like me to point out women who would be sure to go home with you tonight?"

"You have a cute way of fishing for information, Sheila, but I'm going home the way I came. Alone." Unless she'll come look at my building so I can persuade her to take the job, while feeding her cake.

She doesn't seem to notice that although people are curious about me, they're more interested in the perfectly poised woman on my arm. I can't blame them. I delight in her fingers being wrapped around my bicep as she makes warm but short introductions, giving everyone just enough attention before moving us on to the next mob.

"Other than yourself, is there anyone here I *should* pay particular attention to?"

"That depends on why you're here." She stops us short of the next horde and slides a strand of my messy bang back into place. "I mean, you're interested in women, right?"

"What kind of question is that?"

"A perfectly natural one." She shrugs. "Just because it would be a travesty to the female race to lose a specimen like yourself doesn't mean you have to want us back. Would you prefer I point out men?"

She's not as good at reading me as I thought. "*If* I wanted anyone, it would be a female."

"Good. Because there are a lot of women here and just because you don't want to kiss *me*, doesn't mean you don't want to kiss one of them." Light dances mischievously across her amber pools. "That I know of, I'm the only one who requires a relationship to be kissed. Many of the others wouldn't mind giving you their own *tour* of the garden, and it pains me to admit several would be happy to scratch any itch you have with little more than one tiny string attached. And not the monogamy string. One that hugs a neck or wrist and they'll—"

"This isn't my first day living in the real world." I run my fingers over hers, clamping the only woman I want into place. "I know exactly how the game works. And I like the tour I'm getting just fine. Unless you want to up the ante and slide into the bushes with me?"

~16~

It's hard to control myself around Sheila. A problem she doesn't share. The woman is the epitome of control. She taunts and teases, tells me I'm the hottest bachelor to hit this town, then hoses me down by adding, "You'll have a great selection of bush babes to play with while I go help this poor girl."

One minute she's on my arm and the next not even my clutching fingers can hold onto her. Instead of sliding away to a dark corner where I can *show* her I'm not interested in making anyone else's mouth water, she's off saving a tipsy female who's making a fool of herself dancing to catcalls of the men egging her on. I turn to glare at them. For one second too long. Sheila's disappeared. Drunk girl in tow.

Since avoiding all potentially scandalous situations is a life rule, I should just leave this drunk fest that's not anything close to being a *tea*. But Sheila is here, so I walk the stone path she must have darted down. These trails twist and turn, opening up then narrowing again. I slip onto a smaller lane to avoid a crowd Sheila's not in and wind around, fairly sure this is the rose encircling path she took me on earlier.

Reaching the main patio, I step into the foliage enough to survey the scene without traipsing aimlessly through it. A flash of blue catches my eye. I follow it. Sheila's with her mom, the two of them sitting on a stone bench nestling the girl she rescued between them. My phone beeps. I should have silenced it, but the second *my* investigator finds out who Cassie's hired stalker is, I want to know. ***I saw another lawyer today, husband. The one your parents use. In fact, they took me to meet him. Nice man. Call me and I'll tell you all about my new terms.***

Write them down, then do me the favor of shredding them for me. After that, lose my number. I text her back and let my eyes rest on Sheila. The dream I'm wasting my time chasing.

Determined not to manifest any of the emotions my existence normally evokes, I saunter up to the bar, drop a twenty down for a tip since the refreshments are complimentary, and ask the bartender for two virgin lemonades. He provides the cold glasses and I take them in hand, turning away from the bar and running my torso smack into a gorgeous blonde. Her tight crimson dress leaves nothing to my imagination. I lift my eyes, barely managing not to spill lemonade all over her voluptuous cleavage. "Hello. I'm Avery Kingwood."

"I know." Her long lashes wink. "I'm Eva."

"Nice to meet you, Eva." I take note of the jewelry adorning her prize-worthy body. "You caught me at a bad time. I'm right in the middle of something."

"Maybe you'd like to get into the middle of something else?" She runs a painted nail down my arm. "I was hoping you'd be here today because if you weren't, I was going to have to awkwardly bump into you someplace else. And I haven't yet figured out where you spend your time."

"Lately, I've been spending all my free time with Miss Beller, who I need to get this drink to." I make a show of the glasses.

She laughs. "Miss Beller? As in Sheila 'The Prude' Beller?"

"Not a name I've heard her called, but yes."

"Trust me," she steps closer, sharp nail tracing down my neck, "Sheila's not nearly as much fun as I am. What do you say we get out of here and I show you?"

"Like I said, I'm already in the middle of something."

Stepping around Eva, I make a beeline for Sheila. Eva follows, her long silky legs keeping in infuriating step with mine. "I have a couple of friends who would be happy to join us. We're thorough _hosts._"

"I bet you are." I walk faster. "Sheila!" She looks up, a deep grin crossing her face. I want to kiss it off her. "Ready to finish our tour?"

Sheila stands, falling short of Eva's height but not unimpressive in the least. "Hello, Eva. I see you've met Mr. Kingwood."

Eva latches onto my arm. "Avery and I are getting acquainted."

"I'm sure you're trying to get *very* acquainted with him." Sheila looks around. "But where are your minions? I mean *friends*? I haven't seen them today and the three of you together are much better at making acquaintances. Or so I hear."

Eva's nails dig into my arm. "They'll be here soon. Avery's excited to meet them."

Sheila's eyes fall on me. "I hear that's how it works. The men *do* need to be excited."

"Too bad I'm not an excitable man."

The horror of my implication steals my breath, but Sheila's too preoccupied with entrapping Eva to tease me. "I missed seeing your check for the charity drive come in, Eva. Maybe that's what you were discussing with Mr. Kingwood? A way to get the funds you need in order to meet the promise you made?" Her slender fingers fondle the emerald perfectly placed between Eva's cleavage. "Did you hear Mrs. Smithers sold some of her very own jewels and donated the whole of it to charity? I was so inspired I sorted through my own jewelry. I bet many others will do the same." She meets Eva's scowl with a nonchalant look. "Your necklace would be a perfect piece. Donating such a trinket would make you the talk of the town, and I'm sure Mr. Kingwood would be impressed with your generosity. Wouldn't you, *Avery*?"

"Any woman who would part with her favorite jewelry for charity's sake is a gem in my book, *Sheila*."

"See there." She pats Eva's arm. "I'll organize an auction and count on your support when the event is set. And if you don't have cash for the money you've already promised, you can simply put in additional jewels."

I grin through the awkward pause as Eva figures out how to respond. Her nose juts into the air, body moving closer to mine. "I would be happy to donate *all* of my jewels. If they're needed."

"Impressive." Sheila whistles. "Since we're talking charity, which by definition indicates need, I'll remember your generous pledge and happily accept all of your baubles when the time comes." She crosses her hands in front of her. "Until then, I'll let you two get back to the conversation you were having."

"We're finished." I shrug Eva off, her nails dragging down my suit sleeve. "But you and I are not, Sheila Beller. Not by a long shot."

Eva stomps away, her stiletto getting stuck in a crack. Sheila watches the scene with little amusement. I note that the drunk girl from earlier is gone and Katherine is deep in conversation with two other women. I hold the lemonade out to Sheila. "Done saving the day?"

She stares at the glass. "That depends. Did you find Eva engaging?"

"Not as engaging as you."

"Then I accept your drink offering." She takes the glass and nods to a spot over my shoulder. "See that man over there? The one with the white hair and rosy cheeks?"

I slide beside her, into the spot that feels like mine. "Is he the man you're pining for?"

She grins. "I would, but he's pining for my mom. Watch, they keep glancing at each other and sharing secret smiles. They've been flirting this way for months, and though I never thought I'd see my mom with anyone else, I like him. He's nice."

I haven't felt *nice* in so many years I forget what the experience is like. But Sheila makes me want to be good. I place a hand on the small of her back and urge her toward that tiny rose encircling path. "You're okay with your mom dating? No hurt feelings that she's moving on without your dad?"

She inhales. "Dad was the love of her life, but he's gone. I don't see anything wrong with her finding happiness again, maybe even a second love. I only wish I could be as happy as she is."

"You seem pretty happy to me." I nudge her. "It sprinkles out of you and splashes all over the rest of us."

"I'm happy in life, but not happy *with* my life."

"I'm not sure that's possible."

"I'm sure I'm still single with absolutely no prospects." She sighs. "All the men I know are drab or divorced already, and I don't want someone who broke their vows to someone else because I'd never trust them not to do the same thing to me."

My gut caves. I didn't expect to be lucky enough to have a relationship with her, but to hear from her own mouth that I'll never be good enough is a kick in all the terrible places. "People don't get married with the intention of breaking vows."

"No, but they should get married with the intention of keeping them. Do you know John and Mary repeat their vows to each other every morning? Every. Single. Morning. Just to remind the other they still *choose* to love them."

"So you think love is a choice?"

"It's absolutely a choice." Her head shakes. "All this nonsense about *I fell out of love* is because people don't put in the work to make sure they *stay* in love. And don't get me started on the cheaters."

"You have a lot of opinions for someone who's never been married."

She laughs. "You think I should lower my standards? Expect less than absolute devotion all because the bounty of men at my disposal are considerably less than desirable? Because they're obnoxious, lazy, wealth-chasing juveniles?"

I wish she knew what my life was like. "I think your imagination expects too much. Your brother's marriage isn't normal, you've said that yourself."

"But don't you wish it were?"

My heart pinches. Staring into her amber pools physically hurts. I *do* wish I could live with her the way her brother lives with Mary. A dream that will never be my reality. "I used to think it was possible to have the kind of marriage you're dreaming of, but then I grew up."

She studies me. "So that's it then? You've had your heart broken?" I remain silent. She sighs. "Now I understand the brooding. But I've never been in love so I don't know what to say other than I'm sorry you've been hurt. Love shouldn't be so complicated."

"No, it shouldn't." I let my eyes caress her soft skin the way my hands want to. "I hope when you fall in love, it isn't complicated at all."

<h1 style="text-align:center">~17~</h1>

In a perfect world, all the people around us would fall away and I'd stay right here in this moment, staring into Sheila's eyes. I'd give anything for it to have been her who was standing in that bar the night I met Cassie. If the two of them could just switch places.

"Sheila!" A red-tressed man wobbles up, interrupting the conversation my head is having with her eyes. He presses into her space. "Sheila, I've never seen a woman look any better than you."

"Hello, Garland." She moves, reclaiming her space. "Had a few too many, have you?"

"Nah, I've not had anything at all." He waves her off. "But I'll join you for a drink. Or ten." He grins, breath betraying his lie. "What can I get you to start our party?"

"Mr. Kingwood has already taken care of my thirst." She holds up her glass of lemonade. "Have you two met?"

The crimson-haired man thrusts out his meaty hand. "Nice to meet you. Garland Thomas. The boys call me Tom Cat."

"You should hear what the ladies call him." Sheila rolls her eyes when he smiles. "Garland, why don't you introduce Avery to the other men? He's not been able to make his rounds yet and I'm sure he'd like to get to know all of you."

I clamp onto her arm. "Some other time. I don't want to leave you unattended."

She peels my hand off. "Don't you worry, I'll take my little ol' self over to Willis. I'm sure he'll look after me as if I were his own daughter."

"Yeah, he's a good old man!" Garland howls, slapping an arm around my shoulders. "Come on, let's see what trouble we can get into."

She wiggles her fingers as he scoots me away. "Have fun. Eva will probably be along shortly."

I'm not sure if she's dumping me because I don't share her views on marriage or because she's testing me. If it's the latter, I pass the quiz. I'm not a sloppy drunk like Garland and his crew seem to be. Their mouths are spewing nonsense and all I want is quiet. Time to consider the message Sheila is sending me. If there is one.

Garland slaps a hand on my back, gawking at the women walking by and nodding toward them as if I want to do the same. "That Sheila is something else, isn't she? If you want in, we've got a bet going on who nails her first."

"Excuse me?"

"She's hard to get but ripe as a berry in summer." A man twice my age laughs as the six other drunken gawkers grunt their agreement.

"When I took her out," Garland wheezes, "she never even gave me a single kiss. And after I paid for her dinner and took her to some fancy-pants play."

"He still thinks he's going to be the one to get her first, though," the baby-faced one chimes in, hand rubbing over his smooth jaw. "I say it'll be me. Heard she likes them young."

"Heck!" Garland howls. "I'm the only one here she's been on a date with. That shows you what she likes." His chest puffs, sour breath rolling over me. "I'm just hanging back, ready to collect my money when the time is right. But don't let me being the frontrunner discourage you. Put your money in like the rest and take your shot."

"You're talking about Sheila Beller?" I stare each of them in the face. "You're betting on sleeping with her?"

"She's a lot of work!" Their words cover me in a layer of filth, each throwing in their own shovelful. "Not for the faint of heart!" "But there's a nice paycheck attached to her, so the work is worth it!" "Marrying a Beller is the dream that never dies!"

Thunder rumbles from my chest. "Do you want to marry her or nail her?"

"Both!" Garland guffaws. "I figure if I do it right, I'll get her down the aisle too."

"For her money, not because you love her."

"Love?" one of the men says. Laughter rises around me. "Don't tell us you're the romantic type."

Garland slings an arm around my shoulders. "That won't get you far in life, my friend."

"I'm not your friend." I throw his arm off, fists clenching. I need to get away from this gaggle of dunces before I knock their teeth out. Dad would use the fight as a means of revoking my permission to head up the business here, and above all else, I *will* be successful. And now that I've met Sheila, I *will* be staying in Huntington.

The men and women at this party may be the key to my business success, which is why Sheila invited me, but *she* shouldn't be here. Not in eyesight of these men, and certainly not within earshot. Trudging through the garden looking for her, I try to move past an overly chatty circle of ladies but they manage to ensnare me, their rapid-fire questions designed to find out if I'm single or taken, and just how deep my wallet is. I give brief, unrevealing answers. The only woman I care to discuss my affairs with is floating just beyond my reach. Sheila's the epitome of grace. Poised in a way that can't be taught. And she's making me guilty of the very thing she accused other men of doing to her. I stand with these women, mouth moving to give them enough of what they want while looking past every single one of them to what I truly desire.

Sheila's blue dress flows as she glides between guests, always smiling, adding her special touch of joy to every conversation. Faces light up in her presence. Even Eva is under her spell, unable to hide her jealousy and equally unable to tear her eyes from the captivating Sheila. "Excuse me, ladies." I push through the crowd of women. "There's somewhere I'm supposed to be."

Moving across the patio too quickly for anyone else to stop me, I slide into Sheila's left side with enough force to whip her skirt around her legs. She laughs. "Where are you going in such a rush?"

"To you."

I apologize to the people she's talking to, placing my hand on the small of her back and leading her away from them—and everyone else. "How long do you usually stay at this un-tea party?"

"Don't let Mrs. Smithers hear you call it that, you'll break her heart."

"I think someone should break it to her that to have a tea party, one actually has to serve tea."

"There's sweet tea at the bar and iced tea that is heavily alcoholic." She waves me in that direction. "Go. Have your fill."

I stay where I am. She's absolutely testing me, and I intend to pass. Unless she asks if I'm married. I won't lie to her, but I'm not going to voluntarily flunk myself either. "Those types of tea don't count. Ask any good tea drinker and they'll set you straight."

"Are you a tea connoisseur?"

"I spent the biggest part of the last seven years in Europe, where I learned the fine art of a proper cup of tea, so yes, compared to everyone here, I believe I'm the resident connoisseur."

She smiles. "Maybe you should host your own tea party and educate the rest of us. But please, call it something like *Brunch and Beer* so you don't hurt Mrs. Smithers' feelings."

"I should, and then not serve a drop of alcohol *or* brunch." Her laugh unleashes my smile. "I seriously need to know how long you're staying. I'm ready to leave and instead of this afternoon tea ending when it's no longer afternoon, it seems to be ramping up."

She nods. "You've done your duty and graced us with your presence, so you're free to leave whenever you want. You've miffed more than a few of the ladies anyway. Seems you won't give them the time of day, so they're convincing everyone else that you're downright despicable."

"You wouldn't have anything to do with that opinion, would you?"

She places a hand on her heart, playing the shockingly accused. "I took up for you. I told them you're not at all despicable. Only moody, and they should keep trying to get your attention because you're likely to change your mind at the faintest shift of the wind."

"I'm not moody. I was irritated the day we raced and I've apologized for it. Are you holding a grudge?"

"I don't hold grudges." She takes my arm and begins to walk. "To convince me you're not moody, since you've been moody *and rude* more times than just the one day, I'll have to see more of you. Are you up for convincing me?"

"From the way you're grinning like a cat who won the mouse, I'd say we're going to find out."

~18~

Sheila's staying at this un-tea party until her mom is ready to leave. Which isn't happening anytime soon. Willis is keeping her too occupied to notice any of the debauchery around her. I'm trying the same tactic with Sheila, and she seems to be on the same page as me about the two of us staying away from everyone else.

We walk into a quieter, shadowed part of the garden. I slide my fingers atop hers where they're curled around my forearm. "What happened to the girl you saved earlier?"

"Mom talked to her, then I called her a car." She eyes me. "Why? Did you want to drive her home? Try for a nightcap after all?"

"You and your mouth have quite the reputation." I resist reaching out and tracing the outline of her glossy lips. "I've heard, and seen, a lot today."

"Don't repeat a single syllable. Not to me anyway." She walks on. "No sense ruining my perfectly good mood."

"Is it possible to ruin your mood?"

"I'm sure you could manage to."

I pull us to a stop, bringing her around to face me. "I'm sure you're doing your best to ruin mine."

She laughs. "I was only teasing. The women *are* all abuzz over you, but in the very best way. You're handsome, so all you have to do is stand around broodily and the little bees will give you more attention than the flowers in this lovely garden."

"Thank you for making me feel like a piece of meat."

"Just returning the favor." She shivers. "I can only imagine the talk going on in the man circles. A few of them I'm careful not to walk by because I can't stand the idea of what they would say if I did."

65

I rub her arms. "I don't consider males who talk that way to be *men*. And I would *never* talk in a sleazy way about *any* woman. Not even Eva, who would probably consider it a compliment."

Her eyes shade over until I can't see their depths. I don't like it. I want to know everything about her. Look into her soul the way she seems to look into mine. I slide us off the path, into the cover of leafy branches. "All that talk earlier about not lowering your standards, how can that be true when you dated *Garland?*"

Her eyes narrow. "I had *a* date with him. Singular. And not that it's any of your business, but it was six years ago, a disaster, and ended with me calling a cab while he stood outside the theater begging me not to be angry with him for trying to repeatedly grope me. A request I didn't fill." She removes my hands from her arms. "That night ended his chances, and he only had a fraction of a chance to begin with. I'm now fully aware the rumors about him are true, and bet or not, he knows never to attempt touching me again."

"You know about the bet?"

"Of course I do!" she snaps. "Those Neanderthals have had that stupid bet going for years and it hasn't done any of them a bit of good."

"You *know* about the bet?"

Her arms cross. "I tried to get in on the action. But they don't want me betting against them even after I told them if hell freezes over and flying pigs rule the world, I *still* won't so much as allow one of them to blow me a kiss."

"That's your response to finding out they have a pool on who gets to lay you first?"

"The last I heard, the pot is fairly high." She shrugs. "I guess that's something. Why? Did you get in on it?"

Her having the audacity to even ask me that question boils my blood. "What's John say about all this? How can he sit by and let them talk about his sister that way?"

Her finger presses into my chest. "He doesn't know, and you won't dare mention it to *any* member of my family. Are we clear?"

"We're mud." I pull her hand down, cradling it in mine. "They're being more than disrespectful to you and that's not okay on any level."

"They're desperately trying to make themselves valid in a world where they simply aren't." She slides her fingers from mine. "To demand they stop would only give them credit, and I refuse to lend credence by creating drama where there doesn't need to be any."

She motions in their direction, the noise of their laughter wafting over the entire party. "In the course of a day, I never think about any of them. They'll spend their lives with their names only crossing my lips when my path unfortunately meets theirs."

Fear cuts through my chest. She could very easily say the same about me. "You feel as if you have the power, not them?"

"I *know* I have the power. And they all know I can crush them with one little whisper in the right ear." She moves me aside and walks out of the branches, back onto the path. "They're all talk, and talk is cheap. Right?"

"Not when the conversation is with you." My palm glides over her fingers, bringing them to my arm and wrapping them tightly around my bicep. "Most women would be furious, but here you are being too reasonable for that." I pull her close to my side. "One day, you'll have to teach me the art of not being pissed when people do you wrong."

"I never said I wasn't angry. Only that I have the power." She watches the tips of her shoes peeking from under her dress. "Them lusting over me simply because of my bank account takes the fun out of being lusted over."

I take a chance, lowering my mouth to her ear. "If what you want is to be desired, done. I happen to know that an exciting woman like you, wrapped in a whole heap of beautiful the way you are, draws men in like moths to a flame."

She smiles. "That must be why I occasionally manage to find men who genuinely want to kiss me."

Desire to do that very thing right this very moment races through me. "I thought you didn't kiss unless you were in a relationship? From what I've heard today, you've never had a serious boyfriend."

Her face tilts up to mine. "I didn't say it had to be a *serious* relationship. Just a relationship."

"Good to know."

"Is it?"

Her question lingers. Falling over me like glistening snowflakes. Jagged-edged barbs of dream-crushing death. I want so badly to taste her. Clearing my throat, I move us along the path, asking her a question so I can avoid answering my own. "If I heard correctly, there have been exactly two sort-of boyfriends in your life?"

The luster fades from her expression. "The overly informative gossip mill is correct. One was in high school, more of a friend than a boyfriend. Then we both went off to college, where I met someone I thought had potential, but he turned out to be a dud. Since then, I've been doing what every other red-blooded woman in the prime of her life does." My eyebrows raise. Hers mock mine. "Make out with strangers I have no chance of ever seeing again."

"Why didn't you let me in on that action the night of the veterans' banquet?"

Her hand tightens on my arm. "Because you want to keep seeing me. Just like you genuinely want to kiss me."

"Hmm," I trace a finger along the outline of her face. "Now she's a mind reader. Let's step back into the bushes and you can tell me what else I want."

~19~

One of these days I'm going to use my mouth for something other than an orifice in which to stick my foot. Sheila isn't about to slip into the shadows with me and it's impossible to *court* her the way she wants because I can't explain my situation to her, both from a legal standpoint because of the stupid gag I signed as part of my separation agreement, and from her moral perspective since she seems to think all divorced people are failures. It stands to reason that married men aren't on her prospect list either.

I force a smile at the approaching couple, Katherine's hand tucked against Willis' arm the way Sheila's was on mine before I propositioned her.

"You two are so adorable," Sheila sings. "When's the wedding?"

"Sheila Beller!" Katherine's face reddens. "Stop it right now. Willis and I are only friends."

"Yes, Mother." She winks at Willis. "You two *friends* just out for a garden stroll?"

"I'm ready to leave." Katherine huffs, removing her hand from Willis's arm. "I just heard the bar is being restocked and I will *not* stay here and watch people drink themselves into further stupidity."

Sheila nods. "I'm ready to go as well. Are you riding home with me or is your boyfriend driving you?"

"I'm riding with you, *daughter,*" Katherine growls, a family trait, "and you had better not drive like you're on the racetrack."

"I'm happy to drive you home, Katherine," Willis offers. "I've never been on a track and just last year I got a ticket for driving too slowly."

"No, Sheila can mind her manners and drive me home properly." The older woman pats the man's arm. "But thank you for being kind enough to offer."

"Yes, you're too kind." Sheila bats her lashes. "She's right, though. I should drive her. It's time I prove conclusively that speed limits are only suggestions for those who aren't as skilled as I am."

Katherine's eyes narrow. "One of these days, that way of thinking is going to catch up with you. Until then, Willis can drive me home." She looks up at him. "If you're sure it isn't too much trouble?"

He beams. "It's no trouble at all."

Sheila hugs her mom, with a promise to be home on the Potomac to help with some dinner party planning day after tomorrow. I applaud her once they're gone. "Well done."

She faces me. "*Well* is the only way I do things. I'll call you this week to set up a time to see your office building. Since you upheld your end of the bargain, I'll design the space."

"Good." I beam as bright as Willis did. "How about we get out of here and hit up the taco truck? Then I'll take you to look at the building tonight."

"I'll view it during business hours."

"Then we'll just have tacos?"

"I've had too many tacos lately. And just in case you decided to get in on the bet, no one is going to see me leave with you." She turns away, following the path Willis and her mom took.

She's as fast on her feet as she is behind a wheel. Knowing the twists and turns of this garden, she's in the parking lot before I catch up with her. She bypasses the valet stand. I eye the attendant. "Let me guess, she parked herself?" He nods and I thrust out my hand. Of course she wouldn't let anyone drive her car.

The instant my fob touches my palm I take off at a dead sprint, running so hard for her Corvette that sweat beads on my brow and rolls down my temples. "Wait!" I fall against her door, talking to her face through the window. "Are you mad at me?"

She rolls down the glass. "I believe you have a romantic interest in me. You deny it for some reason, in between flirting with me, and I'm willing to let that slide for now. But if I'm wrong and you really *aren't* attracted to me, you're only asking me to hang out at the taco truck because you think there's something in it for you. Hoping to be seen in public with me? Want to mislead everyone and lie your way into a win?"

"Actually, I'd like to hide away in a dark room with you and never come out." Every desire I have surges forth. I move away from her door before I lose control. "You're a rare thing to find, Sheila Beller, so of course I like you. But all I want is to genuinely be your *friend*."

"What was the part about the dark room?"

I hate the look in her eye. She's happy. I know I'm going to hurt her. "The entire time we've been at this party you've been running around dousing everyone else with your essence, and I want it all to myself. For a little while." I place a palm on the lowered glass of her window, fingertips wishing to be running through her hair. "All I want from this relationship is for us to be two people who enjoy each other's *friendly* company. Nothing else."

She studies me, those deep-set eyes looking into me. "We'll see."

I rub the back of my neck. "Just follow me to the tacos."

"Even when I'm working for you, you won't be my boss."

"Working for me by definition means I'm your boss. So I order you to meet me at the taco truck." I grin. "Pretty please?"

"Promise to stay in a good mood and not go all broody on me?"

"You like it." I wink. "Race you! No cheating!"

~20~

The only thing worse than reading Cassie's texted words is hearing them read by the artificial voice in my Rover. I normally keep my phone unlinked unless I need to make a business call, being sure to kill the link directly after. Today, voice texting the built-for-speed woman who's dusting me on roads I don't know, my Sheila Beller tunnel vision landed me in a ditch. It was *her* words I expected to hear. Not Cassie's. ***Ignoring me isn't going to bring our baby back. Call me, Daddy.***

Before I knew Cassie was malicious, I wanted so badly to have a child with her. Now, I'd cut my own throat to keep from giving her my seed. To keep myself from impregnating *any* woman. Even Sheila, the woman who proves joy exists in this life. I feel it when I'm next to her, despise its loss when she's gone, and hate that I can never be for her what she deserves. All I have to offer is nothing. Broken, desolate, financially strapped nothingness.

Having to replace the fender Cassie caused me to ruin isn't going to bankrupt me, but it's causing me a great deal of humiliation. Sheila, waiting on me as usual, didn't fail to notice the Rover's damage when I parked behind her Corvette. I told her a snake caught me off guard, and she informed me that making an excuse for my bad driving was worse than being a lousy driver.

"Want to take our food into the park and eat at the fountain?" The sidewalk is crowded today and we're too much of an easy target out here on the street in our fancy clothes. With any luck, the seclusion of the park will afford me alone time with Sheila; right along with the ability to easily spot my voyeur.

Sheila takes my arm, heading across the street with me to the park. "How romantic."

"It's only meant to be a change of scenery." I bite a hole in my cheek. I wish my marriage license would go up in flames the way my marriage did. Then maybe I could take all this pent-up rage and bury it in Sheila. Pour her over me until all the suffering goes away. "You don't mind getting your dress wet, do you? It's a hot day. I might have to cool you off."

"Is it me you're trying to cool off? Or yourself?"

Two hours later I'm still asking myself that question. I thought I could make her leave since I can't quit her. That she'd bail when I splashed her. But this shocking woman simply slipped off her shoes, climbed into the fountain, and wrapped her arms around my shoulders before falling backwards, dunking us both. I now know that she looks even better wet, and that she's as hard to catch in water as she is on the track.

I wring out my shirt. "It's a good thing not many people come into the park."

"I've never figured out why they don't." She shakes her head, hair spraying droplets across my chest. "In this case, I'm glad they don't. You're prone to stripping, and that's a show I like having the only ticket to."

I trace her lips with my eyes. I wish I could build a bubble around this park, this fountain, the two of us. Because despite the truckload of pain that's attached to me, I want her. "Meet me tomorrow morning." My voice is husky. I clear my throat and tug the damp shirt over my arms. "We've done what you like to do, now it's my turn to show you what I like to do."

Her fingertip traces a droplet down my chest, circling my belly button. "I already know what you like to do."

My body stiffens, not a reaction I need to have on display. I remove her hand, working my shirt's buttons into place and hoping the hem hangs low enough to cover how long it's been since I've been aroused. "I'll pick you up. You're staying at your apartment in town tonight, right?"

"I am." She smiles. "The one you sent those delicious chocolates to."

I pull my eyes off her torso. "It's a good thing you don't live full time in that beautiful Potomac house with your mom, the chocolate might have melted if I had to send your gift all the way out there. And, now that you're working for me, you're going to be in the city a lot."

"I'm working *with* you, not for you." She steps out of the fountain. "And my apartment is going to come in handy since living with you is out of the question. There wouldn't be enough room for me *and* the secretary."

"If you're in, I'll dump the secretary." I need to get a place to live that allows for company. A place with reflective glass and secure entrances. "If you're toying with me, I'm keeping the secretary."

She helps me button the last few buttons, fingers intentionally caressing as she goes. "With me around, I doubt you'll consider any other roommates."

My pulse accelerates. I back out of her reach. "Would you please stop? We can do some lighthearted flirting, but I don't want our *friendship* getting out of hand."

"So you keep saying." She picks up her shoes. "I'll see you in the morning. Sans the moodiness. I've had just about enough of it."

~

I lay atop a sheet that covers the sticky futon in my office, listing the ways my future with Sheila could go. Sometimes, I manipulate the scenario until we actually have a future. Long and happy. Then I face the more realistic outcomes where I confess that I'm technically still married, and we crash and burn before I ever have a chance to tell her I love her. And I do. I don't know when it happened exactly, but the ache of not being near her for nearly two weeks only paled after she walked away from me earlier. I stood by the fountain, staring at the trail of water she left behind. If I could have melted myself into that remnant of her, I would have.

But I'm damaged goods and deep down she knows it. And I know she knows it because every time I grab my phone, checking messages to see if maybe she's thinking of me too, there's never a word from her. All that's ever there is unwanted messages from people sharing my last name, but not my heart.

~21~

In the night, while I'm pacing, memories call to me. I take my daughter's ultrasound picture from the pocket of my suitcase. It's hard to look at the tiny planes of her face and regret conceiving her, but I do. Because I was too stupid to know what my own wife was capable of. Our child was healthy. Strong. So was her mother. Which is why I still don't understand why Cassie took her manipulation as far as she did. I'd already married her. I gave Cassie everything she asked for, even this child. So why get pregnant only to have an abortion? Why lie to me about the procedure?

If Cassie had second thoughts about being a mom, she never talked to me about them. All she did was make a choice about the fate of our child, and lie to me about the death. I'll never forget returning to the yacht my parents had loaned us, making sure Cassie and me stayed well away from their social life. I didn't mind, I enjoyed the freedom. Then I returned from the parasailing trip Cassie had surprised me with and found her in bed, pale and crying. *"Miscarriage."* she'd sobbed. I didn't know it then, but that one word lie changed everything.

My phone rings, and I shudder. I don't even have to look at the screen to know who's calling. Dawn is breaking through the window so I put Dad on speaker and scrub the tears from my face, placing my baby's photo back in its case. "Yeah, Dad."

"Don't *yeah* me. I'm your father. Speak to me with respect!"

I roll my eyes. "I have good news for you, *oh respected one*. I hired a designer to revamp this building. Within a year you'll have tripled your investment."

"You have the audacity to think you're allowed to hire anyone on my behalf? You're not authorized to sign a single contract without Curtis or me approving it first!"

I traverse the hallway, heading for the bathroom. I can argue with him and shave at the same time. "I haven't signed a contract yet, but I thought we were all in agreement that this crap hole needs to be gutted."

"We're in agreement that your *life* is a crap hole," he spits. "If you don't like where you're living, find an apartment. And pay for it yourself. You're not using a single cent of the Kingwood money renovating a building just so you can upgrade your living quarters."

"This building is falling apart. You're lucky the previous tenants didn't sue you."

"Maybe they'll sue you instead." He chuckles, hard and cold. "Like your wife is. Like *I'm* about to."

The razor I was getting ready to shave with falls from my fingers. "Like *you're* about to?"

"Misuse a single cent of my money and I'll destroy you."

"Isn't that what you've been helping Cassie do to me?" I snap. "You sent me here to do a job and just like in Europe, I'm doing it. I'm making you money. A lot of it. And like it or not, I'm a Kingwood too."

"Sharing my last name doesn't make you my son," he bites back. "No son of mine would do what you did to Cassie. What you're *still* doing to Cassie."

After all I've denied myself, after all I've done for this man, his hate and judgement make my anger turn to rage. I sling my shaving case across the room and plant my fist in the wall, pain shooting through my forearm as my knuckles collide with the tile. "Eat out of Cassie's palm all you want, Dad. Set her up as your mistress if that tickles your fancy. But don't you ever say her name to me again. She's dead to me. Keep it up, and you will be, too."

I end the call and run my hand under cold water, watching blood trickle down the drain. The level of disgust in his voice has reached a new high. If he knew about Sheila he'd say so, and it's doubtful that Mom or Lila wouldn't recognize a photo of her. So the escalation of my family's verbal assaults isn't due to their opinion of my love life. At least, not where Sheila is concerned. But something has definitely changed. I'm on the brink of an abyss, and my wife is the one digging the hole.

Retrieving the contents of my shaving kit, I toss the pouch onto the futon in my room and dig through the suitcase for a clean t-shirt and pair of jeans. Straightening, I catch movement through the window. I skulk to the glass and spot a half-bald head disappearing behind a bush. The man's hand is still visible. He's holding a red plastic container. A gas can. "Son of a—"

Feet pounding across the floor, my legs ache as I hit the stairwell at a dead sprint, jumping down the concrete planks four and five at a time until I land on the first floor and race out an emergency exit. The door thunks open and the bushes ahead of me shake. A figure in a black tracksuit pushes through the ornamental shrubs and hits the sidewalk on the far side, the gas can slipping from his grip.

I'm on him as he darts into the street, rounded gut jiggling under his jacket. A horn blasts from my left. A bus swerves to miss me, lurching to a stop in the space between me and the thief. I can't break my momentum, it carries me straight into the side of the bus. Like bouncing off a brick wall, I'm tossed backward onto the sidewalk, blood bursting in my mouth and skin peeling from my forearms. I flip onto my stomach, looking underneath the carriage to where a pair of tennis shoes come unglued from the street and disappear down an alleyway. The bus driver runs to my aid and I shrug him off, pain slicing through my knee as I peel myself from the cement and follow the thief's trail. He's gone.

I have no doubt he's the same man I saw leaving the photographs on my vehicle. That means Cassie *is* behind my gas being siphoned. I already have security cameras on order and once they're installed they'll deter her shenanigans. They won't tell me why she's escalating, though. And so far, neither has the private investigator I hired. He hasn't given me anything other than a bill.

I grab the gas can from the sidewalk, thankful that at least the thief didn't get away with my fuel today, and trudge back through the bushes and into my parking lot. My phone beeps. **You're late. Does that mean you're in a mood I'm not going to like?**

Sheila *would* choose this moment to text me. I take the cap off my gas tank and push the nozzle of the can inside, using my hip to hold it up while texting her back. **Some of us don't have passive income. We have to work. I'll be there in ten minutes.** I look down at the blood seeping through the hole in the knee of my sweatpants. **Fifteen minutes. And I'm sorry. I'm having a bad morning. But please wait for me.**

~22~

Donning clean jeans and a fresh black t-shirt, my knee and knuckles bandaged, I picked Sheila up from the sidewalk in front of her apartment building, where she was impatiently waiting. I sprinted around the Rover to open her door, my knee protesting, but it was the lie I had to tell her about my taped-up knuckles and skinned forearms that hurt the most. "I tripped." I'd muttered while she slid onto the passenger seat with a quizzical gaze. I'd rather have her think I'm a klutz than have to confess to the real reasons I'm banged up.

I'd also rather not call off the renovation project. She'll think I was only scamming her, using the promise of a job to get close to her. In a way, that's true. Doing the renovation with her lets me be near her without lifting anyone's eyebrows. But there's something in it for her to. She gets real-world experience working in the field she went to school for. Giving her that opportunity seems like a fair trade. Flaking on the job she already agreed to seems like the fast track to making her believe I'm unreliable, and I don't need any more actions tallied on the side of caprice.

I'll just have to hire her through A.K. Investments and take the financial loss. It's money I can't spare, especially if I have to meet my family in court. I can sell all my holdings and still not raise enough capital to outspend them. And it's ironic that the only reason I'm still married is to avoid giving Cassie a single penny, and now Dad is going to take away all my pennies.

I glance across the console, watching Sheila's face. She isn't happy. She'd be even more melancholy if I told her I was married, and soon to be bankrupt. I set my gaze back on the road ahead of us, a million thoughts swirling through my mind. "I'm sorry I was late again. And I'm *really* sorry I was rude when I texted you. Thanks for coming after all of that."

"You're not welcome." She stares straight ahead. "Where are we going? There's nothing out here *and* you're driving like you're eighty, so I'm guessing we're not racing."

For me, skydiving is the equivalent of what racing is for her. The airstrip I'm taking her to is where I was the morning of the veteran's banquet. It's why I nearly missed meeting her that night. "I'm driving the speed limit because I'm not you, Racing Queen." I consider telling her everything. That my family hates me and I'm married. But it's too risky. Even if she doesn't join the "We Hate Avery Club," she's already made it clear a divorced man might as well be a dead man. "Where I'm taking you is a surprise, and we're almost there so just sit tight."

Her arms cross over her chest with a force that I feel deep inside my heart. "I thought you didn't like surprises."

I turn off the main road, the wheels of my Rover crunching over familiar dirt. "I don't like *being* surprised. I like *giving* surprises."

I can practically hear her eyes roll. "If you plan on jetting me off to Paris from the little airstrip at the end of this road, think again. I have my own jet, at a real airport, so I'll take myself if I get the urge to have dinner on the Seine."

I steer us into the parking lot and maneuver into a space close to the door before turning hooded eyes to her. "I would jet you off to Paris, but I'd much rather see you jump out of a perfectly good airplane."

She launches across the seat, balling my t-shirt in her fists. "Are you serious? We're skydiving?"

All the terrible parts of my day fall away with the contact. I place my hands over hers. "So…good surprise?"

"A-mazing," she breathes. "I've always wanted to do this. But I'm too terrified!"

"You don't look terrified." My heart swells, glimpses of the hope I dreamt of last night reflected in her eyes. Alone in this vehicle, I let my fingers graze along her soft cheek. "Or is this your scared face?"

"It's my extremely excited face." She loosens her grip and moves back to her side of the suddenly too-big vehicle. "I'd so rather do this than go to Paris!"

"Good. Because ever since you took me to the track, I've wanted to jump with you."

She looks at me. "All the way to a little white chapel?"

If I wasn't already married, I'd race her to any chapel she picked. But I've hit my limit on wife problems. I shake my head. She gets out of the vehicle and heads for the entrance of the only terminal this airport has.

Running to catch up with her, I reach around her to open the rickety metal door. "Stop scowling at me, Sheila. Today is going to be fun."

She crosses the threshold, arms folding. "That remains to be seen. So does whether or not I'll actually jump."

I follow her inside. "You have to be strapped to someone to jump, and that someone happens to be me. So you're jumping."

"As I recall, you don't like doing anything in tandem."

I tug her sleeve. She doesn't move. I tug harder. She topples against me. My arms wrap around her waist, the contact whispering *I love you* through my soul. I brought a cooler, a little lunch packed inside, her beautifully wrapped boxes of petit fours and caramels sitting atop the other food. After we leave here, I'm going to find a secluded spot and figure out which confection she likes best. "There are *many* things I like doing in tandem, just not bike riding."

Her shoulders lift. "Too bad. I want an experienced partner. One I'm not inclined to murder."

"So violent." I grin. "But today you're on my turf. Which means my rules. And I don't own this airstrip or my own jet, but I *am* qualified to be your jump master. So will you please jump with me?"

Her lips are dangerously close to mine. Not her own doing. I keep dipping toward her mouth, catching myself only to end up back in the same spot. I don't just want this woman, I *need* her. "You can trust me, Sheila."

"Can I?" she whispers.

I press my forehead to hers. "Completely."

Reluctantly, I remove my arms from around her and lead us deeper into the building. Her fingers brush mine. "I might be more willing to trust you if you decide to be consistent in who you are. Whether that's the man who makes me laugh or the contrary one, just pick a personality and stick with it."

I glance at her. I'm not conflicted when it comes to how I feel about her, it's the rest of my life that's causing the problem. Like how Dad's only offer to let me use a single dime from Kingwood Properties hinges on me resolving the Cassie problem. Resolve as in, go back to her and *make it work*. I'd rather sell my soul to the lowest bidder. And I'd rather not have to deal with the consequences of telling Sheila about Cassie's existence. I let my fingers lace through hers. "I might have a consistency issue, but I really *am* qualified to be your jump master. I've jumped thousands of times, in twelve different countries, and never had any mishaps. I love this so much, the first thing I did when I got to town was look for a place to dive."

She gives my fingers a squeeze. "I've looked into diving, and haven't done it here specifically because it's *here*."

I understand her meaning. This place doesn't exude confidence in safety, but it's just a little mom-and-pop operation and they haven't had the money to fix it up. I intend to help with that. If I'm not bankrupt by the time I get rid of Cassie, and my family. "It's not as rundown as it looks."

She shudders. "It's bad enough."

I laugh, pulling her close and looping my arm around her waist, resting my palm against her side. This is *much* nicer than holding her hand. "Skydiving is my version of racing. This is where I come to feel the rush. To silence my head. And you're a maniac on the track, racing around at two hundred miles an hour. That's how I know you'll like this."

"Liking it and doing it are two different things." I feel the tension in her body as we near the back of the terminal. "In the car, I'm in control. This is totally different."

"The mechanism is different, but the adrenaline is the same."

If I can get her to do this, it'll be another way we're bonded. Another innocent thing we can do together. Not that I'm being virtuous right now, but at least my lips aren't attached to her face. "There's control in diving. You'll find it, the same as you did on the track. So don't overthink it. Just enjoy the experience." I lower my lips to her ear. "I know I will."

~23~

I've never jumped with anyone. I've never *wanted* to jump with anyone. I've mentioned it to other women and, like Cassie, they all say I'm stupid for calling this fun. But Sheila is different. She's as unique as skydiving itself. I was telling her that when Amalia, the airstrip owner's daughter, stepped out of the stockroom. We hadn't quite made it into the equipment room so I pulled away from Sheila, fumbling through hollow words to pretend my abrupt change wasn't awkward. Sheila didn't buy it, and Amalia stared at us until we disappeared through the equipment room doorway.

I lumber to the locker and pull out my rig, doing my best to avoid Sheila's glare. "If you get up there and don't want to jump, you don't have to. No big deal."

"No big deal?" she bites. "Curious that it's so *suddenly* not a big deal."

I run a hand down my face. Amalia *is* attractive, but Sheila is completely misreading this situation. I withdrew from her simply because I can't stroll around making puppy eyes at her for all the world to see. Especially those closest to my world. Cassie's infiltrated my circles before. She has a way of getting people to feel sorry for her, and when they feel sorry enough, they'll do just about anything for her. For all I know, Amalia is already spy number one. So no matter what I feel for Sheila, I *have* to press it down. I *have* to keep my hands off her.

Deflecting, I start checking the gear. "I think you'll like diving once I show you how to manipulate your body to fly at different speeds and angles. There's even control in the timing of when you decide to pull the chute."

"I believe I'll decide to pull the chute long before we get close to the ground."

I chance giving her a smile. "We're not pulling until you're screaming for your life."

"Perfect," she growls. "Because you're going to have me shouting before we ever leave this room."

She deserves an explanation, but even if I could tell her about Cassie without her walking out on me the second I confess to being married, I wouldn't tell her everything. Parts of it are too painful, others too embarrassing. I'll give her something, though. "Amalia is the owner's daughter. And no, I'm not currently, nor have I ever, dated her." Her stare rips through me. "I'm also not *interested* in dating her." Still nothing but narrowed eyes and crossed arms.

Taking a breath, I set the rigging aside and walk toward her. "I don't bring people here, Sheila. Especially female people. So it probably caught Amalia by surprise to see me with someone."

Sheila won't so much as flinch. Sweat breaks out across my back. She's going to walk out on me without even knowing the real reason she *should*. "My personal life is personal. I don't do PDA. You know, avoiding the whole tabloid rumor thing?"

Her stare moves from me to the scratched wooden door and faded walls, then back to me. "Women tend to choose self-preservation over recklessness. Somehow my wires keep getting crossed. Probably the reason I'm on the fast track to artificial insemination in order to have the kids I want."

My teeth clench. She's like the pop-up weasel game in arcades—you know what's coming but you're still never prepared. "You bring up kids every five seconds. Give it a rest already."

She leans toward me. "By all means, Avery, keep lowering the bar. In fact, thank you for doing so because I'm not doomed to forever long for a child. I can take matters into my own hands. And your behavior just gave me the idea to start a fund for other women so they can *also* afford to silence their biological clocks without having to endure interacting with a man for *any* reason."

I point to the door, giving her the treatment I first received at the track. "You have to take a class before you jump. Two rooms down on the right. Bert's waiting for you, so hurry up. I want to get in the air as soon as possible."

She straightens. "Then you shouldn't have been late."

~

I admit it was a jerk move to pull away from Sheila earlier, but I have no idea how we got from there to it being *my* fault that she doesn't have kids yet. Since the sun came up, this day has been one disaster after another.

I wait for Sheila inside the hangar where our jump plane is being readied, frustration building. "There's a storm coming." The pilot spits out his gum. "If we don't get in the air soon, we won't beat the rain."

I nod. "Get her fired up. We'll be ready to go in a few minutes."

Sheila should have been here a while ago. I flex my busted knuckles, irritation sweeping through me as I step outside and see her, two hangars down and talking to a man I've seen around here a few times. He's slightly taller than me and has blonde hair…that her hands are tousling. "Sheila!"

She folds her arms around his neck, all smiles and touchy-feely without a single acknowledgment of me calling her name. My inferno ignites. Not once has she ever greeted *me* with a hug. "Sheila!" My voice echoes through the desolate acreage.

Her hand finds his cheek. My feet move, fast and sharp over the broken pavement. "Sheila!" She hands him her phone. He types into it and hands it back to her, having the nerve to evil eye me. I move into her side, corralling her away from him. "There's a storm coming. We have to go. Now."

"Dirk, where's your phone?" She reaches over my shoulder, accepting his phone. Her fingers run over the buttons. "Now you have my number too." She circumvents me and leans into him, putting her arm around his torso. "Say cheese." She snaps a photo of them, something else she's never done with me. But I do have pictures of us together. Taken without our knowledge, yet I still couldn't bring myself to throw them away.

She grins at him. "If I don't make it today, send this pic to my mom. Tell her I love her."

I cross my arms. "Nothing is going to happen to you."

She kisses his cheek. "We'll start with lunch, then discuss the possibility of dinner."

He gives her a tight squeeze. "It's *so* good to see you again."

I'm seconds from exploding. If he values his head, he'll take his hands off her. "Sheila, I said it's time to go."

He straightens, meeting my eyes and sliding her slightly behind him. "Sheila, you don't have to do anything you don't want to do."

She rolls her eyes. "You know I've never done one single thing I didn't want to do in my entire life." She walks away, in the direction I just came from. "Come on if you're coming, Mr. Kingwood. I hear there's a storm brewing."

I hold Dirk's stare for two more beats, then go after her. The only point I need to make is already made: she came here with me, and she's leaving here with me.

~24~

Catching up to Sheila at the hangar she was supposed to be in to begin with, I brush against her arm. "Who's the golden boy?"

"An old high school friend."

My blood pressure hits a new level. "The old high school boyfriend?"

"Jealousy doesn't suit you."

She climbs into the plane. I pull the door closed behind me and give the pilot the go-ahead nod. "I'm not jealous. You and your boyfriend are just holding up everyone's day. We only have a short window to jump because of the storm. If we don't get up soon, we're not jumping today."

"Is that the worst thing in the world?"

"We came here to jump. Not to catch up with your boyfriend. You can do that on your own time."

"This *is* my time," she snaps. "And I don't think I'm willing to waste it strapping myself to a man who always has an excuse for why his mood flips at the drop of a hat."

"Picking a fight with me so *you* have an excuse not to jump isn't going to work," I challenge as the plane begins to taxi. "If you're too chicken, just say so."

"Unlike you, I don't make excuses." She's too calm to be anything but irate. "I either do something or I don't. You should try it. It's called being an adult."

The plane maneuvers into place on the runway. Her eyes lock on the door. I study her. She's not only angry, she's hurt. I see it in the roll of her shoulders, the dip of her frown. My jealousy dissipates, leaving a gaping hole of regret.

86

"Sheila, I…" She can't hear me over the roar of the engines. I leave my seat and drop down beside her. "I'm sorry."

"You should be. And you've reached your limit of how many times I'll bite my tongue. Still want to strap to me and jump out of a plane?"

I place my lips to her ear. "Not if we're fighting. It'll ruin the experience for you and I'm hoping you'll want to do this again sometime. With me."

"I'm not sure I want to do it the first time."

"Nothing bad is going to happen." I run my hands over the straps that are supposed to secure her to me. "I've got you."

"You're not going to change your mind halfway down?"

I take a chance and slide my arms around her. "I'll hold you all the way to the ground. Even if you decide not to jump and we ride back down in the plane together."

"Do you promise?" Her voice shakes.

I pull her close. "With everything I am. Because I might be an idiot who doesn't know when to stop running his mouth, but there's nothing in this world that can tear my arms from you."

She takes a deep breath and gives me the okay nod. I strap us together, rubbing my face in her hair and dragging her creamy vanilla scent into my lungs. Standing here with her, simply a man holding the woman he loves, the world and all its problems seem a million miles away. In this moment, I can give her what she wants. I can be the man she makes me want to be. "Try to relax," I whisper in her ear. "Just take in the moment."

"Stay in your nice guy mood and maybe I won't worry so much."

I press my lips against her delicate lobe. "You're in my arms, Sheila. So nice is the only gear I have."

The plane lifts us over the tree line. Clouds in the distance warn of the impending storm, but right here, in this very second, I'm surrounded by all the beauty the world has to offer. I point out the landscape, tilting my head around to watch her face. She's captivated by the sprawling green fields growing ever smaller as we climb. "How are you feeling?"

Tiny shivers bounce along her spine. "I'm awestruck."

I draw her against my chest, hands folding over her stomach so she's tucked in close. "Awestruck is better than being scared."

Her fingers brush along mine. "It's hard to focus on the beauty of the scenery without thinking about crashing into it."

"We're not going to crash," I assure her. "But you don't have to jump. We can just go along for the ride, stay here and watch the landscape pass us by."

Her head shakes. "My heart's beating so hard it might explode, but I want to jump. If I pass out, you'll still be able to land us?"

I rub my jaw along her cheek, my lips desperate to taste her. "I'll be able to get us down safe and sound no matter what you do. Just try not to poke my eyes out if you decide to flail around. It's hard enough to navigate with someone having convulsions, it'll be even harder if I can't see where I'm going."

She moves her head away. "The one thing I won't do is flail. If I can sit still when rolling my car, I can be silently terrified while you get me out of this ridiculous situation. Who in their right mind jumps out of planes that aren't crashing?"

My heart thuds. "How many times have you wrecked?"

She shrugs. "On purpose? About five. By accident? Twice. Which is really good considering the time I've clocked on the track."

Fear trickles over me. "You crash on purpose?"

Her fingers dig into my wrists. "After every wreck, I want to do it again. But they can only rebuild my crash car so many times and the last wreck pretty much destroyed it. Earl is looking for a new one."

"That's it." I move us to the door. "Anyone who intentionally wrecks perfectly good vehicles deserves to be thrown out of a perfectly good plane. And I don't want to hear you scream either."

~25~

Sheila isn't screaming. I'm not entirely sure she's breathing. I roll, hoping to get a reaction from her but there's nothing. "I've got you!" I yell into the wind, splaying out to slow our descent. She should remember this box man position from her class, but she isn't responding. "Hold on!" I maneuver us into a sit, increasing our acceleration but giving me the position to deploy the chute. It unfurls above us, the canopy catching wind and tugging our bodies into a slow descent. A squeak burps from her lungs. "Are you okay?" I thrust forward to see her face. "Sheila! Are you okay?"

She's laughing so hard she can barely speak. "That was…this is…"

"Love," I whisper, gliding us across the sky like eagles.

I steer us toward the center of our target field. "When I give the signal, press back into me and follow my lead. Landing is where people usually get hurt and I don't want an inch of you damaged."

I flare, leaning into the landing. As perfectly as anyone who's done this a hundred times, she hitches her hips and lifts her legs so mine can hit first. I run into the landing, slowing our momentum. At the last second I whirl us around and plop our bodies into the dirt. "You did good, newbie!"

"That was *awesome.*" She scrambles to get up, wiggling all over me like a stuck bug. "Let's do it again!"

"Let me see you." I fight the straps, unhitching us and spinning her so I can look into her windswept face. "You loved it. You *really* loved it."

"The rush…" She gets to her knees, eyes glazed. "You were right. It's unbelievable. Can we do it again? Now? Before the storm hits?"

She's wildfire. Kryptonite. The heel that ruined Achilles. "Come here." I pull her to my mouth, the slow burn of her sweetness dripping down my throat. Honey and hope. She presses against me. I roll her into the grass, control abandoned. Her hands run up my back, driving my hunger harder. I tug at her jumpsuit, the feel of her flesh under my fingers slamming me back into reality. I throw myself off her. "I told you we can't do this."

"It doesn't feel like you were telling the truth." She pants.

"You're not supposed to kiss people you're not in a relationship with. Remember?" She's supposed to starve me. Deny me. So I don't have to live with the memories of what she felt like. "For someone who talks about men lowering the bar, you sure didn't try to stop me just now."

"I was caught up in the moment." She pushes away, tangling in the rigging. "You remember the feeling from the racetrack."

Eager to get away from me, she tears at her jumpsuit, every swipe of her angry hand a jug of ice water to the groin. I sit up, the taste of her still burning through me. "You can slow down. It's not like I can't stop myself from ravaging you. But, why *didn't* you stop me?"

"Because you can stop yourself!" She gets free of the gear. "Where's the truck? There's supposed to be a truck picking us up."

"They'll be here in a minute." A drop of rain splatters between my eyes. "I have a dive partner now, right? We don't have to end every jump with a kiss."

"You can end your jumps any way you like, Mr. Kingwood. Now that I know I like skydiving, I'll find a less moody partner. I'm sure you understand. A lady needs reliability in her life."

She starts walking. I follow her down the only path in the field, hating myself for kissing her. For not kissing her sooner. What I wouldn't give to have control over my own life. Control over her beautiful legs. "Sheila, you knew from the start I didn't want a relationship and you also *know* you're doing everything you can to make it too hard for me to keep my resolve."

"The sooner you stop blaming other people for your own choices, the sooner life will turn around for you, Mr. Kingwood."

"Excuse me for having the audacity to lose control, but I'm not you, *Miss Beller.*" I turn left. "The airstrip is this way."

"I'll find my own way!"

I let her go until I see the pickup in the distance, then run to catch up with her. "I'm not blaming you for my problems. And I'm sorry I lost control." I latch onto her arm, bringing her around to face me. "The high…it was too much for me. *You're* too much for me. But that isn't your fault, it's mine." And my stupid wife's. "If I promise to handle the situation better in the future, will you promise to jump with me again? Please?"

"I'm jumping again with or without you." She tugs free. "And I don't ever want to be kissed by someone who doesn't mean it."

"I never said I didn't mean it. Only that I didn't *want* to do it. *Yet.*" My fingers raise to her cheek. "Sheila, I'm—" Bert blows the truck horn, as if we can't hear him rumbling our way. "It's already raining so there isn't time for another jump today. How about we go to my office instead? You can look at the job, and while you're there we'll check our calendars and set some dates."

"Dates as in *dates?*"

"Dates as in days we can get together to dive. Or race. Or eat tacos at the water fountain." I have a terrible idea. "Can I date you without actually dating you?"

~

My tongue, the harbinger of the apocalypse. And Bert, the third wheel I'll direct all my anger at if he doesn't get back inside the pickup. He reads my narrowed stare and takes cover inside the cab, giving Sheila and me a semblance of privacy as rain pelts us. I thrust my palm against the passenger door so she can't open it, fully aware Bert can hear every word through the glass.

"I'm not trying to mess with your head, Sheila. I'm trying to tell you that despite my best effort to stay away from you, I can't. You're the most amazing person I've ever met." She tugs on the handle. "Fine." I move my hand. She opens the door and slides onto the seat. Not into the middle, right on the edge so I can't get in.

"Rain is picking up, we better move," Bert offers unhelpfully.

"Slide over, Sheila. Or I'll sit in your lap."

"I'm fine where I am. You may ride in the back, Mr. Kingwood."

"I'm fine perched right here." I tap her thigh. "But it might be better if you sit on my lap instead."

"I'll ride in the back." She slides out of the truck, pushing me aside as she marches past. "A little rain never hurt anyone."

I grab her arm. "Right now, it might melt you and not because you're sweet."

She spins into my face. "Watch your tone with me, Mr. Kingwood. You may be used to dating women like Eva who would be thrilled to date you without actually dating you and while happily letting you speak to them in any fashion you like. Do *not* confuse me with them. Speak to me with respect, or don't speak at all."

"On no level have I confused you with anyone."

I wipe the rain that's now falling in sheets out of my face and slam the truck door on the off chance the noise in the cab will keep Bert from hanging on every word. "I didn't mean to be degrading. And if it's clarity you need because me saying dating is complicated *isn't* enough, I'll have you know I've successfully avoided being tempted to date anyone in *seven* years, and now you have me fighting for air."

"On no level is that my problem." She brushes by me again and gets back in the cab. I meet Bert's eyes through the window when she slams the door in my face. He's not about to offer any solutions and I'm not about to ride in the back of the truck. Not if she isn't.

Forcing Bert to slide into the middle seat, I take the wheel myself. Our ride back to the airstrip is anything but slow. I plow into the parking lot near the terminal. "Show her where she can dry off." I shove the pickup into park and get out, leaving him to deal with her. I need time to cool off. Time to process how badly I want to risk everything for a woman who doesn't even know me. One it will hurt too much to lose once she does.

~26~

Thirty-nine calming minutes after blowing off steam in the equipment room, far away from Sheila's studying eyes, I look for her. My fist aches after another punch landing on a block wall, leaving my already raw knuckles freshly bloodied. There won't be any lies about the injury this time around. I'm going to take her someplace quiet, feed her lunch, tell her absolutely everything, and hope the desserts are enough to gain a little understanding.

No one is around in the main terminal except Amalia. She's at the front counter tinkering with the broken baggage scale. "The woman I came in with, have you seen her?"

She taps the scale with a screwdriver. "Last I saw, she was heading for hangar two. But the man renting the space for his plane left, and I think she left with him."

Amalia isn't making eye contact. Her dad probably told her what happened out in the field. "She came with me, she's leaving with me."

"Actually," Amalia swallows, "his car left ten minutes ago, and before that she told me to tell you she had a ride. And that's where she went. So…"

Anger is the easiest emotion to feel. I hear it in the screech of my tires, the decibel of the music blasting from my speakers. Wherever Dirk took Sheila, I hope if he kisses her, she tells him my tongue was there first.

~

Sheila's ghosting me. I've called and texted, even drove by her apartment building three nights in a row. Her flashy red car isn't there. I hope that means she went home to the Potomac, not off to Rome with the dirtbag who took advantage of my mistakes. I never caught up with

93

Dirt the other day, but I know where his hangar is. As soon as I fix my two flat tires, I'm going to bury my anger in his face. Sheila won't approve, but it's hard to stay composed when every waking moment is designed to crush me.

It doesn't matter how hard I throw myself into work, the dull ache of loss never leaves. I've lost my family, my child, and now I've lost Sheila. The only person I can't seem to lose is Cassie. I used to block her calls but she would just call me from a different number. Changing my own phone number didn't work either. No matter what I do, she gets to me when she wants to. Even siphoning my gas, and orchestrating the two flat tires that greeted me this morning.

I planned to drive by Sheila's apartment building early, to see if I could catch her before the day got into full swing and I was once again buried in work. But two flat tires foiled that plan. The slices in the sidewalls are clean—and obvious. For the first time since I walked away from my marriage, I call Cassie. "Stealing my gas wasn't immobilizing me so you had your lacky slice my tires?"

"What are you talking about?" She yawns.

I hold the phone away from my ear, her voice clinging to me like a layer of poison sap. "I doubt you have the guts to stick a knife in my tires yourself, but I did notice some things moved around inside my office and that's right up your alley. Did you manage to pull your nose from my parents' backside long enough to pay me a visit?"

"I'm at home, *husband.* Where you should be." she slices. "But you're too busy playing with your new toy. Did you at least tell this one about me?"

She's baiting me, trying to get me to implicate myself. "If you want the divorce, you know my terms."

"And you know I'll rip the head off your toy if you don't agree to *my* terms," she threatens. "I'm no dainty Sheila Beller, so sign the divorce papers or give up pretending you're not dragging this out because you still want me. Give me the divorce, or come home to me. Either way, *I* get what *I* want."

My hand tightens around the phone. "You so much as mutter Sheila's name again and it'll be *me* ripping *your* head off."

According to the investigator whose credentials I'm starting to question, Cassie hasn't been outside California since I arrived in Huntington. He also denies finding a reason that she'd be upping her game right now. She isn't dating anyone and my parents are paying for her upscale apartment, along with all of her other expenses, so he doesn't think money is a factor. I believe otherwise. I believe she married me thinking I'd be her ticket to the family fortune, then she found out my parents despise me and got worried that she'd end up with a disowned husband and a kid on her hip.

Disowned I may be, but I'll bury her before I let her mess with Sheila. And it's clear to me now that siphoning my gas and slicing my tires are ways to keep me from seeing Sheila. While the immobilization puts a damper on certain parts of my business dealings, it doesn't shut me down. And my company failing would mean less cash for Cassie. Me losing the fragile position I have at Kingwood Properties does the same. No, she wants me working, she just doesn't want to share what she thinks is hers—my money.

~27~

If Cassie knows Sheila's name, it's curious that she's worried about Sheila taking any part of my theoretical pie. A simple internet search would inform her that Sheila's net worth is well above my own, and that her family as a whole puts mine to shame. If Cassie's lacky is stalking me the way I think he is, he'd also be able to confirm that my visits to Sheila's apartment only last long enough for me to drive through the parking garage. Those minutes are hardly testament to an affair, and after all these years, I don't see how any judge could rule in Cassie's favor even if I *was* dating Sheila.

To gain access to Sheila's building, I had to inquire about taking up residency. There aren't any units currently open, so the manager added me to their waiting list and before I left, I set up a time to come back to preview his personal apartment, lying that I didn't have time to do it that day. I implied that having a garage code would make my return convenient and he obliged. I've never relied on my family credentials before, but this was one time they came in shockingly handy. Not only did I gain access to spy on Sheila's vehicle, but the apartment building doesn't track the use of non-resident codes. At least, no one has called yet to ask why I've entered at odd hours, never attempting to contact the manager. Nor have they deactivated the code. A lot of good that does me. Today I have no choice but to hole up in my office and do exactly what Cassie wants me to do—work."

"Mr. Kingwood?" Gladys's voice scratches out of the intercom in my office. "Miss Beller is here to see you. Should I send her in?" I rub my face, sure I heard her wrong. Then a sound hits my ears that can only be one thing. One person. One beautifully fantastic person.

I bolt upright, toppling my chair as I break for the office door. Latching onto the frame, I lean over the threshold and find the source of the melody. Sheila's sitting in the plastic-chaired lobby, laughing over something on her phone. I ache all over.

Summoning my composure, I walk toward her, one steady foot in front of the other. "What's so funny?"

"Dirk." Her nails click over the screen. "I owe him lunch. And dinner. He'd like to collect both on Tuesday now that I'm back here for the week." She stands. "Is this a good time to view the building?"

"Why are you going out with him?"

"Because I want to." She frowns at the state of the shabby lobby. "That's what adults do. We make decisions. Unlike whoever threw this ramshackle place together."

I head for the elevator. "It gets worse. We'll start upstairs."

For the conversation we need to have, it's imperative to be away from Gladys's ears. For all I know, she's giving both Cassie and Dad daily updates on my movements. Which is precisely the reason I didn't ask her to order any of the treats I bought for Sheila. I sourced those on my own, and have the ones I meant to give her after our skydiving trip in the top of the mini-fridge in my room. They're probably ruined by now.

I hold the elevator door for her. "You coming?" She steps inside and I hit the "door close" button, taking us up to the third floor. Too short of a trip to figure out why she's suddenly here but long enough to know I'm not forsaking this opportunity. "I'm sorry about the other day. I was a huge jerk."

"Are you apologizing because you want to kiss me again and you're afraid if I spend time with Dirk I'll fall madly in love, robbing you of another chance?"

"So that's why you're here." I let her out of the elevator ahead of me. "Should I even show you the building or do you just want to hear me confess to being jealous so you can go on your merry way?"

"Since you won't date me unless I agree to hide in the gutter like a filthy rat, I don't care if you're jealous or not." She walks on. "Show me what rooms you want renovated, *then* I'll go on my merry way."

"Good, because I'm not jealous of Dirt." I brush past her. "You can fall madly in love with anyone you want, just so long as it isn't me."

I parade her through the rooms on this floor, sinking lower with each step. I'm so used to defending myself that my initial reaction to everything is to lash out. An impulse that's going to make me blow this *one* chance I have to tell her how I feel.

"I'm sorry I'm rude." My fingers rake across my forehead, embarrassment kicking in as she looks over the office I've been sleeping in. I didn't push the sticky fake leather futon back this morning and my toiletries are scattered on the desk. There's even a pile of dirty laundry in the corner. All the markings of a loser, an assessment my dad would be the first to agree with. "I'm having a hard time right now and this…us… I'm trying to keep everything steady so we're both okay in the end."

"Tell me about your vision for this floor." She leaves my pathetic room and walks back into the main hall. "The same number of offices? Or are you expanding some of the smaller ones?"

"I don't mean to say things that upset you."

She points toward the empty space by the elevator. "I see a central ovoid desk over there. The offices on either end joined with the smaller ones next to them for anyone requiring larger rooms. The others remain as they are, with updated fixtures and fresh paint, of course."

I step in front of her, placing my hands on her shoulders. "I'm so jealous of Dirk it's driving me mad. And I know that isn't fair, but I can't help how I feel." My thumbs stroke along her neck, my throat tightening. "Please don't go out with him."

She shrugs my hands off. "I think a terrarium behind the desk will make a nice focal point when you walk in. You can put a skylight in above it."

"You're dating him, aren't you?"

"I'm committed to having two meals with him. One of which I *wouldn't* be committed to had you not behaved like a fool. But he drove me home, so I'm taking him to dinner." She steps into the elevator. "I'm proud of you for finally admitting you're jealous."

I stand in the way of the elevator door so she can't leave me. "Will you come here before you go to lunch with him?"

"Why?"

I place my palm against her cheek. "I'm going to wager you're not the kind of woman who will kiss two men in the same day. Come here tomorrow morning? Let me have my chance to kiss you first?"

She darts around me, leaving the elevator, and enters the stairwell. I jump in front of her, blocking the stair platform. "Move, Avery. I have sketches to make."

"You haven't seen the whole building yet, so you can't be ready to run off."

Her hand waves me aside. "I'm assuming the other floors are laid out like this one, and I'm currently rethinking letting you benefit from my expertise. This may be my first *professional* job, but I assure you I have an eye for design that you'll be hard-pressed to top."

"Just a few days ago you had an eye for me." I cup her face. "Please, Sheila. Tell me you won't kiss him. Because even your lips landing on his cheek again like they did the other day is going to be bad for his health."

Her fingers wrap around my wrists, nails digging in as she pulls my hands off her. "I'm not a toy. I'll do as I please. And I'll do it guilt-free."

Her word choice strikes a nerve. It's hard enough opening up to her, I don't need her ridiculing me with my wife's words. I run a hand through my hair. "I'm not playing games with you. Life just sucks right now. The only time it doesn't is when I'm with you. But when I'm with you all I can think about is what happens when you walk away. Which *is* going to happen because I'm not the man you'll ever want a future with. So I'm stuck between not finding out what it's like to be with you and already being with you enough to know losing you is a whole new level of suck."

"You're stuck between the truth and the lies you tell yourself." She studies my features. "I feel something when I'm around you, and when you're not being intentionally vile I'm certain you feel it, too. Yet you deny us the chance of exploring what that something is. Why?"

~28~

Why do I deny myself the chance to be with Sheila? For starters, I'm married to a woman who's blackmailing me. Then there's the impending financial ruin and the manipulation she's using on my family to make them hate me more. And oh, I'm *married*. And that's worse than being divorced. "You don't want to taint your perfect little world with me, Sheila. I know it, and deep down you know it. That doesn't mean I don't want to strangle Dirt until he's too dead to lay a finger on you."

Silence pounds against my ears. She stares at me, eyes tracing the bead of sweat sliding down my neck. When she speaks, her voice is soft. "Did you know the FBI doesn't investigate missing adults?"

"Are you planning to disappear me?"

"Just before John and Mary wed, she was abducted. By a friend of hers. An evil human who preyed on her vulnerabilities."

"You think I'm preying on you?"

"I'm telling you I don't live in the imaginary world you've set me in. Losing Mary was devastating. I honestly thought she was dead." She swallows. "If Mary died, I would have lost my brother, too. He would have destroyed everyone connected to what happened to her and in the process destroyed himself. I did everything I could to keep that from happening. Including *persuading* the FBI to lend me two agents."

"Money is a powerful motivator. Even government agencies will do just about anything for enough of it."

Her head shakes. "You're missing the point, Avery. Because of what happened to Mary, to this day I cultivate relationships with every law enforcement agency in this state, including the FBI. I've built a network of people I can call on and I do them all sorts of favors so they'll be there when I need them. So don't judge me by the labels *you* give me. Judge the fact that I know what trouble looks like and I see it all over you. It's

100

taking everything in me not to find out on my own what that trouble is, and I'm only doing so because I want to give you the chance to tell me. I want to give *you* a chance."

My mouth goes dry. I guess I should be flattered that she likes me enough to want to know my secrets. But I'm not flattered. I'm terrified. I lean on the wall. "My life is hard, Sheila. Really hard. It's nothing you need the FBI for, but it is something I can't mix you up in." I reach out, running my fingertips along her arm. "You are the queen of perfection. Your hair, your laugh, your clothes…" I meet her eyes. "Then there's the sunny disposition. The one that goes away when you're with me, and it makes me sick that I do that to you. But the truth…"

I don't like to show emotion to anyone. I remove my touch and stare at the ceiling, battling tears. "The floor of rooms you just looked at are the truth of how messed up my life is. I'm living in this wretched building and not bothering to find another place because I'm on *probation* with my own father. It doesn't matter that I've worked my tail off since I was fifteen or that I spent years in Europe doing his bidding. He's dead set on leaving the entire company to my brother, which means I get cut out completely."

"What did you do to make him put you on probation?"

I married someone he thought was *beneath* us. Then I left her, which he also thinks is *beneath* us. "He doesn't respect me and I don't respect him either. Which makes working for him a heck of a conundrum." I bounce the back of my head off the wall. "I can make *him* money and do everything *his* way, or I can fight to have this side of the country belong to me. I already have a business set up, I dabbled a bit in Europe on my own and did well. But if I do that here he's already threatened to sue me, which means I have to sue him first. Or try a hostile takeover, maybe." I rub my eyes. "I don't even know what that means. And I don't *want* to do any of it. I don't want to fight my own family, and most of all I don't want to fight you."

"Then why do you?"

"I just told you." I stare at her. "Figuring out what to do about my current state of screwed is bad enough on its own; dealing you into the mix makes it even harder to know which end is up. The same way joy spills out of you and sloshes all over everyone, death comes out of me."

"That's a bit dramatic. On both accusations."

Tears burn against my lids. "You don't know what my life is like. My family *hates* me. I've tried to be their poster boy, but even if the ghost of Midas possessed me and I gave them gold, I wouldn't be good enough. And the worst part is, I actually still love them. Even my dad."

She steps toward me and I wipe away the water leaking from my eyes, pushing off the wall and avoiding her touch. "My problems aren't yours, and I don't ever want them to be. Which means I have to stop begging like a fool and let you go, and it pisses me off. I'm *moody* because I can't have you and there's nothing I've ever wanted more." My voice is thin. "If I could just be near you…"

"You are near me." She forces me to face her, hands on my arms and body close to mine. "You should really look into therapy to get rid of your aggression over the unsavory fact that life is messy because *when* you date me, I want this Avery. The one who's honest with me, not the one who's angry and lying to both of us."

"What can you possibly see in me that makes you want to date me?"

She grins. "You have really good abs. Really, *really* good abs."

~29~

I'm not so shallow as to believe that my physical appearance is enough to make Sheila forsake her good sense. And I'm fully aware that I've only told her a tiny piece of my reality. But in this moment, she's accepting me for the failure of a person that I am. In this moment, I get to hold her hand as we traverse the stairs.

If only this stairwell could be our den. If only I could kiss her in every room on every floor, occupy every space Gladys isn't in and leave the walls with the memory of my lips on this beautiful creature.

I stop us short of the door to the main floor. "When I asked about the un-dating thing the other day, I was asking to spend time with you, like a couple, except for the whole physical thing."

"Why leave out the fun part?" Sheila opens the stairwell door, a grin on her lips and a shine in her eyes. "You want me. The sooner you admit your desires, Mr. Kingwood, the better."

"The man on the moon can see that I want you, Sheila." I tug her toward the side exit so we don't have to pass Gladys's desk. So I can keep holding her hand a little longer. "Are you sure you have to leave? It's only two in the afternoon. Plenty of time for me to admit some other things."

"Save them for next time because sadly I have to leave. I have an appointment."

"Can I come with you?"

She smiles. "I'm going to see a lady doctor. Probably not something you want to sit in on."

"Depends on where I get to sit." I pull her into a hug. "Is everything okay? You're not sick or anything, are you?"

"I'm having my eggs checked."

"Eggs?"

103

She rests her head on my chest. "Have to make sure I'm fertile ground. In case some nice man wants to knock me up. Or a test tube. At this point I'm not picky."

Babies are another reason I can't tell her the whole truth. I'm legally bound to keep quiet about Cassie's abortion, so it's impossible to explain why I can't bring myself to father a baby, no matter how much I might want to give Sheila a houseful of them. The fact I'm even *considering* wanting to give them to her is disturbing.

I let go of her and walk us out the exit, rounding the building to where she's parked without touching her skin again. "I'll be waiting for you tomorrow. Don't see Dirt without seeing me first."

"Even when we're a couple, I won't be taking orders from you. You may ask for things, and I may or may not grant you those things."

"Ditto, babe."

Her eyes roll. "Avery, I'll be here for you if you're having family or business problems, but if you're playing a game with me, I'll win. So choose your moves wisely."

I smile. "Is kissing you until there's lipstick smeared all over your face a good move?"

She slides those sleek legs into her car. "You're not finished apologizing to me. When you are, you may kiss me. Until then, I'll take two dozen more petit fours and a dive trip."

"Done." I close her door before I climb in there and do more than kiss her. I'm not giving her the stale cake from the refrigerator. I'll order fresh ones. "I'll see you tomorrow."

She rolls down her window. "My friend's name is Dirk. Not Dirt."

I walk away, cupping a hand to my ear. "What was that? I can't hear you."

~

Since ten this morning, I've been on a fifteen-minute cycle of checking the lobby and circling the parking lot. It's now twenty after one and there's no trace of Sheila on the horizon. I should have known yesterday was too good to be true. She's out with Dirt, comparing us and finding he's the better choice.

If the Rover was back from the garage I'd go out looking for her, but the tire shop hasn't delivered it yet. I'm stuck here waiting for her, for my vehicle, and for the security company to finish installing outside cameras. "Hold my calls, Gladys." I storm by my unusually tall secretary's desk. "I'll be on the third floor doing some demolition."

Smashing my hammer through a section of drywall that needs to be replaced, I brood over my ill-fated attraction to Sheila. Not only am I married and on the hook for a tire bill my wife denies being responsible for, I'm now expected to somehow make up with Sheila while she lets another man wine and dine her. One who has a history with her. I don't even have to close my eyes to see her arms wrapping around him, her lips finding his cheek. She's comfortable with him in a way I've never let her be with me.

The day after Dirt whisked Sheila away from the airstrip, I added him to my investigator's list. If I see in black and white why he's better than me, maybe I'll stop obliterating walls I had no intention of tearing out on my own. If I find there's dirt in Dirt's life, I only hope it's as bad as mine, or worse, so I can use his problems to gauge what Sheila's reaction might be to mine. The way she dumped me at the airstrip, walking away without a word, doesn't inspire confidence.

"Mr. Kingwood?" Gladys's voice breaks through my destruction of the third-floor lobby.

"Over here."

Coughing, she waves a hand through the dust. "Miss Beller is here to see you."

"I can see that." Sheila's beside her, wearing a light-yellow skirt and pale pink shirt. She looks like spring. "What can I do for you, Miss Beller?"

Gladys's head shakes. "I don't know about her, but what you can do for me is stop demolishing things. The mess is starting to find its way downstairs."

"I have a cleaning service coming tonight."

"They can't help you not work yourself to death." She pats Sheila's shoulder, the way a mom would encourage a daughter. "He's done more business in the short time he's been here than we normally do out of this office in a year. See if you can talk him out of also doing the remodeling himself."

She pads away and I grab my t-shirt off the half standing wall. "Don't get dressed on my account." Sheila wipes a bead of sweat from my neck, tracing her nail over the dirt smeared across my chest. "I didn't realize it was casual Tuesday or I would have worn something different."

"Instead, you wore another beautiful outfit and came by to rub it in my face that you stood me up."

"When did I stand you up?"

"You were supposed to come here before your lunch date with Dirt."

Her arms fold. "I never told you I was coming. And I had an appointment this morning, so I couldn't have stopped by even *if* I wanted to soothe your unstable ego."

"What appointment?"

"None of your business."

I tug the shirt over my head. "You had an appointment yesterday, too."

I'm not asking if her eggs are good, she'll never let me fertilize them. "Where did you and Dirt eat?"

"Dirk and I ate at a place where friends go to eat."

"Did you have a good time?"

"I was having a *very* good time until you put your shirt on."

"Answer one of my questions and maybe I'll take it back off." I lower my face to hers. "Did you eat tacos with him?"

She pats my cheek. "I only eat tacos with handsome dark-haired stallions. Unless said stallion isn't my boyfriend. In which case, I'll be taking Dirk to the taco truck tomorrow."

"We've been through this." I wipe a paper towel over my sweaty face. "I'm not exactly boyfriend material."

"You missed a spot." She pulls the towel from me and proceeds to linger close enough that I can taste her vanilla perfume, her delicate fingers caressing my flesh. "Did I mention Dirk's ready to be married and start a family? Same as me?"

Of course he is. "He sounds swell."

"He's remarkable." She tosses the towel in the trash. "He gave up his career to come home and care for his ailing parents. I knew they were both sick, but I didn't realize they needed around-the-clock care."

"Sounds like he doesn't have time for a family."

"Sounds like I'll be finding out." She picks up the portfolio she carried in. "I made some initial sketches last night, Mr. Kingwood. Is there someplace less dusty where I can show them to you?"

"Don't start being formal with me again." I tug at her shirt. "I hate when you do that."

"If you're not boyfriend material, our relationship is strictly business, no need to be anything *but* formal." She taps the portfolio. "Considering what you've been up to today, I might have to revise these plans a little, but I think you're going to love this design. Shall we go to your office?"

I circle her waist with my hands, lifting her onto the nearest desk. "This is why you're not going to date him." I press my mouth over hers. She kisses me back. I keep it slow at first, building until she's as wild and hungry as me. I break away, moving to her neck, sliding my lips along her skin, feeling the erratic beat of her pulse as I climb to her ear. "I'm ready to go downstairs and look at your design ideas now, Miss Beller."

~30~

Tension born of desire builds between Sheila and me. She's been working in my building for two full days now and I'm falling down a slippery slope, the heat of hell lapping at my feet. I try to fight the attraction but my lips beg to be on her the second we're alone. And today, begging is all my drooling mouth has been able to do. She's tired of me treating her like she has the plague whenever Gladys is around. So much so that I nearly came clean, spilling the entire truth of why I can't openly date her. But doing that is more of a threat than Dirk, and he's already a danger to the precious little time I have with her. She's still talking to him, and talking to *me* about him. "Dirk told me the funniest joke this morning. Do you want to hear it?"

Gladys was just in my office, so of course she's bringing up option number two—the man who *doesn't* ignore her when other people are around. "I don't want to hear his name, let alone his words."

"Your loss." She shrugs, placing a list on my desk. "You'll need to order flooring soon, and you'll also need to hire installers. Gladys and I are tired of you trying to do the work yourself."

"We'll order it tomorrow."

"*You'll* order it tomorrow. I won't be here."

My stomach drops. I drum a pen against my desk drawers. "We still have a lot of work to do on the design. We haven't even started plans for the main floor, and that's what people will see first."

She grabs her coat. "There are drawings in my portfolio; it's on your desk along with the list of flooring choices."

I stand. "When are you coming back?"

"Next week."

"Next week?"

108

She walks out of my office, tossing Gladys a polite goodbye. I rush into the hallway, fully aware my secretary's eyes are glued to my every move. I squirm when Sheila turns around. She's daring me to get personal with her in front of Gladys. "Um…I'll get the flooring ordered and look for installers. Enjoy your three-day weekend."

"I said I'll be back next week, not Monday." Sheila whips around and pushes out the first set of doors. My feet move. Her head shakes. Such a slight movement to deliver a decisive blow. I'm not allowed to walk her to her car. She doesn't want my inconsistency anywhere near her.

It's possible she'd feel differently if I told her I was dumping money into a building I don't own to have an excuse to be near her, but somehow I don't think she'd find the sentiment endearing. If anything, the notion that I'm letting Dad benefit from every penny spent on this renovation while simultaneously using him as an excuse not to date her will only confuse her more. It might also send her digging for her own answers. Another option that doesn't work in my favor.

Despite my shortcomings, seeing her sketches come to life matters to me. I want this building to look exactly how she drew it. After I watch the Corvette leave the parking lot, I go to my office and begin ordering flooring—paying extra for overnight delivery. I'll have the contractor she suggested work around the clock, and since I don't sleep at night, he can add me to the crew. I'll do everything I can to make sure that by the time she comes back, whenever that is, we've actualized as much of her vision as possible. And I'll order her some spicy chocolates. With any luck, I'll get to lick the remnants off her.

~

It's Tuesday morning and I still don't know when Sheila's coming back from the Potomac house. She hasn't responded to my messages, not in a way that says she wants to talk to me. All I've received are a few short words letting me know she arrived safely and received the chocolates I sent her. It's just as well, I've paid the contractor good wages and if I was up all night talking to her, I wouldn't have been able to throw my own back into the work.

Every wall in this building has been painted, the various tiles are installed in bathrooms and lobbies, and most of the rooms are carpeted. I've cleaned the floors three times already but am going over them again with a steam mop. When Sheila does finally show up, I want everything to look nice for her. A clean slate. One that starts now. Her approving whistle just turned the corner and hit my ears.

"Someone's been busy."

"Thanks to you!" Gladys is thrilled about the changes to the dusty building she's been cramped in for so many years. "After you left, Mr. Kingwood and all the contractors he hired worked twenty-four seven. Gobs of people in and out!"

I turn off the steam mop and walk down the hall in time to see her grab Sheila's hand. "Upstairs is even better. The walls are back up, and it's clean."

Sheila's amber gaze falls on my face. "It seems I need to go away more often."

I meet her halfway, hand outstretched. "Whether or not you were here to distract me, I would have gotten the work done." Her fingers slip into mine and I pull her toward me. "I missed you."

Gladys backs away. "I'll let you show Miss Beller the upper floors."

Leading Sheila into the elevator, I contemplate for a moment what it means that I've been this open in front of Gladys. I haven't told Dad I started the renovation and he hasn't brought it up in his scathing morning lectures, so it's doubtful she's reporting my actions to him. As for Cassie…Sheila is beside me, the two of us enclosed in our tiny metal cocoon. After being apart from her again, I know that whatever trouble comes from me being with her, I'll face it. Because loving her is the only thing that matters to me. I drag her into my arms. "Please don't go away anymore."

She smiles. "You really did miss me."

"Miss?" I tilt her chin up. "I had to eat tacos alone."

"That's the only reason?"

"No." My mouth moves toward hers. "But it's a pretty important one."

Her lips move with mine but I feel the distance. The lessened fervor. The stiffness in her fingers as we stroll hand in hand through the building. I turn us toward the room I've been sleeping in. My things are still here with the old futon, but the room is painted and neat as a pin. "What do you think?" I'm proud of the work. Proud to have the colors she selected surrounding me.

"I think we need to go over the layouts once more and get the fixtures ordered."

I take the hint and steer us back toward the elevator. Slowly. No urgency to get there. "Why the snail's pace?" she whispers. "Trying to decide if the elevator or the stairwell offers better cover for you to kiss your girlfriend?"

My throat tightens. This is why she's distant. She wants answers. "There's a lot we need to talk about before you start calling yourself my girlfriend, and I'd rather not discuss those things today."

Her feet plant. "Why? Because you have no intention of ever committing?"

I face her, holding both her hands in mine. "Commitment isn't an issue. I'm yours. But," a chill runs up my spine, "you want marriage. And kids. I can't give you either of those."

She removes her hands. "You *won't* give me those things."

I drag a hand down my face. "If anything in my life was a matter of simply doing what I want, I'd be filling your head full of all the things you want to hear, and I'd probably be painting a nursery."

"But you *won't*." Her eyes narrow. "So I can't do this with you. Because every time I let you kiss me, you take a part of me. A part that should go to a man who *wants* a future with me."

I move forward, heartsick when she steps away from me. "My feelings for you do *not* end where commitment begins. I want a future with you. It's just that I can't give you the one you want. Not right now." I close my eyes, blocking out the sound of my phone ringing. It's "Dead March," the ringtone I set for Cassie.

Blowing out a breath, I meet Sheila's stare. "I don't know if I'll ever be able to give you what you want."

She turns on her heel. "Then you should answer your phone. I'll show myself downstairs."

I follow her. "I don't want to answer the phone. I want to talk this through with you."

As annoyed with the constant ringing as I am, she shoves her hand into my pocket. "Don't!" I snatch the phone before she sees the screen. But she doesn't have to see it to know it's a woman calling. My reaction told her everything.

~31~

My elevator ride back down to the first floor is much different than it was on the way up. Sheila is still beside me but so far away I might as well be back in Europe. "The phone calls aren't what you think they are." I mutter as the doors open. "Hence the ominous ringtone."

Her shoulders square. "Your personal life is none of my business. I'll spend this week finalizing designs and placing orders, then I'll hire some installers to come set fixtures while I'm gone next week."

"Gone?" I follow her to my office. "You're jumping ship because I won't marry you?"

She places her shoulder bag onto my desk. "I didn't ask you to marry me."

I slam my door shut, irritated that Cassie chose to call me right when I was on the verge of having an important conversation. "The job continuing on *without* you is the very definition of you jumping ship."

"If I were running and never coming back, you might have a point. Although your phone has you quite distracted, try to pay attention." She circles around my desk, focusing her eyes on me. "I said I'll be gone next week, not forever."

"Your mom's annual retreat?" I forgot about the hostess duties she told me about. "What day are you leaving?"

"Saturday morning."

The distance between us crowds my lungs. "So I have four days with you?"

"You have nothing with me." She returns to her bag, taking out more sketches that her beautiful long fingers drew.

I slide into my place at her side, fingers encircling her wrist. "Will you listen to me for a minute?"

"No, but the woman calling you might." Her wrist slips from my grip. One of these days I'm going to learn to hold her tight. Right against my heart.

"I don't want to talk to her, Sheila. She's…" My wife. "A business contact."

"Sounds like you two have a great deal of *business* together."

Sweat pools under my arms. "I…made a bad decision with her. I knew better than to get involved with someone below me but—"

"Below you?" She gapes. "If the great Avery Kingwood refuses to give anyone without money the time of day, pretend I'm a pauper!"

My tongue is a knife. Each syllable cutting deeper. "You've said yourself we have to be careful because people prey on us, that's all I meant."

"Spin your words any way you like, but not once have I ever disregarded someone over their bank account. My brother married a woman who was *beneath* him and she's the best thing that ever happened to him."

"And you're the best thing that's ever happened to me." I enclose her in my arms. "Please don't walk out on me, Sheila. Please." She pulls free and I turn away, emotions boiling over. It feels weak to cry. Especially in front of her.

I wipe my face, circling away from her and back to my desk. "How long did you say you'd be gone?"

She studies my red eyes. "I can be back as early as Tuesday."

I bite the inside of my cheek, offering her the extra chair I pulled up to my desk so we could sit side by side. "But you might stay gone longer?" She nods. I sit down. "Then we better get as much work done this week as we can."

"Avery."

"I have a right to want the job finished." I meet her eyes and wish I didn't. There's a hint of tears. I've done exactly what I knew all along I would. I hurt her.

I leave the safety of the desk and go to her. "I care about you, Sheila. And I'd give anything not to disappoint you, but I don't know how to keep from hurting you."

"Date me." She places her hands on my shoulders. "Give us a chance. Give *me* a chance. Let *me* decide if you're right for me or not."

So many times I've counted death as my only hope. Now I'd die just to hear her say she loves me. "Before I met you, the only time I felt alive was when I was diving. Putting my life on the line, seeing how close I could get to the ground before letting the canopy save me. Now all I have to do is think of you and I feel that rush." My fingers sweep along her cheek. "You woke me up, and now I have to face what that means. I *will* face every obstacle, I just need time."

"You don't have to face anything alone," she whispers. "I'm here with you. Together we'll figure out who *we* are and we'll make a future of we both want."

I press my lips to her forehead. "You already know who you are and what you want. I wish I could be as solid as you. But there are things…reasons…"

"Other women?" Her face tilts to mine. "Are you seeing other people and leading us all on? And don't lie to me. I *will* find out, and then you'll find out how much I don't like being made a fool of."

I smile. "You're the only woman who's ever given me a reason to consider who I am and what I want. And unfortunately for both of us, what I want is you. Only you."

Her arms wrap around me. "And I want you. So why are we not together?"

I rest against the top of her head, closing my eyes. "We *are* together. I just…want to have my affairs in order before I demand that you kiss me in every public space. In front of Dirt so he knows to keep his hands off you." I tip back and look into her face. "I'm not standing on solid ground and if a sinkhole opens under me, I don't want you falling into it. Yet I can't stay away from you. So tell me how you want to do this, and that's what we'll do."

Her hands slowly move from around me, running up my stomach and over my chest. "I can't stay away from you, either. Which is why you're coming to the Potomac with me. But there will be no PDA. I don't want to have to explain you until I'm more certain of you than I am now." Her lips brush mine. "Let's explore this spark. Monogamously. And discreetly."

I cock a brow. "You want to date me without actually dating me? Ouch, Sheila. That hurts.

Her eyes narrow. "Consider this your trial period. Impress me, because I'm nowhere near convinced that you're worth all this trouble."

~32~

I can't think of a single thing I've done right, before *or* after meeting Sheila. And I'm certain the fact that she's seen me naked has nothing to do with her still being in my life. Yet here I am, living on the edge of dreams with an amber-eyed divinity.

Sheila owning the racetrack means we can race whenever we want, and it has me thinking I should just buy the airstrip. We could start our days with a dive, work hard during business hours, then I could chase her around the track each evening and spend the nights holding her. It's a fantasy that plays in my head each time we fall from the sky straight into a fevered kiss that pulls down my barricade inch by mouthwatering inch. I *will* give this woman everything she's ever asked for, including children.

After talking with my lawyer and financial advisor this morning, a plan to get rid of Cassie and get my family off my back is coming together. The plan doesn't allow me to buy the string of car lots Garland's family owns. Not that I want to be in the car selling business. I only looked into the company's financials because I heard a rumor that Garland was looking for investors. I don't want to be his partner. I want to own him. So I can fire him.

The car lots would be a gift for Sheila. I'd strip Garland of his family legacy, avenging her, and then give her the keys to any vehicles she wanted. Not that she can't already have her pick. It's just that it would be nice to provide her with something other than food. That's why I'm not entirely pulling the plug on buying the lots. I won't go through with the deal, but I'll go as far as to make Garland *think* I am. His dad is like mine. Garland doesn't get to decide what the company does, and so far as my corporate lawyer says, Garland's dad is inclined to sell rather than take on a partner.

"Babe?" I rush through the double doors of my building. Gladys is out taking her husband to the doctor, so Sheila offered to work reception for her while I went out to view a potential property for my dad.

"Babe?" I traipse through the hall. "I haven't been gone that long and we don't get too many calls, so you can't be abandoning your post already." There's a clanking sound, followed by rustling. "Sheila?" I drop our bag of tacos on Gladys's desk and trace the sound to my office. "There you are!"

My smile fades. Sheila is rifling through my desk, hands sharp and fast as paper clips spill across the floor. "What's going on, Sheila?"

"You had a visitor."

"Who?" I take a step, her anger choking the life from my limbs. "Who was here?"

"You were served."

Bile rises in my throat. "Served what?"

"You're being sued." She thrusts a manila monstrosity into my face. "By your *wife!*"

My lungs compress. "I…I can explain."

"You're *married.*" She stomps around the desk. "*Married!*"

Blood pools in my feet. She throws the envelope I refuse to accept onto the floor. "I'm getting divorced." The words fall weak and pathetic from my lips. The office door slams behind her. "Wait!" I drag myself forward, throwing the door open and leaning on the frame. She's already at the exit.

I sprint after her, a plea on my lips. "Just listen to me. Please?"

"Whatever you have to say, say it to your *wife!*"

~

I call Sheila all day. All night. She doesn't even bother to pick up for the satisfaction of hanging up on me. Each time, I'm forced to plead into her voicemail. And each time, an image of her deleting the messages without hearing my words burns through me. That's how I treat Cassie's voicemails. Ignore them. Delete them. Pretend she doesn't exist even though the constantly twisting knife in my back digs deeper with every breath. This time it's gone too far. I feel the blade pressed against my lung. Severing my spine. Ready to destroy what's left of me.

"Please call me, babe." I lean against my office wall. "Please, Sheila. I need to know you're okay. I need to know *we're* going to be okay."

No sooner than I lower the phone, a voice wafts through my open door. "Good morning, Gladys." It's a ghost. A thief come to steal the very breath from my lungs because it can't be Sheila. She'd never come back here.

"Good morning, Miss Beller." Gladys's voice sounds as real as Sheila's.

"If you need me, I'll be working from the second floor today." Her timbre comes to me on whispers of air. I close my eyes. The click of footfall passes close. I open my eyes. The apparition floats past my door.

"Sheila?" I stumble toward her, phone still glued to my hand. "I've been calling you. Why aren't you answering my calls?"

"Ask your wife."

"Ask his what?" Gladys chokes.

This isn't a dream. Sheila's really here. Standing in front of me. Denying me. The way I always knew she would. Anger rises hot and dark. I stuff the phone in my pocket. "Don't feel bad, Gladys. Outside of my family, no one knew I was married. And now it doesn't matter because after eight long years, I'm finally getting close to settling the divorce." I look to Sheila's still defiant profile. "A concept Miss Beller doesn't understand. Please get her a dictionary so she can look up the meaning of the word."

The elevator door opens. I step inside. Sheila walks to the stairs. I exit the metal box and follow her, slamming against her back when she abruptly stops just inside the stairwell.

A vision of calm, she turns, staring directly into my face. "I intend to finish the job I started. Not for you, but because I've decided to make office design my niche. I won't work for *your* company again, of course, but I can't very well leave this job undone and expect anyone else to take me seriously. Now, leave me alone while I work because it's bad enough that I've run around with a married man, I don't want to go to jail for murdering one."

"D-I-V-O-R-C-E." I spell it out.

"It's comical you think being a man who breaks vows to a woman he professed to love in front of God and family is better than being considered a married man." She turns and resumes her path.

"Yeah, I'm real twisted." I huff. "Are you going to continue being hardheaded or are you going to give me a chance to explain?"

"I don't want any connection to you whatsoever, which is why I'm now doing this job for free." She pushes through the second-floor door. "I refuse to accept your money. All you have to do is pay for the materials, unless *me* paying for them will get you to leave me alone while I work. In which case, I'll gladly foot the bill."

She unloads her bag and begins shuffling folders onto a table covered in empty paint cans. I help her move them aside. "You know how much I've struggled since meeting you, so why are you acting like I wronged you when I said from the start I can't date you?"

All but ignoring me, she pulls out a catalog and takes a picture of a desk. "I was going to have my brother design custom pieces, but now I'm not." She stuffs the catalog against me. I don't take it. It falls to the floor. "I'll email Gladys the item numbers. You can order from the catalogs like everyone else."

"You came on to me as much as I came on to you, so don't blame your hurt feelings completely on me."

"I flirted with you because there is no ring on your finger." She's intentionally not making eye contact. "At the time, I didn't realize you were a liar who takes off his wedding ring. I now see you for who and *what* you are."

The same as Garland. I'm clipped. Cut from her life. My name never to whisper over her lips unless I throw myself in her path. "I don't wear a wedding band because I tossed it into the Atlantic Ocean long ago. And maybe I'm wrong for not telling you about the divorce, but having a conversation about my soon-to-be ex-wife is a heck of a lot more complicated than saying *Hey! I'm Avery Kingwood, a twenty-nine-year-old divorcé.*"

"It didn't sound complicated at all." She opens the second of her infuriating folders.

"It was impossible to say that to you, Sheila. Because you told me how you feel about divorced men. You would have shut me out like you're doing now."

"Don't blame me for your failures. That brooding anger is the guilt you feel for betraying your wife. I was only the unsuspecting dope." She moves from the table and opens a window, the smell of fresh paint still overwhelming on this floor. "Normally I'm not so naïve, so kudos to you. You've perfected your game. Shame you didn't get in on the bet. Or maybe you did after all? I'm sure I was gullible in that regard as well."

My already broken heart shatters. "After all the time we've spent together, you really think I was playing you?"

"I think your cards showed too soon, Mr. Kingwood." She turns, the breeze whipping against her silhouette. "The bet is to get me in bed. Even if doing so requires marrying me. So, you lose. But I'm curious. Is your wife also a bet? One you took too far?"

~33~

Sheila's accusations cut deep. It's been three hours since I walked away from her but I'm still raw. "Miss Beller, may I take you to lunch?" I force the words out as soon as my feet step beyond the elevator.

"No." She's found a chair and has it pulled to the paint can table, her attention staying on the list she's making.

Rounding the clean side of the table, I look over her shoulder. She's writing out instructions for the future installers in meticulous detail, attaching copies of her sketches and item numbers from the catalog to ensure pieces end up where she intended them to go. "May I at least have ten minutes of your time?"

"No."

"We need to talk."

"No." She checks her phone. "I have to go. Please see yourself out ahead of me, or stay behind until after I'm gone."

No choices left, I stomp down the stairs ahead of her. I throw open the door and make for my office, eyes landing on Dirk waiting in the lobby. "What are *you* doing here?"

"We've not had a chance to formally meet." He holds out his hand. "I'm D—"

"I know who you are," I snap. "Why are you here? In *my* building?"

"He's taking me to lunch." Sheila steps off the elevator and glides past me, taking his arm and giving *him* her smile. "You're early. I'm impressed. Too many men have egos that won't allow them to meet a lady on time."

"No ego is worth keeping you waiting." He gives the smile right back to her.

She walks toward the door, giggly and beautiful with him. "Sheila." The rumble of my voice makes me shiver. She walks on, not heeding the warning rolling from my chest. "Shei-la."

"Do you like tacos?" she asks as Dirk opens the door for her. "I know a great taco place."

"Sheeeeila!"

"Mr. Kingwood!" Gladys's tall form blocks my view of my sun. My Sheila. "Mr. Kingwood!" Gladys grips my shoulders, shaking as her lips spill my name. "Your hand!"

I don't remember having the pen. Never felt it break. "I'm fine." I pick the largest shard of plastic out of my palm, blood streaming down my fingers and dripping all over the freshly cleaned floors.

"Your shirt..." Her hand pauses over my side. "The blood..."

"A lot of blood vessels in the hand." I push out the door Sheila just left through, my shirt looking like I slaughtered a hog. Sheila's already gone, her Corvette whipping out the parking lot while Dirk follows close behind. He wasn't here to pick her up, he was here so she could rub him in my face.

I head to my vehicle, Gladys screeching behind me about medical attention. "Go home for the day," I yell back. "We're not doing any more business until I settle some things."

~

I'm still waiting to settle those things. I don't know where Sheila went yesterday but it wasn't to Alberto's. Someone else was there though, and his red hair prompted me to do what I said I wouldn't. What my financial advisor is furious over. But in the heat of the moment, signing the deal with Garland's dad made sense. It seemed like a way to show Sheila that I *am* serious about her. That I *am* the man who's right for her. Not Dirt.

Now that I'm sitting across from Garland in an office that's technically mine and with absolutely no idea how to run a single car lot let alone a chain of them, I feel like an idiot. I *needed* the capital I spent on this deal. I *needed* to do a grand gesture that Sheila would actually respect. Not cement myself in a franchise that takes away my ability to start over with A.K Investments once I resign from Kingwood Properties and hand over everything it takes to divorce Cassie. Sheila will see this folly for what it is, and she'll be as disgusted with me as I am. These aren't even racing cars!

I stare at Garland's red face, watch the color deepen under my scrutiny and wonder what Sheila ever saw in him. I wonder what she's going to think when I don't fire him. Because that's something I can't do. Not right now. I need him to run this dealership until I find someone else. "As of now, you still have a job. But if you ever look at Miss Beller inappropriately again, I'll bury you."

His mouth flops open, eyes wide with surprise as the realization of what this meeting is about sinks in. "You're with She—"

"It's Miss Beller to you. Don't ever let me hear you address her otherwise." I sit forward, resting my elbows on the desk. "Call your friends and cancel the bet. They don't need to know why, only that you're a moron who shouldn't have ever started the wager to begin with."

He swipes a palm down his sweaty face. "Should I tell them it was won?"

"It wasn't. All that's happening is you're growing a conscience." I wait. He nods. "If you value your life, you won't breathe even a syllable of this conversation." He nods again. I wave him away. "Get back to work. You're not on salary anymore and I'm not paying you to sit around."

Even if this business venture explodes all over my face, Sheila's already hurt, so thick skin or not, I don't want to be the cause of rumors murmured about her. What I want is an opportunity to explain my situation to her before she leaves for the Potomac tomorrow. A trip I was looking forward to taking *with* her. One Cassie ruined with impeccable timing.

Sheila's not taking my calls again, and she's already showed up in my office to prove to me that she's strong enough to endure being under the same roof without the slightest inclination to fall into my arms. She proved she can erase me. *Replace* me. But as cool as she remains on the surface, she's beyond angry. And there's only one place she can blow off that kind of steam.

She's not going to be happy that I'm rolling up behind her on the racetrack, but if the woman won't come to me, I have no choice but to chase her. "Um…" Earl's voice crackles into my ear. "I don't think you're supposed to be out there running with her."

"What makes you think that?" I jerk left as she slams her brakes, then right when she spins around.

"Earl, she's not going to…" The front of her car rocks, the engine revving. I roll to a stop. Smoke billows from her rear end. I hold my breath. She guns it, barreling straight at me. "Tell her to stop!"

"I don't think she's listening!" he yells. "You might want to move!"

Tightening my wet palms on the wheel, I dodge right. Sheila barrels down my neck, adjusting her path as I try to avoid hers. Jerking hard, I spin off the track in a cloud of sod. She whips around, charging. I push out the window, clinging to the hot metal of my door. There's no place to run. No guarantee I'd even make it if there were. Her snarling beast gains ground. I hold up my hands in surrender, tucking against the car. Her fender lurches to a stop an inch from my shaky knees.

With trembling fingers, I yank off my helmet. "Are you insane?"

"This is *my* track," she roars. "Stay off it!"

"With a psychotic woman behind the wheel, everyone needs to stay off it!"

"Psychotic?" She shoves out her window.

"Yes! Psychotic!" I storm toward her, all fire and fury. "You could have killed us both." I tug off her helmet. "Don't ever do that again." Her lips move, shouting at me. My mouth falls over them. Her gloved hands dig into my neck, pulling me closer. Our bodies meld together, the luxurious taste of her melting down my throat. She drives the kiss deeper. I give her everything she wants. Everything *I* want.

The toe of her boot rams into my shin. "Ouch!" I limp back. "Kick me all you want but you kiss me back *every* time. So go ahead, *Miss* Beller, keep lying to yourself about what I mean to you. Your tongue tells me the real story."

Her face is pure fury. "This fling might have died hard, but I assure you it is dead. You mean nothing to me."

"Kiss me again and prove it."

Without words, she whips back to her car. I thrust my arm across the window. "Is Dirt your new stallion? Does he hold your hand and call you his girlfriend like a twelve-year-old boy? Is that what makes you happy? A baby-faced punk drooling all over himself?" Tears flood her eyes, crashing through me to douse the anger I only summoned to cover my own hurt.

I reach for her. She slaps my hand away. "Even if Dirk were the loser you describe, I would still be happy because he isn't hiding like a snake in the dark, his lying tongue ready to strike whatever truth suits him."

I lower my voice. "You're not a plaything in my toy chest. My marriage has been over almost from the beginning with zero chance of reconciliation. The lawsuit is yet another of Cassie's attempts to get money, and until I met you, I was willing to let hell freeze over and have flying pigs rule the world before I ever gave her a penny."

"Aw." She fake frowns. "Did you marry someone beneath your station? That explains why you've been preying on me. You're worried she'll clean you out. Attaching to me would keep you in the lap of luxury."

Attaching to Sheila keeps me in the lap of happiness. The kind of joy that bubbles from someplace unknown. "Money has nothing to do with my attraction to you. I want to be happy. *You're* what makes me happy."

I'd give anything to see a moment's hesitation on her face, but there's no emotion showing in the whole of her body. I swallow against the choking stench of death. "Sheila, will you please have faith in me? I can explain. I'll tell you everything that happened in my marriage."

Her resolve stiffens and she slides into the car without a word. I lower my face to the opening. "I'm not Dirk the golden boy, but I'm not a lowlife serpent either. I'm a man who makes mistakes. Should those mistakes crucify me?"

She throws the car into reverse. "Ask your wife."

~

Cassie's pretty face smiled back at me through our vows, and then I lived in wedded hell. Surviving only to live through this whole new kind of hell. Sheila's leaving for the Potomac today so I have no choice but to beat on her apartment door at the crack of dawn. If I have to die knowing she's choosing Dirt, I'm not going to do it while getting steamrolled. He's no more deserving of her than I am.

"Open up!" My knuckles rap against the wood. "I know you're in there. Your car is outside."

She opens the door, suitcase in tow. "What could you possibly want? There's nothing to say. Hence the reason I've ignored your phone calls for the last hour."

I hold out a manila envelope much like the one she shoved in my face, but this one doesn't have anything to do with Cassie. "I only came to bring you this. I was going to meet you on neutral ground, but since you won't answer my calls, I had to come here."

She pushes me aside and walks on, not glancing at my envelope. "It's clear I can't finish the project I started. You'll have to find a different designer."

"Will you just take this?" I push the envelope into her left hand. "It's information you need to see before running off into the sunset with Dirt. He's not the golden boy you think he is."

"Can't stand on your own merit so you besmirch everyone else to make yourself look better?" She presses the envelope to my chest. "I'll take my chances. Compared to you, Dirk *is* a saint."

"Such an angel he was arrested for DUI. That sound like a man you want to be mixed up with?" She has the nerve to laugh in my face. "He's in more debt than our country. Still find it funny?"

"Hilarious." She bats her eyes. "Thank you. The laugh is appreciated. Now, if you'll excuse me."

I grab her suitcase, rolling it down the hallway myself. "Don't worry, we'll have plenty of time to talk while I drive you to the Potomac. And I won't have to borrow money from shady lenders in order to pay for the gas either."

She slows to a crawl. "I'm going to count to three, and if you're still here, I'm calling security. Not for my own protection, but yours. One. T—"

"Three." I laugh. "How do you think I got up here? You're not the only one who knows how to grease palms. So call security. Tell them you're mad at me because your boyfriend isn't worthy of the pedestal you're putting him on."

"Dirk's in debt because his mother has cancer and his father had open heart surgery. Twice. He's taking them to the best medical professionals and those expenses have drained him, and the stress has landed him on the wrong side of a binge a time or two." She yanks her luggage away from me. "He's been fully open with me. What you and your little envelope think are bombs are only confirmation of what I already know."

She walks on, in complete control of her luggage. "In the midst of all he's going through, he also makes time for me."

"I made so much time for you I barely got any work done." I fight her for the suitcase. "This is going in my vehicle anyway, so you might as well give it to me."

"Let. Go." Her voice pricks over my flesh, loosening my palm from the handle. "Make sure our paths *never* cross again."

~35~

If I were a smart man, I'd heed Sheila's warning. But no one has ever accused me of being smart. They accuse me of everything else. And I'm tired of it. Sheila's going to hear me out, give me a full ten minutes of quiet while I explain my side of the marriage situation.

Giving her a half a day's head start, I drive to the river house. The estate sits at the end of a private lane, perched two hundred yards off the Potomac's mighty shore. High stone walls lord over the sloping lawn, daring flood waters to breach the security they've long provided. I imagine Sheila watching from the turreted roof, as menacing as the brewing storm.

Ringing the stronghold's doorbell, I listen intently as scuffling kicks up on the other side. The noise fades. I ring again, straining to hear through the slab, but the voices trailing from the back of the house drown out the commotion. I'd try to find my way around to the other guests but it's probably Sheila on the other side of this door, deciding exactly how she'd like to chop off my manhood. "Hello?" I knock this time, the wood solid under my knuckles.

The door finally opens. "Sorry, we, um…" Mary's hair is tousled, her cheeks red.

"We were busy." John holds the door open further. "You must be the reason my sister is in a mood."

"In the flesh." I step into the house at his invite, a pit opening in my stomach. "May I talk to her?"

"That's up to her." Mary eyes the two gift bags I'm holding, unimpressed. "She's usually never in a mood, so you must have done something terrible."

"She didn't tell you?" I should have brought flowers.

John's dark green eyes scour me. "All she's done is hog our son and mutter about men being arrogant fools. So, arrogant fool, what did you do?"

He's only a couple of inches taller than me, but if I were the type to be afraid, I'd choose this moment. "I doubt I'm any more arrogant than she is, but I'm definitely the only fool between the two of us." I run a hand through my hair. "I'll tell you everything after I talk to her."

His arms fold over his broad chest, same as Sheila's fold when I'm irritating her. "She's busy entertaining our guests."

"She invited me, so technically I'm one of those guests." I shake the two gift bags. "I have something to give her."

His eyes lock on, hard and steady. Mary nudges him. He blows out a breath. "This way."

"Thanks." I follow as he slips an arm around his wife and leads us under the arched beams that open into the main house. When Dad first gave me the green light to move here, the little research I did on this family led me to the origins of their home. It's old, built by generations long gone and never once occupied by anyone who wasn't a Beller. These walls have seen a lot. And surely they've heard more laughter than the cold echoing halls of my family's palatial estate. A truth that makes my feet plant. "Wait." I peer out the provincial French doors overlooking the expansive patio where people are scattered about. Sheila's so close, but I'm not going to barge in and ruin her day again. Especially without confessing to her brother. "Sheila's mad at me because I'm married."

His head snaps around. "You're what?"

"Getting divorced." I brace my core for impact. "I've been trying to get divorced for seven years, so it isn't a new thing, but your sister seems to think I've done something wrong to *her* when what happened between myself and the devil formerly known as my wife happened long before I met her." I take a breath. "Sheila thinks *I'm* the devil. But that's only because she never met my wife."

When he's quiet, it's even more suffocating than Sheila's silence. Mary's dark stare and closed lips are enough to cause a stroke. "You heard the part where I said I'm getting divorced, right?"

"For seven years?" His jaw ticks.

"Seven years, one hundred sixty-three days." I sigh. "I'd count the hours and minutes but it's already depressing enough."

"That explains things." Mary smiles at her husband. "Everyone says *I* wear rose-colored glasses, but it's you Bellers and your curses that are the naïve ones."

"Careful, sweetheart." He grins. "You're one of the cursed."

"I bet if I were divorced instead of widowed, you wouldn't have gotten near me."

"I bet you're wrong." He swings her into his arms. "This is where you belong. Nowhere else. And *with* no one else."

Somehow, I don't think me picking Sheila up and toting her around like a baby will make her swoon. I imagine that ending with blood dripping down my face and nothing in my hands but the teeth I managed not to swallow.

Sheila bolts through the door. "What are you doing here?"

Katherine enters behind her, pulling the door shut. "What my daughter meant to say is, welcome to our home, Mr. Kingwood. We're delighted to have you."

"That's not even close to what I meant to say."

"I'll use my imagination to fill in the blanks." I deliver the first gift bag to Katherine. "Thank you for having me. I heard you like pralines. I had these specially made and added enough for you to share with your guests."

"I'll share them if I don't eat them all myself before the day is over." She winks. "Thank you for such a thoughtful gift."

"You're very welcome." I hold out the second package to Sheila. She crosses her arms. "Please take it."

"Sheila." Her mom growls, glancing out the doors behind her to be sure their visitors are more interested in their cards and croquet.

Sheila's arms unfold, sliding down to clasp her hands together, that infuriating polite tone lifting her voice. "I can't possibly accept such a generous gift. We'll make a game of it. Choose a number from one to twenty, Mr. Kingwood. The guest who draws the number gets your gift."

~36~

My gift is only meant for Sheila. I say as much but she won't budge. John nods to the console table by the door. "Leave it there. Her curiosity will get the best of her soon enough."

"Doubtful." She looks bored.

I set down the package containing nothing but a signed copy of my divorce papers. Ones I'm willing to submit if she'll have me. To know if she'll have me, she has to talk to me. I'll tell her the truth of what happened between Cassie and me, she'll read the divorce papers and make her decision based on knowing everything about me. Like how I'm quite possibly going to end up broke *and* jobless. "Is there someplace private we can talk?"

"The one thing my mother looks forward to every year is hosting this event for our *close* friends and family," she answers. "Part of my responsibility is helping her host. So no, I can't sneak away to do anything with you, Mr. Kingwood. Especially in private."

"You've already helped me by readying all the rooms and greeting everyone." Katherine nudges her. "I think we can spare you for a few minutes."

"Maybe take a walk along the river?" Mary suggests. "The storm looks to be passing us by and the air will help you both have clear heads."

"Sounds good to me." I accept the suggestion. Sheila doesn't.

"He's pursuing me," she announces. "But he's married already."

As I did, Sheila's now learning that when you drop a bomb, you better be sure the information you're dropping is worthy of an explosion. Katherine is shocked, but she's taking cues from her son. He's clearly the hothead in this family. And Mary is taking up for me. John places her back on her own two feet and she takes Sheila's hands in hers. "Divorce isn't ideal. But I can imagine scenarios where you have no choice."

131

Sheila shakes her head. "Honoring your marriage vows should be the only choice you give yourself."

Mary sighs. "Think back to the time in John's life when he almost married the wrong person. If he had gone through with it, knowing what you know about her now, do you think he would have been justified in divorcing her?"

"Perfect example." Sheila smiles. "I hadn't wanted to bring it up in front of someone who is neither friend nor family, but no matter what *she* did John wouldn't have divorced her."

His head shakes. I see the kindred spirit of sadness in his eyes. He's still haunted by his near mistake. Which means he understands me actually marrying mine. "I can't stand here and say I wouldn't have gotten a divorce. I very well may have."

"You don't believe in divorce any more than I do," Sheila protests.

"It isn't a matter of belief." He sighs. "There *are* circumstances where divorce is best. I can't say I would have fallen on my sword and stayed married. Most likely I would have divorced her."

"I don't believe you."

"You would have wanted him to stay in a loveless marriage?" Mary questions softly. "You would have sat by and watched him be drained of all his joy, trapped in a miserable life, all to stay *socially acceptable?*"

"It isn't about social acceptance," Sheila snaps. "It's about commitment. And neither of you know what kind of a marriage Avery had, so stop trying to make him a martyr."

It's true, they don't know. Especially her. "If you'd talk to me, I'd tell you what kind of marriage I had."

"If you'd stop talking to me, I'd be able to get back to my guests." Her eyes flit to John. "Just because your wife justifies all your actions doesn't mean you can excuse his."

"My wife uses her head in conjunction with her heart." He growls.

"Trust me when I say my heart is *not* what Mr. Kingwood is trying to win."

"What does that mean?" He glares at me. "What is she talking about?"

Setting John off by telling him about the bet isn't the worst thing I can think of. If she's game for it, I'm down. "Want to clarify? Or shall I?"

Her eyes narrow. "It means Mr. Kingwood is the deep end, and I have no intention of drowning. So if you'll all excuse me, I have guests to get back to."

She leaves with a swift turn, showing remarkable control in not slamming the door behind her. The others stare at me. I shrug. "That went better than I expected."

"Come on." John chuckles. "I might kick you out yet, but for now you're welcome. No matter what my sister says."

~

Sheila scoops Mikey out of Willis's hands and takes a seat beside the older man. The patio is full of people, but the chair next to her is empty. I move toward it. Her eyes snap to mine, amber hardened, no longer the color I love to get lost in. Mary sees the trouble, snatching her son away from Sheila so the baby isn't caught in the middle of our drama. I take a breath. "Sheila, will you take a walk with me?"

Like my own family, this one doesn't want to air their dirty laundry in front of company. Me being the laundry, I can't help but have a front row seat to the warning tones in the whispers passing between Katherine and Sheila. Mary steps in to save the day, addressing the guests who are all watching what's about to become a scene. "The weather does look nice now. How about we all take a walk?"

Sheila climbs to her feet. "Only the ladies. The men can stay here."

~37~

Since John and Mary don't ever leave each other's line of sight, I fell into a group of men who tagged along behind the huddle of women Sheila managed to tuck herself in the middle of, laughing and making them all happy little butterflies while I'm stuck back here with Uncle David, listening to fishing stories that sound more like fiction than fact. "I'm going to sit down for a while." I nod to John, who already left our men's assembly in favor of sitting on a bench by the river where he's bouncing Mikey on his knee and watching his wife.

"Okay." David slaps my shoulder, leaning in close. "You just make sure you don't compliment that wife of his. I made the mistake once of saying how pretty she is, I thought he was going to gouge out my eyes!" The old man laughs.

"Duly noted." I throw in a smile to offset my tone and make my way to John.

"I hear if I call your wife pretty, you'll gouge out my eyes. She's beautiful." I plop down beside him. "Start gouging, I won't fight you. I welcome the end of my misery."

"My sister making you develop a death wish?"

"In your sister's eyes, I'm already dead."

"She'll get over your divorce situation. In time."

"I don't expect her to get over it, I just want her to talk to me about it."

He tips Mikey onto his shoulder. "Talk to me instead. Start with the investigation into Dirk." I look at him and he grins. "I heard her mumbling something about your *nerve*."

Like me, John doesn't call massive debt and a DUI clean, no matter what excuses Sheila wants to make. "All I wanted was to prove to her that golden boy wasn't so golden."

"And you wanted to sink him so she didn't pick him over you." John looks into the face of his now sleeping son. "If there had been competition when I met Mary, I would have taken him out by any means necessary, and without blinking. I told her as much and, well…" He smiles out to where she's standing twenty yards ahead. "She eventually forgave me for being an ogre and married me."

I drag my hands down my face. "How do you get away with being overbearing? I can't sneeze without making your sister mad when all I'm trying to do is *not* sneeze. I'm drowning, and I'll be long dead before Sheila throws me so much as a smile, let alone a life jacket."

John has everything I want. A wife. A child in his arms. A family who loves and supports him. I wish I could say he's smug about it. That he doesn't deserve it. But he's a man who knows he's blessed. He doesn't take anything around him for granted. Especially his wife. While we sit far enough away from the commotion so that his son can nap, he's intentionally close enough that his wife can look in on both of them. Each time she waves or tosses him one of her knee-melting smiles, he soaks it in, makes it part of him, and passes it to his sleeping baby with the softest touch.

"Mary looks at you like her whole world lives inside you. I'm not asking for the playbook on that kind of admiration, but the least you can do is tell me how to make your sister blink."

"Chase her?" He points to the lawn where the entire party begins to play a game of tag.

I stand but Sheila shakes her head, not looking at me but announcing loudly, "Mr. Kingwood doesn't want to play."

John laughs. I glare at him and plop back down, leaning on my knees to watch Sheila graciously stand next to an elderly woman so the lady can tag her and play the childish game without feeling she's too old and slow to join in. "Not one time has Sheila asked me the circumstances surrounding the divorce. All she does is accuse me of breaking vows like it wasn't the hardest thing I've ever had to do."

He rubs Mikey's stomach. "The curse of every Beller is struggling to find their one true love. Sheila thought she knew what that looked like, but you just shattered her dreams, so whatever she dishes out, take it."

The dreaded romanticism this family exists on *and* my own special kind of voodoo is a pandemic of wrong. "The idea of true love, that there's one person in the entire world who completes you and that once you find them you'll live happily ever after is complete fantasy. Life is hard. And I don't care how much money you have. Suck is suck."

"I feel for you, I really do. But just because life sucks doesn't mean you sour your soul and give up. I'm speaking from experience." He points to the screaming laughter of the tag players. "I almost shut myself off and missed out on Mary. For different reasons than my own, she'd done the same. One tiny decision on either of our parts could have made us miss out on even meeting. That's why she puts up with me when I overstep or act like a Neanderthal. We're both grateful for the chance we were given. She knows I'm completely devoted to her, and to absolutely proving myself to her."

"How do you prove yourself to someone who won't even speak to you?"

He shrugs. "My guess is Sheila's scared. And probably embarrassed."

I understand why she's embarrassed. She lowered herself to be with me. "What is she scared of?"

"No Beller has ever been divorced."

"Which means I don't fit in with the Bellers and therefore have no shot with Sheila." And here I've been dumb enough to think my life ended before.

He stretches an arm along the bench, his massive hand engulfing my shoulder. "Be understanding of Sheila's reaction to your situation and let her come to terms with reality in her own time. Do that, and she might end up smiling at you the way my gorgeous wife smiles at me."

"Do you believe the words coming out of your mouth or are you enjoying spouting mush to give me false hope?"

"What I believe is you wouldn't show up here knowing I'd be here unless you're either an idiot or in love with my sister. I'm banking on it being the latter, which makes me respect you."

"I wouldn't rule out idiot."

He claps his hand against my back. "You seem pretty hopelessly hopeless. For a little while, I felt that way with Mary. So my advice is to just hang in there."

"Sheila isn't a pushover like Mary."

"Let my wife hear you say something about one of hers and you'll be the one she pushes over." He grins. "Everyone sees the sweet side of her, but I'm here to tell you when the woman tells me to jump, I don't ask how high. I jump as high as possible and keep going until she tells me to stop."

I laugh as she heads our way and he bounces out of his seat, ready and waiting for anything she might ask. She scoops Mikey into her arms and John wraps his around both of them, facing me. "I've listened to you, now you listen to me. If you hurt my sister, I will break every bone in your body and sink you to the bottom of the Potomac."

"Noted." I also note Mary not saying a word. Her eyes tell me she'll help him. "Any chance either of you can get Sheila to come over here?"

~38~

Steady as the water lapping at the river's edge, I quiet my pulse as Sheila makes her way across the lawn to my stone bench. Despite her disdain, she isn't the type to let one of her *guests* sit alone. She'd rather let someone else keep me company, but John and Mary whispered in Katherine's ear, and Katherine whispered in Sheila's.

"Do not speak to me," she bites. "Why are you here?"

"I can't tell you if I'm not allowed to speak."

"Leave." She turns her back to me, standing far enough to the side to give the appearance of talking to me while watching the dwindling game of tag.

"I'm here because you invited me. And I wanted to make good on my promise to spend this weekend with you."

"Forgive me for thinking it was implied that your invitation was revoked. In the future I'll spell things out for you. L-E-A—"

"D-I-V-O-R-C-E." I pat the bench next to me. "Will you please listen to what I have to say?"

"If every inch of this lawn was on fire and the only safe spot was beside you, I'd gladly burn."

"Wait for it." I stand, sliding in front of her. "Because if you keep this up, there might be a fire."

Her chin rises. "Rejoin the others. Keep a smile on your face while staying away from me. Do not look at me. Do not speak to me. Do not breathe at the same time as me. Then in one hour, make up an excuse and leave."

She walks toward the house and I break all her rules, starting with walking next to her. "You want me to lie to your family? And here I thought you were so against liars."

"Lying comes easily to you, so I have no doubt you can look each of them in the eye and do your excuse justice."

"I didn't lie—"

"So help me if you don't shut up, I'm going to get a lighter and set this whole place ablaze myself."

"Life isn't puppies and rainbows," I whisper in her ear. "The sooner you learn that, the better."

~

Gathering in the general location of the backyard, factions of guests scatter about in various activities. I sit down for a card game when Sheila picks up a croquet mallet, but I'm too distracted watching her to pay attention to the cards. "Excuse me." I leave the table, catching Katherine's eye. "Is there a room available for me?"

Her smile is sympathetic. "We have plenty of rooms. I'll show you to one so you can rest up before dinner."

I retrieve my duffle from the Rover and then Katherine winds me through the house and up the stairs, happening to mention which room is Sheila's when we pass the corridor leading to a part of the house that overlooks the side lawn. After depositing me in my designated room, she leaves and I sit on the edge of the mahogany bed, staring at the wall until the clock strikes seven, summoning me to dinner.

Though we're eating in the formal dining room, the seats aren't assigned. Katherine is at the head of the table with John at the opposite end, Mary on his right while Willis sits on Katherine's right. Sheila is in the middle of the length of table facing the doorway. I walk toward her right. Her slender arm traces along the back of the seat. "Sorry, this seat is reserved." She points to the end of the table. John's left. "That one is open."

"Which lucky person gets to sit here?" I lean close to her. "Why can't it be me?"

"My guest isn't here yet, but he will be soon." She removes her arm, heading off the questions scrolling across everyone's faces. "When he arrives, my date will be sitting next to me."

My heart sinks as the doorbell rings. She jumps up. I hear my voice mutter something imperceptible while she dashes from the room. I make a move for the door. "Mr. Kingwood," John's voice booms. "Have a seat next to me. I saved it just for you." His tone isn't a request. I turn back to the door and Sheila's already gone.

"Fine." I walk over and huff down into the chair. "But if I were you, I wouldn't relish the idea of what's getting ready to happen."

He grins. "Keep it tame enough not to upset my mom and I'll enjoy the fireworks just fine."

"The two of you will *not* ruin this dinner party," Mary scolds, eying her husband. "There seriously can't be two of you in this world."

"He's nothing like me." He taps her nose. "I wouldn't have sat down. I'd be punching Dirk's lights out before he ever crossed the threshold."

"See?" I shrug. "I get shafted and you get to act like a gorilla on steroids. Want to tell me again that you're cursed?"

A hush falls over the room as Sheila reenters. Her hand gently rests on Dirk's bicep, I imagine my own hand squeezing his throat. "Be nice," Mary begs, people already glancing my way to decipher my reaction.

My chest heaves but I remain silent, fixing my eyes on Dirk as he greets Katherine with a hug. His familiarity with this family ties my gut into knots. "It's wonderful to see you, Dirk. I'm sorry to hear about your parents, they were always the sweetest people."

"Thank you." He hugs Katherine for the second time. "They'll be happy to hear you think so kindly of them. Almost as happy as I am that your daughter invited me to dinner."

Sheila grins. "Don't be modest. I invited you for the remainder of the weekend. Only one dinner with you just won't do."

His hand slides into hers. "My bag is in the car. I'll stay as long as you'll have me."

Envy tears through me, forcing my mouth open. "That's a confusing statement coming from someone who is supposed to be caring for his parents. Did they make a miraculous recovery when Miss Beller beckoned?"

He doesn't answer. Awkward silence builds as everyone waits. Sheila leads him to his seat, addressing the allegation *for* him. "Dirk prefers to tirelessly do most of the caregiving himself, but his parents have a nurse who stays with them, so I talked him into coming." She sits next to him, shoulder leaned into his. "He deserves a weekend away where someone will take care of him for a change. That someone being me."

I barely hear John's whisper. He slides Mikey off his lap and into Mary's arms. "Don't make me drag you outside." He laughs into my ear as if he just told me a joke. My fists clench in response.

"The food smells wonderful, Mom." Sheila ignores our entire end of the table.

"It should, you planned it." Katherine's tongue clicks. She knows exactly what her daughter is doing and she isn't happy about where this is going.

Sheila raises her water glass, making eyes at Dirk. "Here's to our health. May our years be many, and blessed."

I push my glass into the air, fixing my stare on Dirk. "To our health. Except some of us prefer something stiffer in our glass. Isn't that right, *Dirk?*"

"I don't allow drunken parties in my home." Katherine snaps. "If anyone needs something heavy in their glass, they'll have to go elsewhere."

I nod at her. "We should toast to your wisdom. You're an example to the rest of us."

"Then it's too bad you didn't know my mother sooner, Mr. Kingwood." Sheila sips her water. "She could have helped with your moral development."

"Too bad, indeed." I take my own sip. "How about you, Dirk? What are your views on strong drink?" I ignore Sheila's fiery glare and stare at her date. Out of everyone here, he's the only one eating. "Do you believe stronger penalties would deter people from driving under the influence? Or would that not make a difference in a drunk's decision to get behind the wheel?"

He chokes down his freshly served roasted potatoes. "Me? I, um…"

Sheila hands him her water to sip. "This isn't an appropriate topic for dinner."

"Actually, I'd like to hear his answer." John levels on him. "Making a choice to drive after you've been drinking is a serious matter."

Sheila waits, but Dirk's lips aren't moving. She looks from him back to us. "He was twenty-one years old and made a *single* poor decision. Other people in this room think they should get a pass for what they did at twenty-one when their decisions were much worse, and affected way more people."

I cross my arms over my chest, mimicking John's current posture so she knows this end of the table doesn't welcome her *date*. "A drunk driver puts hundreds, maybe even thousands, at risk by getting behind the wheel. Most personal decisions, like who you marry, don't."

"Sheila." Dirk pushes from the table and stands. "May I see you in the other room, please?"

"How about you sit back down and let her eat." I snap.

"I'm rapidly losing my appetite." She gets up and links her arm through his. "Let's go. We can always enjoy a late-night snack together later."

~39~

John *strongly* encourages me to stay in my seat while we wait for Sheila to reappear in the dining room. She walks in without Dirk. I release the fork I'm bending. I'd clap through her announcement of his *unavoidable* departure, but the traces of humiliation slicing through her features pierce deep. Everyone knows why he left. And I'm the fool who embarrassed her because of my own jealousy.

I attempt to strike up a conversation while she lifelessly pushes food around her plate, but she doesn't even bother to give me a dirty look. Fishing for a reaction will only draw more attention to her unusual somberness. While the people around us eat and talk among themselves, my penance is to sit here, reflecting on how I managed to do the very thing I'd rip out my own heart not to do. I've obliterated the joy that *is* Sheila Beller.

Under the guise of setting up games in the family room, she leaves the table. Ignoring John, I climb to my feet. I don't need his permission to go to her. I'm going.

Walking softly over the hardwood, the low murmurs from the dining room concealing my footfall, I come up behind Sheila. "Need any help?"

"No." She pulls a stack of board games out of a cabinet. "The others are having dessert. You should be with them."

"I didn't come here to be with them." I place my hands on her shoulders. "I came to be with you."

She shrugs me off. "There's no chance of that happening. Especially after what you just did to Dirk."

"All I *did* was ask him a question," I defend. "It isn't my fault the coward ran off. If I were him, I would still be sitting beside you gladly giving an account for myself, especially over something as serious as drunk driving."

"As serious as you lying to women because you think having female companionship is okay as long as you do it in the shadows so your wife can't see?"

I hold out my hand. "Yes, Sheila. As serious as that. So let's go back in there right now and I'll clear everything up in front of everyone."

Moving away, putting a card table between us, she looks at me for the first real time all day. "I knew the instant you arrived at Mrs. Smithers' tea party. The jaw of every woman gathered in the garden hit the floor, followed by their straightened postures and bright smiles tossed in your direction. There was a moment when I felt like them. Happy. Full of butterflies and nervous that you wouldn't choose me. Then you did. I just didn't know you'd already chosen a wife. So no matter if you kept your affair with me secret, the stain is still as much on your soul as Dirk's DUI is on his."

I lean across the table, trying to get closer to her. "I don't consider you an affair. And I didn't set out with reckless abandon or the intention to break any vows, let alone the law. So don't lump me in with the likes of *him*."

"Dirk is a man who dropped everything and raced out here simply because I asked him to." Her eyes flood. "Not only was he treated poorly, but I had to stand in this room and make excuses for how it is we came to know his personal business. I had to confess that I *did* invite him only to make you angry, which makes me a monster. So no, he shouldn't still be here sitting beside me after I treated him in a way I thought I would never treat anyone." She leans on the table, mocking me. "Pat yourself on the back. You win again. I lowered myself to the point of possibly losing forever the one man I could actually be with. He may never forgive me no matter how much I try to make this up to him, and I don't blame him. I blame you."

I snatch her hands from the table. "If he cares about you, he'll forgive you. But the very fact that you admit to using him to make me jealous proves he isn't the man you're meant to be with."

She yanks free. "After the horrible display at dinner, I can only imagine how embarrassed Mom is over me, so please, for the remainder of the weekend, stay away from me. Don't ruin this for her."

"I…" Voices echo down the hallway. The others are coming. I lift the stack of board games from the table. "I'll spread these around. If you need help with *anything* else, please ask. I'm here for you."

She turns away. "I don't want you here. And I certainly don't *need* anything from you."

~

After an hour on the other side of the room from where Sheila played monopoly with her cousins, I slipped away. The more I leave her alone, the perkier she becomes. And I need some time to clear my head.

Walking the perimeter of the estate, I take in the peaceful swashing of the Potomac, slowly winding my way through the dark and back to the house. Stillness greets me. Most everyone has trickled off to their rooms for the night, but there's light in the family room. I peek inside. A few smiling faces beckon me to join them, but the only face I care to see isn't here. "I'm going to turn in. See you in the morning."

Trekking to the patio instead of the stairwell, I take in one more thick draw of country air, hoping it might help me sleep. Shadows move to my left. "Sorry." I turn away from the couple entwined in the chair.

"We're decent." John's chuckle fills the night. "Mikey is with us. We like to sit outside when it's warm, and he's fighting sleep tonight so go ahead and join us."

I sit down and see the bundle in Mary's arms. She's perched on her husband's lap, a pretty smile scrolled across her lips. "He's one good baby. I don't think I've heard him actually cry."

"He's sweet tempered." She nods. "He cries occasionally, but not much."

"A testament to the fact that you two are good parents." I return her smile, a familiar ache tugging at my heart. Only, the sorrow is now mixed with longing. I want a child with Sheila.

"Here." John pushes Mikey toward me. "Wouldn't you like to hold him for a while?"

Holding him will only worsen my pain. I shake my head. "As much as I'd love to help you get that alone time you're after, there's no chance I'm taking him."

"Scared holding a baby will make you want one of your own?" Mary smiles. "Sheila's ready for children."

"I know." I sigh. "The golden boy will make a good dad. As long as she doesn't let him handle the money. Or drive."

"Dirk?" John scoffs. "The man tucked tail and ran when the heat was turned up."

"Can you blame him?" Mary scolds. "The two of you ganged up on him. I felt bad for him *and* Sheila."

John shrugs. "You'd feel worse if she married the coward."

"Just because he left tonight doesn't mean he'd bail on her when she needs him," she defends. "He came here because she needed him to. And when he got here she needed you two to be civil."

I wonder if she's on his side or on *everyone's* side. I rub my face. "All he had to do tonight was answer a simple question."

"Instead, the coward let my sister do his talking, and when he didn't like the defense, he got mad and left." John rumbles. "Even if you can't win, a real man stays and answers the stupid question."

"Case in point." I tap my chest. "I have a stain on my soul so I can't win, yet I'm here."

"Don't sell yourself so short," Mary's hand presses into my arm, confirming she's on everyone's side. If only her touch could soothe me the way Sheila's does.

"I don't have to undercut myself, Sheila explained my undesirableness to my face."

Mary sighs. "I know you men don't like to back off, but women need time. We need to think things through and process what it is we really want."

I look at John and he shrugs. He has nothing to add because he only gives Mary her time now because he has her. Because they made it through their darkness and ended up together. I'm scared I'll never have that with Sheila. I lean back in my chair. "I don't have a problem giving Sheila space. I have a problem knowing Dirk is the better man."

"Right now, I think you're both fairly worthless." John pulls the baby out of Mary's arms again and pushes him into me. "He won't bite, so earn yourself some points. I'll be back for him in an hour."

"Two." Mary giggles as he hops out of the seat with her cradled against him. "Unless I hear Mikey screaming. Then I'm coming back, and you're dead."

"Told you." John winks. "She's not nearly as sweet as everyone thinks."

They disappear before I realize they're not joking. "Wai—!" The kid is sleeping. I drop my voice, holding him tight to my chest. "What am I going to do with you?"

His tummy rises and falls. He doesn't have a care in the world. "Stay little." I kiss his chubby cheek. "The world isn't any fun after you grow up."

"Don't tell him that." Mary slips out the door and scoops him from my arms. "You didn't really think I was leaving my baby with you, did you?"

"I did." John pouts from the doorway.

"All I know about this man is that the divorce he didn't bother to mention to Sheila isn't final and he has absolutely no table manners." She pushes past her husband. "You two may be peas in a pod, but the only one of you I trust, I'm married to. Now come help me put him to bed before he wakes up and decides Mommy and Daddy don't get *any* quiet time tonight."

~40~

John follows Mary around like a puppy on a leash. I don't blame him. If Sheila would come for me, I'd jump at the chance to follow her orders. If they would be orders to do something other than leave her alone.

Head in my hands, I consider what to do next. I need her to give me a chance to explain myself. At least then I could walk away with her knowing I love her. That I wouldn't have put her in this position for any other reason.

The beep of my phone gives me a glimmer of hope. It could be her, waiting for me on the turreted roof. I glance up to the top of the stone walls, pulling the phone out of my pocket with a miserable smile. **Make room for me, I'll be on your girlfriend's doorstep by morning. With all my love, your adoring wife.**

My heart stops. I wasn't followed to the estate, I've been watching for a tail since the day I caught the man leaving photos on my windshield. There hasn't been anyone puttering around my office building since the cameras went in either. Admittedly, I've been careless with open affection toward Sheila since I nearly lost her to Dirt, but the only place we talked about me spending this weekend with her was inside the privacy of my office. Where the paperclips were moved. Where a stack of folders were in the middle of my desk instead of on the side. Cassie bugged my office.

Lurching from my chair, I make good use of the half bath inside the back door of the estate, the contents of my dinner emptying into the ceramic throne. If my building is bugged, Cassie's heard…everything. My love for Sheila. My agony. Every intimate word, Cassie heard.

Dragging myself off the floor, I text her back. **Don't come here. I'm coming to you. And when I get there, you better hope you're as smart as you think you are because this is over. I'm putting an end to you.**

Sheila wants me to leave and now I have to, but I'm not going to beat on her door and tell her all the ways in which a relationship with me has compromised her. I'd like to prolong the finality of my fate for as long as possible, storing the tiniest seed of hope in my chest, watering it with my own blood to see if there's any possibility that one day, she'll forgive me.

Taking a pen out of my duffle, I rip a sheet of paper out of the notebook on the neat desk by the window. As I write, my slow strokes mimic the swash of the Potomac.

> *Sheila, I came here in the hopes of having a chance to open up to you, but it's clear that isn't going to happen. You need your space and I respect that, so rest assured that by the time you read this, I'll be gone. But I beg you to do me the favor of reading this fully before ripping it to shreds.*
>
> *There are many reasons I didn't tell you about the divorce. One being a conversation we had all the way back at Mrs. Smithers's un-tea party. It was brief, but I'll never forget how it felt to know in that moment that I'd always be a disappointment to you. It made me not want to confess.*
>
> *Before that, it was my family. They feel the same as you and never miss an opportunity to berate me. But they don't know certain facts about my marriage. Facts I'm not free to discuss with them due to my separation agreement. And whether or not I ever tell them, I do want to tell you. All along, I intended to sit you down and explain my situation to see if you could accept me under the conditions of my life. I never had a chance to get that far. Things got out of hand faster than I expected. I'd like to get them back on track. On Tuesday, I'll be waiting at our fountain in the park. Please meet me there so I can fully explain everything to you.*
>
> *I care about you. Now and always.*
>
> *- Avery*

Dull steps take me to her door. It's two in the morning. I press my palm to the smooth white wood, close my eyes, and imagine her standing on the other side, her hand pressed against mine. Sliding my hand down, I pass my letter through the thin crack under her door. Then, with two deep breaths, I walk away.

At the end of the hall I hesitate, envisioning Sheila unfolding the plain white paper, eyes eager, feet even more so as she runs after me, stopping me. Not letting me go. But there's only silence. I maneuver through the darkened house, retrieving the gift bag from where it still sits untouched. There's no point in leaving my signed divorce papers here. In my heart, I have to believe that if Sheila knew the depths of Cassie's deceit, she wouldn't want me to mail these in. "Don't turn your back on me." I whisper into the darkness. "Please, Sheila. Don't let go of me so easily."

~

The precision with which Adelle just cleared my building of bugs is impressive. She drove up in her inconspicuous blue Honda, walked in the front door, put her finger to her lips, and slid through the rooms with the stealth of a panther. Not a sound was made until the two bugs she found were disabled and resting in my open palm.

Sheila was always careful not to be in my *room*—the location of the first listening device, whether for modesty, appearances, or lack of trust in me. But we had plenty of intimate conversations in my office, where Adelle found the second bug. I attempt to recall the teasing banter, arguments, me begging for forgiveness, and all the moments when Sheila gave it, letting my mouth reap the reward of her lips.

Though I'm thankful I didn't expose her in my room, what that device heard is too painful to consider. Cassie got to overhear my sorrow. The long, tormented nights where I grieved the loss of our child, the witching hours when I openly manifested the heartache of not being the man Sheila deserves. Whenever I let my emotions overtake me, Cassie listened.

I knead my fingers along the tense muscles in my neck, locking eyes with Adelle. "My girlf…a female acquaintance of mine, I need to make sure she's not being watched. Or bugged."

Her blue eyes scour mine. "I'll need your friend's name."

"You can't repeat her name to anyone." I wait for the nod confirming the confidentiality we discussed on the phone. Since my last private investigator still hasn't provided any intel on Cassie, I chose a different one. "My friend's name is Sheila Beller."

Adelle laughs, eyes twinkling as the sound spills over her lips. My jaw clenches. "This isn't a joke. I'm worried."

The corner of her mouth twitches. "I highly doubt Sheila has a bug problem, but I'll check into it."

"Then you know her?"

"That's confidential."

"That's a confirmation." I stare at the equipment in my hand. "Sheila's already pretty upset with me, and this… I'm going to tell her what's going on, I just need some time to figure out exactly what *is* going on. So could you not mention this to her?"

"You think there's more going on than just your wife wanting to know if you're having an affair?"

"I'm not having an affair. My wife is only my wife on paper, and once I get back to California I'm going to remedy that. But the soon-to-be-ex has something brewing." I hold up the listening devices. "Can you track who bought these?"

"I'll try. They're low rent though, so whoever decided to purchase those isn't a professional. I'd wager they're not even a real investigator because no one I know would use dime store junk like that."

"Does that mean these don't work?"

"It means someone has to be close by with a transmitter to pick up anything. I'll go through your security footage to see what vehicles park within range."

I have a beat of hope. Unless there is enough manpower to have someone sit outside my building twenty-four hours a day, Cassie hasn't heard all my moments, only some of them. "Can you check the security footage of Sheila's building, too? I have access to the parking garage and can get you by the doorman."

She takes the devices from me, mouth tilting in a smirk. "I'll check on your girlfriend, but I highly doubt an unsophisticated stalker has gotten anywhere near her. The only reason *your* access to the building still stands is because Miss Beller told me to leave it active. She likes the little treats you send her."

My mouth goes dry. She grins. "Her connection to you is the only reason I dropped everything and ran over here. Now I'm going to open an investigation into your wife. If at any time there's something our mutual friend needs to know, I'll tell her. Until then, your bug problem is our little secret."

I shouldn't be surprised that Sheila's known all along how often I roam through her parking garage. I'm just grateful she only had Adelle watching her back instead of having me investigated. "If you find out we're not going to be able to keep this secret, will you tell me before you tell Sheila? I need time to invest in body armor."

$$\sim 41 \sim$$

With Adelle's promise to give me a heads up, I go through the motions of living while waiting for Tuesday to roll around. Before I leave for California to face Cassie, I need to speak to Sheila. In the meantime, I had Dad check the current location of my wife. I knew my ask wouldn't be well received, but after he belittled me for not knowing where my own wife is, he confirmed her whereabouts. I have photographic evidence that she's still in California.

Going to the fountain in Miller Park at dawn on Tuesday, I wait as patiently as possible, every footfall jump-starting my heart only to crash it against the rocks when it's not Sheila. I call her every hour, forced to leave messages on her voicemail each time. My last one was at fifteen till midnight. "In case you didn't make it back from the river today, I'll wait for you again tomorrow. Please come, Sheila. *Please* give me a chance to explain myself."

Another day of sitting by the fountain having every footfall send my pulse into a frenzy leads to a Thursday morning of me sitting at my desk, poring over financials instead of making the decision to waste another day waiting for Sheila. She's not coming. Ever.

I'm not just hurt anymore. I'm angry. It's one thing to be rejected, but to be dismissed without being heard is another. Sheila's lack of even trying to understand my side reminds me too much of my own family. I get what John said about how she must feel, but I have feelings too.

Gladys creeps into the room and slides an envelope onto my desk. "Here are the remaining drawings and instructions for completing the renovation." Sheila's neat handwriting is scrolled on a sticky note tacked to the front. *No payment needed. The project was a learning experience. With best wishes, Sheila Beller.*

Reading the words "best wishes" makes my stomach turn. It's as if we never meant anything at all to each other. Sheila Beller is washing her hands of me. "Gladys, send Miss Beller a referral letter and a thank you for the work." She may be done with me, but I'll uphold my end of the bargain. From afar.

"Anything else?" Gladys asks, her voice betraying how broken she is for me. I wish she wasn't. But it's hard to hide your feelings from your secretary.

That Gladys is upset for me only stokes the flames of my anger toward Sheila. Toward Cassie. My family. All of the people who think they can treat me like I'm nothing. "Go home for the day Glady's." I need time alone. "Take next week off, too. I'll be in California."

She nods, making a benevolently swift exit. I wait for the door to close. For the beep of her setting the newly installed alarm when she leaves. Then, I stand, whirl around, and grab the leather chair Sheila picked out. I slam it against the walls of my prison, crashing and banging until it's nothing but ruble. I don't want to buy this building from my dad, I want to destroy it. I want to rip everything Sheila's touched from my life, including the shattered pump in my chest.

~

Only one place has ever released my anger, soothed the aches and offered comfort. The one place without boundaries or limits, where the rush pushes back until my mind clears. Where senses awake and the earth explodes in vibrant color as I hurl toward it, everything and nothing existing all in one moment.

Tension pulls from my muscles as I relax into the freefall. I could deploy my chute, slow down, stall my canopy, and accelerate again. But I'd rather stay right here in the freeness of the fall. I close my eyes, letting the automatic activation device earn its worth. It can deploy my chute; I don't have the will to save myself.

My body lightens, its mass screaming toward the ground, head clear, heart empty. I hear the beep of the altimeter, but the AAD—isn't on! I pull out of the dive, fumbling for my handles. The ground is too close. I send up the main canopy but it doesn't deploy. I yank the cutaway and go for the reserve. It thunders out above me, struggling to catch wind. There's no time. It snags a draft, but my body still slams into the ground, sod exploding around me. I flip, the reserve catching another gust. The wind flings me upward, slamming me back to the earth. Blood bursts into my mouth, filling my throat as I roll and thump through the field, the wind a demon shoving me where it wants me to go. I let it take me. I have nowhere else to be. No one else to be with.

~

Skydiving fatalities are rare. Today, I'm not the exception to that fact. An ambulance was already busting through the jump zone before I landed. If you can call what I did landing.

"Thirty-eight stitches?" Bert's pale as he drops a fresh change of clothes on the hospital bed where I'm downing a cup of pain pills.

"A new record for me." I slip out of the hospital gown when the nurse leaves, tugging on the t-shirt he brought. "Thanks for this."

"No problem." Worry lines stretch across his brow. "I brought everything that was in your locker. If you need something else, I'll run out and get it."

"This is fine." I assure him, feeling very little of anything. Both from the painkillers and the emptiness inside me. "The ground broke my fall without snapping any bones, so they're not admitting me. I'll be able to leave soon."

He stares at the line of stiches springing from my brow and curving toward my mouth. "I bet you got one heck of a concussion. What happened up there?"

"I was reckless." I tug on the pants, not caring if he sees my backside. "I didn't check the rig before I jumped. I must not have packed it right after the last trip and…forgot to turn on the AAD."

He rubs his face. "I checked the rig. The main chute was in a bind, and the AAD computer was tampered with. Looks like someone popped the unit open and jammed something into the circuitry. So I'll ask again. What happened up there?"

"I wasn't trying to die on your watch, if that's what you're implying."

"Amalia said you were somber when you came in, and that you told her you wouldn't be back for a while."

I face him. "Because I'm leaving for California tomorrow. I didn't tamper with my gear, but if someone did, I need to get your security footage." He's probably wrong about the AAD. Most likely, the damage came from the crash. But on the off chance that Cassie would have someone… She wouldn't go that far. Would she?

I rub my stitched face, a bad case of hallucinations stabbing me in the gut. "After this concussion stops making me hear angels calling my name, I'll come by and go through what's left of my rig."

He grins. "You mean that woman screaming your name is an angel?"

My head snaps up, Bert fading as I focus on the voice crashing through our tiny corner of the emergency room. *Avery Kingwood! Where's Avery Kingwood?*

"You hear her?"

He chuckles. "Everyone in the state hears her."

Dizzy on my feet, I rip open the curtain, twisting it in my fist to stop the world from spinning while I process the scene at the nurse's station. A perfectly groomed apparition is draped over the counter, grabbing the computer screen while two nurses swat her away. "Sheila?"

~42~

Sheila runs toward me, the force of her body slamming into me while her arms engulf my neck. "Avery. You're alive!"

"I'm…" Not sure I didn't die. "You're here to check on me?"

"Have you been seen by a doctor yet?" She pulls away, tugging on my non-hospital clothes. "Nurse! Why isn't he being treated?"

"I have been." I wipe her tears as her fists wrench into my shirt. The tighter she grips, the more pain I feel. But it pales in comparison to the joy of seeing her. "Babe." My hands find her cheeks. "I'm okay. They stitched me back together."

"You are *not* okay." Her voice shakes. "Where's the doctor?"

"She's come and gone." I hug Sheila to my chest, stuffing my face into her hair and dragging her scent into my lungs.

She pushes out of my embrace. "Where's your chart? I want to see your condition for myself."

"Take a look." I open my arms. "I'm a little banged up is all."

"Your chute didn't open! You could have *died*. That's more than a little banged up!"

I wince as the stitches pull against the smile my mouth can't help having. My concussion might be playing tricks on my mind, but if this is hell and she's in my nightmare, I don't even want to see heaven. "My reserve chute opened, so no major damage."

"The ground crew said it sounded like a gun going off when your body hit." Her fingertips brush over the row of stitches. "Don't lie to me, how badly are you hurt?"

"With you standing here, I'm not hurt at all." I move her palm to my cheek, splaying her slender fingers over my swollen flesh. "I've missed you so much."

157

She swipes her hand away, eyes drying with each passing moment. "I'm only here because I thought you were hurt. Or worse."

If my corpse had met her, she'd still be crying. She might even have a nice thing to say about me. Instead, she's pulling further away. Maybe this *is* hell. "By rushing in here, are you telling me you care about me despite ignoring me?"

Her hands fold. "Mr. Kingwood, I'd be concerned for anyone who was in an accident like yours."

I rip my eyes away from hers and head for the exit. This isn't hell, it's purgatory. "Avery." She's behind me, voice clipped.

"How did you know I was here, Sheila?"

"Should you be out here walking around?" She cuts off my path. "I think you should go back inside."

I step into her. "*How* did you *know* I was *here?*"

Her eyes dart to the asphalt underneath our feet, then snap back up to meet mine. "Dirk called me. He was at his hangar when the ambulance deployed."

Tension tightens my jaw. "Did it take you this long to get here? Or did he just wait until he thought maybe I'd died before he decided to give you the news?"

Her shoulders straighten. "You need to get back inside. I want to see your chart—"

"Why?" I yell. She jumps and I reach for her. She retreats. I follow her. "Why, Sheila? Why the sudden concern?"

She spins. "Never mind. I can see that you're perfectly fine. Same old Avery."

"And I can see that you're still the same old Sheila." I plant my feet and watch her slide into her Corvette. It's parked beside the building, as if she raced into the parking lot and abandoned it. In a daze, I watch her drive away. I don't know why she came here, but I do know I'm tired of being nothing but a blot in her rearview.

~

Sheila doesn't get to race in and out of my life, her terms the only ones that matter. I beat on her apartment door, prepared to harass her until she either talks to me or I get arrested. It could be the concussion driving me, but I did wait until the pain medication wore off before committing to coming here so whatever happens, I'm ready for it. I even have enough ego to face her brother, so let her call him.

"I know you're in there." I knock louder. "I'll wake up all the neighbors if I have to. No one will get any sleep tonight if you don't talk to me."

Her door opens a crack. "There is nothing you have to say that I want to hear. Leave. Now."

"You don't know if you want to hear what I have to say because you have no idea what I'm going to say." I don't bother to hush my tone. "You may not want to deal with me, but you came to check on me today. Let's talk about why."

She starts to shove the door closed, but I catch it, overpowering her to keep it open. "I don't want to get inside as bad as you're fighting to keep me out." I keep my fingers in the door but release the resistance I'm applying. She lets the door smash my hand. I grind my teeth, the pain nothing more than what I've already experienced today. "Sheila, you should want to talk to me as much as I want to talk to you because you *were* upset over me being hurt. Which means you care."

"Is having you force your way into my apartment the penalty for caring whether a man lives or dies?"

"I don't have to cross the threshold to say what I desperately need you to hear." I wrench my skinned fingers from the door and shuffle back a step. If she closes me out, I'll just bang again. "Will you please listen? For a few minutes?"

"If I do, will you go away and never bother me again?"

I swallow. "If that's what you want, yes. I just can't go away before I say this."

"Then talk." The door opens, her robe-clad arms crossed. "Make it quick."

All my anger falls away and I simply say what I came here to tell her. "I met my wife at a bar—"

"I don't care."

"My buddy wanted to have a blowout to celebrate his twenty-first birthday, so we went to this wild rave kind of place and before long, the party was way out of hand." She retreats into her apartment. I stand on the threshold, the door wide open ahead of me, and continue. "There was this girl by the door. She looked as uncomfortable as I was. Since I was leaving, I offered to give her a ride home."

"*Details* aren't going to change the fact that you're *married*."

"She left her number on my dashboard. I didn't ask for it, but she was sweet, so I called her and we spent the next two weeks together. I thought she was amazing. Kind of the way John seems to think Mary is the best."

"He thinks that because she is."

"Mine wasn't. She was the fake kind of sweet." I run a hand through my hair. "I didn't know. So I married her, *then* introduced her to my family. They were mad we eloped, assumed she was after my money, and didn't hold any punches when letting me know how stupid I was."

Back then, I didn't realize stupidity was the least of my worries. "Cassie, my wife, fooled my family the way she fooled me. So about a week into our marriage, they weren't snubbing her, only me, because I've always been on the outs with them so it wasn't a stretch to hold something new over my head. But they liked Cassie enough to *want* to introduce her into our society, they just didn't want to do it before making it seem like I'd been dating her for a while. They wanted time to set the stage."

Sheila sits on her creamy white sofa. "This has nothing to do with me."

I take a breath and stay the course. "My family kept the marriage a secret and sent us off on an extravagant honeymoon to get us out of the way before rumors spread. By the time that overly long honeymoon ended, I knew I had made a mistake."

"Avery—"

"Sheila, please." I drag a hand down my face. "Let me finish. Then I'll go and you won't ever have to see me again."

I lower my voice. Her neighbors don't need to hear more than they already have. "The instant Cassie was my wife, I gave her access to my bank accounts, credit cards…everything. Because all the things you say about love and marriage, I believed those. I lived that with her. Became one with her. But she wasn't who I thought she was, and all of the sudden I was lying next to a shell of the person I married. It looked like her. But everything below the surface was different."

"That's your opinion."

"It's my truth." I stare into her amber eyes. "I tried. I went out of my way to satisfy Cassie's appetite for all things grand and expensive. I did the *fake it till you make it* because I wanted so badly to have my marriage work. I swear to you, I did *everything* I could. And I would have kept trying. But…" My throat tightens. If I knew Sheila would accept me, I'd tell her about the death of my child. But it's too painfully personal to share otherwise. "Something so heinous happened that I had to leave. And no, I can't tell you what it was. That's part of my separation agreement. I'm not allowed to talk about the *incident*."

"That's ridiculous."

"I know, but Cassie drew up the papers and at the time, all I cared about was getting as far away from her as possible. So I signed. And all I can tell you now is that outside of thinking I'd lost you forever, what happened back then was the most unbearable pain of my life."

She leans forward, resting her chin in her cupped hand. "Avery, I'm sorry you had to go through such pain. I'm not sure what possesses people to cheat, but it's clear that's what she did to you. And now you've done it to her. With me. Congratulations. You're even."

~43~

If Sheila hadn't already dropped me faster than a hot penny, I'd tell her that she's wrong. I'd tell her what Cassie did to me was much worse than cheating on me. I'd start with telling her about the little psychological games Cassie played, and end with her convincing me her abortion was a miscarriage. But I'm not allowed to talk about that last part and I'm not going to spoon-feed Cassie what she needs to bury me with if I at least don't get Sheila in the end.

I chance stepping inside the apartment. "Is this okay?"

Sheila nods. "Close the door."

I click it shut and cross the room, sitting next to her on the white sofa. "Sheila, I never manned-up because I was too scared of how you would react to the marriage news. It took losing you to make me realize how one-sided that was. No matter your reaction, you deserved to know." I owe her so many apologies. "I had no right to ask the things of you that I asked. I'm sorry."

"At least you understand that omission *is* a lie."

I lean into the fabric, taking in the scent of her that's all around me. "I don't know what I'm supposed to do. No one even knows I'm married, and whether I am or not, my parents are embarrassed of me. They act like my presence taints their life, and unfortunately the separation order I have makes it impossible to tell them who that sweet little girl they think they're protecting really is." That, and my pride. I didn't deserve their mistreatment then and I don't deserve it now. "In the separation agreement, Cassie agreed to no alimony. That made me think it was all good and fine to sign. But that little piece of paper is why the divorce is dragging on. She's finding loopholes and making false claims in order to void the deal and take everything I have. I've been fighting tooth and nail not to give her one single penny, and a whole lot of good that does me when my family supports her like she's on their payroll."

"Are they trying to keep her quiet?"

"In the separation agreement she also agreed to not tell anyone about our marriage, so if she whispers into a dead man's ear that we're married, I'll call a news conference and tell everyone why we're divorcing in the first place." My jaw tightens. "Lying little b—"

"So you have a two-way gag? She has you in a hole and you have her cornered?"

I press fingers into my temples. "It feels a lot like I'm in the hole *and* the corner."

Part of me has always wished that a reporter somewhere would care enough to find out what ever happened to the *other* Kingwood son. Marriage licenses are public record. But for all I know, my parents have used some buying power to seal mine. So no matter how much hope I harbor, my reality is that the mistakes I've made have directly affected Sheila, and nothing I do now can make that right.

I sit forward on the sofa. "I'm so embarrassed, Sheila. Here you are sizing up the vultures and letting the fools get in on a bet they have a snowball's chance of winning, and all it took was one pretty girl batting her baby blues to sink my battleship."

"Only one?" She smiles. "I have a feeling many lashes have been batted your way."

I meet her eyes. "The first time I met you, I looked into your beautiful face and knew I was in trouble. I tried to fight the attraction, but everything you do pushes me over the edge. And now that I've had a taste of you, I know I'll never get over you."

She studies me, silently taking in my features. I move closer, relishing being near her. "I know I'm a mess. I'm far from perfect and not at all what you had in mind. But please don't shut me out. If you don't want to date me, I understand. I'll stay in whatever lane you put me in. Just don't leave me entirely because I *do* want to date you. I only said otherwise because I was worried what you'd really think of me. But of all the people I've lost in this divorce, you're the one who hurts the most. I don't want to be kicked out of your life."

Her hand rises to my face. My pulse quickens. She smiles, fingers stroking along my stitched jaw. "Maybe I judged you too harshly."

"I deserved it." I place my palm over her hand, pressing her into my busted face. "Is there hope for us?"

She leans in. "Kiss me and find out."

Her words steal my breath. I swallow. "I hardly need an invitation to kiss you but—" Her mouth engulfs mine, hot and sweet. My arms run around her waist, tight and close, the way I always want to hold her. I work my lips over her jaw and down her neck, sliding up to the curve of her ear. "I'd make a thousand bad jumps just to have this one moment with you."

"I want all your moments, Avery," she breathes. "And if you make a bad jump again, you better die because I'm going to kill you."

~

If kissing Sheila is too far, there's no return from the abyss of making love to her. My physical pain from crashing into the earth is dulled by the rhythmic bliss of our fevered bodies moving together. On her sofa. In her bed. Savoring. Releasing. Frenzied and tender. My head murmurs all the words my lips won't say. All the words she deserves to hear. Syllables I wait until she's fast asleep to utter. "I love you." I press my lips to the back of her wrist, feeling the comfort of a deep sleep descend upon me for the first time in a long while. "One day, I'll tell you that in front of God and family."

~44~

Dawn paints soft golden strokes across Sheila's sleeping face. One bare shoulder peeks out at me, the rest of her nestled into the teal cocoon of her bed. I press my lips to her skin, one more taste before slipping away from this extraordinarily stubborn woman.

The last tendrils of bliss fall away as I snap back into reality, passing the sofa, the place where our hands and mouths first sent our senses careening into overdrive. Tension gave way to pleasure, and I both offered and begged for more. Against all odds, I win the stupid bet. But before I can truly be with Sheila, I need to rid myself of Cassie.

~Sheila~

I've often wondered what my *first time* would be like. Avery exceeded all my expectations. He was gentle, generous, and forsook no part of me. Last night, he loved all of me. And that *is* what it felt like. Love. The thing I've been trying not to feel because Avery worries me. There's a darkness in him, and it calls to me.

I'll never forget seeing him strip outside the banquet hall. Not because his body is pure divinity, though it most certainly is. It was the look on his face, the way his eyes glinted, and the set of his jaw. He seemed to be challenging the air itself, daring it to touch him. And I wanted him. I wanted every single inch of him.

I stretch my arm across the bed, the sheets next to me empty. I sit up. "Avery?" Silence answers me. I slide out of bed and grab my robe, pulling my arms through the silk sleeves. "Avery?" I check my in-suite bathroom. The door is open. He isn't inside. I leave my room and traverse the hall, tiptoeing near the end before jumping around the corner to land in the kitchen. "Found…you." My laugh dies on my lips. He isn't here.

165

Turning in a slow circle, my eyes glide over the empty living room, legs beginning to shake. I walk to where my nightshirt is folded and resting on the creamy fabric of the sofa. Avery's doing. Last night, everything we had on was torn off and strewn about. Now all his clothes are missing, right along with him.

I sink into the soft cushions, tears coming hot and fast. I can't believe I was this stupid. I press my face into my hands, choking back a sob. The front door clicks open. I look up. Avery is sneaking in. He spots me and plasters on a smile. "Morning, babe." I don't respond and he squints, dropping the bag in his hand and rushing to my side. "What's wrong?" He sits beside me and cups my face. "Why are you crying? Did I hurt you last night?"

His hands move over me as if he's checking for an injury. I jerk away. "Where have you been?"

"Getting us breakfast. Alberto opened the truck for me…" He points toward the bag he dropped, realization hitting. "You thought I *left?*"

"You did leave."

"To get us food." He wipes my tears, smiling. "Last night was perfect. I wanted to give you a perfect morning, too. So I swiped your apartment key and got Alberto out of bed."

"You should have told me."

He slides his arms around me. "You were sleeping, and I wanted to surprise you." His head dips, eyes meeting mine. "I would *never* sneak out on anyone. Especially you."

I shake my head. "You literally just snuck out on me."

He leans into the sofa and drags me onto his lap. "I understand why you don't trust me, I haven't exactly given you a reason to believe in me, and I do regret last night. But don't insult me by arguing semantics. I did *not* spend the night with you and then bail."

My heart crushes, tears falling anew. "You regret me?"

"No, babe." He nuzzles my neck. "Being with you was as close as I'll ever come to living a miracle. It's just…I took something you wanted to save. You had a plan, and I barged in with zero self-control and took your virginity away."

"I *gave* it to you because I wanted to be with you." I tilt my face to his. "You know I've been crazy about you since you stripped in that parking lot."

He brushes the hair from my face. "I'm crazy about you, too."

I take a breath and rest my head on his shoulder. "I don't regret last night. I wanted you." I curl my fingers through his. "Thank you for not making me feel awkward. I've never seen you so gentle before."

"The bear you think I am is a result of the battle I've had constantly raging inside me. It's gone now. From here on out, you get nice Avery. The man who won't storm over here in the middle of the night demanding you talk to him."

I bite my lip. "But that ended up being pretty fun."

"And now we get to skip the bad parts and go straight to the fun." He squeezes me tight. "We've crossed the sex line, but I don't want you to think I expect that to be part of our relationship. I'm in this for *you*. Not to get my rocks off. So tell me what you want our relationship to be and you've got it. I'm yours to command."

"I don't want a soldier. I want the man who likes to argue with me."

"You only like arguing with me because you always win."

"True." I twist in his arms and press my lips to his. "When I said I wanted to save myself for marriage, I meant I wanted to save myself for someone I love. The assumption being I'll marry the man I love." I run a finger over his stitches, recalling the fear that gripped me when Dirt told me about Avery's accident. "I don't regret last night, Avery. Because I lo—"

He presses a finger to my lips. "We should eat. Our tacos will get cold, and Alberto's already mad I made him get up early just to feed us. Must be a real pain to have rich people spoiled to only eating your food."

He slides me off his lap and crosses to the door where he dropped the bag of tacos. I stand. "I want you to know how I feel. You don't have to feel the same way but—"

"Babe." He stops me. "One day, I want to hear a four-letter word from you that starts with *L*. But I haven't earned it yet." He places the bag on the dining table. "Let me earn it. Let me *prove* to you that I'm not the man you thought I was."

"I already know you're not."

He stares at me. "Five minutes ago you thought I slept with you and snuck out like a thief in the night. So no, you don't have a clue who I am. You haven't seen me at my best. But I *will* make you believe in me. I'll earn every bit of your trust." He lifts a remarkably unscathed taco from the bag and reaches for my hand. "Let's get you back in bed. I want to start this thing off right by feeding my *girlfriend* breakfast in bed."

~45~

Avery

It's easy to forget about life beyond Sheila. She has me spinning. I could barely keep my hands off of her before, and now that she's practically demanding they be on her, I'm all too happy to oblige. We've consummated our relationship in every nook and cranny of her apartment.

"We make a good team." I whisper against her sleepy head after heating up the sheets one more time.

She grins. "I guess that means I'll help you finish your renovation. In person."

My heart thuds. One long, mournful beat. I postponed my flight to California so I could stay here with her, but I *do* have to go. And by the time I return, I may not have *any* projects I can afford to hire her for. I only hope she meant what she attempted to say earlier—that she loves me. Because whether or not I have two pennies to rub together, I'll have joy if I have Sheila.

I graze along her collarbone, tasting the remnants of the packet of hot sauce I dabbed on her earlier. Now her flesh is as spicy as her attitude. "We'll find a lot of things to do together, and they'll all be luxury, not work."

She kisses my itchy stitch line. "Did you seduce me just so you could fire me?"

I roll onto my back, weighing what I should tell her with what I should express only after I have accurate information to relay. "In a perfect world, you'd be my partner. Officially or unofficially, whichever you prefer." I draw her fingers to my lips, kissing them one by one.

"Partners at work. Partners in life. All our free time together. The *let's never be apart* sappy crap you complain about your brother over."

She stares at me, amber pools drinking me in. Seductive. Scary. I sit up and drag her across my lap. "I've worked with a lot of designers and so-called experts over the years, so while I might be looking for an excuse to have you close, I'm not lying when I say you're the best. Building design and visualizing how the space should be organized for the best flow is in your blood. So, will you work with me *and* allow me to spend all my time running wild with you?"

She sighs. "So that's it then? We're becoming one of the annoying couples who can't bear the thought of ever being apart? We'll gross everyone out with our PDA and live in an oblivious bubble of bliss?"

I smile. "We're going to make your brother and his wife look like chumps."

"Those are fighting words in these parts."

"The only Beller I'm afraid of is you." I kiss her. "Don't break my heart. Tell me you'll be all gross with me."

She runs a hand over my shoulder. "Occasionally, I'm going to need space. I'll let you know when, and it won't be often, but you should be fully aware I'm nowhere near as sweet as Mary."

"You can have all the space you need, just never let go of how we feel right now." I devour her lips. Her jaw. The formerly hot sauced earlobe. One move leading to another until I'm lost in her once again.

~

I want to love Sheila at full speed, out in the open, and in all the ways my heart tells me to. And there's only one road that leads to that reality.

"We need to hydrate." I pour us two glasses of water and lean on her counter by the sink, gulping mine down while she sips hers. She isn't going to like what's coming next. "I need to see my family. I'm going to miss you like crazy, but I have to talk some things out with them."

"You're going back to California?"

"Unfortunately." I trace a finger over her brow, down the tip of her nose, and let it fall onto her lips. "The California Kingwoods aren't as hospitable as the East Coast Bellers, but I have to go tell them about you in person before they see our kissy faces plastered all over the tabloids."

I try to replace my finger with lips but she dodges the kiss, her scowl growing. "You just said you didn't want to leave my side."

"I don't." I exhale. "Before I dive in and lose myself entirely in you, I need to settle some things, then I'll be back and you'll never get rid of me."

Her hands slide around my waist. "I'll come with you. It'll be nice to meet your family."

My jaw ticks. "I already know the lecture I'm going to get from them. I don't want you to be part of it."

"If I'm dating you, I *am* part of it."

I cup her face. "It's hard enough to look in my mom's eyes and see her disappointment, I can't add yours to that."

She runs her hands down my bare chest. "I'm not disappointed in you."

"You're not thrilled with me either." I lean back, giving her access to whatever she wants. "If you were to side with them, feel enough disdain to leave me, I couldn't handle it." I swallow. "I pretty much couldn't handle you ignoring me before. Now, after we've gotten to this place…I'd lose it, Sheila. I'd absolutely go insane."

"Then it's a good thing I'm *very* hardheaded." Her hands slide to the waist of my jeans. "No one can taint my view of you because I know who you are."

"Says the woman who's had a low opinion of me since the day she made me get on that stupid tandem bike."

"Not true." She grins. "My low opinion started the night before."

"Exactly." I run my palm around the nape of her neck, lowing my mouth to hers. "I just got you believing I'm not atrocious. I'd like to keep it that way."

"Which is why I'm going with you." She unzips me. "There's strength in numbers. And my darling personality is sure to win them over."

This is one time she isn't getting her way. I take her hands from my zipper and bring them to my lips. "I need to go alone."

"Fine." She pushes away, leaving my hands cold. "While you're gone, I'll tie up my own loose ends."

"What loose ends?"

"Dirk." She saunters down the hall toward her bedroom.

My blood boils. She disappears through the doorway and I'm hot on her heels. She tosses a look over her shoulder. "Don't worry, I'll get together with him and take care of things. How long did you say you'd be gone?"

"I can't leave worrying about you being with *him* while I'm gone."

"Then stay and come with me when I thank him for telling me you were in the hospital. Quite possibly, you're right and he only did so because he thought you were dead. Still, I'm grateful."

"I thought you were done using him to make me jealous?"

She slides onto the bed. "Not if your jealousy is going to make you abandon your plan of visiting your family without me. Before you decide, know that I can very easily dig up a few more Dirks."

My eyes narrow. "I advise against it. If I have to come back early because you're letting other men sniff around, you're not going to like the outcome. It'll be a nuclear war. And I don't care how perfect you are, Sheila Beller. I *will* win every *war* we have."

"You severely underestimate me." She slides off her robe, her naked body radiant in the soft glow of the bedside lamp.

I pin her to the sheets, feathering kisses over her neck, reminding her why *I'm* the one she wants. "You can win the battles, Sheila, just so long as I win the war." She bites my shoulder. I laugh. "Obviously all I get is a participation trophy, but you can pretend it's the title." I rest my forehead on hers. "Let me handle Dirk. I'll properly thank him for sending you to me. Best decision he ever made."

~46~

Avery versus Sheila battle number eighty-seven is too close to call. She insisted on coming with me, I insisted that wasn't an option. We fought about it in the most fulfilling way, then I left for California.

My commercial flight touches down and I text her. **Made it. And you win. Call Dirt if you want. Just remember I'm coming back. See you soon, babe.**

I don't have to wait for her reply to know what it's going to be. She's going to tell me she already called him. Because the one thing she doesn't need is my permission. And it's sexy that she isn't afflicted with being too nice to speak her mind. I don't have to guess with her. She tells me what, when, why, and even how. If only my family would do the same. In a way that makes sense.

Driving toward the estate where I grew up, I'm struck by how different it is from anything the Bellers own. Their place on the Potomac, as old and grand as it is, pulses with homeyness. It's warm. Inviting, even to the uninvited. And Sheila's apartment, as lovely as it is, isn't in the most upscale building. There are two others that are more posh, but she chose a cozy atmosphere over elegance. Here, where an ornate iron fence surrounds the mansion grounds, every blade of grass in the meticulously landscaped lawn is chosen for the wealth it portrays. Water features and marble statuettes dot the miniature gardens dispersed around the Mediterranean architecture where the sun bakes the tile roof. And to make sure no one considers the house understated, a hedge carved into a crown sits in the center of the driveway's turnabout. Surrounding it, roses grow from a pebbled bed, trained to trellises in the shape of *K*.

Wide marble steps lead to the grandiose front entrance that's meant to intimidate visitors. Or at least have them licking their chops. I park and step out of my rental, pushing up my sunglasses to take a better look at the ostentatious exterior. If I wasn't in a hurry to get back to Sheila, I would have made the cross-country trip in my own vehicle. More time to contemplate how to approach what they're going to throw at me once I cross the threshold. But now that I have Sheila, anytime I have to go *anywhere* without her, I'll fly. "Get in quick. Get out faster."

I ascend to the main doors, knowing better than to go around to the garages. I'm not part of this family anymore. At least not a part they'll allow to walk in a back entrance. I'm surprised I made it through security at the front gate.

I ring the bell and wait, staring at the columns lining the porch like this is the Colosseum in Rome. It will take the butler a while to get here. The fact that they even have a butler is ridiculous, but the fact that they only have *one* is worse. The poor man runs all over this house because anyone else opening a door or fetching a glass of water would be ludicrous.

The door opens slowly. "Oh, Master Avery." Mason steps aside. "I didn't know you were coming."

"No one did." I sling my duffle over my shoulder and walk inside. "Are they home?"

"In the study." He reaches for my bag. "Your brother and sister only just arrived. They're having a family meeting."

"Glad I wasn't invited." I withhold the bag. "I'm going to go shower before I see them. I assume my room is in the same place?"

"It is." His lips twitch, moving into what can almost be misconstrued as a smile. "Shall I send up any refreshments?"

"Nah." I head for the stairwell. "I'd rather see them on an empty stomach. Less chance of hurling."

Mason is the real kind of butler, suit and all. And he doesn't keep secrets from the *masters* of the manor. I reach the second floor, nearly escaping into my room before the clack of mom's shoes hits my ears. I don't even have to look to know it's her. I recognize the stomp. "Hi, Mom."

"Did you really think you could sneak into my home?"

I face her as she closes in on me. "Last I checked, this was the *family's* home, and you insist on keeping rooms for all your kids, even though Curtis and Lila are married and have houses of their own."

"You're married too," she snaps. "And if you'd act like a man for once in your life, you'd have your own home to keep that beautiful wife of yours in."

"That's a little anti-feminist. These days, women keep themselves." I lean toward her. "They don't even need us to have babies."

Sheila's informed me more than once she'll be a mom with or without so much as the hint of a husband, but I can't mention her while the flush rising up Mom's neck is about to spew out of her mouth. "Your wife needs you. With or without the baby, *she needs you!*"

"I haven't touched Cassie in years, so if she's pregnant—" Mom's hand lands across my face.

"I knew you were impulsive." Her nostrils flare. "We spoiled you, gave you too much. I'll regret what that nurturing turned you into for the rest of my life."

"Nurturing?" I rub the freshly stitched jaw she hasn't asked about. "We have very different versions of my childhood."

"Do *not* speak to your mother that way!" Dad storms down the hall, my siblings in tow.

I drop the duffle to my side. "I didn't know I was interrupting a reunion."

"You don't do anything without a motive." Curtis's eyes narrow. "Get away from Mom."

I take ten steps down the hall, away from all of them. "I didn't except a parade, but the gang-up is a bit much." And curious. Just like the damage to my rig. Someone told them I was coming, and that someone might have actually stooped low enough to tamper with my gear.

Lila confirms my suspicions on who *someone* is. "Cassie told us everything. We know what you did to her."

"Then maybe you should fill me in on exactly what my murder-minded wife told you."

She blanches and mom gasps. Dad folds Mom into his arms, dark eyes piercing enough to kill me where I stand. "We were ashamed of you before. But now that we know you got Cassie pregnant, then blamed her for the miscarriage all so you could leave her destitute and alone on a foreign shore..." Fury ticks the vein in his neck. "That poor girl was devastated by you. *Humiliated.*"

I win. The separation order says *neither* of us can talk about the baby. "You think I'd blame her for having a miscarriage?"

"You left her!" Lila yells. "And she's suffered in silence all this time because you made her. You're a monster. I hate you!"

My gut roils. I already knew their true feelings but haven't ever heard them stated so plainly. I move past them and into my room, looking each of them in the face before I close the door. "It was my child, too. *I* lost a child, too."

~47~

The death of a child, even an unborn one whose tiny fingers you've never touched, rips a hole in the fabric of your being. In my mind's eye, my baby is still a baby. Soft and small. She'd be almost eight now, but I've never been able to imagine her as anything other than a tiny pink bundle cradled in my arms. A child willingly conceived and, because of Cassie, voluntarily ended.

I compose myself and enter the den, facing my parents, my siblings, and their spouses. Byron is shorter than Lila, pale-faced with a stomach pushing over his belt more than the last time I saw him. Darla is the same height as Curtis, lanky and bronze like Mom. She's pretty with those almond eyes and full lips, but she's borderline too thin. Cassie was a waif, too. Always worried about her nonexistent fat. It's probably why she didn't want to carry our child. "When did Cassie tell you about the baby? I'm assuming you haven't known for the last seven years or you would have already confronted me about it."

"We don't care about your stupid gag order." Lila presses a tissue against her cheek, other hand tightly clasped inside Byron's. He and my brother are both shaking their heads. Mom won't look at me. Dad's still trying to gut me with his stare.

"That's the problem. When it comes to me, none of you care."

Mom's head snaps up. "Don't you dare say that to me! I carried you inside me for eight and a half *long* months. And never once imagined your father blaming me for the fact that you came two weeks early."

"My daughter didn't have a chance to come early."

Curtis strolls to the center of the room. "What do you think a miscarriage is? Women can't help what their bodies do. Your baby came too early to survive. That isn't Cassie's fault."

176

"If that was how it happened, no, it wouldn't have been her fault."

"Maybe if you'd been there rather than off skydiving you could have helped her," Lila blares.

"I wasn't skydiving. I was parasailing. Big difference."

"And he complains no one loves him enough." Byron's cheeks wiggle.

"I've never complained. Only stated the facts." I pan the room. "I'm guessing in her harrowing tale of betrayal, Cassie didn't incriminate herself? Only me?"

"For some insane reason that girl still loves you," Dad bites. "She thinks deep down you love her, too."

"She's wrong."

"We know." Mom sniffs. "Do you know how hard it is to listen to her bawling her eyes out over *you*?"

"Do you know how hard it is to stand here listening to all of *you*?" I glare at them. "Have you ever *once* considered there's more to the story?"

"Like you saying she *killed* your baby because she wouldn't stop doing Pilates?" Curtis growls.

Bitter air curls through my lungs. Nothing should surprise me anymore, but I'm still shocked at the depth of lies Cassie continues to spew. "Listen to the words coming out of your mouths. This isn't the *Twilight Zone* and the *Upside Down* doesn't exist. I didn't leave my wife because she had a Pilates-induced miscarriage."

"Ahem." Mason appears in the doorway, hands folded behind his back. "A Miss Sheila Beller is here to see Master Avery."

"Did you say Beller?" Dad chokes.

"He did." Sheila strolls in, slipping a red scarf from her neck. "Sorry my visit is unexpected. Telling Avery I was coming would ruin the surprise." Her eyes twinkle. "And he loves surprises."

While my spirit tries to reenter my body, my hand clamps down on her wrist, sweeping her out of the room and down the hall. "What are you doing here?" I pick up speed, shuffling through a door under the stairwell before anyone has a chance to regain consciousness. "I told you not come," I whisper-yell, heart thundering. "You're not supposed to be here!"

"Whatever we do, we do together." She plucks my fingers from her wrist, flipping on the light, nose crinkling at the storage area we're crammed in. "If you're having a hard time, I'll help. And if I can't..." She cups my cheeks. "I can at least put a smile on your sad face."

"No..." My eyes close. "You being here is going to make this infinitely worse. You have to go."

Her hands leave my face. "Because dating me is the cause of the problem?"

I pull her toward me, resting my forehead on hers. "You're not the cause, but a severe exacerbation." I kiss her nose. "I've missed you so much I nearly came home a thousand times already, but I need to settle things with my family so I can come back home to you for good."

"Home?" She relaxes against me. "Then the East Coast *is* home to you?"

Her question has an easy answer. One I never feel able to say. But it's the whole reason I'm putting myself through this family reunion. I press my lips to her ear, hoping the words find their way to all her secret places. So she knows I love her. "Home is wherever you are, Sheila Beller."

~48~

Sheila followed me to California because she doesn't trust me. Of *that,* I'm certain. Yet here she is, once again on the verge of telling me she loves me. I want so badly to hear the words, but only after all is settled and done with my family, and she's had time to review my divorce papers. When we exchange those precious words, there'll be nothing left unsaid between us. She'll have the whole truth, and all of me. If she wants it.

I press a finger to her lips, teeth grinding against the sound of Mom's voice calling out for us. "Not yet, Sheila. Not here."

"When, then? Where?" Her eyes follow the sound of Mom's footsteps ringing off the travertine floor. "For me, the time to say the words has long passed. You don't have to feel the same but—"

"When we get back home, we'll have this conversation." I cover her mouth with mine, showing her one more time how I feel.

Reluctantly, I pull my lips from hers. "Did you…" My throat constricts. "Did you hear anything when you arrived?"

Her head tilts. "Echoes of shouts from where your *butler* asked me to wait. In case the yelling was over you telling them about me, I decided to not follow Mason's suggestion to remain in the foyer."

"I don't think he was suggesting."

She shrugs and I can't help but smile. This woman is fearless, and no doubt the guards at the gate are still trying to figure out what spell she cast on them. "I haven't had a chance to tell anyone about us. I'm working up to it, but they aren't hearing anything I have to say."

"Well," she snakes out of my arms and opens the door, "seeing is believing."

"No!" I wrangle her back into our hiding spot, red flags shooting out of her in every direction. My pulse hammers, head throbbing. I step away. "This has nothing to do with how I feel about you. It's…they expected me to get chummy with your brother, not you."

Her arms cross. "A poor expectation any way you present it."

"They'll think me getting mixed up with you is the kiss of death for our East Coast business."

"Mixed up?"

"Involved." I swallow. "They consider your family of a slightly higher station and therefore have this weird reverence that rich people get and…" My jaw clenches. "No matter what I say about how I really feel, they'll say I have ulterior motives. They'll want to put an end to us. All because they don't want your family to write mine off if I mess up, which they'll believe is inevitable."

Her hands unfold, running the length of my arms until her fingers lace through mine. "You're like a child being told not to eat the chocolate bar because it'll make you fat, when you've eaten three already and lost ten pounds."

If only life was as easy as eating chocolate. "You thought I might come here and never come back to you." I drag her mouth to mine before she can dispute doubting me like all the others. "I think that means I keep eating the chocolate despite being told not to, and now I'm two hundred pounds overweight and still stuffing candy in my face."

"But our romantic involvement is a choice we *both* made."

"They'll say I coerced you."

"I'll set things straight." She smiles. "Like how my family is more than of a *slightly* higher station, and how, if you hurt me, it won't be only your East Coast business I give the kiss of death to." She presses her lips to mine. "My vendetta will be global."

"Good to know."

I want to do battle *with* her. As allies against everyone who has ever hated me. I scratch the stitches on my jaw. Stitches no one has asked me about, but she's kissed and checked them even while standing here miffed at me. "Sheila, they think I've done something *else* to disgrace them, and all that's happened since I got here is arguing. I don't want you in the middle of it."

"What do they think you've done?"

I close my eyes. "Cassie broke part of the gag order. She's saying some things that…don't paint me in a very good light."

"What kind of things?"

I look at her. "The kind I'm not telling you about."

"Then I'll tell you *my* news." Her hands fold, a sure sign she's going all *proper* on me. "I met with Dirk after you left. You'll be happy to know he's fully forgiven me and said I could count on him to be there for me in the future should I need him in *any* way."

"Is this your way of letting me know you're keeping a man on the side just in case I blow it?"

She smiles. "He has no idea how to launch a global war. *If* I needed arms to fall into, I'd choose someone much more lethal."

"My arms aren't going to let you down." I wrap them around her. "You don't play fair, and I will *always* be jealous of anyone you give your time to. So stay here, and maybe my family will behave themselves in your presence. If not…" I lower my face to hers, staring into her beautiful eyes. "Please believe in me. No matter how bad things get out there, believe in me the way I believe in you."

Sheila's the epitome of poise and grace. It feels good to stroll into the den hand in hand with her. I'm hedging my bets on these gape-mouthed idiots being too money-struck to berate me in front of her. If I'm wrong, the strength of character the meticulous woman next to me possesses won't allow her to believe them. She'll know I'm not the terrible person they make me out to be.

"Sorry we rushed out of here. My girlfriend is teaching me that not all surprises are bad." I stare at their stunned faces. "Everyone, meet Miss Sheila Beller. Sheila, this is everyone."

I'm almost tempted to give proper introductions, but they don't deserve to be introduced to her. At this point, I don't care if she ever knows their names. I'm more curious to see how long it takes Dad to blow a gasket. His face is red, neck purple with tiny veins bulging out.

I offer Sheila a seat on the long leather couch opposite his chair and sit next to her, raising an eyebrow at Mom, who's perched on Dad's armrest. Cassie did that on my chair once and Mom called it unladylike. If she'd seen Sheila jumping in a fountain with me, she'd be as furious as Dad. "My parents aren't quite as loving as John and Mary, but I guess they're closer than I remember."

"No couples are as close as my brother and his wife." Sheila smiles, using her obnoxiously polite socialite tone. "But it *is* nice to see married couples enjoying being with one another. And it's also nice to meet *everyone*." She dips her head to the still stunned group. "We'll go around the room, each of you tell me who you are and what your attachment to Avery is." She winks at me. "*My* attachment is already clear. He wasn't gone long before I simply had to gas up the jet." She meets Mom's stare. "I can't imagine the absence you must feel with him being across the country. Not to worry, though, my family and I are taking *excellent* care of him."

The Kingwoods aren't her first encounter with wealth-obsessed one-percenters who actually believe the size of a bank account is equal to character. She knows how to play these cards, starting with the fact that I highly doubt she flew out here private. From what she's said, her brother and Mary primarily use the family's plane. But her travel arrangements are minuscule compared to the tension bubbling under the Kingwoods' flowery words and overly reverent remarks. If one more person says what an *honor* it is to meet Sheila, she might shoot off enough of her own steam to obliterate the walls.

I tighten my grip on her hand, our entwined fingers escalating the boiling ire. She stokes the flames, her free hand finding its way to my knee. Mom breaks first, grimacing face taut. "Where are you staying while you're in town, Miss Beller?"

"I'm open to suggestions." Sheila smiles at me. "Where do you recommend?"

Dad tugs on his collar. "You mean you came all this way and didn't book a place to stay? Young lady, what will you do if all the hotels are full?"

"In my experience, having money means something is always available," she toys. "I'm sure you understand how that works, your *station* being close to my own."

"If you can bear staying in this big drafty house, we have guest rooms available." I save them, they'll never match her wit and they'll soon figure out she's not remotely bothered by their obvious disdain of our affection. "Since you're loaded, we'll give you a room for double the normal price."

Mom's gasp echoes down the hall. "Don't be ridiculous! This isn't a hotel!"

I shrug. "I was only trying to get us a piece of the Beller money. If you want to put her up for free, so be it."

"We apologize for our son." Dad's throbbing temple is one big purple vein. "He has a twisted way of offering hospitality, but I'm sure you don't want to be cooped up here with us anyway."

"Byron will make some calls and get you booked in the best suite he can find." Lila sniffs.

Byron dips his head. "I'll do it right now."

"No need." Sheila stands. "This home will accommodate me just fine. If I require more space, I'm sure I can find it on my own." She tugs me to my feet, eyes on my parents. "My bag is in the car, have it taken to whichever room you decide is best for me. In the meantime, Avery is going to give me a tour of the grounds." She nods to my siblings and their spouses. "I hope to see all of you at dinner."

I can't blame her for testing them. If they're going to treat her like a golden goose, she might as well act like one. I sweep her out of the den. "They're going to pick a room as far away from mine as possible."

"I was going to tell them to send my bag to *your* room, but I thought that might put them in the hospital." She pulls me to her. "Where can we rendezvous? I didn't come all this way to get locked in a tower and never see you."

"I know some places." I slip us out an exit and head for the tree line, checking her legs. "I love those shoes but next time, wear running shoes." I take a cue from John and swing her into my arms. "It won't make me stare at your legs any less, but it *will* help us get to where we're going a whole lot faster."

~50~

If when you die, you're stuck repeating the last moments of your life, I want to die after making love to Sheila. The *last* place I want to die is sitting down to dinner with my family. We *dress* for dinner in this house, something I've always hated. But Sheila came prepared even though half the people at her river estate wore the same clothes to dinner they'd had on all day. I was one of those people. So was her brother.

"Sorry about all the formality." I pull out her chair. Mom asked Sheila to sit on her right. Dad asked me to sit on his left. The opposite end of the table from my girlfriend.

Sheila taps the chair next to her, looking around the table. "You'll have to excuse us. We're still in our honeymoon stage, so we simply have to be touching at all times."

I sit down before anyone says a word. The seats next to my siblings are empty. "Where's Byron and Darla? No concerns the married-ins are both missing? Together?"

"Byron went home," Lila bites. "He doesn't like eating with you."

"Why on earth not?" Sheila laughs. "I'll admit he can be a bit messy over a platter of tacos, but I've come to find it endearing."

"My husband doesn't want to associate with a man who abandoned his wife." Lila straightens, inclining a nod to my brother. "And he's not the only one who lost his appetite."

Mom leans toward Sheila. "These days, we're all ill. We're sick over this thing between you and Avery. It isn't you, it's him. He shouldn't be acting the way he is with you. It just isn't right."

So they *are* willing to trash me in front of her. As much as I hate it, it's the first thing they've done in a long time that I can respect. "When Sheila and I want an opinion from any of *you* about *our* relationship, we'll ask."

185

"The situation we're *all* in isn't easy." Sheila softens toward them, pinching me under the table. "I'm not asking you to divide your loyalty, it doesn't offend me that you still care for Cassie. I only ask that you accept me as well. For as long as Avery and I choose to be together." She levels those amber eyes on me. "Which we hope is forever."

Mom swivels in her seat, dragging Sheila's attention to her. "Tell me, when you two disappeared earlier, did he take you to the gazebo in the woods?"

"Mom!"

"I'm asking because he used to take his wife there, too." She drives forward. "He and Cassie were always running off, as much in love as anyone I've ever seen. The two of you together remind me of that. The only difference being, he's *married* to her."

"Barely." I huff. "And not for much longer."

Mom continues to speak to Sheila as if I'm not sitting right here. "Miss Beller, will you force us to watch him sneak in and out of your room at night? Will you prefer to sneak into his room? The room where he and Cassie *still* have their marital bed?"

Cold sweat rolls down my back. "I'm not with Cassie anymore. And the woman Sheila is right now, in front of you, is the person she always is. She doesn't lie and scheme and turn into a bi—"

"You courted Cassie the same way," Dad snaps. "Painted her a picture of a happy life she thought would *last forever.* Then you married her and when life crashed against the rocks, you abandoned the girl. Told her you never wanted to see her again and left her stranded in a bungalow in Tahiti."

"You couldn't very well expect me to leave her on the yacht."

Curtis jabs a knobby finger at me, directing his comments to Sheila. "This is why we're ashamed of him. His actions are unacceptable, and he isn't remorseful."

Lila frowns. "I'm sure you think we're monsters. But when Cassie called us, we ran to her, flew her home—"

"And Avery has done nothing but fight us ever since." Mom places a hand over Sheila's, lowering her voice. "He refuses to even acknowledge he *has* a wife, let alone acknowledge she's hurting. So neither of them can heal nor move on, because he won't take the necessary steps to allow them to."

Sheila's grip on my knee loosens. Mom retrieves a worn tissue from her dress sleeve. "We've set up numerous counseling sessions but he never shows, only his poor, destitute wife."

Sheila's eyes turn to mine and I nod. "The day I left her stranded without a penny to her name in a country she didn't know, I told her to her face I'd never see her again and so far, I've managed to keep that promise."

Dad glares at me. "That's why we've taken her well-being into our own hands. She had a *medical* issue that was so painful it's hard for her to work. So we help her as much as she'll allow."

I plant my hands behind my head. "She lives in a posh building, but because she isn't in the penthouse, they act like she's suffering. And did you catch the part where she doesn't work? Funny how she has clothes, furniture, food, and everything else she could possibly want without taking *too much* from them. You know, she's a saint and all. Never too much charity for that one."

I can't tell what Sheila's thinking. She's looking through me. Into me. All the places at once but nowhere all the same. Her hand is still resting lightly on my thigh but probably only because she's too in shock to move it.

Mom puts a hand on Sheila's arm. "We understand what it's like to be young. To be in love. Or at least to think you are." Sheila's head slowly turns to face her. Mom smiles softly. "We're not trying to embarrass you. We only want you to know who he is."

"We never dreamed he'd choose someone like you to…soothe his carnal urges." Dad swallows. "If I'd thought for a second he would endear himself to you this way, I would have never agreed to him taking over our East Coast affairs."

"We value your family, Miss Beller." Curtis weighs in. "We hate how this ordeal with Avery and his wife has extended to you. If only there was a way to let you feel how utterly sorry we are."

"If only," Sheila mutters.

"Yeah." I unclasp my hands and fold them in my lap, being sure not to touch her slender fingers. "If only."

Silence heightens around the table. All eyes are on Sheila except mine. I stare at my plate, feeling the weight of her hand on my thigh inches below my point of focus. There's nothing left for me to say. All I can do is wait for her.

"I don't regret being involved with Avery." Her strong voice is razor sharp. "I can't speak *for* him, but I know how I feel *about* him. And those feelings are the only reason we're involved the way we are. The point is not the failure of his marriage, or even the terms under which it came to an end. The relationship he and I have is based on *us.* Surely you know that."

Mom hardens. "You may care about him, but he isn't a man who will faithfully love you. Surely *you* know that."

Dad clears his throat. "Not only is he *still* married, he's made a train wreck of our lives. So much so, I have deep regret for being the one who raised him."

A sob hits Mom's throat. "It's such a misfortune that you've had to meet the curse we loosed on the world."

Sheila's hand leaves my thigh. I open my mouth, then close it. She worries enough about curses and here I am labeled as one. She stands, hand resting on my shoulder. "How can you call your own flesh and blood a curse? You are his *mother.* You should love him unconditionally."

She isn't abandoning me, she's defending me. I whip my face to hers. Her cheeks are cut of pure stone, a marble warrior. She looks at each soul around us. "Do any of you even care about how miserable he was in his marriage? Would you rather he suffer the rest of his life?"

"Miserable?" Lila scoffs. "Is that what he told you? Now your feelings for him make sense. He lied his way into them."

"I don't believe he's lied to me at all." She lies, having told me to my face that my omissions count as lies.

"My son was happy, Miss Beller," Dad bites. "Very."

"He and Cassie traveled the world," Curtis adds. "His request, not hers. He said he wanted people on every shore to witness her beauty."

She looks at me. I shake my head. That's something her brother would say but I'm not that kind of guy. Though I want to be. For her. She shrugs. "So? He was smitten and dead set on showing her off. Wasn't it the party gathered here who conspired to send him and his bride away so he could enjoy her beauty in parts *less* known?"

"You can't blame us for wanting to wait an acceptable amount of time to make such an announcement!" Mom defends. "He barely knew her when he eloped."

Sheila motions for me to get up. "My brother only knew his wife a short period and not once did my mother and I think of sending them away. Avery and I will take our dinner in my room."

I stand beside her. She slips her hand into mine and we turn from the table. "Miss Beller." Mom's tissue makes another appearance. "We're not proud to broadcast the truth of this matter, but after seeing him sneak off with you…" She chokes back tears. "We couldn't bear it if he did the same to you that he's done to poor, poor Cassie."

Dad's eyes meet mine as he stands. "We're admitting our greatest shame to you, Miss Beller. So we don't have to see you experience the pain we've watched Cassie endure."

She breaks his focus on me and makes him look at her. "You do so without considering the pain of your own son. One day, you'll wish you'd been smarter. Consider where you'll find yourself when that day comes, Mr. Kingwood, and hope your son is more forgiving than I am."

~51~

Sheila defending me was arousing. The protectiveness seductive. I made love to her with more fervor than I ever have. Lingering, giving, losing myself in her only to find who I truly am. I beat out the rhythm of my love while she only went through the motions, her spirit slipping away. The more I devoured, poured myself into her and fought to hold on, the faster she retreated.

Lying beside her breathless and broken, I pray for morning to never come. But like all my prayers, the answer is no. "Avery," she whispers against my ear. "Wake up."

"Not yet." I haven't slept all night. "I like the dream I'm having."

"It's light outside." She props on her elbow. "You have to get out of my room before the house wakes up."

"Didn't you pretty much give their so-called moral code the finger last night?" I roll over. "So what if they see me leave your room?"

"I was angry, shocked… I shouldn't have disrespected your parents in their own home."

"Why not? It isn't like they have any respect for anyone else."

"They certainly don't have any for you." She slides out of bed, pulling a robe around her that I've never seen before.

I sit up, rubbing my face. "So you're kicking me out because they don't like me?"

"No." She sighs, facing me. "Are we lovers, Avery? Or are we *in* love?"

"Even if I use the *L* word, my parents wouldn't be okay with us sharing a bed."

"But at least I'd know how you feel." She moves to the door. "Be stealthy on your trek."

I get out of bed and tug on my pants. No matter what I do, I'm choosing pain for someone. And she's choosing pain for me after defending me then abandoning me. "I brought Cassie into their lives, so like it or not, I'm responsible for the hold she has over them. One I can't seem to break because they'd rather break me. And *that* is exactly why I asked you not to come here. But you don't trust me, so here you are. And now I'm expected to appease you? To pour out my heart and say a bunch of words after which you're *still* going to kick me out? That isn't fair."

"Not fair is you saying you're committed without actually committing. Saying you're getting a divorce without actually getting a divorce. And saying you *can't* tell me how you feel when what you really mean is you *won't*."

"I *won't* have this conversation with you in *this* house. You've seen how my parents react to us," I defend. "They cringe if I even smile at you."

"So Cassie was good enough for you to defy your parents over, but not me." She opens the door. "Thank you for explaining."

"That's not what I meant and you know it." I ball my shirt in my fist, crossing in front of her, stopping to stare into pools threating to drown me. "I've asked you for very little, Sheila. Time. Trust. But you can't be bothered with giving me any of that because you're too worried about getting what *you* want. Well, babe, I hope me leaving helps you get it."

My bare feet beat over the carpet running down the length of hallway leading away from her room. By the time I reach my own room, I'm furious. I slam the door shut and throw my shirt. It lands on the bed, next to a black box wrapped with a gold bow. Guilt washes over me. *This* is why Sheila sent me here. She bought me a gift.

Sitting down next to the box, I slide the gold strands aside, lifting the lid. White satin lines the inside, and nestled against the fabric is a plastic doll wearing a cutout of her face. I flick the mask. The head topples, red liquid seeping from the neck to stain the once white cushion. My fingers twist around the decapitated doll. Under its body is a message revealed by the crimson liquid. *Ticktock.*

Rage pours through my veins. I yank out my phone. Cassie answers on the second ring. "Mess with Sheila and *you're* the one who's going to end up like this doll!" I hang up. If I have to hear her voice I'll explode. My next call is to my lawyer. "I'm sending you pictures. Bury the wench."

Teeth clenched, I send him pictures of the mutilated plastic and copy each member of my family on the message. I want them to know why I'm going to leave Cassie penniless in a ditch.

You are not running off with Sheila Beller, so whatever game you're playing, stop it! Dad's the first to send irrefutable proof of his blindness. Lila is second. **How dare you stage this to hurt Cassie after everything you've already done to her. Enough is enough, Avery!**

Curtis's rebuke lights up my screen as I stomp through the house to hunt down Mason so I can find out how the box found its way to my bed. By the time Mom graces me with a response, I already have the man in hand and have his story validated by gate security.

~

Dragging Mason into the sitting room adjacent to the breakfast nook where the unbelievers are waiting for breakfast to be announced, Curtis and Lila still missing their spouses, I nudge Mason forward. "Tell them. Tell them how Cassie sent her box to the front gate."

"The package was delivered by courier. The guard house sent it up and I placed it on Master Avery's bed." His eyes flit sideways. "As I couldn't locate him at that late hour, I left it there for when he *did* return to his room."

"I returned this morning," I bite. "And where I was last night is no business of anyone in this room."

"You're excused, Mason." Mom sends him away.

"Making him leave doesn't change the facts."

"Do you think we're stupid, Avery?" she bites.

Before I can give her the answer she deserves, Lila gives her own explanation. "Having your sick plan orchestrated by courier doesn't throw us off. We see right through you, and all I can say is I'm glad I have *one* brother who knows how to treat women." Her hand falls on Curtis's shoulder. "I have *one* sibling I can be proud of."

"Good for you!" I snarl. "I don't have *any.*"

"Don't have any what?" Sheila strolls in wearing slacks, a high-collared blue silk shirt and painful-looking stilettos.

I haven't showered yet and I'm not wearing a shirt. "I was just going upstairs for a shower. Want to come with me?"

"No." She moves past me, past all of us, and stands by the window, one of the many ornate fountains of our estate silhouetted behind her unflinching form. My family watches, appearing elated her demeanor toward me is cool. They want her to drop me. To stab her stilettos straight through my heart. All *I* want is not to see flashes of her decapitated head.

Crossing the expanse of hardwood, I lower my voice for only her to hear. "Those shoes look like they'll be painful when you give me what I deserve."

"Are you remorsefully expecting it? Or hoping for the pain?"

"You see how I grew up." I shrug. "Being obnoxious is in my blood."

She eyes the room's furnishings and the way Mom is dressed as if she's attending a gala. Everyone in the room shuffles to look away, pretending to share sections of the newspaper, no one willing to engage her. "This place certainly lives up to clichés." She eyes yesterday's jeans that I'm still wearing. "I suppose I feel sorry enough for you to ignore your rich boy problems."

I press my lips to her ear. "My problem is you seeing me as a boy, not a man. Why couldn't you have just stayed away like—" Choking sounds catch my attention. I turn to Dad. Curtis rushes him a glass of water while Mom slams her section of the paper against the armrest so hard Lila nearly jumps out of her own gala-ready gown. I turn back to Sheila, prying my hand from the delicate skin of her cheek. "I can't even touch you without giving them aneurisms. How am I supposed to be manly for you under these conditions?"

Her hands fall to my waist. "You're a man. One who needs a few lessons from a woman. By the end of the week, they'll be asking Cassie *who*. Then, you and I are going to have a conversation, in this house, about our future. Agreed?"

I lace my fingers through hers. "Yes, but I don't want to be in this house at the end of the week. I want to take you home." Someplace safe. Away from here.

She smiles. "Then I better start dazzling your family now."

Our fingers locked together, she leads me to the center of the room. "Mrs. Kingwood, I'd like us to spend the day together. You too, Lila." Sheila graces them with an affectionate smile. "We'll have breakfast out, then maybe we can go to the spa. My treat, of course."

"Breakfast out sounds wonderful," Mom answers politely. "But how about we take you shopping instead of going to the spa?"

"Shopping is good with me any day." She faces Dad. "Mr. Kingwood, I'm looking forward to spending time with you as well. After my day out with your lovely ladies, we'll discuss what you might like to do."

He nods. "While you're shopping, I'll take my *son* and go play a few rounds of golf. Avery's never been much of a player, but Curtis and I will take him along. Surely he can manage to at least hit the ball."

"Doubtful." I hate golf almost as much as I hate spending time with them. "Sheila needs a chauffeur, and for obvious reasons, that will be me."

Her head shakes. "I do my own driving. You're free to do whatever you'd like today, though it doesn't sound like golf is a great option." She turns those eyes back to Dad. "I can't say I enjoy golf, but I have been known to hit the ball. We'll play tomorrow. For money, of course. It wouldn't be any fun without a friendly wager."

~52~

Sheila

Leaving Avery behind is gut-wrenching. Especially when leaving him alone with his dad. The man is atrocious. Hopefully I've proven I'll not tolerate his demeanor, otherwise the wager we make tomorrow will be anything but friendly. Golf is one of those games that bores me to tears, but Mom plays so indulge her when she doesn't have anyone else to play with or when she promises not to complain about how competitive I am. Everything I do, I play to win.

Today, I intend to win over Avery's mom and sister. If we can build a bridge, or at least begin to draw up the plans for one, I'll count this excursion as a success. An outcome that's only possible in Avery's absence. Too often his temper gets the best of him and the outbursts do nothing for resolution.

Based on everything I've seen so far at the Kingwood estate, falling in love with Avery was the easy part. He stirs a desire within me that's unmatched even by my love of racing. I adore the way he tries to hide how much fun he's having only to succumb to it every time, his walls crumbling away to reveal a man who shares my passion for life. Avery gets me like no one ever has and makes me genuinely warm through and through when he never gives up. I've ignored him so many times, sure he'd quickly abandon his pursuit in favor of a woman less scrupulous, but steadfastly, he's been there. Sending me cakes and chocolates, calling me and driving through my parking garage at all hours of the day and night. The man doesn't sleep. He works, and he pursues me.

His dedication is why I was crushed when I found out he was married. My fantasy about being his wife had already haunted my dreams so many times that I believed it was our inevitable fate. That Avery and I would play this game, teasing and tempting one another until the dam broke and we fell into each other's arms. That's why I always went back to him. I'd push when he pulled, and pull when he pushed. I thought those trials would prove our love. To both of us. But he'd already given his love to someone else, and I couldn't bear to hear him tell me about her. Not even when what he had to say about Cassie was negative. Her very name on his lips sent daggers into my heart.

Last night, I *did* want to talk to him about her. About the way he was so mistreated by his family. But all he wanted was to forget any of it happened at all. So I let him. And I wondered if he didn't want to discuss it with me because I had sounded just as bad as them when I judged him and refused to let him speak to me about the state of his marriage.

"Turn up here, dear." His nauseatingly smiley mom chirps from my shotgun seat. "Lila isn't feeling well, she needs to go home."

I glance in my rearview, glad I chose a Mustang so there's room for Lila, although she does look slightly uncomfortable in the close quarters. "An illness keeping a woman from shopping must be a severe one."

She presses a hand to her stomach. "I'm just a little nauseous."

Following their directions, I pull into the parking garage of an impressive high-rise, a sea of Bentleys surrounding my fastback. "I'll wait here." I eye Mrs. Kingwood as she wraps her head in a scarf and dons oversized sunglasses, Lila following suit before either of them steps out of the vehicle. "Feel better soon, Lila. I'd like to see you again while I'm in town."

"Walk up with us." Mrs. Kingwood looks around, pulling her scarf tighter. "We'll visit upstairs for a bit and then see how everyone feels."

Hackles at full attention, I follow the women into the building. I seem to recall Avery mentioning Lila's *house* was nearly as large as his parents'. "This is where you live, Lila?"

"We'll be going to the fourth floor." She smiles as the attendant presses the elevator button for us. "The upper floors are nicer, of course, but Cassie's modesty won't allow us to pay for better accommodations."

My gut drops, ears burning as Mrs. Kingwood wrings her hands. "Cassie refuses anything better, thus we're forced to traipse around like common beggars."

"Beggars?" I bite back the anger. "Nothing about this building is common and I doubt even a royal would complain about sleeping in the lobby." I thought their play would be spewing more dirt about Avery. Not this. "I shouldn't be here."

"You should." Mrs. Kingwood's fingers lightly close over my forearm. "I want you to understand who Avery is, and it's clear *our* words aren't enough to convince you. So do yourself this favor and hear it straight from his wife. Don't, and there's nothing more we can do to help you."

I open my mouth to tell her I never asked for their help but close my lips once Lila steps off the elevator and begins lightly rapping her knuckles against an apartment door. The handle turns and ever so slowly the door opens, revealing a frail form that doesn't need to look up from the space of floor its eyes study for me to see how scared Cassie is. Her shoulders are slumped under the plain blue dress she wears and her locks fall like golden curtains to cover most of her porcelain face. She's barely a year older than me yet every bit the child I never was. Her tentative blue eyes raise. "Please, come in."

With Mrs. Kingwood's grip still on my arm, I cross from the elevator to the threshold, coming to a stop just inside the door. Avery's mom peels off to hug Cassie, she and Lila coddling the girl between them. Suspicion rises as they sit on the velveteen sofa, urging Cassie to tell me her story. "Miss Beller is a friend, you don't have to fear telling her the truth."

"But Avery…" Cassie's eyes dart to theirs. "He'll kill me. You saw his threats this morning."

My blood cools. "This morning? *I* was with Avery this morning, and doing a very good job of making him angry. He didn't threaten anyone."

Lila's nostrils flare. "That's because he's good at hiding his treachery. But he *did* threaten to hurt her. I can show you the text messages."

"No." Cassie sniffs. "It's my fault anyway. I asked if I could come see him. I know not to, he's warned me about being near any of you, but…"

I raise an eyebrow. "But you'd rather not have me see messages that supposedly prove claims against him?" I perch on a nearby chair. "Curious."

Her hand twists tightly around her wrist. "I don't want him to get in trouble."

Mrs. Kingwood's eyes flit to mine. "She loves him. Don't ask me why. I don't know what any woman could possibly see in him. But Cassie believes she'll love him through this *stage*, and he'll one day come crawling back to her. As much as I hate the thought of her being subjected to him further, I happen to agree. Else why drag out the divorce?"

Since the night I first met Avery, I knew he was destruction wrapped in a dangerously handsome package. But a fun kind of destruction. A man that would ruin me in the best of ways. "Cassie, you seem to have a story to tell. Let's hear it."

Her words prick over my flesh, the beginning of her story a near replica of Avery's. It's when she gets to the honeymoon that things veer off track. "His little outbursts. The recklessness. Anger summoned at the drop of a hat. It's all my fault. I *made* him that way."

"No, you didn't." Lila comforts. "Avery's always been that way. Even when we were kids." Her eyes snap to mine. "The boy should have been institutionalized."

The shake of Cassie's head forces tears from her eyes, the ever dutiful wife defending her husband. "He wasn't like that before. It only happened after I let him down. The miscarriage…it broke him."

"You were pregnant?"

She sniffs. "It's why he left me. He told me not to do Pilates, but he also told me not to lose my figure. So I kept doing Pilates. That's why I lost the baby. And why he left me. I just couldn't do anything right."

Mrs. Kingwood hugs her close. "The miscarriage wasn't your fault. If anything, it was his."

"It was mine." Cassie wipes her face. "But he'll forgive me. He tells me so when he calls at night. Sometimes it's late, but I don't care, I always answer because to hear him say he loves me…" She musters a small smile. "I'd stay awake forever to hear those words. And I always let him know I still love him, too." Her head dips. "He promises we'll be together again. But I've waited so long already. That's why I'm pushing for the divorce." Her face pops up to meet Mrs. Kingwood's eyes. "You know I don't want the divorce, it's just that…it's so hard to be without him."

Mrs. Kingwood sighs. "Avery has been leading you on, and now we've figured out why." Her eyes turn to me. "Last month, Avery told Cassie that he wanted her to move to Huntington with him, but that she had to wait because having her around just then would *mess up his business.*"

My heart sinks. Her face tightens. "We knew he was *with* other women; he likes to call and tell Cassie about them. We just never dreamed…"

Cassie's tearful eyes stare at me. Knowing, watery eyes. "Everyone thinks I'm weak, but he was with other women even when we lived together, so…it's okay with me. I just want my husband back."

All the times Avery rejected me, drawing me close only to push me away again, come into focus. It wasn't an internal battle he was fighting. We weren't testing each other. Avery never wanted to get this involved with me because he never intended to divorce Cassie. He pursued me because he wants my money. My contacts. So he could go into business with people like Garland. Dirk spilled the news of Avery's dealership acquisition and I pushed the unease from my mind when I arrived at the Kingwood estate and heard the raised voices. I shoved it further away when I saw Avery's crestfallen face. But I shouldn't feel sorry for him. He does, after all, now hold the title of "Bet Winner."

I kneel in front of Cassie, taking her shaking hands in mine. "If what you're saying is true, then instead of wanting him, focus on yourself. Focus on healing. Then make new dreams, ones that do *not* include Avery Kingwood."

~53~

I pack my suitcase and traverse the deluxe halls of the Kingwood estate. Avery was right, I should never have come here. I should have listened when he said he wasn't right for me. If I'd walked away sooner, I wouldn't have to make this shame-filled walk to his bedroom now. But for as much as he slipped underneath my normally accurate radar and used me, I still can't force myself to leave this place without giving him the dignity of a note.

In his room, surrounded by walls that bore witness to his wedded glory, I press an envelope to his pillow. Cassie's own head may have rested here. I touch the fabric, allowing the walls to now bear witness to Avery's mistress. His business arrangement. The woman who will *not* hang her head low because of him.

> *Avery,*
>
> *It's now my turn to write to you. But not with the same sentiment as you wrote to me. I will not be waiting for you, and I don't want to talk to you.*
>
> *Give Cassie the divorce, reconcile with your family, and let them guide you to a place where you can heal from the suffering in your life. Both what you've caused and what might have been forced on you. Because outside of someone being tortured themselves, I can't imagine what drives a man to such abuse as what you've inflicted on me. And on Cassie. I met her today. She's broken. But even after all you did to her, she's willing to take you back and loves you still. At first, I didn't think it was possible for anyone to be so forgiving. But as I sit here and write this letter, I realize love is trickier than I ever imagined. So I forgive you too. Knowing I'll heal and move on. Knowing I'll use the lessons*

learned from this experience to prepare my heart, make it harder to penetrate the next time it's persuaded to take such a leap with a man. So thank you, Avery. For never saying the word I longed to hear. I count that as a kindness, not giving me the memory of the endearment passing your lips, and therefore not forcing me to have to despise the sound.

Best of luck to you, and to Cassie without you.
Sheila Beller

Eyes on me as I descend the stairs, Lila and Mrs. Kingwood wait by the door. I lift my head, nod to them, and keep walking. If I speak, I'll only cry, and despite their efforts to reveal truth to me, they didn't do so out of concern for my well-being. They aren't kind people, and my leaving is all the thanks they'll get from me.

~

Typically, driving is what clears my head. But this time, the gaping wound in my heart leaves it cloudy. I gambled and lost, and only one person can soothe my devastation. "Mom." Despite the hour, I tap on her bedroom door. She doesn't answer. I knock louder, her name ripping from my lips. "Mom!"

The door pulls from my reach, her sleep-crusted eyes wide. I fall into her arms. She holds me up. "Oh, honey. What happened? Is it Avery?"

My knees buckle, sobs jerking from depths I've never known. She guides us to a soft landing, cradling me against her, her own tears beginning to fall. "My dear, sweet girl. Tell me what happened. Did you and Avery break up?"

I'd only just told her about him before I left for California. She'd guessed our relationship already, or some version of a relationship based on the fateful weekend he tried to spend here. "I love him." My tears drip onto her shoulder. "I love him so much."

She holds me against her. "He doesn't feel the same?"

"Not even a little."

Her lips press to my temple. "It's impossible not to love you even a little."

"Tell that to the man I gave everything to." Sobs cut off my air supply, my pathetic words coming out in a torrent of gulps. "I slept with him and now…"

Her arms cinch tight. "You're pregnant?"

I wish I was. A sobering realization. After all the lies, if I were pregnant with his child, I'd be happy. "The last test I took was negative."

She unburies my face and wipes my tears. "I know how badly you want a child, but if he's not the right man for you, he isn't the right father for your child."

"If I was pregnant, it wouldn't be his. Probably. I was mostly careful."

"Mostly?" Her brow knits. "There are mistakes, then there's just plain foolishness."

"Sometimes there's both." I settle back against her. "But he's not the reason I took a pregnancy test. I went through a round of IVF."

"I thought so." She strokes my hair. "Or guessed, anyway."

"How?"

"You've been moody." Her head rests on mine. "At first I thought you were depressed, then I noticed it was only sometimes, and I just guessed it was probably hormone injections."

It wasn't the shots making me moody, it was Avery. "Sorry for not telling you." Tears trickle over my chin. "I didn't want to get your hopes up. It was bad enough having mine up and dealing with the disappointment."

She sighs. "To be honest, I've been angry with you for not telling me. For not letting me be a part of it. Mostly, for you going through that alone. I was kind of hoping you let Mary and John in on it? Or even Avery?"

At one point, I considered asking him to be a sperm donor. Instead, I chose from the ranks of anonymous donors. "I wanted it to be a surprise. So I could give you the baby news in a creative way, how Mary and John told us about Mikey." They served us dinner, all blue food. Instead of guessing, we thought they had finally lost their minds. Then John served his now famous triple layer fudge cake with the words spelled out for us. They gave us auntie and grandma gifts from their unborn child while an ultrasound video of him played on their big screen.

"Before I left for California, I told my doctor I wouldn't be doing a second round. I thought Avery and I were…" On our way to marriage. "I let you down. And came very close to disgracing this family in every possible way."

"Nonsense." She leans us against the wall. "There's no disgrace in falling in love. And certainly no disgrace in bringing a life into this world. So pregnant by Avery or some unknown donor, I'd support you and extend my unconditional love straight to the gift you carried in your body." She presses her cheek to mine. "Tell me what you need. How can I help you through this?"

I curl in her lap. "Make me get over him. Please, Mom. Get rid of the hole inside me."

~54~

Dawn brings little relief. Memories flood back, too real and raw to process. Mom's last words as she curled beside me in her bed pound against my heartache. *The right man is out there, honey. One day you'll meet him. I'm just sorry it isn't Avery.*

I'm sorry too. Sorry for the longing his touch left on my flesh. Touch he gave with little investment. More than once, he even blamed me for his omission of the fact that he's married. And I pitied him. Chastised my sharp, judgmental tongue all while he begged me to keep seeing his side of things without the slightest nod to mine. So now I have another dating rule. "Never abide a man who can't be bothered to even *try* seeing my perspective."

"What, honey?" Mom yawns.

"Nothing." I roll over and face her. "I haven't slept in your bed since I was twelve."

"Try twenty-one." She sits up with a wink, taking her phone off the nightstand and staring at the screen. "I put this contraption on silent mode, but now I have thirteen missed calls from John and twelve from Willis."

"All from last night?" I check my phone. I have calls from John but mostly Avery. He called for three straight hours before I blocked him. "I have voicemails, but I'm not checking them."

She slips on her glasses, tapping at the screen. "This is useless. I'm going to call them from the phone in the den. Willis probably called John and had a search party sent out since I didn't call him this morning like I normally do."

"Way to rub in my face that you've found love twice in your lifetime while I can't manage to find it once."

"Willis and I aren't in love."

"Just go call your boyfriend." I get out of bed. "I'm going to take a shower. With any luck, I'll wash off some of this self-loathing."

The shower heats and I step inside, water scalding a path down my body. I lean on the wall. Tears want to come again, rush as fast and hot as the stream around me. But I'm not letting them. I've cried enough for Avery Kingwood.

"Sheila!" The voice cracks and booms, only muted by the fist pounding against the bathroom door. "Sheila!"

"Is the house on fire?" I stay where I am. Mary pushes inside, slamming the door on her shouting husband. "I know you two don't practice privacy but *I'm* not a lunatic, so how about you leave the way you came?"

"Are you okay?" She shoves a robe at me, eyes full of tears. "He isn't going to stay out long, so put this on. Are you okay? We've been calling for hours…"

Her face is swollen. Eyes red. She's been crying almost as much as I have. "What's wrong? Mikey sneeze two times in a row?"

"This isn't funny!" She opens the door as soon as the robe covers me. John rushes in. Not crying. Angry. And I've only seen him worse once—when Mary was abducted.

"What on earth is going on with you two?"

"Did that son of a—"

"She's fine!" Mary yells over him. "I just saw all of her. No bruises."

"Bruises?" I cross my arms. "Why would I have bruises and who are you calling a son of a—"

"It's all over the news." Mary's eyes glaze. "*All* over. And we thought—"

"We didn't know you were home," John explodes. "We only came here to leave Mikey with Mom so we could go get *you*."

"Get me from where?"

Mom comes to the bathroom door, Mikey cradled in her arms, her own eyes as glazed as Mary's. I throw up my hands. "What is going on? What's all over the news?"

"Avery." Mom's throat bobs. "Sheila, it's Avery."

Feet beating a watery trail through the house, I rush into the den where Mom has the television blaring. John's behind me, threatening to kill Avery. That means he isn't dead. Though John could probably find a way to kill a man twice.

I stare at the television screen. Avery's face is plastered in the top right corner, video of him being shoved into a police car narrated by the newscaster. "Billionaire Avery Kingwood has been arrested for putting his estranged wife in the hospital, after what police are calling one of the worst cases of domestic violence they've seen in recent years. The apartment where the young Mrs. Kingwood lives is described by one paramedic as a battleground." They cut to a live feed of the high-rise I visited. "A spokesman, the Kingwood family's lawyer who will *not* be representing Avery Kingwood, released a statement saying the family is devastated by the actions of Avery Kingwood and that they will be tending to the needs of Cassie Kingwood, as she is their sole concern at this time."

I sink to my knees as the scene cuts to a crowd of people standing outside of a hospital. "Friends of the Kingwood family are speaking out against the man they call unstable, citing Avery Kingwood deceived everyone by pretending not to be married. They speculate that he planned to end his young bride's life to keep his secret."

John crouches beside me. "Was he violent with you?"

"No!" I push him away, head spinning. "He could be forceful at times…but not physically, and certainly no more than the rest of us." I climb to my feet. "This can't be true. Avery wouldn't—"

"His family apparently thinks he would," John roars. "The police apparently think he *did*." Mary puts a hand on her enraged husband, calming him. He takes a ragged breath. "I want to know what happened in California and I want to know right *now*."

I fight the tears burning my eyes, compassion for Cassie, the childlike creature who sat weeping softly between her in-laws, slamming against me harder than it did when I knelt in front of her. "What happened in California is *me*." I stare at the faces of my family. "I went there, showed up out of the blue and made everything fall apart. Avery told me not to come. If I'd only listened…it's all my fault."

"You did *not* make him beat his wife," John shouts. "He did that all on his own."

"I told him I talked to her." Knots form in my dry throat. He went to her apartment because of my letter. "I have to go to her."

John blocks the door, Mary by his side and Mom at mine. "Move." I shove John. "She got hurt because of me!"

"She got hurt because of him." He stands firm and solid, Mary's eyes narrowing on me because I touched her husband. "If he *ever* laid a single finger on you, I'm going to snap him in half."

"The only thing he did to me is what I *let* him do to me. What I *wanted* him to do to me. So move. I'm going to California, or Avery isn't the only one who's going to be arrested today."

"I'll go with her." Mom passes Mikey to Mary. "That man—"

"Isn't going to lay a hand on me and we all know that."

"Money doesn't make you immune to abusive men," Mary bites. "He nearly *beat* his *wife* to death. What makes you think you're any better?"

Mom puts her arm around me. "Reporters are going to be glued to this. On top of everything else you're dealing with, you don't need to be photographed and dragged into the middle of his trouble."

Tears race over my cheeks. "I'm already in the middle of it. I need to go to Cassie. Alone. I'll wear a headscarf and keep my identity concealed as much as possible, but the Kingwoods aren't like us, they won't stop my name from being leaked. All of you have to be okay with that because I'm going, with or without your consent."

"Then go." John moves away from the door. "You didn't make him lose control, but by all means, go back to California and see the *wife* he beat up. He's in jail, so he can't hurt you."

"But we'll be watching, and if he gets out…" Mary looks up at her scowling husband. "I'll only keep him on a leash for so long."

"*If* I need any of you, I'll call." I push past them before they block me again.

"We're not worried about the press," Mom calls after me. "We're worried about you."

I glance back at her. At all of them. "If I need you, I *will* call. Keep the plane ready."

~55~

The last time I drove to the Kingwood estate, I did so thinking Avery was mine. A man who was never free to be mine to begin with. Something he told me over and over. Yet I listened to what my heart sang instead. Or maybe it was only lust, my biological clock ticking loud enough to block out the truth. Either way, I have to do penance for my carelessness. First with the family. Then I'll go to the hospital to apologize to Cassie.

The air around me thickens as I top the steps and approach the door. Mason stands before me, ominous and dull. "I'd like to see Mr. and Mrs. Kingwood. And no, they're not expecting me, but I'm here nonetheless. Judging from the other vehicles assembled behind me, I'm assuming the whole family is here."

He allows me to enter and escorts me toward a buzz of people. Dipping through a doorway up ahead is Darla, a woman who refused to keep company with the family while I was here so as not to be seen as complicit in Avery's affair. I'm sure she'll be happy I've come hobbling back with my tail between my legs. All of them will. Because today there is no holding my head high. Today, I wash their feet.

Mason announces me to the stone-faced room. Before my presence was known, they were laughing. Quite jovial for people who just had one family member go to the hospital and another to the jail. "Excuse me for intruding." I pan the room. "I…" My tongue loops back on itself. Sitting in an oversized plush chair with a glass of wine in hand, legs crossed and a dangling foot gently swaying, is Cassie. "I thought you were in the hospital?"

"The Kingwoods are going to take care of me here." Her voice is strong, not like the last time I saw her.

I study her unswollen cheeks. Not even tears have puffed her eyes. I cross the floor, lifting her golden-tan arm to inspect it. "Avery's in jail for *beating* you."

"As he should be." Mr. Kingwood's voice slices with warning. "He's where he belongs, and as far as I'm concerned, he's no longer my son."

"But the news says he *beat* her. Badly." There's a bruise on her wrist and three minor scrapes on the back of her hand.

"I hid from him." She displays a cut on the underside of her other forearm. "He banged me around, then destroyed my apartment." Her eyes fall, suddenly that little girl I met. "I'm really sore, and the Kingwoods thought I should come here."

"Of course we did, dear." Mrs. Kingwood moves to her side and drapes an arm around her. "You're one of us. Family. And we take care of our own." Her eyes level on me. "She's already told the police everything. There's no need to relive it again. For anyone."

Guilt knifes deep inside me. "I'm sorry, Cassie." I look around the room. "I'm sorry to all of you. It's just…the news is claiming something very different than what I'm seeing."

"Are you some sort of domestic battery expert?" Lila snaps.

"I'm not. But when she looks as if she tripped over her own feet and her worst complaint is she's *sore,* one tends to question what actually happened verses what may very well be sensationalized in the news." I face Cassie. "Did he put his hands on you?"

"He…" She shudders. "Dragged me by the hair. Then…"

I wait while she's petted, tears in everyone's eyes but hers. "He assaulted her." Lila moves to her mother's side. "In case you're confused, this isn't the Stone Age. Even though she's his legal wife, rape is still rape."

I step back, the weight of the word crashing over me. "He…"

"He made sure everything revolved around him while the rest of us suffered," Curtis answers. "And now he's proven once and for all he's scum not fit for the bottom of our shoes."

Shame washes over me. "I…I'm…"

"You're in love with him." Cassie wipes her now falling tears. "I could tell when we met. And I know how it feels to want to think the best of him."

"Impossible since there's no good in him," Lila declares.

Mr. Kingwood's chin lifts. "We've tried with him, Miss Beller. My daughter-in-law is proof he's beyond help."

"Of course." I swallow, settling my gaze on Cassie. "I didn't come here to upset anyone. I came to support you. In any way I can. I only asked about the details because of what's being reported." My excuse feels lame.

She blows her nose. "I always thought his rage would never amount to anything. A few broken chairs…my favorite painting…but not me." Her face lowers and a single tear blobs onto her loose gray slacks. "I never thought he would break me."

Silence thickens the air. For once in my life I have nothing to say. Mrs. Kingwood sighs. "Miss Beller, though we appreciate you coming, and we're sorry for what Avery *is* and for what he's done to both of you, we're moving on. Cassie is going to live with us. We'll take care of her. And I suggest you follow our lead in removing all traces of Avery from your life."

"Tell her honestly, Mother." Lila stands arm in arm with her overly righteous husband. "We're removing him and *anyone* associated with him."

It isn't often a Beller is turned away, and since I'm here as friend, not foe, the Kingwoods closing ranks against me pricks. "I don't see a problem with our paths not crossing in the future." I look away from Lila, catching amusement flitting across Cassie's eyes before they drop back to her lap. Uncertainty burns through my gut. If she's lying, and convincingly enough to manipulate everyone in this room, there's more to deal with than Avery's guilt. He may very well be innocent.

My spine stiffens. "No matter the man, I cannot erase a life. Nor can I fathom gathering for such a *joyous* afternoon when a tragedy just occurred. It's sensational, really."

Mr. Kingwood springs to his feet, neck purple as forceful words blow from his mouth. "You want sensational, I'll show you sensational!"

He storms from the room. With a shrug, I follow, conflicted on why I'm even here.

Outside his bedroom, Mr. Kingwood stops, pointing to a jagged blood-tinged hole in the drywall. "You see this? *This* is why no one cares what happens to Avery. Before he attacked his wife, he attacked his *mother*."

My knees go week. Curtis closes in behind me, hand on my elbow to steady me. "Dad managed to stop Avery before he was able to get to Mom, but Avery wasn't holding back. That punch was intended for her."

The hallway begins to spin. I press my eyes shut. "I'm sorry."

His voice is soft. "We don't need you to be sorry. We need you to wake up, and realize my brother isn't the man any of us thought he was. We need you to not condemn us for trying to put his wake of destruction behind us. We want to live without worrying when Avery is going to fly off the handle next. Or who he's going to hurt when he does."

I nod, nausea washing over me. "May I have a moment?" He removes his hand and I fight for composure, focusing on their steps retreating down the hall. Once they're out of earshot, I sink to the floor.

~56~

While tears fell down my cheeks and my breath came in shallow spurts, laughter commenced from the party below, the echoes swirling up to where I sat against the wall with the crumbling red smear. Many faces in the room I didn't know, friends and family of the Kingwoods who will no doubt sell a story about me to the press. I take out my phone, texting John. **_Call Mr. Ronceverte. We have stories to kill._**

I have no doubt the instant I left the Potomac my family set to work getting our contacts to put their ears to the ground. Tales we don't want told are usually squashed before they're whispered, but in a case such as this, where the story has already hit the mainstream news, it'll be challenging to eliminate me from the conversation.

Dazed, I wander the hallways, ornate rooms beckoning to my unseeing eyes. I pass them by, steps trekking to the one place I don't want to be. My hand slides onto the knob. I twist, cringing as the unlocked door gives way, allowing me entrance to Avery's room. "Oh…" I slam back into reality. Cassie is sitting at what used to be his desk. Now a mirrored vanity adorns the spot, but everything else is the same. "Sorry. I didn't realize you were in here."

"Who else did you expect to find in my room?"

I recheck my surroundings to be sure I'm in the right place. Cassie grins, putting down the golden hairbrush she's running through her silky locks. "It's fitting I take Avery's room, don't you think? I know it's drab, but Mom and I are working on ordering new bedding. I'm just having a hard time deciding exactly what color scheme I want." Her painted pink nail taps her lip. "What do you think? Purple or ruby red? I want something rich feeling. Regal." She turns back to the mirror and picks up the brush. "No royal blue. It'll wash out my eyes."

"I'm sorry, didn't you just get out of the hospital? Today?"

She runs the bristles through her long hair. "Those boring people wanted to keep me. Poke this, check that. I cried to Dad and, well, no one tells Pa Kingwood no."

"Those *boring* doctors and nurses have a job to do after someone is attacked."

She shrugs. "Avery's in jail. It isn't like he can hurt me anymore. Besides, dwelling on the past isn't healthy."

"Your attack is hardly the past."

"When you've been dealing with Avery for as long as I have, trust me, you're eager to make him part of the past." Her eyes meet mine in the mirror. "Aren't you ready to put him in your rearview?"

I've already abandoned Avery. And I don't want to judge Cassie's behavior because everyone deals with trauma differently, but hardly forty-eight hours ago she sang me a completely different tune. And redecorating in the short amount of time she's been here is peculiar. "If you're set on having this room, I suppose changing it up a bit is a good idea."

She smiles, eyes roaming down my body and back up. "With your fashion taste, I shouldn't ask for your decorating opinion. I think I'll change to a new color scheme every few months anyway. You know, always change things up to keep it interesting."

"How will your in-laws feel about that?"

Her eyes twinkle. "They won't mind. They've already been so very, very helpful."

My shoulders square. "Now that you've rid their life of the only person stopping you from having unrestricted access to their wallet, I'm sure they have been." Her façade slips, ire searing through her reflection, attempting to burn my flesh. I'm immune to dirty looks. If she wants a rise out of me, she'll have to do better. "Is this a game to you, Cassie?"

She blinks, returning to her childlike state. "I've gone through hell with Avery. The least this family can do is buy me some sheets."

I study her, watching for the subtleties of lying, but her head dips, hiding her face from me. I fold my hands. "I hope that, with the aid of time, you're able to overcome what you've been through. Until then, take care of yourself, Cassie."

I'm not naïve. I contemplate the reality of simply seeing in Cassie what my heart wants to believe as I return to the rest of Avery's family. Mary didn't waste time bouncing back from her attack, so why not expect Cassie to do the same?

"I'm leaving." I announce before anyone has time to utter a syllable. "As we've determined already, I won't be back. And while I don't know the truth of who Avery is, what he's capable of, or what he actually feels, you don't either. As his family, you should find out before you cut off your own arm." I meet their stares one by one. "It wasn't pleasant meeting you, but I wish you all the best nonetheless."

~

"I have information about the Avery Kingwood case," I inform the uninterested officer at the police station's front desk. There's a scarf wrapped around my head Audrey Hepburn style, and sunglasses sit on my nose larger than the ones the Kingwood women favor. "Please point me in the direction of the right detective."

"Name?"

"I'll give it to the detective." I take off my glasses. "Surely one has been assigned to the case. If not, the arresting officer will do."

"Name?" His tone is flat.

"I've got it." A man whose blue tie is half undone steps out of a doorway behind the toneless officer and motions for me to follow him. "I'm Detective Gill. And I was present when Mr. Kingwood was apprehended. That good enough for you?"

"Perfect."

I wait until we're behind a closed door before removing my scarf. "My name is Sheila Beller. I'm happy to give you references and wait patiently while you look into me. Then I want to know everything you know about Avery Kingwood and what transpired in his life over the past twenty-four hours."

"Demanding." Gill's lips tick up. "What exactly makes you think you're entitled to even get the time I'm giving you now?"

"Entitled is the exact thing I am." I hand him a note I wrote in the car. "Call this number and give them this message. I'll wait."

He eyes the ten digits, my name scrawled across the bottom with the sentence, *Forever in your debt once more, and I expect you to collect.* "Cryptic. Whose number is this?"

"Call and find out."

His body shifts forward, eyes leveling on me. I meet the scrutiny unflinching, hands folded in my lap. His jaw ticks, curiosity outweighing his instincts. "While I call and relay your message, make yourself comfortable."

He slides the chair back, keeping his stare fixed until he rounds the desk and disappears back into the hallway. Thankfully this won't take long. My FBI friends will plead my case with gusto, and then I can get on with finding out the very things I'm afraid to know.

~57~

Gill swings the door, a laptop tucked under his arm. "You've got some friends in high places."

"I prefer not to call on those friends, but today it's necessary."

"If you say so." He sets the computer down and taps on the keyboard. "Want some coffee?"

"No, thank you."

"One steaming hot cup coming up." He winks, sliding the laptop across the table. "I'll add a little sugar and cream, then take you out later for a real drink."

He leaves and I turn the screen toward me. Avery's file is displayed for my perusal. There's little information outside of his mugshot. I study his face. Per usual, his expression is impossible to read. There's too much conflict in him. Too much darkness.

"Here's your coffee." Gill slips into the room and places a Styrofoam cup in front of me, dropping a folder into my lap. "Oops." I meet his eyes. He grins. "It takes a while for the paperwork to get done, and even longer to be detailed in the system. What's not there you'll have to ask me for over dinner."

"I believe my friends only intended to compel your cooperation, not your audacity." I flip through the sparse file of papers. "The arrest was made at the airport?"

"Right before Mr. Kingwood boarded a plane."

"What state was he in? Combative? Bloody?"

Gill settles back into the chair across from me. "Are you writing a novel?"

"If I were, you'd be cast as the hero." I float him a smile. "Was Avery wearing fresh clothes when you found him?"

"Hard to say." He shrugs. "Pictures are in the file, so you tell me if those are fresh or not. As for his state of mind, he was angry but compliant. And no, there wasn't any blood on him."

I scan the photos one more time. The file has more than a mugshot, but still there's not much to draw from Avery's expression, or his appearance. "Surely you've seen these cases before. Did he look like a man who just finished brutalizing his wife?"

"Domestic violence isn't a look. We see it from every race, gender, and walk of life." He checks my finger for a ring. And not discreetly. "Mr. Kingwood's right hand is busted up and, at first, he denied the charges. Now he isn't talking."

"Has anyone been to see him?"

"Only his lawyer. And you. I'm assuming that's what you're asking for next. Is he that good of a *friend* that you really want to see him?"

"I'm afraid it isn't a matter of want as much as need." I ignore his attempt to find out the nature of my relationship with Avery. "So Mr. Kingwood *does* have a lawyer?"

"A public defender." Gill leans toward me. "And not one I'd want defending me if I was innocent. So either your buddy isn't innocent, or he's unaware of how serious the charges are."

There's a third option with Avery. He's too cocky to realize how dumb he is. "I just came from seeing Cassie Kingwood. She isn't *beaten*, yet the news says the police department is hailing this case as one of their worst. Why?"

He shifts, a look of concern flashing across his face. "These kinds of things happen with high-profile cases. People sensationalize."

"So the news is blowing things out of proportion?"

"Does that shock you."

"Not in the least." I take a breath. "What does the apartment look like? Worthy of being named a battleground?"

His chair creaks as he rocks back into it. "Yep. And if you saw Mrs. Kingwood, you know what *else* he's accused of doing to her?"

Bile rises into the back of my throat. "I do."

He frowns. "That's why the news is reporting what they're reporting. Some of the first responders talked, including one of our officers."

I nod my understanding. "I'd like to see Mr. Kingwood now."

He gets out of his seat. "I'll do you one better. I'll get you in to see him *and* take you to dinner tonight."

"Rain check on dinner." I sigh, willing to eat with him in order to discover more about his thoughts on Avery, but not tonight. "It's already been a long day and it's quickly becoming longer."

Gill leads me to an empty room where a cheap laminated table fills the center of the small space. Three silver-legged yellow plastic chairs flicker under the fluorescent light. "Sit on this side." He nods to the left. "The shackle bolts are on the other. I'll make sure your friend is chained down in case he decides to take a swing at you, too."

"He would never hit me."

"I bet his wife said the same thing."

<h1 style="text-align:center">~58~</h1>

I fixate on the oatmeal walls, waiting for Gill to return with Avery. I check the clock. It hangs over the door, beckoning me to leave. It's been twenty minutes already. "I've gone mad." I stand, ready to escape. The door swings open. Gill walks in. Alone. "You didn't bring him?"

"I did." Gill nods to the hallway. "He isn't coming willingly."

Scuffling assaults my ears, the growling threats of two men rumbling through the space as a uniformed officer shoves Avery into the room. Gill buckles Avery's orange-clad knees, pushing him into the chair across the table from me. "Sit. And be nice to the lady."

"I came." Avery glares at me while the officer chains him to the bolt in the floor. "I sat. And now I'm going back to my cell."

"You sure he's your friend?" Gill straightens. "He's saying he doesn't know you."

I didn't realize they'd tell him who was here. My heart clenches. "I've endured worse than being denied."

The uniformed officer shakes his head. "If I were you, I'd be the one denying I know him."

"That's advice I've received twice today." I meet Avery's glare with my own. "Leave us. I want to speak to Mr. Kingwood alone."

They leave despite Avery's protests. "This is against protocol! I can't be left alone with a random civilian!"

I cross my arms. "I'm hardly random."

"I want to go to my cell!" he yells at the closed door. "You have to let me!"

"Avery." I slam my palms on the table. "I understand you being angry with me and I'm sorry for my part in what happened. So hear me out because on my life, I never dreamed leaving you that note would

219

drive you to…" His eyes snap to mine, snarling mouth frozen. "If I would have stayed, told you in person…maybe you could have gotten all your rage out with me instead of seeing Cassie and having things escalate."

"Did you just say you'd rather have me hit you than her?" He leans toward me, words low and slow. "Did you just say—"

I step away from the table. "I'm saying I'd rather you not hit anyone. I'm saying I'd rather not be associated with a *rapist*."

Anger spills from his pores. He struggles against the shackles, yanking, writhing, peeling his wrists raw. "Officer!" His voice echoes off the walls, booming back to my ears. "Officer!"

I note his damaged hand. Envision it smashing through the wall where his dad and brother rebuked me. Not through a face. Even the animalistic display he's putting on now doesn't allow me to believe he'd physically hurt anyone. "Avery!" I yell over him. He stops fighting his restraints, chest heaving.

I take a breath, sitting across from him and extending my open palm. He yanks his balled-up fists as far away as the cuffs will allow. My teeth grind against the sorrow raging through my heart. "Why are you doing this? You do realize sitting here screaming like a maniac only makes you look worse?"

"Worse than what?" he snaps. "Everyone already thinks I hurt women, and the only thing worse than that is listening to you say you want me to hit *you*. To spare *poor* Cassie."

"That's not what I said." At least it's not what I meant. "I'd rather have *talked* to you, de-escalated the situation and spared her because I don't think you would hit me. And I'm not entirely sure you hit her, but something happened to her and she's saying…" Nausea crashes over me. "Avery, did you rape her?"

Silence spreads dark and inky around us. He stares at me. The wall. So many emotions at war inside him I can't read any of them clearly. The only thing I'm sure of is my own agony. "Tell me what happened, Avery. I need to hear it from you. All of it. The whole truth."

His jaw grinds. "You shouldn't be here. I don't want your name dragged down with mine."

"I'm not worried about my name, I'm worried about you. Even if you *did* hurt Cassie, be honest with me about it. So you can get the help you need." I can't stop myself from scooting forward, reaching for him again. "This is your life on the line."

His hands don't move this time. "You're worried about me? After all this? After everything you wrote in that letter, you're worried about me?"

No matter what's happened, I can't turn my feelings for him off like a switch. I press my palm over his fists. "Please, Avery. Tell me everything. From the time I left until this very moment."

He stares at my hand. "You first. Tell me what Cassie said to make you leave me. I know what she's told my family to make them hate me, but I never thought she would get to you. I thought you'd be smarter."

Tears flood my eyes. "I'm sitting here after you're accused of beating and *raping* your wife. So what exactly gives you the impression I'm smart?"

~59~

I remove my hand from Avery, fold both my palms into my lap to keep them from touching him. "One important thing that Cassie told me was, she still loves you."

"She only loves herself," he spits. "What else? I know you didn't back down over her saying she loves me."

"I *should* back down over your *wife* saying she loves you. But it was her wanting to reconcile even though you blame her for the miscarriage that got to me," I snap back.

His eyes go distant, looking past me into a memory. "I'm sorry I didn't tell you about my daughter. Losing her was the worst day of my life."

"It was the worst day of your wife's life, too. Then you compounded her sorrow by leaving her stranded." I keep my voice steady. "Tahiti, was it?"

His eyes narrow. "Now I'm glad I didn't tell you about my daughter."

"Yes, well, I kept my end of the bargain. Now you tell me what happened when you punched a hole through your mother's wall."

His face pushes toward mine. "Your letter was in my fist. I punched it into the wall so my *mother* could have a memento of the day she ran you out of my life."

"That's all?"

"All?" He huffs. "No, Sheila, that's not all. I yelled. A lot."

"And when you went to Cassie's apartment?"

Fire licks behind his eyes. "I called you a hundred times. I was ready to get on a plane *with* you so *we* could go *home*. But you were long gone. And I was pissed."

"And?"

"And it got worse every time you didn't pick up the phone," he snaps. "You ran scared, so I went to Cassie's apartment to find out exactly how she managed to spook the unflappable Sheila Beller."

"And?" I growl.

He leans toward me. "Cassie was her usual arrogant self. She threatened to call my daddy and mommy if I didn't leave, so I didn't leave. Then she broke a few things, so I broke a few things. And that's *all* I did." He plops against the back of his chair. "It's not like she paid for anything in that apartment. My parents keep her well funded so I wrecked what already belonged to me anyway." He leans the chair back on two legs. "Happy? You didn't sleep with a rapist. Now you can run back east and pretend you never knew me."

I believe his version of events more than I believe Cassie's. Whether or not it's only wishful thinking remains to be seen. "You going to her apartment was my fault."

He lunges to his feet, the chains jerking him back down. "I went there on my own. Because I was pissed off. And seeing her face made it worse. She may have everyone else eating out of her palm, but I know who she really is, and right now, she's getting *exactly* what she wants. You hate me, and my parents are ready to move her into their estate."

"She's already moved in," I whisper. "She's in your room."

His shoulders slump, body sliding into the chair and head falling to the table. His forehead bangs against the surface. Slowly. Harder. "Stop!" I kick free of my chair, round the corner and fall over his shoulders. "Avery, please stop."

"Leave." His motionless head remains on the table. "Leave and don't come back." I try to pry him up. "I said leave! Right now, Sheila. Leave!"

"I believe you when you say you didn't hurt her."

"Why believe that when I'm clearly such a violent and selfish person?" His face rolls to the side. "Don't answer that, just leave. I don't want to see you. I'm done with you. I'm done with all of you."

~

Each time I walk away from Avery, it's harder to convince my feet to go. Alone in my hotel room I sob for him. For his unborn child. For all the broken pieces of my bitter fantasy. I want to believe Cassie made up her story, that the Avery I came to know when he simply lived life with me *is* the man he is underneath. Yet I'm forced to contemplate his guilt. Forced to admit the anger that's always there, bubbling just under his surface. My love may want to give him every excuse, but I refuse to be blind. I *will* get the truth.

My first order of business is hiring Avery a proper lawyer. Whether or not this case goes to trial, I'm not going to be kept from the details. And Avery is going to have to deal with that very real fact because no matter how much he fights the officer shoving him down the hall, he's going to face me again today.

"When are you going to learn your lesson?" I wave an arm around the same windowless oatmeal room we occupied yesterday. "There's only one way out, and those men with guns behind you aren't letting you take it."

Avery yanks his elbow from the officer's grip. "I told you I don't want to see you anymore."

"I don't particularly want to see you either, but if you want out of here, I'm your only hope. So sit down and shut up."

His chair's plastic creaks under his thudding weight. "Do you see me trying to get out of here? My parents may have cut me off, but if I wanted to post bail, I could."

Ignoring him, I place a hand on the officer's shoulder. "He won't need to be bolted up. In fact, you can take the cuffs off entirely. Mr. Kingwood is leaving today."

Avery groans as his chains are removed. "Did someone die and make you the boss?"

"*I* made me the boss." I walk the dimpled officer to the door. "Thank you for putting up with him. Now send in his lawyer, please."

The man shuffles down the hallway and I take my time closing the door. Even longer to pull a chair from the table, its silver legs scratching over the tile. "If you'd rather me not be here while you meet with your lawyer, I'll respect your privacy and leave. But he *is* representing you. So cooperate with him because I've posted your bail since you couldn't find the time to do it. You'll be out of here soon, and I expect you to play by whatever rules my lawyer gives you."

He rubs his wrists. "What part of leave and don't come back confused you?"

"The part where you professed your innocence and I believed you." I smirk. "If you're lying to me, I'll find out in the process of you receiving a fair trial. Since this is your first offense and you're probably not a threat to mankind, you deserve to be free while you await said trial. Something I cleared with my mother to be sure I'm not blinded by the dreaded *L* word."

"You're still compelled to use the *L* word after all this?"

I grip the back of the chair, remaining on my feet. "I'm compelled to do what's right, love has nothing to do with it."

He leans back in his seat, not giving me any idea of how he feels about me outright saying the word he wants to erase from the English language. "The bonehead lawyer they gave me can't find his way out of a paper bag, so I'm doing time regardless. I thought I was going to have to represent myself to go inside, but I'm pretty sure this lawyer is going to do worse than I ever could."

"I don't know why you want to be in prison, but you're clearly the one with a hearing problem. I said I brought *my* lawyer." The door opens and a silver-haired stout man walks in. "Hello, Mr. Ronceverte. This is Avery Kingwood. Despite the words that may come out of his mouth, he *does* thank you for dropping everything to fly out here for him."

"You're the one who called him, you thank him."

"I don't need thanks." Ronceverte slides his briefcase onto the table. "Miss Beller warned me you may resist representation, but let's at least have a conversation, hear your side of events, look at the charges you're facing and see if we can agree to a course of action. Then you can make a decision on whether or not you'd like my help because either way, I'll sleep well tonight knowing I kept my word to Miss Beller."

"At least you're honest in admitting you're only here doing the bidding of the illustrious Beller family."

Mr. Ronceverte sits down. "I hope you'll be just as honest because the only bright spot I can see in this for you is the fact that you have a Beller in your corner."

I avoid direct contact with Avery's eyes, but I know they're glaring at me. "Since everyone is playing nice, I'll go finish making our exit arrangements."

$$\sim 60 \sim$$

In my now usual full Audrey Hepburn disguise, I wait outside the building with Detective Gill. He knows Avery is being released, but few others do. Which is a few too many to trust word won't spread to the media.

I scan the parking lot as we wait on the steps, two vehicles idling below us. The tinted-window SUV has a driver and awaits Avery and Mr. Ronceverte. The rented Corvette is mine. It isn't as nice as what I own, but I couldn't resist the comfort of the familiar wheel. An appreciated perk on a day like today.

"You sure your friend is innocent?" Gill breaks into my thoughts.

"No." My chest tightens. "But I believe it enough to think he won't hurt anyone if he's released."

"For your sake, I hope that's true." He stands closer to me, watching Avery approach. "When am I getting that dinner?"

"I could use a distraction this evening."

"I'm your man." He smiles. "What time?"

Avery stops in front of me. "You two look cozy. Care if the felon interrupts? I need to have a word with Miss Beller."

Gill stands taller. "What you need is to learn to control your temper, or you're going to find yourself right back here."

"Control my temper?" Avery's dark eyes roam over me. "Or my temptation? The latter is pretty hard in certain company."

"You'll manage to do both." Ronceverte clutches Avery's elbow, nodding to me. "I'm taking him to the hotel."

I ignore Avery's antics. "Fresh clothes will be waiting for him. If you need anything else, let me know."

The first news van screeches onto the far end of the lot. Ronceverte tugs him. "We need to move. Now."

Avery won't budge. "Sheila? Are you coming?"

I pull my sunglasses over my face. "I'll be in the car behind you. Now go!"

"Dinner?" Gill shouts as we run down the steps. "I'll pick you up at eight!"

"Dinner?" Avery growls.

"Shut up and get in the car." I skirt around the Corvette. Avery grudgingly jumps inside the SUV and we all peel away. I shift gears, taking a right out of the parking lot while the man I hate myself for loving exits left.

~

Prepared for the media storm, I booked Ronceverte, his paralegal, Avery, and myself into a small but expensive hotel. With only eleven floors, the space is manageable. The top floor is communal, consisting of a spa, pool, and fitness room. The tenth is three large suites. I rented each under different names to ensure no one connects the occupant of that floor—me—with the fifth where I booked the entire floor under Diane Mineral, Ronceverte's paralegal's name. Avery and his defense team will hole up there.

With doormen already posted at every entrance, I only hired security for the stairwell and to monitor the fifth-floor elevator. No one gets off on that floor without being precleared by Ronceverte. My floor, however, is devoid of security. Another attempt not to have anyone link me to Avery. I'm also not visiting his floor. All my communication is solely with Ronceverte or Diane, who have the hard job of keeping Avery from being seen *or* heard while he prepares for the deposition.

The fifth-floor curtains aren't even allowed to be opened, and I've been keeping my own closed. The manager assures me the reflective glass won't allow photographs to be taken, but I'm not prepared to test the theory. What I trust is an array of bulky sunglasses, hats, and headscarves while I sneak out employee exits and walk back alleys. The two times I've snuck out to meet Gill for dinner, he never spotted me until I chose to reveal myself. But there's one person my disguise isn't fooling tonight. Avery knows it's me under the wide-brimmed hat as soon as he steps onto the elevator. "Is it okay if I ride with you or would you prefer the wife beater take the next one?"

"I'm not your wife, so I'm perfectly safe and don't care which elevator you take."

Jamming his finger against the elevator's door close button while glaring at the security guard, daring the man to say a word to him, Avery moves his hand over the tenth-floor button. "I assume you're on your way up to your room?"

"You assume correctly."

"Been out having another date with the good detective, have you?"

"Where I've been is none of your business. And you should be more careful walking around the hotel, everyone has cameras these days and they'd love to get a picture of you in the gym pumping iron to feed the image of you being aggressive."

"How do you know I'm going to the gym?"

I take off my smothering disguise. "The only two things on the floor above me are a gym and a pool. You're not wearing swim trunks, so I'm using deductive reasoning."

"You should be a detective instead of dating one." He leans against the wall of the slow-moving elevator. "Not that *my* business is any of yours, but I'm not walking around here without common sense. I had the hotel manager clear the top floor for me because you forgot about the spa. Women are always lurking around up there."

"At least you know you're not in a position to give them a show. Impressive. Since you've been prone to stripping in the past."

"That all depends on who's watching." He turns to me. "Going to the spa today?"

I focus on the elevator lights, watching them fade and glow as we pass the ninth floor, choosing silence instead of banter. Avery breaks first. "I'm losing my mind being locked up here. It's been a week. I have to have some way to blow off steam."

"Are you asking me if you can pick up one of those lurking spa women to *blow* off steam with?"

"I'm telling you the weights are the only things coming close to keeping me sane." He pushes off the wall and rubs his face. "I swam. Ran up and down the halls of the entire fifth floor. Nothing helps. Maybe I can run up on your floor, too?"

"Maybe."

"I bet it's nice living up there in the high life with all the peasants below you."

"I should have put you and Ronceverte up there and taken a lower floor for myself. I forgot about your repulsion to those who have less than you."

"You know that's not true," he nips. "I was only making conversation. So stay up in your tower, Princess. That's where you belong."

The elevator door opens, releasing me from the torture. I step into the hall and place a hand over the door. "I plan on coming to the deposition. If you prefer I not be there, say so."

"Why do you want to be there?"

"I don't. But look around, Avery. No one else is standing with you. So no matter how much I don't want to be that person, I can't walk away and leave you completely alone." My heart makes me return to this nightmare every day. "Your family will be at the deposition and they'll be sitting with Cassie. If you prefer to face that alone, I'll respect your wishes. But you don't have to walk in there tomorrow with only a paid lawyer by your side."

I let my eyes rest on the curve of his perfectly scarred brow, the stitches now removed. "I've stayed in town so you'll have someone for the tough times. And yes, I'm keeping my name out of the press, but if you need me to openly stand in the light with you, I'll do that, Avery. All you have to do is ask."

"Why?" He steps toward me. "Why are you willing to do all of this for me? And don't tell me because it's the right thing to do."

"You know why." I look at my shoes. "I keep telling myself you'd do the same for me, but no matter how much I try to convince myself, I know it isn't true."

"It is." His fingers slide under my chin, raising my face to his. "Sheila, I'd do anything for you."

I turn away, his mouth dangerously close to mine. "Sorry." He drags a hand over his jaw. "I wasn't going to kiss you."

"I've heard that before."

Standing this close to him, I feel the sadness rolling off of him. I meet his eyes. "Are you okay?"

"No," he whispers. "The pictures Ronceverte showed me of Cassie's apartment..." His throat bobs. "I didn't do that. I broke two vases and she threw some things, but it didn't look like that when I left."

"And the damage to her body?" Tears flood my eyes. "If even one bruise is attributed to you, you're not the man I thought you were."

"Really?" He steps away from me. "Because it isn't her bruises, her apartment, or even jail time that concerns *me*. You were long gone before any of that ever happened, and I wish I still had the letter to prove it." Palm flattening against the elevator he slams the buttons, teeth grinding as the door slides between us. "You're not exactly the woman I thought you were either. I guess that's why you have a new boyfriend now."

~61~

I'm filled with guilt. The words Avery spoke to me yesterday struck a chord inside my heart. I *did* abandon him. More than once. I also judged and refused him, behaving more like his family than I ever care to admit. It's no wonder he's angry.

I sit next to him, feeling the pang of loss even deeper as hostility writhes under his surface. Not even the dawn of a new day has sobered him. "There's your boyfriend." He smirks as Detective Gill enters the hall outside the hotel conference room we're using for the deposition. "You'd better go say hi and give him a big kiss so he'll say something nice about me today."

"Look around and think long and hard before you say another word and drive away the *one* person who's willing to sit next to you."

"I didn't ask you to come." Avery slices into my ear, breath hot against my neck. "The only reason I'm not making you leave is because this is a chance for you to hear some facts so you'll believe me when I say I didn't lay a finger on Cassie."

"I've already told you I believe you."

"Yet I've seen you *once* since I've been out of jail and you implied during our chance meeting last night that you *do* think I hit her." His arms cross. "Quit talking out of both sides of your mouth and put on a pretty smile for your boyfriend, he's staring at you."

There are two officers present today and Gill is sitting with them, staring at me to see what the status of my relationship with Avery is. Something I wish I knew myself. "I'm confused, Avery. Surely you understand that." His mouth opens. Closes. Eyes fixing on the door behind me. I turn in time to see his parents float into the hall, a weeping Cassie nestled between them. They walk to the far end, all three of them

231

ignoring Avery's presence as they pass by us. They give not so much as a glance while his eyes remain glued to Cassie.

I study Avery's face while he watches his wife being coddled by his parents, his mom dabbing Cassie's eyes while his dad offers reassurance of her safety. He finally has an expression I can read. Torment. I slide my hand onto his arm. "For what it's worth, I'll be here beside you the whole time. No matter what truths come out today, I'll be here."

He removes my hand. "Be here for your own nosy benefit. And go sit with your boyfriend. I don't need anyone beside me."

The slump of his shoulders betrays his hurt. No matter what comes out of his mouth, he's upset beyond what I can imagine. My own family would never shut me out. They would be beside me, yelling and screaming if necessary, but they'd be here *with* me. Especially when there's a shadow of a doubt, and from what Ronceverte tells me, he thinks Avery is actually innocent. Not defense lawyer innocent, genuine innocence.

"Gill is staring at me because when I have dinner with him, we talk about you. So he's trying to figure out if you and I are more than the good friends I told him we were."

Avery's eyes break from watching his wife. "Are we?"

"I don't know," I whisper. "But I'm sitting beside you."

"I guess I should be thankful." His dark eyes roam over my face, hand sliding toward mine. "I *am* thankful. Without you—"

"You'd have one less person to argue with." I tightly grip his sweaty palm, desperately wanting to ask him about Garland. I need to know if I was only a bet.

"Thank you." He whispers against my ear, keeping hold of my hand as Ronceverte ushers us into the conference room ahead of Avery's family.

"Of course." I keep my face forward, not trusting my lips if they turn toward his. "Just don't make it a habit. This is a one and done for me."

We take our seats, fingers still tightly wound together under the table where no one can see him rest the back of his hand on my knee. "I'm just happy it's not a done and done, Sheila." His breath electrifies the soft hairs along my neck. I close my eyes. His lips are so close I feel them brush my lobe as he whispers. "I'll never lie to you or hold anything back again. Cassie *will*. Remember that."

His fingers tug free, his touch ripped from me as easily as he gave it. I open my eyes. Cassie is directly across from him and the sole recipient of his attention. Today is her turn to speak. Her chance to tell her truth.

A dull throb starts behind my eyes as she begins to paint a picture of the man whose touch I'm dying without. I focus on her words. On the details of the attack. I glance his way, hoping to see contradiction in his face, but there's only a cold, hard stare of a man harboring hatred for the woman he once professed to love so much, he married her.

"Stop looking at her that way." Ronceverte slides a notepad under Avery's nose, his voice low and tense. "Write. Draw. Wiggle the pen around. Just do something other than stare." Avery doesn't move, break his glare, or utter a single syllable. Ronceverte looks at me, but I can't speak, not while Cassie's three feet from me, sobs of despair wrenching from the hurt he inflicted. If he didn't do what she's describing, this woman deserves an award.

Ronceverte pushes a box of tissues from our side of the table over to Cassie's lawyer. "I believe your client has had enough for one day. We'll reconvene tomorrow, same time and place." He inclines a nod to the Kingwoods. "You three may leave ahead of us."

Coddled between Avery's parents, Cassie leaves the room still being pierced with Avery's glare. The instant she's out of sight, his hand slides to my knee. I jump to my feet, slamming his hand against the underside of the table as my chair tips and clangs against the floor. "Sheila…" I hear my name roll off his lips, but I need air. Speed. To drive until I lose the images Cassie's words carved into my skull.

~62~

One high-speed trek after another and I'm no less mentally drained than before. Cassie's portrayal of Avery is still raw as I pull into the hotel's parking garage. It's one thirteen in the morning and I'm exhausted in every possible way.

Trudging by elevator security, I kick off my shoes and wait for the doors to reopen on my floor. Everything I'm feeling is so small compared to what Cassie lived through, *if* she lived through it. And if she did, I'm partly responsible for her pain.

Exiting the elevator, I mindlessly open my door, weighing the truth I want to believe against the heavy sorrow of her words. Tossing my heels into the apartment's dark interior, I make my way to the bar, stopping in my tracks when the shoes skitter back across the floor. I turn, scanning the shadows. A form materializes. I back away. It stalks closer. "Where have you been, Sheila?" Avery approaches, one step forward for every two I retreat. "Where. Have. You. Been."

I make it to the small dinette before he catches me, his body advancing until my back presses against the wall. "Have you been with Gill?" he rumbles, palms flattening against the plaster on either side of my head. "Having a nightcap?"

"You need to leave."

"Are you having lunches with him, too?" His face lowers to mine. "That's how you started with me and Dirt. Bait us in with lunch and have us hooked by dinner."

"You need to get out of here before you do something you'll regret."

He rocks backward, icy glare freezing me in place. "You're scared of me."

"I'm not sure what you're capable of anymore, and I want you to leave before I have to find out." I slide along the wall. "I'm not Cassie and I'm not a rag doll. Touch me and it will be the last thing you ever do."

"Because you'll fight back?" He cuts off my retreat. "Do it, Sheila. Fight back. Fight the way I expect you to fight if *anyone* ever tries to hurt you."

"*You're* hurting me!" Tears flood my eyes.

He pushes away from me, fisted hands tense at his sides. "All along, you've believed every disgusting word out of Cassie's mouth."

"She didn't give herself those bruises."

"Didn't she?" he bites.

"You're the one who left her, Avery." I lift my back from the wall and inch around the dinette, plotting a course past him and to the door. "Even without the physical damage, you emotionally destroyed her. You're not doing either of those things to me."

I break for the door, hand grappling for the handle as a roar rips from his lips, carrying a single heart-stopping message. "She *killed* my child!"

I turn, watching his form crumple to the floor. I can't see his face, but I hear the tears he's shedding. "She had a miscarriage, Avery. That isn't murder."

"Abortion." He sobs. "She lied. There was never a miscarriage. She scheduled an abortion and sent me off on a day trip so I wouldn't know." His body tilts forward. "She murdered my baby girl and now she's killing what's left of me."

I walk toward him, stunned, and drop to my knees beside him. His pain digs into my heart. I drape an arm around his shoulders. I'm not scared of this man, I'm broken for him. "Why would Cassie lie? Was there a problem with the pregnancy?"

"She just didn't want to be a mom." He uselessly wipes his face. "She said she did, so we got pregnant on purpose and I was so happy…" The more tears he wipes away the harder they fall. "She let me believe it was a miscarriage. I held her. Mourned with her. Put aside my own devastation so I could be strong for her."

"How do you know it was a scheduled abortion, Avery?"

He lifts onto his knees, shoulders shrugging my arms away from him. "I was worried about her, so I did some research, tried to find out what therapy might help, but she refused to *waste* her time. She started getting out of bed every day with a song on her lips, like nothing ever happened." He climbs to his feet. "Just because I was still devastated didn't mean she had to be, but I wanted a copy of her medical records to send to a doctor in the States. I'd read there can be complications for a woman after a miscarriage, and I didn't want anything to happen to her." His cold eyes stare at me. "That's what a man does for his wife, loves her unconditionally. But she didn't want my love. She wanted me to shut up and leave her alone. Kind of like you."

He stomps out of the apartment. I scramble off the floor. "Avery, wait."

He swings around. "Why? So you can tell me I didn't hear her doctor explain to me with his own mouth *every* step of the procedure *she* paid for with *my* money?"

"I want to help you." I reach out, but he moves away.

"I don't want your sympathy, Sheila. I don't even want you to care that she *murdered* my child without giving me a chance to have a say in the matter because *you* don't want to be with a man who would abandon his wife, and that's something I'll always be guilty of and never regret. I left her high and dry, and with every hope in the world that she'd fall off a cliff and break her lousy lying neck."

I clamp onto his arm, wrapping my fingers in the fabric of his shirt. "Why didn't you tell anyone the truth?"

"We made a deal." His hand folds over mine, fingers plucking mine away one by one. "Unlike some people, I keep my word."

"Then you're stupid." Tears slide from my eyes. "Signing a separation agreement doesn't make it right for you to lie to everyone for so many years."

He leans into my face. "I agreed never to speak the truth about the abortion because it was her *private* medical information, and she agreed never to tell anyone we were married because that's what my *parents* wanted to begin with. I let everyone have what *they* want, and then all of you turn against me because none of you can be bothered to even care about my side of *any* story. Why do I want to waste my breath on people like that?"

"I'm sorry." I cup his face. "If what you're saying is true, I'll apologize a thousand more times. But you have to set aside your foolish pride and tell your parents the truth."

"The truth?" A tear escapes his eye. He removes my hands. "The truth is that they, like you, think so poorly of me that you find everything Cassie says plausible. Each of you turned on me with so much ease, *I'm* starting to believe I'm the monster she says I am."

"You're not." I reach for him.

He steps away. "I blew up my world for you, Sheila. And all I asked in return was for you to trust me. I *asked* you to believe in me." He steps into the elevator. "*Cassie* is who you believe in."

"And *Garland* is who you believe in." My teeth grind. "I hurt you, but you hurt me, too. Yet I'm *here*, Avery. At your very worst moment it's *me* who is standing here with you."

"For how long?" His eyes narrow, hand slamming against the elevator buttons. "Every time Cassie speaks, you take her word as gospel and bail so fast it speaks volumes about how you really feel. So take your pity and the *L* word you keep wanting to throw around, and shove them!"

~63~

Avery's tale of betrayal rips through my soul like nails on a chalkboard. It's dawn and the living nightmare I'm trapped in won't allow me to sleep. Slipping on the shoes Avery kicked back across my floor, I grab my purse and bypass the elevator. The stairwell will get me out of the building faster, and it's high time I reacquaint myself with the garish Kingwood estate. Avery might be too proud to speak the truth, but I'm not.

Women have abortions for many reasons, and Cassie is in within her rights to do so, even without Avery's consent, though I do understand why such a thing has gutted him. I'd be devastated myself if the roles were reversed. However, Cassie has gone to great lengths to not only cover her deed but paint it with a different brush. I intend to find out why.

"Sorry about the early hour, Mason." I push past him, unbuttoning my coat. "I need to speak to Cassie immediately."

"She's still sleeping. As are *all* the Kingwoods."

"I'm sure they are." I walk ahead, not giving his lips time to speak what they're going to say next. I already know I'm not welcome here, the guards at the front gate made that clear. But after a friendly negotiation, they let me inside. I'm not negotiating with Mason. "Feel free to go have your breakfast. I'll show myself up."

Adrenaline courses through my veins as I take the steps two at a time, sweeping down the hall to Avery's door. "Cassie." I knock, not waiting for a response before letting myself in. If she doesn't want uninvited company, she should lock her door. "Good, you're awake."

She jerks upright. "What are you doing here? Mom! Dad!"

"Oh, please." I pull out the vanity chair and sit down. "I'm not going to hurt you and you very well know that."

"Your head is twisted up in Avery." She tugs the satin magenta sheets up to her chin. "For all I know, he sent you here to kill me."

"Billionaires don't do their own—or anyone else's—dirty work. We hire people for that." I fold my hands in my lap. "I want the truth of your relationship with Avery. Every single sordid detail. And if it doesn't match with the story he told me, one of you will find out exactly how vengeful I am when people lie to me. Now talk."

She's a chameleon. Scared and frail one minute, vicious and pouncing the next. Disgust flashes behind her irises and she lets the sheet slip, revealing her chiffon teddy. "Entitlement only makes you a brat, not a threat. So go ahead, try to play games with me." She rubs her legs over one another, showing off her body. "I'm better." A sensual finger traces over her collarbone. "Smarter." A finger runs up her neck. "And I don't push, I shove." Her tongue runs over the end of her nail. "Just ask Avery. He likes *everything* about me."

"I'm not capable of being intimidated and I'm not interested in playing games, so tuck your cleavage away and tell me what I came to find out before the *very* thin amount of patience I have left runs out."

"And what will you do when it does?" She slides off the bed, swaying as she crosses the room and pushes her face down to mine. "Hit me? If that's the way you like it, go ahead. Show me what tricks you learned from Avery." Her morning breath washes over my cheeks, hands pressing against the back of the chair and hair brushing my jaw as she leans close to my ear. "Mom told me he took you to the gazebo. I taught him those tricks. Did he tell you that? Does he still call my name the way he used to?" she taunts, voice low against my lobe. "Do you like it? Pretending you're me?"

I steel my nerves, remaining where I am and allowing her to do the same. *This* is how I get to see the real Cassie. "For a narcissist, the separation agreement was clever. Then again, it only worked because you chose your mark well. A lesser man wouldn't have abided by it."

"You don't know what you're talking about." She stiffens, straightening herself away from me. Fast enough for me to realize she's hiding more than an abortion.

I remain unflinching. "The options before you are simple. Tell me everything. Or don't. Either way, I *will* know the truth. So choose wisely."

She opens a vanity drawer and retrieves a doll, its body in one hand and head with my face plastered on it in the other. "Did Avery show you his handiwork? If anything were to happen to you and the police find this dolly along with the one he made of me... Well, our dear sweet Avery is going away for a very long time."

"You're threatening me?"

"What's going on in here?" Mr. Kingwood bursts in, tying a thin red-flowered robe around him. "You will leave this house! My wife is already on the phone with the police!"

"The police?" I whistle, watching fear trace Cassie's brow as she drops the mangled doll back into the drawer. "Seems all the inhabitants of this lovely house are *very* brave." I stand, using my hip to close the drawer for her. "Maybe it's mold. You should have the walls checked."

"Miss Beller—"

"Please, call me Sheila." I wave him off as Cassie drops back into her victim role, falling to his side in a fit of sobs.

"The police are on their way!" Mrs. Kingwood makes her appearance. White fluffy robe thrown around her.

"Good." I smile, moving toward the door. "I could use a few good officers right now."

<h1 style="text-align:center">~64~</h1>

When you ask a question, you better be able to handle the answer. And now that Cassie has laid a threat at my throat, she's going to find out there's no one better than me at asking questions. Whether or not *she'll* be able to handle the answers doesn't concern me. I can. And I can afford the privilege of haste.

"If you're going to arrest me, I insist you frisk me first." I smile as Detective Gill enters the room I've commandeered at his station. It took a little persuasion to gain unfettered access to the space, but setting up somewhere else was out of the question. The supplies I need are already here, and time is of the essence.

Gill's head shakes, arms crossing over his broad chest. "You're lucky the officer responding to that call this morning knew who you were, or I'd be taking handcuffs off you right now."

"I hear handcuffs are more fun when they're on."

"Don't tempt me." He relaxes and walks further into the room. "So what's this I hear about you being given a first-class police escort to your own personal war room?"

I have to admit it was fun breaking speed limits with the blue lights in front of me instead of behind, but much less entertaining to find out that my friend Adelle had already been conducting an investigation into Cassie. While I'm thankful Adelle had a head start, I'm equally irked that I wasn't informed. The moment Avery called her, I should have been notified. Then I wouldn't be standing in this room admiring the work my ragtag team has done in under two hours. I would have stopped Cassie long before now.

I scan the space with Gill. A picture of Cassie is taped to the center of the whiteboard, two teenage hackers Adelle already had on retainer are tucked behind computers, and a middle-aged woman in a pantsuit is talking into her earpiece while furiously scribbling on a notepad. Being Mr. Ronceverte's paralegal, Diane was also already hard at work. I simply had to borrow her services and alter the angle of her efforts. "It was a lucky thing indeed that the Kingwoods had the guts to call the police on me."

"You're really going to go to battle with them over their son?"

"This has very little to do with Avery anymore." I walk over to the photo of Cassie, staring into blue eyes that will soon have no secrets. "The last time I did this I was searching for a psychopath who abducted my sister-in-law. Comparatively speaking, tearing apart *this* psychopath's life should be fairly simple."

Gill stands beside me. "Well, I'm your unofficial personal assistant, so introduce me to the gang and let's get this over with. You owe me dinner that doesn't include talking about your maybe guilty ex."

"He's innocent." I press a sticky note onto Gill's button-up. "While you've been napping, my highly capable computer geniuses have been turning over the stones of Cassie's life. The first intriguing tidbit they unveiled is a juvenile arrest record."

"Let me guess, it's sealed?"

"The she-devil was able to enter adulthood with a clean slate. A convenience all the better to trap a future husband with." I show him to the corner of the table I reserved for him. "Unfortunately for her, seals can be broken. An investigator friend of mine has already been working on doing just that. I expect to have the information before the end of the day."

He peels the note off his shirt and studies it. "Whose email is this?"

"Diane's. She's going to compile our information and keep us coordinated, so report everything to her." I nod to Mr. Ronceverte's paralegal. "Once we know the details of Cassie's misspent youth we'll have a better idea of where to place our focus."

I turn to the bright teenage eyes that are chomping at the bit to show each other up. "Do either of you have a location on my mother's plane?"

"I do." Alton's fingers fly over his keyboard. He turns his screen my way. "This little blip is her. As soon as she lands in Tahiti, I'll let you know."

"I've got her phone *and* Willis's pinged, too." Dina crosses her arms. "After they land, *I'll* keep track of them."

Mom and Willis are going to hunt down Cassie's abortion doctor. Not only do I plan on obtaining a copy of her medical records, I also want to hear from the man's own mouth the account of his interaction with both Cassie and Avery. They each point fingers. It's time for the truth.

"Mrs. Mineral," I say. Diane reminds me of Gladys. She's a little thicker around the middle and not quite as tall, but they're nearly twins. "Have you heard from Mr. Ronceverte?"

"Oh, yes." She smacks her lips. "He said Mr. Kingwood is in a particularly foul mood today, a downgrade from the horrid mood of yesterday."

I lean on the table beside Gill. "Sounds about right."

Her pink-tinged cheeks dimple. "I told Ronceverte that so long as the depositions are delayed, we don't care what the overall attitude of his predicament is."

"Then I *am* rubbing off on you." I force a smile, though the last thing I feel is jovial. While I prepare to hijack the entire deposition, Avery is simply going to have to wait. I'm finished playing by his rules. Lying by omission and keeping secrets has destroyed many more lives than only his.

~65~

I peruse the tenant list for Cassie's high-rise, two names flagged for an in-person interview. One is Cassie's neighbor and the other is the male spotted pacing outside Cassie's apartment on the surveillance video my little hackers delivered. I forwarded the information to Adelle, and Diane's coordinating with her and Ronceverte's office back home to run down profiles for the rest of the occupants. "Gill, feel like taking a drive with me?"

"Anytime." He grabs his suit jacket and nods to the door. "Lead the way."

I don't often ride shotgun, but for this part of our day, Gill is in charge. He can drive while I continue my flurry of text messages and required reading. And for the interviews, he'll conduct them while I sit quietly, studying the people's body language while they answer his questions. Starting with the neighbor who *didn't* call the police.

Cathy Poca's age doesn't show, but the twenty-years-her-senior neighbor of Cassie's isn't hiding her disdain for the younger resident. "All I heard that day was the *usual* clatter."

Gill leans forward. "What do you mean by *usual?*"

Her face tightens. "That one is always thudding something. All hours of the day and night, bang this, crash that. Then there are the muffled voices and the…*screams.*"

"What kind of screams?"

Her eyes dart to mine. This woman is prim if nothing else. I sigh, breaking my silence. "Pleasure screams?"

"If you call that pleasure." She grunts. "I reported her to building management, but I've seen more than one of those *managing* men coming and going, so of course they never enforced rules. Not for *her* anyway. I

244

got cited for parking over the line of my parking spot even though the space I was half in also happens to be mine." She lifts her chin. "We each have two designated spots and I've always parked in the middle of mine. Until *she* showed up here and I filed the first complaint."

Her description of Cassie falls in line with what I've experienced. At first glance the young Mrs. Kingwood seems harmless, but a deeper look reveals the ugly truth behind her blonde locks and shiny smile.

~

"What do you think?" I ask Gill as we make our way to the top floor where the pacing man lives. "Split personality? Psychopath?"

"I think you have yourself a con artist." He shrugs. "Cassie Kingwood could be any of those other things, too, but any way you slice this one, your friend got himself mixed up with the wrong woman."

"Two of them." Avery doesn't know the half of how horrible Cassie is, and in the process of me revealing all her dark secrets, he's going to meet my lethal side.

The moment Gill introduces himself, the balding pot-bellied man in front of us breaks out in a sweat. My stomach drops, intuition kicking in. "He's having an affair with her." The man's terrified eyes expand at my accusation, clumsy feet propelling him backward, deeper into his apartment. "Oh, goody. It's more than just an affair."

"I thought I was handling this," Gill snaps. "Do you mind?"

"Lead the way." I motion for him to enter the apartment ahead of me. Technically, the now sobbing man hasn't invited us in, but he hasn't expressly forbidden it either. So he better dry his tears. I'm not leaving until his soul is laid bare.

~

Numb from head to toe, I hand Gill my phone as we exit Cassie's building. The email on display is a copy of her juvenile file. It reads like the Who's Who of childhood criminals. The story I just heard from the sobbing dimwit upstairs proves this file should have never been sealed. Then again, Avery hasn't bothered to fact-check a single detail of Cassie's life so the state of the file wouldn't have made a difference for him. When it came to loving her, he was blind. "Why do men value beauty so highly that they'll sell their souls for it?"

"Until I met you, I couldn't answer that question." Gill opens his passenger door, hand catching mine before I slide onto the seat. "When you see forever in someone else, it makes you want to do anything for them."

"In his case," I nod to the high-rise where officers are leading Cassie's lover from the building, "only one of them wanted forever."

"Which is why I'm only doing half-stupid things for you." Gill stares at our hands, slowly releasing my palm. "Until I see that forever looking back at me."

An increasingly agonizing part of me *wants* to imagine a life with him, but like Dirk, he doesn't give me the spark that's always there whenever I'm near Avery. I slide into the car and enter an address into the GPS. "This is where we're going next. Cassie's parents' house. She isn't the orphan she told her husband she was and I can't wait to hear the parental rendition of everyone's favorite liar."

~66~

Fifteen long hours into Operation Crucify Cassie, a name I decided on after enduring a sickening interview with her former high school janitor, my team is exhausted. "You look like you've been dragged backward through a ditch by a bull." Diane hands me an espresso, our investigative existence fueled by thick black liquid, pizza, and overly greasy fries.

"If I have to eat another slice of that pizza, I might hire a bull and give the ditch a try."

"I've got us covered." Gill produces two white paper sacks. The smell of lo mein pulls my feet forward. Diane had the forethought to hire a local barista to set up shop for the entire police station, but she let our young friends choose the food.

Gill slips us out the door and out of the building. "You're lucky I'm not feeding you from the vending machine. You running amok is going to get me fired."

"Your job is secure." I slide into his shotgun seat once more and wait for him to take his place in the driver's seat, pushing the chair back and slipping off my shoes. "Trust me when I say I want this over as much as you do."

He divides the takeout boxes. "So you can get back together with your ex?"

"I don't know." Avery and I are only apart because I left him. He's made it infinitely worse since, but I could have made a different choice the day I first met Cassie. I could have *asked* him to account for all of her accusations instead of believing them. I'm only now realizing that I didn't because of my own insecurity. My fear that a man will never truly love me because he won't be able to see past my dollar signs. Even Gill's tune changed once he found out the kind of clout I have.

I meet his eyes. "I'm sorry I didn't tell you right away that Avery and I had been involved."

Gill leans back in his seat and skewers a piece of chicken with a plastic fork. "I get why you didn't. I just don't get what you see in him."

"Avery isn't…" I sigh. "What you're seeing is the worst of him, and honestly, he has good reason to be angry at the world. But I know a different side of him. A gentle side. A man who would throw himself off a bike just to soften my fall." Remembering all the good parts of Avery hurts. In so many ways, I let him down. And only *some* of the reasons I did are his fault.

I look around the half-alive lot, clacking my chopsticks toward the light pole shining over us from ten feet away. "We're not supposed to be talking about Avery, and I changed my mind about dinner. This scenic location is perfectly romantic."

Gill's hand slides across the console, brushing my arm. "I've had less romantic dates."

"And I've had worse *un*-dates." I shift, facing him. "While we're out here under stars we can't see, why don't you tell me more about yourself? After all the nauseating stories we endured today, I'd like to hear about the life of a normal human being."

"Who said I'm normal?"

"Unless you want my next war room to be directed at you, I suggest you at least pretend."

As he talks, I watch his lips, wondering what they feel like. Wondering if they would hold enough comfort to put an end to my ache for Avery. Gill's handsome, and if I weren't already in love with someone else, I'd have it in me to flirt with him mercilessly. "So no engagements, serious girlfriends, or wives? I'm highly impressed."

"I aim to please. And speaking of impressive…" His fingers trail to my face, tips running over my cheek as his lips come ever closer. I press a hand to his chest, noting the muscle rippling under my palm. *He's* impressive. And if I saw him naked, I might just forget all about Avery Kingwood.

I pull away. "Sorry, but I can't…"

"I'll be here when you can." He rests a hand on my knee, squeezing before moving back to his side of the car. "Break's over. Let's get back to work because the sooner we get this over with, the better."

Outside the car, he slides his hand into mine. "Any chance I can convince you to move here?"

"After I flay Cassie Kingwood on her cross, I doubt I'll ever step foot in this state again."

"Then I'll come to you," he whispers.

~67~

Avery

Since my last fight with Sheila, I haven't left my hotel room. All I can do is lie on the bed and stare at the ceiling, her face—full of fear—staring back at me. She thought I was going to hurt her.

"Open up!" Ronceverte's incessant knocking blasts through the thick slab of door. I don't move. Not when all I have left of Sheila lingers above me. I try to hold onto the picture. To remember a time when I could comfort her. When she would have believed me when I said I only came to her room that night to make sure she was okay. "Open! The! Door!"

"Go away!" I clench the bedsheets in my fists, her face fading with every intrusive sound. "Go! Away!"

"I'm not leaving! Open the door!"

With those last words, she leaves me. Dark and cold. Alone. I slide off the bed and pull a t-shirt over my head. If Ronceverte is here, it means the depositions are finally moving forward. But I'm not bothering with a suit. I'll go through this whole sham just the way I am. I'm going to prison anyway, and I don't care that it's over something I didn't do. Any life, even one behind bars, is better than the one I've been living.

I throw the door open. "What?"

"Get undressed." Ronceverte rushes past me, one meaty hand undoing his tie.

"Excuse me?"

"Get undressed and get in the bed." He peels back my sheets. "Now!"

250

I fold my arms. "I don't know what kind of payment you're used to, but this isn't happening. Get out of my room."

His face scrunches. He looks at the bed, then back at me. "I'm not propositioning you! I'm trying to get your deposition delayed another day, but to do that I need to lie and say you're sick, so get in the blasted bed and cough so I can *pretend* I'm not lying."

"No." I drop my arms. "I didn't want the delay in the first place, so stop whatever it is you're up to and just tell them I did it. Whatever Cassie says, I did it." I lean on the wall. "Slap handcuffs on me and get this over with before I'm too broke to pay you."

"You're not paying me, Miss Beller is. If…" His face falls.

"If what?"

If I'm not guilty. That would be Sheila's stipulation to paying for my defense. If I'm guilty, I'm on my own. The princess will wash her hands of me and walk away as if she never knew me. "I'm going to prison, you might as well cut your losses now." I point to the door. "Get out. I'll take it from here."

He sits on the bed with a sigh. "Miss Beller is working on something. Until she finishes her project, we're to delay the proceedings by any means necessary. So please just work up a cough for me."

My teeth clench. "Are you telling me *she's* the reason this is dragging on?"

"*You're* the reason this is even happening," he snaps. "*She's* the solution. So cooperate."

"I will." My eyes narrow. "Make your call. Tell Cassie's lawyer I'll be waiting in the conference room."

He stands, jaw ticking. "You'd do that to Miss Beller? You'd ruin her plan after everything she's done for you?"

"Like you said, I'm the one who made this mess to begin with. No need to soil her dainty little hands any further."

"She's hardly dainty," he scoffs. "My own paralegal isn't allowed to tell me what your girlfriend is working on. All I know is Miss Beller went to your parents' home and got herself arrested, then—"

"Arrested?" I growl.

"Seems your parents aren't too fond of her."

His shouts fade the farther away from him I get. I shove the first security officer and glare at the other until he puts his hands up. They may want me to stop for my own good, but if my parents made Sheila spend a single second of her life behind bars, I'm going to *earn* my way into prison.

~

I never intended to use the spare key fob I swiped from Ronceverte's driver. I just wanted to have it, to feel like I wasn't trapped. Now that I need to find Sheila, make sure she's okay and then deal with my parents, I'm glad my fingers took the bit of molded plastic when they had the chance.

Circumventing reporters that have been waiting in the lobby since being tipped off to my whereabouts, I take employee corridors and navigate the parking garage. I dash to the blacked-out SUV, jump inside, and fire up the engine.

Swerving through traffic, I cover pavement in a blur, twisting and turning through the city until I finally see the police station entrance. Taking a hard right, I drive into the first open spot and slam the vehicle into park. Three steps away from the SUV I'm intercepted by two uniformed officers. Behind them, Detective Gill. I fold my arms. "I have business inside."

"You sure do." Gill smirks, one of the officers pulling out his handcuffs. "Avery Kingwood, you're under arrest."

"For what?" I step backward, jerking my wrist free when the young officer grabs it.

Gill's face lights up. "Resisting arrest."

"Oh come on!" I yell as the second man spins me around, shoves me over the hood and bends my wrist behind my back. "I don't care if you arrest me, but you're not doing it until I find Sheila Beller."

"How do you think I knew you were coming?" Gill chuckles. "You made one already furious woman even angrier."

Teeth grinding, I let them push me into the building and through the halls. All Sheila's doing. And here I thought I was coming to save her. "Last I checked, socialites don't get to decide who gets arrested."

"One of them does." Gill takes my arm, pushing me through a doorway and into a long room where plush chairs surround an oval table.

"She advised me to inform you that she *will* hold anything you say and do against you. Your only right is to remain silent. I suggest you do that."

The handcuffs cutting into my wrists, I do everything *except* be quiet. "This is your final warning." He glowers. "The second thing she told me was to advise you that if another living soul hears your voice today, the next time you jump, *neither* of your chutes will open."

"Then I want to press charges against your girlfriend for threatening my life."

He rushes me, slamming me into the wall. I fight, but my wrists are bound. He wraps his hand in my collar, hitching the t-shirt up until it's tight and choking. "You're not worth the spit it took for her to issue that threat, and when this is over, you're going to stay away from her." He shoves my head into the wall, forearm cutting across my jaw. "Go ahead, fight me. I'll gladly arrest you for real."

Ronceverte barges in. "What's going on in here?" Gill lets me go, flames in his eyes. No less of a fire than what he can see in my own.

Fixed on Gill, I raise my wrists to Ronceverte. "Get these off me and I'll *gladly* tell you what was happening. The lawsuit will have a nice fat payout for you."

Ronceverte shakes his head at both of us, landing a glare on Gill. "His wife and his parents are right outside this door. Get those cuffs off my client. Now."

My mouth goes dry. "What is Cassie doing here? Where's Sheila?"

"You'll see her soon enough." Ronceverte slams his briefcase onto the table. "Congratulations. You're getting your wish. The deposition is happening."

The door opens. All our heads swivel. It's Cassie, swollen red eyes peering from between my parents' shoulders. Even after all these years, the red nose and tear-streaked face seem impossible to fake. But I know better.

Gill yanks the cuffs off and leaves. I rub my sore wrists. "Good. Everyone's here who needs to be here so let's get this show on the road. I have women to beat."

~68~

Ignoring my parents' shocked faces and Ronceverte's pleas for me to stop aggravating the situation, I call Cassie out. "How much money do you want? That's why we're here. You made your play and you'll get all my money, but that's not enough for you. So let's hear it, how much of my family's cash will it take to make you disappear?"

"Disappear?" She sniffs, pressing her face into Dad's chest. "He's going to kill me. Make me go away for good this time."

"He's going to do no such thing." Dad glares at me.

"Not now." I fold my arms. "I missed my chance at your apartment."

Ronceverte slams his heel down on my foot, the sound covered by the thwack of the door bouncing off the wall behind me. I swing around. It's Sheila. An amber-eyed ball of fury. "You two set up over there." She directs the two teenagers behind her to the end of the table on my right. While the teenagers open up laptops, the *click click* of their fingertips flying over keys the only sound beyond Sheila's voice, Mr. Ronceverte's paralegal is sent to his side while Gill and a pot-bellied, half-bald middle-aged man are directed to a row of seats along the window wall of the room. I stare at the man. I know him.

Realization pushes me to my feet. "You." He ducks his head toward Gill. I make a move for him.

Sheila latches onto my arm. "Hall. Now."

Abandoning choking the gas thief for a chance to talk to Sheila, I follow her into the hall, slamming the door behind me. She whirls around, inches from my face. So close I can feel the heat of her breath against my lips. "In thirty seconds, you are going to walk back in there, sit down, and shut up. No matter what happens or what *anyone* says, you *will* keep your mouth shut."

"What *you're* going to do," I lean in to her, "is tell me what's going on. First I hear you got arrested because you broke into my parents' house. So I come here to get you, then your *boyfriend—*"

"Keep. Your. Voice. Down."

"Tell. Me. What. Happened." I press my nose into hers, the contact sending my pulse into overdrive. "Why is the man who stole my gas sitting with your boyfriend?"

She removes herself from my space. "Everything you need to know is getting ready to be revealed. That can happen a lot sooner if you do as I've asked."

"You didn't ask, you told. I'm not some fool to be ordered around like a pawn in my own life." My chest heaves. "They're all sitting in there smirking at me like I'm the devil, and you're out here like your place is to boss me around when just a few nights ago *you* looked at me the same way."

"Since the night you broke into my room and *earned* yourself every look you suffered, I've found the truth. And before you have the gall to think I'm here to defend you, let me assure you today's favorable outcome where you're concerned is only a side effect of the stupidity of others." She steps back into me, curled lip showing bright rows of teeth that look anything but friendly. "Your *parents* called the police on me. Your *wife* labeled me pathetic and thinks the game she's been playing is already won. *You* didn't respect me enough to supply a single truth to let me make an actual decision about who I would tie *my* life to. You also didn't stay in your hotel room like I *ordered* you to. Now my hand is rushed. So be quiet while you ingest what I'm getting ready to dump all over your wife." Her hand snakes around me, opening the door. "The next tears Cassie cries are going to be real. You're welcome. Now go sit down and be a good little boy while I show you how to get your way without throwing tantrums."

~

I sit in silence among the hushed whispers from every corner of the room. Sheila waves an older couple inside. They hold on to each other, wide watery eyes a mix of fear and shame. Cassie's horrified shock at seeing them crossing the threshold is rewarding, though I don't know why she's afraid of them.

"Dad? Mom?" slips out of her mouth.

I sit upright. "You told me your parents were dead. That you were in foster care—"

"Never." Sheila escorts the couple around the table, where a perfectly placed glare shuts my mouth. "Cassie, your parents are here to support you. They've been briefed on the dire situation you've put yourself in and like all good parents, they love you nonetheless." She turns her attention to *my* parents. "You'll want to move now. Not only does she have her actual family with her but after you hear what I'm getting ready to spill, you're not going to want to be anywhere near her."

My heart lurches to my throat. Sheila's hand is sliding across the back of Dad's chair, her lips leaning close to his cheek, those ever-watchful Beller eyes tracking every little tic. "Unless, of course, you've been in on her scheme the whole time?"

The vein in his neck bulges. "What lies are you trying to put on our family? No one is in on any scheme."

She smiles. "Now there's a statement you certainly don't want to make."

Dad and Mom begrudgingly relinquish their seats to Cassie's parents but remain standing behind Cassie. Sheila's head tilts. "That's a strong show of support for a woman now flanked by parents she professed to be dead. And to be clear, the longer you stay with her, the more I'm going to be persuaded you *are* in on her scam. Is that the case? You hired a con woman to seduce your son?"

"Con woman?" I choke. "Cassie's...you hired her to seduce me?"

"Of course not!" Dad's hand flails at Sheila. "You can't barge in here spewing lies."

"You heard him." Cassie's chin rises. "Take all your people and get out of here."

"You poor dear." Sheila tsks. "It must be unnerving seeing your boyfriend walk in when you haven't told anyone you're dating him."

"Boyfriend?" I gawk at the balding man.

Sheila places a ballcap on his head, conjuring the vision of the man tucking an envelope under my windshield wiper. "Cassie's lover is many things. Photographer. Stalker. Tire slasher. And my favorite," she turns her eyes on me, unholy fire burning behind them, "he feigned an interest in skydiving and managed to get a few minutes alone with your rig."

Numbness snakes through my limbs. He tried to kill me. For *Cassie.* "I don't know what she's talking about," Cassie screams. "I don't know that man!"

"Shh," Sheila coos. "You don't want to say anything to further incriminate yourself. I have plenty to bury you with already."

~69~

All this time, Cassie thought she was a sly fox. Because she was. Because I let her be. But now, I can *see* the fear seeping from her pores, those calculating blue eyes trying to decide if chewing off her own leg will save her. It won't. Not from Sheila.

Sheila moves forward, nodding to the two teenagers. "Since boyfriend Oliver is being denied and Cassie is cozy without swapping out the Kingwoods for his strong grip at her back, let's go ahead and introduce our next guest." She pans the room with a pretty smile. "Isn't modern technology wonderful? The doctor is joining us all the way from Tahiti."

The room floats around me, an out-of-body experience as a laptop screen swivels toward the room and a leathery-faced man I haven't seen in over seven years stares at me. There's noise coming from Cassie's side of the table. Screeching. Something inhuman that I haven't heard from her before. Sheila's silhouette turns toward the sound. "Dr. Elkins is here to teach you a very valuable lesson, Cassie. Cash beats sex. Every time."

"Sex?" I blink Cassie into focus. "You slept with him?"

"Patience," Sheila nips. "I'm going to cover *everything* in excruciating detail."

I close my fists against my thighs, dragging air through my nostrils as Sheila's words fall over me, every syllable driving my parents farther away from their vigilant post at Cassie's back. They thought she was so pure. Now maybe they'll finally see from my perspective.

"Dr. Elkins had an affair with Cassie Kingwood. He met her in a bar. On a night that, according to her, Avery Kingwood drank too much and passed out in a hotel room."

I remember that night. We hadn't been married two weeks and Cassie wanted to go out dancing. We had shots before leaving the yacht and by the time we made it to shore, I was puking. She'd already booked us a room, so I went there and don't remember anything else until I woke up at noon the next day. I always wondered about that night. Those shots shouldn't have knocked me out, but the only other explanation would be that Cassie drugged me. I refused to believe it for a long time, but now…

"Cassie painted an ugly picture of her husband that night." Sheila continues despite the protests from Cassie's lawyer. "Dr. Elkins felt sorry for the young mistreated girl. Though married himself, he allowed her to cry on his shoulder and from there, one thing led to another."

My fists unclench, sweaty fingers digging into my legs to stop the trembling. Sheila plows forward. "Dr. Elkins, after Cassie Kingwood got pregnant and you met the husband of your mistress, did he seem like the drunken abuser she described?"

"Quite the opposite." The doctor's arms fold. "I found it hard to reconcile the man I met with the one she described. But by that point it didn't matter. She ended the affair."

"But you were sleeping with her long enough you thought the baby might be yours?"

"Miss Beller." Cassie's lawyer tries once again to stop Sheila's warpath. "I don't know how it's done in the east but here in the west, we don't allow theatrical productions in our proceedings. Whatever this is, you're wasting your time, and I'll have you brought up on charges if you continue."

"And I'll have you brought up on charges if you breathe again while Miss Beller is speaking." Mr. Ronceverte looks bored. It seems to be the way he operates. Underneath, he's wound tighter than a bow string. "She's under my employment and doing this spectacular production on my behalf. Furthermore, today is *my* day, not yours. So listen and learn. Maybe you'll benefit from seeing how we win cases in the east."

Sheila straightens. "Now that we've established the floor is mine—"

"This isn't allowed!" Cassie rages. "Avery! Stop her!"

A warning shows in the set of Sheila's jaw. I clamp my mouth shut. Her lip ticks in approval. "He isn't going to help you, Cassie. So turn your eyes to the screen."

"He came on to me." Cassie tugs tissues from the box in front of her, pressing them to her cheeks. "I said no. But Dr. Elkins forced himself on me."

"Forced?" My gut clenches. If that's true, maybe she was too ashamed to tell me what happened. That would change…almost everything.

Sheila's palm slams down in front of Cassie, cutting off my thoughts. "You weren't *forced* into anything and you did *not* have a miscarriage. You paid Doctor Elkins to perform an abortion, which he's here today to attest to."

Sheila withdraws her hand from the table amid gasps from my parents, her next blow aimed directly at them. "Avery found out. *That's* when he left her. And that's when *Cassie* put a stipulation into their separation agreement that the abortion couldn't be discussed. Grieving the fate of his unborn child, he agreed to those terms."

Like a lioness stalking her prey, Sheila paces the room, watchful eyes on Cassie's now sobbing form. "Her motive was to silence Avery so she could manipulate the rest of the Kingwood family in order to get what she set out to get before Avery ever met her."

I curl my fist back into my thigh. She looks at me. "It's no twist of star-aligned fate that the two lovers met. Enclosed in the booklets Mrs. Mineral is passing out, you'll find details of all the facts we've so feverishly worked to gather. For those of you who haven't seen it, there's a copy of the separation agreement."

I glance at Cassie. She looks as ill as I feel. "She can't do this. Tell her, Avery. This is *ours*. It's supposed to be secret."

Sheila slides a booklet in front of my face, breaking off my ability to see Cassie. I take it, placing it on the table and lowering my eyes to the pages as Sheila moves on. "The privacy section of the separation agreement is highlighted for everyone's convenience. You'll also find sworn testimonies from all the witnesses you'll hear from today. Including the man who actually destroyed Cassie's apartment and tossed her around enough to give her the bruises and cuts she later accused Avery of." I look up. Sheila's eyes are on me. "Please save all your questions for the end because trust me, you're going to have plenty."

"This is ludicrous!" Dad waves away the booklet offered him. "I don't need to see separation agreements or hear testimony of someone coerced to say whatever lies you've cooked up about our daughter, Miss Beller. We've seen Avery's behavior. Have you already forgotten the hole in our wall?"

She faces him. "No, I haven't. Nor have I forgotten you're exaggerated claims of what transpired that day. In fact, combined with today's steadfast behavior, you've released me from any guilt I might have had over you being collateral damage in your *daughter's* imploding world." Her amber eyes are ice cold. "Next time you choose a side, make sure it isn't opposite me."

"Sheila!" The crackle of her mom's voice breaks through the storm of words penetrating my skull. I glance at the screen. Katherine's puff of white hair tickles the edges.

"Is that your mom?"

Sheila nods. "She and Willis are on an impromptu vacation. As luck would have it, Tahiti is nice this time of year."

"Sheila!" Katherine shouts. "Your phone! Check it. Now!"

Diane Mineral's face goes pale as she scans Sheila's texts, the two of them huddled together. Sheila's hand trembles as she waves the two teenagers over to her. I lift from my seat, but Gill beats me to Sheila's side. I plop back down, burying myself in the booklet to keep my emotions in control as best I can. Cassie is worse than I ever imagined, and Sheila's the one shining a light on what an imbecile I am. I don't deserve her. Because Dad's been right all along—I'm a living, breathing mistake.

~70~

An eternity passes before Sheila comes back into the room. When her entourage left, part of me hoped they'd never come back. But Ronceverte told me they would, to wait silently and today would be worth all the pain. So I waited. Though it's hard to imagine anything good coming out of this day.

Silently, Sheila strolls around the table, steps steady as she passes behind my chair. "Avery Kingwood is honorable. He kept his end of the separation agreement in spite of the overwhelming hardship it brought to his life. Meanwhile, Cassie Kingwood has continued to manipulate everyone around her. She tells his family she loves him and wants him back, yet tells the man she's sleeping with *he's* her one and only."

She stops directly in front of my parents, who have made their way along the wall, slinking closer to the door with every ticking minute. "Modesty didn't keep her from taking you up on your offer to move to a better apartment. Her lover did. He has money and was her next mark."

"Liar!" Cassie screams.

Sheila ignores the outburst. "If Cassie let you move her to a nicer floor, her *poor little me* story would fall apart."

"She's lying!" Cassie pleads to deaf ears.

Sheila nods to the man sitting in the corner staring at Cassie like she's the best thing his world has ever known. I know the look, I had it once. "She needed someone who would do anything for her. Poor Oliver here was so smitten, he was willing to commit murder for Cassie. When that didn't pan out, he staged a crime in order to put the final nail in the coffin of his lover's husband."

Cassie glares at Oliver before looking at Sheila. "You can't prove any of this."

"It's already proven." The snap of Sheila's tone forces me to look at her. Something is wrong. Her control is slipping.

I whisper her name, but if she heard me, she's ignoring me. "Cassie, you separated Avery from his family. You played on their sympathy until you realized they were never going to *announce* your marriage. A fact lending itself to you being forgotten forever *if* Avery managed to get his way in the divorce. Something you feared would happen with *me* in his life." Sheila begins to pace. "Obviously he preferred me, and you wagered it wouldn't be long before his parents did also. So you staged the beating, forcing the Kingwood family's hand into public acknowledgment while letting you remain the poor little victim who gets exactly what she set out to have all along: access to them and everything they have."

Cassie climbs to her feet, pleading to my parents, who have decided to not make eye contact with her. "I would never do that. Never!"

Sheila stalks toward her. "You did. And now that I've dissected your life, I'm going to splash the intimate details of it all over every media outlet from tabloids to prime time. *Everyone* is going to know how you duped your rich husband into marriage and got pregnant to exploit him because you already had a plan to get rid of the child."

Sheila's ice-cold face presses right in front of Cassie's. "I'm going to take away all your hiding places. Ruin everything you touch. And make your life pure hell from this day forward."

"Make her stop." Cassie falls into her seat, throwing herself at the mercy of the only ally she has left. Her lawyer. "She can't do this. Tell her she *can't*."

"He knows I *can*," Sheila bites. "So say goodbye, Cassie. You're going to prison."

The hush falling over the room is so thick I can't even hear the beat of my racing heart. Sheila hones in on my family's lawyer. "Advise your client to sign every single paper Mr. Ronceverte slides in front of her face. No exceptions."

He looks to my parents and Sheila snaps, prompting Ronceverte to slide the other lawyer a folder. "You *are* her legal counsel. Review the file, and advise her to sign."

Sheila's jaw ticks. Whatever is in that folder, she doesn't like it. "Sheila." I whisper her name again but all her energy is trained on Cassie.

Sheila's eyes narrow. "You'll confess to framing Avery. The charges against him will be dropped and he won't bring any of his own against you in this particular matter. Agree, and I'll call off the reporters. Fight me, and spending time in prison for framing your husband will only be the tip of your losing iceberg."

Cassie pushes away the first piece of paper handed to her. Sheila's eyes glitter. "You're going to make all kinds of cuddly new friends in jail."

"Keep the reporters," Cassie spits. "I can't wait to tell them what you've done to me." She reaches for her biological dad's hand. "And to my parents."

"The reporters will be far more interested in what *you* did to your parents. And I can't wait to give them all the sordid details." She places a blue-clad document in front of Cassie's father. "Your daughter is obviously a disappointment. After everything she's done to you in her lifetime, this does little to help, but I'm afraid other than putting an end to her, this is all I have to offer you."

I'm as shocked as Cassie that Sheila would pay off the mortgage for Cassie's parents. But the act isn't a bribe. It's power. Sheila is proving once again why she's afraid of nothing. *She* is the thing to be feared. "When I'm done with you, Cassie, the media scrutiny alone over having a lunatic child will cause your parents to lose their jobs. It goes to reason next will be their home. I don't think that's fair. They've suffered enough in dealing with the heartache you've caused them, so for my part in locking their lunatic daughter away, I'm gifting them the security of a home."

"You're the one who forked out money to pay *my* parents' bills, so who's the lunatic?" Cassie smirks.

"The one with two lovers and a husband all cozy in the same room."

I glance to the screen where Dr. Elkins' feed has just gone back live. He's not physically here, but Sheila's still counting him in Cassie's tally. I lower my eyes, ignoring the tsk of Sheila's tongue as my parents slip out the door. I'm not surprised they're bailing. When it comes to me, I've never been worth their effort. All they care about is their image, and the solid evidence Sheila is stacking against Cassie isn't something they can refute.

Sheila continues her assault. "Cassie, my offer to allow you to sign away repercussions expires in one hour. Until then, we'll listen to testimony of other witnesses and read through our tasty little packet of goodies. At any time *before* the offer expires, you may stop the train by agreeing to my terms and going outside to issue a statement to the waiting press in which you confess to inflicting the damage to yourself as a ploy for attention, completely exonerating Avery and giving him a public apology." Her nails rap over the table. "If you're not willing to agree to every single demand, I suggest you brace yourself. When I throw a blow, you feel it. Way down deep in your bones."

Silence answers Sheila. Not a peep from anyone in the room, especially Cassie, until the door opens again. Then I hear the inhalation. The death rattle of a dying wench. "What is *he* doing here?"

I glance to the visitor. Gill is helping an old man wheel his oxygen tank to the row of seats by the windows. He has the old man sit next to Oliver, propping the man's cane against the wall. My eyes flit to Sheila. The smile on her face holds no joy. "Having your juvenile record unsealed was quite a treat."

"Her what?" My head aches. "Is anything you told me about yourself true?"

"It's doubtful she's ever uttered a single truthful word in her life," Sheila nips. "Cassie started her criminal career as a compulsive thief."

"Thief?"

Sheila nods. "As a pre-teen, your wife liked to break into school lockers. When that gig ran its course she switched to shoplifting, stealing bikes off the street, and once she even stole a jeep. Her parents were forced to send her to a home for rehabilitation in order to keep her from being locked up, hence the bills they *still* have from the debts she *kept* racking up because much to their chagrin, no amount of therapy ever worked for her." Sheila nods to the elderly man fiddling with his oxygen line. "Not even the deal she made with her high school janitor was enough to cover all her deeds."

"Stop it!" Horror rips from Cassie's throat.

"Sign," Sheila demands. Cassie doesn't move. "After talking kids from her rehab into operating a countywide theft ring, she had sex with the janitor in exchange for his help fencing the items they stole."

A tear slides down Cassie's face. "Stop."

"Cassie is *very* persuasive." Sheila bulldozes forward. "How did a fourteen-year-old girl know how to perform the nauseating favors she introduced her janitor to? He's described them in great detail and I must say—"

"Stop!" Cassie covers her ears.

"Sign," Sheila challenges. "Or I'll have him describe to this room the actions I had to Google search in order to be sure they were even possible."

I have a flash of myself in place of the old man. Bile burns its way up my throat. Cassie's hand makes no move for the pen, eyes gathering one last bit of strength to level a glare on Sheila. I want to yell. Scream. Tell them all to stop, and puke up the rot festering in my soul. But Sheila's unyielding. Her hands fold in front of her. "If you're sensitive or have a weak stomach, I suggest you leave the room. Our janitor's vivid memories are gruesome enough, but the videos…they'll make pornography blush."

I do my best to tune out as Sheila describes how Cassie flirted with the janitor, left him notes, and sent him naked photos until the predator took her bait. Later, she set him up to take the fall for the theft ring she masterminded. He didn't fight the charges because if he did, she threatened to expose their relationship. So he went to jail for her. Much like I was prepared to do.

To the janitor's sick credit, he was smart enough to keep everything Cassie ever gave him—even videos of her with other boys and girls. "Detective Gill has secured the videos." Sheila's entire body is a wall of stone. "On them, Cassie's sultry, albeit childish, voice talks the others through the deeds while she smiles and plays to the camera so her *lover* will be entertained." She places a new pen in front of Cassie. "His days are numbered, so he had no problem telling me all your dirty little secrets, and I have no problem airing them. So sign. Or don't. Either way, you lose. The only remaining question is how badly."

Cassie's hand moves for the pen, stalling overtop, fingers lingering in the air. Sheila straightens. "In exactly five seconds the grainy, graphic video footage you shot is going to begin to play and everyone in this room is going to watch you—"

"I'll sign your stupid papers." Cassie's shaking hand begins to scribble her name over the documents. "You'll pay for this. I swear—"

Sheila stands over her. "Threatening me is what got you into this mess to begin with. As you're already going to regret that mistake for the rest of your life, I suggest you remain silent from this moment forward."

~71~

Sheila

It seems we've been in this stuffy room for hours, the walls closing in. Air hangs thick, every breath a struggle as I watch Cassie blindly sign away every claim she ever had to Avery Kingwood. No doubt she'll later say she signed under duress, but what comes next will seal her fate. Try as she might, she'll never mount a winnable defense.

Diane waves me to the corner where she's taken up residence beside Alton and Dina. Since the moment Dr. Elkins confessed to Mom that he didn't abort Avery's child, that instead, he'd made a deal with Cassie to forge the paperwork so they could sell the child, my team has been feverishly tracing the credibility of Dr. Elkins' claim. We have the proof of his flight to the United States. Proof of his meeting with a midwife at an oceanside rental house, and her testimony that she did help deliver Cassie's child.

According to Dr. Elkins, Cassie had already made arrangements to sell the baby to a couple from Idaho that she'd met in an online chat room. The day after she gave birth, the couple visited the rental property and completed the transaction.

As shocking as it was to find out Avery's little girl has been alive all this time, I'm more stunned that Cassie worked out this entire scheme before ever getting pregnant. Like Avery, Dr. Elkins was a mark. She knew she could tempt him into an affair and tap into his greed when their physical connection ran its course. She also knew she'd be able to force Avery to leave her for, at the very least, the amount of time it took her to carry and deliver his child. After that payout, she could still use him, whether they reconciled or not. Had she not threatened me, or had I never met Avery, Cassie would have gotten away with this.

Diane hands me her phone. It's filled with photographs of Mary and John sitting beside a beautiful blonde-haired girl, a miniature Cassie. Only the nose is Avery's. And she has the wide shape of his hauntingly dark eyes, but they're lit with joy as Mikey sleeps in her arms. Tears fill Diane's eyes, a whisper on her lips. "Look at her little soccer outfit."

I nod, fighting my own tears. "We've confirmed she *is* his?"

Alton shrugs, each of us keeping our voices low. "The parents have documentation from Dr. Elkins and the paper trail checks out, right down to the money the couple paid."

"The good doc did a paternity test day one to make sure it wasn't his kid," Dina adds. "Kingwood's isn't back yet but the girl looks like him. Well, the parts of her that don't look like the she-devil."

I glance over my shoulder. Avery's sitting with his head down. He hasn't moved for the last half hour, and now I have to crush his soul even more. And since his parents snuck out like cowards, I'll have to go see them one more time. To let them know the *mental health* retreat they paid for, allowing Cassie to stay away from them for four months, was her manipulating them into paying for the house where she delivered and sold their granddaughter.

I give Diane her phone back. "Tell Mary and John to keep the child secure and away from all media. I'm going to end this as delicately as possible, but I have a feeling it's going to be more like setting off a bomb."

The least I can do is take Avery out of this room, away from prying eyes. I have no doubt this will break him before it heals him, and Cassie doesn't deserve the pleasure of seeing more of his pain.

Hands trembling, I approach his side and lower to his ear. "Let's step outside."

"No." His eyes lift to stare at the woman soon to be his ex. "I'll leave when she does."

"She'll be gone soon," I whisper. "Ronceverte has been covering the details of what she's signing in detail for a reason. I needed him to delay. But I don't anymore, so please, Avery, come outside with me. It's important I talk to you before—"

"If you have something to say, say it." He doesn't budge. "It isn't like you haven't said every other flipping thing you could today. Why stop now?"

"It's about Dr. Elkins."

"Say it!" He bangs a fist on the table. "Attention, everyone! We're not done yet. Miss Beller has more to add to this party." His eyes level on me. "What is it this time? She was banging the math teacher, my best friend, and the dog catcher, too?"

"Quite possibly your best friend." I straighten, blinking the tears from my eyes. If he wants the dirt spilled in front of everyone, I'll pour it all over the floor. Same as my bleeding heart.

"It seems the only thing greater than Dr. Elkins' lust is his greed." I pace away from Avery, watching Cassie. I want to see her face the moment she realizes I *know*. "Circling back to where this day began, we all remember Dr. Elkins." His face is once more on Alton's screen. "Doctor, is it fair to say you didn't bother telling Avery Kingwood about the affair because you were afraid his wife would retaliate?"

The man sighs. "When she ended our relationship, she sent me a picture of my wife at the grocery store with our three daughters. The threat was clear—say anything to her husband and she would tell my wife." His tongue clicks. "I enjoyed my time with her and may not have wanted it to end, but I love my wife and children. I would never do anything to hurt them."

"Except have affairs," I chide. I doubt Cassie was his first, but I'm not here to discuss his morals. "Tell me about the abortion, Doctor. Were you relieved when she asked you to perform it?"

"In some ways, yes." He exhales. "The chances of the baby being mine were high. And when she offered to pay me extra so her husband wouldn't find out, well…like I said, I have a wife and three daughters. They wouldn't find out, *he* wouldn't find out, and I would be paid amply for services rendered."

"Would be?" There's no turning back. "You never were paid, were you?"

"Not for the abortion," he answers.

"Why not?"

Cassie's eyes dilate, lungs compressing with each syllable out of her cohort's mouth.

"I was never paid for the abortion because there was never an abortion performed."

"But I heard the heartbeat." Air rushes from Avery's chest. "I saw the ultrasound! She didn't fake being pregnant!"

I face him. "She faked having an abortion. The same way she faked having a miscarriage." Confusion twists his brow. "She *planned* for you to find out about the supposed abortion, Avery. Because she knew you'd leave her." I turn away from him, leveling on Cassie. "You were okay waiting a while for your marriage to either be outed or to have a lucrative divorce. There was money enough to live on. In addition to what you skimmed from his parents you had an additional five hundred thousand. Well, four hundred after you gave Dr. Elkins his cut for delivering then selling your baby."

The noise behind me is gut wrenching. Feral. I just detonated a bomb inside Avery's chest.

~72~

Three days after Avery reunited with his daughter, Sophie turned eight. John and Mary stayed by his side until paternity was proven and he won the court case against the adoptive parents, officially gaining custody of his child. After that, my family came home, leaving the Kingwoods to deal with the Kingwoods.

After my rebuke to their faces, Avery's parents went to him and remained with him when John and Mary left Idaho. That was nine months ago. It was the last time anyone around me mentioned Avery Kingwood's name.

Since the devastating day inside a stuffy room when I simultaneously ruined and saved his life, I've come to realize my purpose in Avery's life was fulfilled. No matter how much it hurt to lose him, I did what I was meant to do. I put an end to Cassie. In part. She *did* plead guilty to every charge laid at her feet, but Avery brokered a deal to have her reprimanded to what's barely a minimum-security prison. When I saw the press conference on the news, it was as if he was twisting a knife in my back. Still, I allowed the leniency. Because Avery may have put Cassie in Martha Stewart's old cell but she *is* incarcerated, and she's out of *my* life. And I do have a life now. One I've chosen with my eyes wide open.

I walk toward Alberto's taco truck, taking the sealed envelope from my pocket and running my fingers over the creamy paper. Inside is the sex of my child. This morning, before Gill left to fly back home to California, he took me to the obstetrician's office, and now I have a secret burning a hole in my pocket. A three-month-old tiny bloom whose gender won't be known until they're born. At the end of the week I'm moving back to the Potomac estate, where a room already painted a mellow yellow awaits our arrival. There, my child will be born and raised.

On the banks of the river where I spent endless hours roaming the edges, skulking the length of our property and following the perimeter back around while day turned to night. There, I mourned. Shrieked. And learned to not regret my many mistakes. I embrace them as the part of me they'll forever be. Just I as embrace the new life growing inside me. This is how it was always meant to be.

Standing in line, fingers pressed to the fabric of my dress, I stroke along my abdomen. "Sheila!" My name rings out from across the street, dislodging the envelope from my grip. "I'll get that!" A figure darts into traffic, eliciting a string of blowing horns as his frame closes in.

Struggling to steady my breath, I lower, swiping the envelope from the concrete before his hand can touch what's sacred to me. "Hey." Avery smiles, bending down to my eye level.

"Mr. Kingwood." I steel my nerves and push back to standing, sliding the envelope into the pocket of my dress. "What brings you to the east?"

"Home." He's still smiling. Bright white teeth gleaming in the sun. "I bought a house."

"How grown-up of you."

"I bought the airstrip, too." His prideful brows raise. "And the jump plane. I even bought a race car."

"And here I thought you were reconnecting with your family and your little girl." I turn back to my place in line, sweat building under my arms.

He falls in beside me, stuffing his hands into his pockets. "Her name is Sophie. She's here, too. Well, not this weekend, but she'll be back tomorrow and my parents are flying out next week. Not to stay, just to see the house."

"Sounds like things are returning to normal, then."

He stares at my profile. "I've learned there is no normal. There's only life."

"No truer words." I tuck my arms to my sides. I don't want him to notice the baby bump. Mom says it's hardly there, but I see the change.

I move forward in line. He moves with me, head dipping. "I've been dealing with a lot. Shedding tears that as a man I'm not proud to admit, but I've worked out as much as I'll ever be able to work out with my parents. You know, scars and all." He pauses. I remain silent. "They've promised never to take anyone else's word over mine. Except for yours." I see the smile from the corner of my eye. "You have everyone shaking in their boots."

"*Some* people should be afraid of me."

He swivels in front of me. "They are. *I* am. But I've wanted to see you so badly I've been stalking this taco truck hoping to run into you. It was starting to look like you lost your taste for tacos."

I step out of line and walk. He follows. "Our table is free." He points at it as if I don't know which one we used to sit at. "Eat with me? I'll grab some food and—"

"No, thank you."

"I'll buy." He plows forward. "We can eat in the park, by the fountain like—"

I stop my feet and force myself to face him. "I'm glad everything worked out for you, Mr. Kingwood. Since you bought a house, I assume that means you'll be running the East Coast operation for your family again. I'm sure we'll end up bumping into each other at one event or another. Until then, take care."

Spinning, I resume my steps and pick up the pace. He doesn't fall back *or* hide the scowl. "Just so you know, a sugar-coated blow off is still a blow off."

"I'm glad you understand that."

"Sheila." His hand drags down his face. "*Please* sit with me? Or take a walk in the park like we used to?"

"I have somewhere to be."

"Are you seeing someone?" His hand lands on my arm. "I haven't been able to ask around for the latest gossip because I've been trying to keep a low profile, but I need to know. Do you have a boyfriend? Or…" His voice wavers. "More than just a boyfriend? Because I've looked at your finger a thousand times already and still can't convince myself there's no diamond on it. So just tell me. Is the place you're running off to another man?"

I may owe Avery an apology for some of my past behavior, but I do *not* owe him a personal update. "Your question implies you're looking to rehash the past and I have no interest in doing so. I've spent the last nine months accepting our fate. I've found my closure. I suggest you do the same."

"I'm not looking for closure."

"Yet we've both moved on." I turn away and cover the final ten feet to my Corvette, opening the door and sliding inside.

He taps on the window. "I don't want to say goodbye and pretend to be only an acquaintance."

I crack the window enough to not have to yell through the glass. "If that were true, I would have heard from you in the past nine months."

He stares at me. "Sheila, that day…things were crazy. They've *been* crazy. And I—"

"You've been where you needed to be." I offer him a weak smile. "The rest is water under a bridge neither of us are prepared to cross. I wish you and your daughter the very best. Now step away from my vehicle."

~73~

After so many months, I was sure Avery was gone forever, soon to be nothing more than the whisper of a memory. I didn't anticipate having to navigate running into him. Especially not while pregnant. Now that I know he's back in town, I feel even better about my decision to move permanently back to the estate. With any luck, I'll get through the rest of this week without having another chance meeting.

Since he professed to be stalking the taco truck, I've stayed away from it. I've avoided even the simplicity of strolling through the park on a warm afternoon. But I have so few days left to see the city and it's balmy tonight. "Mommy can't sleep again, little one." I scratch my stomach and pick up my keys. "No racing allowed right now, so how about we take a walk?"

It's past midnight but all I need is a light sweater while traversing the cobblestone through the park. Moonlight bounces off dewy grass, littering the lawn with stars that twinkle as I pass by. I follow the winding path to the soothing waters of the softly cascading fountain. Dipping my fingers into the cool liquid, I glide the tips around and watch the ripples. "You're not supposed to do that." A throaty voice rattles across my flesh. "The city frowns on people getting into the fountain. I know because I got in there once with this amazing woman."

"I have pepper spray," I announce flatly, peering into the darkness beyond the lamppost.

Avery steps under the light, jean-clad legs and a blue jacket zipped up to his throat, dark hair mussed in all directions and his hands stuffed into his pockets. "You still think I'd hurt you?"

The agony of still being attracted to him washes over me. I look back to the rippling water. "I'm just letting you know I'm armed. I don't need the *you shouldn't be out here alone* lecture that men are always swift to give."

"I wouldn't dream of lecturing you." He sighs. "But statistically, most people with pepper spray either end up spraying themselves or can't get to it fast enough to stop the attacker."

"If you're going to use that as an excuse to lurk around, please don't. I'll be fine."

"Yeah, but if I leave, *I* won't be fine." His footfall is slow. Heavy. "What are you doing here this late?"

"Minding my own business."

He moves closer. "Are you looking for me?"

"If I knew you were here, I wouldn't have come."

"Really?" He takes a steady, deliberate step. "Or is that what you're telling yourself so you don't have to face the fact that you're here, in the middle of the night, because deep down you want to see me?"

I face him. "Deep down, I hoped to never so much as hear your name again."

I was coming to Miller Park long before I knew him, and me being here tonight has nothing to do with him. "Where's Sophie? I thought you said she moved here with you. If so, you should be with her right now instead of stalking women in parks."

"She started school Monday, made a new friend, and informed me this morning she *had* to spend the night with her friend or she'd just *die*. She also constantly reminds me she's almost nine. I'm learning that means she cares more about hanging out with her friends than her dad." He scrubs his jaw, fingers lingering over the spot his stitches once were. "Because of everything she's been through, it's hard to tell her no. I'm…"

I watch his silent face. Dark watery eyes glisten like the dew-covered grass. He's petrified. "You're scared to tell her no because she's already been through so much in her young life." He nods, pulling pity from my depths. "How is she adjusting to finding out you're her dad?"

"She says she's fine." He pinches away tears. "We're both in therapy, by ourselves and once a month together. Two different therapists each. So far as anyone is telling me, she's handling everything like a boss. But people don't always tell me the truth, so it's hard to know for sure." He looks away. "I try to gauge by her smile. Unhappy kids wouldn't smile, right?"

My heart betrays me at every turn. I ache for him. And hate myself for it. "I think as long as you're paying attention, you'll know if she's truly *not* okay."

He turns back to me. "That's what Mary said. I was asking John but, you know, they're a package deal. I can't ask him anything without her answering. Pretty awkward when I want to talk to him man to man."

Heat flushes my face. "You talk to them?"

He nods, face falling. "I asked them not to tell you."

My knees buckle. I lower myself to the fountain wall, hand protectively pressing against my stomach. My family lied to me. By omission. Same as Avery always did.

He crouches in front of me. "You told me before that I acted like a child, and I did. Pouting and throwing tantrums because people weren't being *fair*. But all that got me was a boatload more misery." He takes my hands in his. "I was angry all the time. I acted out, treated you horribly, made mistake after mistake and hurt you. Because of that, I had to get help before I could see you again. And I knew the day John signed off on my being allowed to speak to you would be the first day I could actually lay eyes on your beautiful face. Else I would have begged and pleaded before I ever straightened myself out enough to be able to make you all the promises I intend to make."

My head pounds. "John said you could talk to me?"

He smiles. "Not even for one single second. Mary said it was okay, though. And for all the hype your brother has, his wife calls the shots and he falls in line. So here I am."

I yank my hands from his. "The only person who can give you permission to speak to me is *me*."

He rocks back on his heels, hand resting on my knee. "Will you give me permission? Because there are so many things I need to say to you. The first of which is thank you. Thank you for giving me a life. A daughter. Sophie wasn't in a bad home, the people were good to her, so she would have been okay, but…"

"She's *your* daughter." I remove his hand from my traitorous flesh. "She belongs with you."

He swallows. "The day you told me she was alive… I've relived those hours so many times. I can't believe I didn't know…about anything."

I take a breath. "Cassie didn't want you to know. My guess is that if she ever got into trouble or ran out of money, she would have told you about Sophie. Blackmailed you for whatever she needed."

"And to find out where my little girl was, I would have done anything Cassie asked." He stands, sitting down on the fountain wall beside me. "I can't believe I ever fell for her."

"She gave you what you wanted, Avery. A person. Someone who loved you."

He swallows. "I guess for anyone paying attention, it wouldn't have been too hard to figure out I didn't really have anyone close to me."

I close my eyes. "The important thing is that you have someone now. You have Sophie."

His hand slides toward me, fingers lightly brushing over my linen pants. "My friend, the one whose party I was at when I met Cassie, was he involved with her? Did he set me up?"

I shrug. "He's how she got the invite to the party, but exactly what he knew is something you'll have to talk to him about. He was in rehab, so I didn't press for details. All he said was she wanted to meet you, so he obliged."

"For a few *favors*." He grumbles. "How'd she know I'd fall for her?"

My teeth clench. I'm so tired of talking about her. "Typical damsel in distress bit. Works like a charm."

He leans close to me. "So does being the opposite of distressed. You've never played the part of a damsel to get a date."

"I doubt I've had as many dates as the women who do." I stand, moving away from his closeness. "I realize she hurt you so you want to talk about her, but I don't. All I know, I've already revealed. And I *am* sorry I had to be the bearer of all your bad news, but you deserved to know the whole truth. And I deserved to be out of the danger of her threats."

His head lowers. "You deserved more than that. So don't apologize to me for anything. I'm the one who owes you." He looks up. "Without you, I wouldn't have Sophie."

"We're even, then." I drag my teeth over my lip, having never planned to tell him this. "You were right about Dirk. Adelle checked into the debt you made a fuss over and unearthed Dirk's gambling problem. He wasn't in debt because of his parents, his right hand was stealing from his left in order to pay off bookies."

~74~

Avery's gloating. "I told you there was something off about golden boy." I fold my arms. He grins. "Adelle is good. I've already hired her to check out all of Sophie's teachers, friends' parents, soccer coach…everyone."

I unfold my arms, head telling me to leave while my heart says stay. "I'd like to say that's overkill, but after what she's gone through, safe is better than sorry."

He nods. "I can't fault her *parents* for wanting a child, only for the illegal adoption part of it. But I didn't cut them out of her life. She still talks to them and they get together. That's where she was the day I saw you at Alberto's."

Sophie's adopted parents are decent. John and Mary *did* tell me that much. That, and the fact they'd told Sophie in the first place that she was adopted, so having a new dad show up wasn't too much of a shock. "It's good of you to include them in her life."

He goes distant. "I include Cassie, too. Show Sophie pictures so she knows where she came from."

My gut churns. "If I were Sophie, I guess I'd be curious as to what the people who birthed me looked like, no matter their despicable nature."

"You think so?" Tears glisten in his eyes. "It's hard to know if I'm doing the right thing by being open with her or if it's too much for a little girl. The therapists say she's smart, the kind of kid who'll do better having all the facts to process." A tear slides down his cheek. "I just have this fear inside. I don't want to mess her up."

I tamp down the urge to wipe away his tears. "It sounds like you're doing your best, Avery. All you can do is show Sophie no one is perfect."

"You're perfect." He stands, body moving close to mine, his warmth revealing just how cold I've been. His voice is low. "I really need you to answer my question because my heart might fall out of my body if you're engaged, but not knowing if you even have a boyfriend has me close to hyperventilating."

I don't want to walk this road with him. "You've proven yourself to be unflappable. I doubt any news I give you will elicit even shortness of breath."

"Try me." He whispers. "Tell me all your news, Sheila. What has your life been like these last months?"

"Why?" I meet his stare. "Will knowing my personal affairs make you sleep better?"

His hand glides to my jaw. "Having a complete home will make me sleep better. And my home will only be complete when you're in it."

"So that's what this is?" I remove his hand from my face. "You came back here thinking I'd jump in bed with you again? Be a ready-made mother for your child?"

"Don't accuse me of things. Just ask. Because no, I didn't expect to come back here and get even the time of day from you." He runs a hand through his hair, making it stick out even worse than before. "I did come back *hoping* you'd talk me. We left a lot of things unsaid, and I know I hurt you, but you hurt me, too. I got past that, and I…I want to be with you, Sheila."

"Says the wolf." My eyes narrow. "Before you fired Garland, did you collect your winnings? Or was that part of your purchase agreement? He knocked some off the price to compensate for the way you blew him out of the water?"

His jaw ticks. "*Don't* accuse me of things. *Ask* me. Or go ask Garland if you think he's more trustworthy than me. I got a crap deal on those lots and spent money I didn't have just so I could fire him. So I could do *something* to prove to you that my list of what I care about starts and ends with you. And now Sophie, because *you* gave her to me."

"*Cassie* gave her to you." I bite, tears threating my eyes. "And that is the *only* reason I'm letting you reward her with a cozy jail cell."

"Reward?" He snaps. "After what she did, I wanted her buried *under* the jail." His eyes well. "I want to erase her. But you're right about one thing, *she* is Sophie's biological mom and I can't erase that fact. So I lobbied for the cozy lockup because Sophie asked me if she could visit her mom, and I didn't know how to tell her no." Tears slide down his cheeks. "She hasn't gone to see the psychotic woman yet, but if or when she does, I can't let my little girl walk into a prison full of rapists and murderers."

I take a breath. "I'm sorry that you're stuck in the middle of such tough choices, but if Cassie so much as utters my name again, I'll rip her out of that day spa and bury her myself."

He gives me a mocking bow. "I'd expect no less."

I turn away, traversing the cobblestone. He falls in beside me. "Did you ever care for me? Like really care about *me*, as a person, or were you only looking for someone to check off the husband box?"

I plant my feet. "How can you ask me that?"

He shrugs. "You don't trust me. You never want to hear my side of anything. And you make walking away from me look easy."

Fury builds in my chest. "If you want me to treat you differently, maybe you should do basic things. Like find the time to call me at least *once* in *nine* months. Or tell me when your crazy ex beheads a doll she made of me!"

"You didn't call me either, and the doll came the morning you met my crazy ex. You remember that day? The one where you talked to her for five minutes and then dumped me?"

His rebuke lands as squarely as it should. I inhale deeply, calming the anger I thought I was done with. "I admit I was wrong. I absolutely treated you unfairly. But she *threatened* my life, Avery. How could you not tell me?"

He looks up at the starry sky. "Before the doll came, I was just plain scared that you'd do what you ended up doing anyway. At the time the doll came, I didn't have proof that Cassie had tampered with my rig but I suspected she'd hired someone to try to kill me, so I *did* take the threat seriously." His eyes lower to mine. "I should have told you right away. Then maybe you wouldn't have left me, or at the very least you wouldn't have left me because of the lies she told you." He shrugs. "In the end, I'm not sure there was a scenario that didn't lead to you bailing on me."

I cross my arms. "I didn't behave in a way that I'm proud of. From the moment we met until the last one. I pushed you and I was wrong to do that." A tear slips from my eye. "I should have respected your wishes and left you alone to begin with. But then you wouldn't have Sophie. So I accept my role, my responsibility, and I'll endure any rebuke you want to press against me. But I only bailed on you because I didn't know the truth. You were never honest with me."

He steps closer, hand raising to my cheek. "I don't want to put any of the blame on you. I know that my decisions led to your actions. And I also know that you were there for me when it mattered most." His lips press against my forehead. "I'm sorry that I covered my heartbreak with anger. I'm sorry that you tied my past into a neat little box and I plucked at all the threads that directly affected Sophie. And I'm *really* sorry I haven't called you. Most days I didn't think you wanted me to. The others I was too embarrassed to try. But if I'd known you wanted to hear from me, I would have called you every single day. I would have stayed on the phone with you all night and came home a heck of a lot sooner."

I move away and pry his hand off skin so flush with the want of his touch it hurts to remove him. Desirous, traitorous flesh. "It's over now, and we've both moved on."

"Speak for yourself." His hand comes back to rest along my cheek, thumb wiping away my tears. "I'm not over you. And living without you is misery."

I close my eyes. "Avery…"

"Look at me, Sheila." He whispers. I open my eyes. He smiles. "We put each other through a lot. Mostly because of me. But I'm not afraid to tell you how I feel anymore." Slowly, he lowers himself in front of me, one knee underneath him. His fingers dive into his pocket, pulling out a red velvet satchel. "I want to have the life we talked about. I want to eat, sleep, and dream you. I want to be the man who wins the greatest prize of any bet in the history of mankind." He takes a heart-cut diamond out of the velvet cocoon and holds it up to me. "Sheila Beller, will you marry me?"

~75~

My head pounds, moonlight reflecting off all the tiny surfaces of the diamond strobing into my skull. Avery twists the ring in his fingers, worsening the effect. "I started to get it cut into the shape of a car, but I wanted to give you my heart." He smiles. "Cheesy, but…do you like it?"

I don't answer. I retreat. Breath coming in short, shallow gulps as I go back the way I came, heading for the comfort of my car. His footfall closes in. Anger propels me. He walks faster. I spin into his face. "You can't not speak to me for *nine* months, then waltz in and get on your knee like that makes it all better!"

"Marrying you doesn't make the past better, but it will sure as heck make the future a whole lot brighter." He sighs. "Look, I don't expect you to trust me, Sheila. I haven't done anything to inspire your confidence. Which is why I'm fully prepared for your rejection. Obviously I'd rather have a different outcome, but I *will* prove myself to you." One hand moves up my arm, over my shoulder, and underneath my hair to cup the back of my neck. "If it takes ten years for you to trust me with your heart, so be it. I'm not going anywhere. I'm perfectly content waiting for you. So talk to me? Let me be around you sometimes? And if you're ever ready, let me date you? Actually *date* you."

"No." I pull away. "How can you say any of this when you never even wanted to hear me say I loved you?"

He reaches for me, face falling when I step further away. "You have no idea how badly I wanted to know you loved me, but how could you when I hadn't told you the whole truth? *That's* why I wanted you to hold off. I didn't want you to say something you'd regret once I confessed to my whole lousy situation. But I'm not in that predicament anymore. I resigned from Kingwood Properties, have you to thank for putting my family and my ex in their places, and I also have you to thank for the fact that I have Sophie. *You*, Sheila. No one else gets credit for her. Only you." His lips tick up. "She's dying to meet you. I might have given her the impression you're a superhero, so she hated all the houses we looked at. She said you deserve a castle, which I'm supposed to build."

"If I want a castle, I'll build my own."

His smile breaks fully across his handsome face. "I told her that. And talked her into buying an older house because I thought it would be a fun project for the three of us to renovate. So we can make it ours. *Yours.*" He walks toward me. "Marry me."

Furiously disoriented, I wind through paths, unable to lose him. I veer off the trail and go through the shrubs, managing nothing other than leading us straight back to the fountain. He spins me to him, his heartbeat against my chest as steady as the trickling water behind me. "I saw you that day."

I fight tears. Stupid pregnancy hormones. "What day?"

"*That* day." He growls. "You threw a hand grenade in my lap and when the smoke cleared, you were gone. I ran outside and I *saw* you with him. *Gill.*" The name hisses through his teeth. "You were in his arms. I called your name and you just got in his car. You drove away from me." His eyes glisten. "For all I knew, Gill was driving you to that little white chapel you were so eager to get to. So I just stood there in that parking lot and watched you leave me again. And then I made the only choice I could make. I went and got my little girl."

I bite my cheek. "You were so angry with me just before and I…I just assumed you'd rather me not be there anymore."

"The only place I ever want you to be is with me." His face falls. "After I got back to California, I went to see Gill. He wasn't wearing a ring so that helped, but I still had to put myself in therapy before I could get to a place where I didn't feel like an absolute failure at everything."

"Avery," I wipe his tears. "You've never been a failure. You've only been surrounded by people who fail you. Including me. I'm *so* sorry."

His watery eyes meet mine. "If I wouldn't have been afraid to tell you the truth from the beginning, things might have been different for us. And honestly, I'm still afraid. That's why I haven't knocked on your door. I'm afraid you already have someone else, or that you don't, and will reject me anyway." His smile doesn't reach his eyes. "Despite being afraid, I got this idea that it would be romantic to see you at our taco truck and propose to you right there on the sidewalk where we had our first date. So when I saw you there…I've been waiting so long for that moment."

My stomach flutters and I push away from his chest, unable to quell the tears. "Who wants to be proposed to at a taco truck?"

He sighs. "Apparently you don't."

I take another step away from him. "Who wants to be proposed to by a man they haven't seen or spoken to in *nine* months?"

He waves a hand at me. "Clearly not you."

"That's right, I *don't*." I press a hand to my stomach, tears blurring my vision, casting him in a hazy shadow of moonlight. "I don't want to be proposed to by a man who will *never* say he loves me."

"But I do." He reaches for me.

I back away, my legs bumping against the fountain's cool stone. "You proposed without saying it once. So live in whatever city you want to live in and buy as many houses and planes and cars as you want. But stay away from me."

~76~

Sorrow takes a toll on a body. Mix in outrage and hit it with a dash of pregnancy and you get a well-baked wobble. One that leaves you vulnerable to the arms of the nearest bystander. In this case, Avery. He wraps around me, holding me upright and steady against his chest. "Let it all out, Sheila," he soothes, brushing the hair from my face. "Cry all you need to and let me hear everything you've ever wanted to yell at me so I can try to make amends for my mistakes because I've been in love with you since that horrible un-tea party. So be angry with me. Slug me a thousand times if that's what makes you feel better. But when it's all said and done, I'm going to get back down on my knee and beg you to marry me because I'm madly and insanely in love with you."

Fluttering kicks up within me. My baby. My future. I swivel out of his arms. His hands fold over my shoulders, pulling me against his chest. Tears stream down my wet face. "How dare you come here and spring this on me like I'm supposed to swoon. I don't want someone I have to yell at."

"Then don't yell at me."

"I don't want to have to scream to get them to say they love me."

"*Whisper* and I'll say I love you."

I turn back to the comfort of his arms, meeting his eyes as he embraces me. "All you've ever done is make me fight with you to get the faintest notice."

"It only *appears* that way to you. But I'll fix that. I'll fix all of it, Sheila." A millimeter more and his lips will be on mine.

I drop my gaze, removing my lips from his realm of possibility. "I can't do this. I've worked too hard to learn from the mistakes I made with you. I have a different life now."

His mouth lowers to my ear. "I have a different life, too. And I've learned lessons I never knew existed. So trust me when I say that I love you because those are words I've said to you a million times already. When your head was turned. When you were asleep. Every time you drove away from me." His lips find the corner of mine. "I listened to my heart beat those words every single time we made love. I love you, Sheila. In a way I never knew was possible to love someone. You make me want to pour myself out for no other reason than to be a better man, and I'm begging you for another chance because even if you let me stand in your presence for eternity, it won't be long enough." He moves back to my ear. "We were happy once. For one brief moment in time, we were happy. I want to be happy again."

There's no strength left in me, the effort of fighting my own desires draining my very soul. Avery's arms tighten, hands steady as he lifts me against him. Water floods over me, time warping into a thick, slow mass as he steps into the fountain and sinks us into the water. The cold shocks my senses and I claw over his shoulder like a soaked cat. "What are you doing?"

He laughs, jiggling the ring as he slides backwards, attempting to cut off my escape. "Proposing to the woman I love in the least fitting place possible. Sheila Beller, love of my life and the most beautiful, immaculate woman I've ever beheld, will you please save my soul and marry me?"

"No." I crawl over the side of the fountain, water splattering behind me. *"No!"*

"But I thought—"

"You thought *wrong!*"

Water sloshes from Avery's shoes as he runs to catch up with me. The clarity of the freezing water keeps the right path under my feet. I reach the comfort of my car and yank the door open. He throws his dripping body in front of the entry. I wipe the mix of tears and water from my face, teeth grinding. "Get away from me before you have *two* exes in jail."

He smiles. "*You* I'll bail out. Then we can get married in the field where we landed that first time. We can skydive down to the ceremony, or you can stand there in your dress and I'll dive down to you. Then you'll drive us out there in one of your cars and I'll lay the throttle down and love you like you've never dreamed of being loved because *I love you*, Sheila Beller."

The last crumbs of strength drain from my body and I double over, leaning onto my knees. "Saying you love me now, over and over, doesn't make up for the past."

He lifts me to him, holding me upright in a warm embrace. "*Nothing* can make up for the past. That doesn't mean I'm not going to try." He presses his lips to my temple. "You're trembling."

"That happens when you get dunked in a fountain in the middle of the night."

He lifts me gently, carrying me to the passenger door. "Yeah, I should have thought that through." He slides me into the car and dashes around to the coveted driver's seat, getting the engine revved and the heater going.

He angles the vents to me and I press my palms against them. He looks around. "If I wasn't as soaked as you, I'd offer you my jacket. Any chance there's a blanket tucked somewhere?" I shake my head, tears dripping. "Hey." He turns my chin to him. "It's going to be okay. We'll figure everything out. And though I'll never be as good of a driver as you, I promise to spend my life trying to beat you on the track, just so you can gloat about how I can't. I also promise to remain terrible at gambling, and I vow to worship you every day of your life. Because the only thing I'm afraid of, is losing the one woman who loved me in spite of me. And you did, Sheila. I know you loved me once. So even if you don't anymore, that's okay. I'm a better man now and I'll prove that to you. You *will* love me again. And then I'll marry you, wherever and whenever you want."

Words twist from my depths like a phantom stealing the breath from my body, syllables passing my lips to make him stop. To snuff the light from both of us. "I'm not marrying you, Avery. I'm three months pregnant. Do the math, the baby isn't yours."

There's restorative power in a hot shower. Crying into a stream of molten liquid never ceases to cure the moment's sorrow. I step out of my bathroom, wrap a fuzzy robe around me, and smell the delightful aroma of food.

Following my nose, I enter the kitchen, where Avery is unwrapping hamburgers and placing them on a platter already piled high with fries. I expected him to leave after he helped me to my apartment, the shock of my revelation finally silencing him.

"Hey, babe." He half smiles, still pale and pasty. "Not many places open this late. Steve at the guard station grabbed this for us."

"I know who Steve is."

"Your refrigerator is empty." His eyes bob to my stomach. "America's junk food isn't great for the baby, but you have to eat. You're not worried about your figure, are you?"

Cassie saying she worried about hers due to him floats through my mind. "I eat plenty and my refrigerator is scaled down for a reason."

"Pregnant women can't have reasons to only eat salad and hard-boiled eggs." He sets a place for me at the table and pulls out a chair. "You don't even have peanut butter and pickles."

I sit down and shove fries into my face. "I'm not Cassie. Whatever she craved that you dutifully prepared for her at three in the morning can't be forced on me."

"I can't help that I have a past." He sits next to me and eats a few fries of his own. I take a bite of hamburger two sizes too big for my mouth. He wipes mayo off my bottom lip. "You could have led with the pregnancy news, stopped me before I went and spilled out my heart."

"And you could have called me at some point in the last nine months."

His teeth clench. "Phones work both ways. But now I know why *you* didn't call *me*. Who's the father?"

"Not you."

"It better not be Gill."

"He told me about the visit you paid him."

His eyes narrow. "So you *are* talking to him. Is it his?"

"My baby isn't an *it*, and when an ex-con shows up on a detective's doorstep, said detective feels the need to let the party being argued about know."

"I'm hardly a convict and *he's* the one who was arguing. I only told him to stay away from you."

"An order you have no authority to give. I'm not now, nor have I ever been, *your* property."

"Doesn't mean I'm not going to tell the man who arrested me where he can shove himself." His eyes scan the apartment. "He moved in on you when you were vulnerable. When we were *both* hurting. It wasn't right. And if he's such a good guy, where is he? Why isn't he here with his pregnant girlfriend?"

I push the suddenly nauseating food away. "The day I saw you at Alberto's, I'd just dropped Gill off at the airport so he could fly back to his place in Cali."

Avery's so still I'm not sure he's breathing. His red-rimmed eyes beg my heart to relieve his pain. "You've always been between Gill and me, Avery. Because of you, we never had a chance to become anything other than good friends. The baby isn't his."

He exhales, blowing the breath all the way out and sucking in another deep breath. "I'm guessing Dirk is out, too?

"Avery…"

Tears well in his eyes. "I don't want your pity. I just want to know who took my place. Who gets to raise a child with the woman I love?"

I leave the table and grab tissues from the box on the counter, pressing one into his palm. He crumples it and wipes his face. "I've hated me for a long time, but never so much as *that* day. And this one."

I place a hand on his shoulder. "Stop crying, Avery."

"I can't help it." He sniffs. "You're the belle of my ball, Sheila. Staying away from you was the hardest thing I ever had to do, but I *had* to. I've been a man in distress since you met me. And you've saved me over and over again despite getting nothing out of it but heartache. I couldn't do that to you again. I had to be sure I *wouldn't* do that to you again." His fist slams into the table. "I thought I was doing the right thing. And nobody told me…" He throws the tissue. "John should have told me!"

I tug him from the seat. He shakes his head, resting his forehead on mine, his tears falling against my cheeks. "No matter where you are in this world, I will always love you, Sheila Beller. Whoever you're with, whatever you're doing, I love you. And if there's ever a time you'll allow me to be in your life again, I'll be here. Husband. Boyfriend. Friend. Annoying acquaintance you tolerate. However you'll have me, I accept. Just please don't forget about me, Sheila." His eyes close. "Please don't let me go."

Lifting onto my toes, I draw his mouth to mine. Kissing him is a like a warm breeze. It sweeps over me. Through me. Lifting the ache from my soul. I want him. "I love you too, Avery."

He smiles, tears shaking loose as he gives a sad laugh. "I've waited so long to hear you say that." He wipes his tears from my face. "If your baby daddy won't eat tacos with you, I'm your man. Day or night, whatever you need, I'm yours. Promise me you'll remember that."

I lift his hand from my face. "All I need is an explanation of this ring." A sob breaks from my chest. "I swear if you married someone else I'm going to kill you, Avery."

He wipes his face with his damp shirt sleeve and slips the black gold band from his ring finger. "I bought your engagement ring six months ago. And I went ahead and bought my wedding band, too." He places it in my palm. "In the midst of trying to become an overnight dad and working out the rest of my damage in therapy, the single truth of my heart is that I belong to you. So I bought the rings and started wearing mine. I only took it off once I got back to Huntington, but I keep it in my pocket at all times, right next to yours. I put it back on when you were in the shower. In case… I just want you to know that I *do* love you."

I read the inscription. Etched inside the metal are the words *Diving. Racing. Loving. Now and Always. Sheila & Avery.* He lifts my chin. "Did I leave anything out?"

"Tacos." I whisper.

He smiles. "I'll get that added to the inscription tomorrow. Anything else?"

Tears drip from my lashes. "It would have been romantic to be proposed to at our table, and to ride tandem in the park with you after."

He hugs me, shoulders jerking with his sobs. "This is why I'm not going to be able to get over you, you like my dumb ideas."

"I don't want you to get over me, Avery." I pull back and look into his face. "That way I don't have to get over you, either. Unless you don't want to have another baby because Sophie has a sibling on the way."

Lights turn on behind his eyes and he drops to knees, pressing his face into my stomach. "You had in vitro." He breathes against me, clouds rolling away and fresh air building around us. "You're having *our* baby."

I bury my fingers in his hair. "Took you long enough."

"Yeah." He wipes his freshly falling tears. "We're going to have to work on your communication skills." His grin grows, eyes looking up to mine. "After you mentioned having a child this way, I checked on being a sperm donor. I didn't think you'd ever actually go through with it because I know what you really wanted was a partner, but if you *did*, I wondered—if my swimmers were there for you to choose from, would you? Fate."

"You're serious?" I laugh.

He presses his face back to my stomach. "I'm going to take your mommy to eat tacos tomorrow. Then I'm going to get on the dirty ground and beg her to marry me. And whether she says yes or no, we're going to go for a bike ride in the park afterward. Then, I'm going to take you home and introduce you to your big sister." He looks up. "I bought a big place, with plenty of rooms to turn into nurseries."

"Nurseries? I'm not having quadruplets." I lower to my knees in front of him. "I've had it confirmed, there's only one bun in my oven."

"For now." He salutes. "I've had it confirmed, when you're ready for another, my soldiers are at your service."

It's been a long time since I've laughed. Truly laughed. And just as long since I've heard *him* truly laugh. "Corny?" He grins.

"Very." I smile.

He wraps his arms around me. "Love me anyway?"

I nod. "Unfortunately."

He digs the diamond ring out of his pocket. "Marry me? It's okay if you say no. I'll ask again tomorrow. And the day after that. And the day after. And the—"

"Avery?"

"Yes?"

I slide my arms around his neck. "Will you please shut up and kiss your fiancée?"

A Note From The Author

"I have always imagined paradise will be a kind of library." ~ Jorge Luis Borges

Thank you for taking an emotional ride with Avery and Sheila! I hope you found as much enjoyment from their story as I received when writing it.

My deepest gratitude to Anita and Christie from Proof Positive. These ladies tirelessly edit my work and help me articulate my thoughts clearly. Without them, you'd be balling instead of bawling!

I can't thank my son enough for his love, encouragement, and support. As I age, legacy becomes increasingly important to me. While I intend to leave many books in the world, my son will always be the best part of me. And he'll forever be the reason I put one foot in front of the other…

For my days of doubt, God gave me my husband. His strength remains at my back and his lips at my ear, encouraging me to run when I don't think I can walk. Joe, I love the way you love me.

And you, my reader, are never far from my thoughts.

I consider you with every breath, and dedicate myself to honing my craft in order to fill your library with stories you want to read.

ABOUT THE AUTHOR

Lee Dawna is a romantic thriller author living in the rolling mountains of West Virginia. An avid traveler and outdoorswoman, you may bump into her along a remote trail where a meandering stream whispers her next story.

Connect with her on:

Instagram https://www.instagram.com/leedawna_author/

Twitter https://twitter.com/LeeDawna_Author

Facebook https://www.facebook.com/leedawnabooks

Find all her links in one place at https://www.linktr.ee/LeeDawna

Brace for a special Halloween Day Thriller Release!
Descend is a small-town serial killer thrill!

Want to know what happens when Johnathan Michael Beller grows up? The next installment of Beller Ties will be released on March 1st, 2022.

www.ingramcontent.com/pod-product-compliance
Lightning Source LLC
Chambersburg PA
CBHW061606190726
48288CB00007B/2195